Karla's Choice

A John le Carré Novel

NICK HARKAWAY

PENGUIN BOOKS

PENGUIN BOOKS

UK | USA | Canada | Ireland | Australia
India | New Zealand | South Africa

Penguin Books is part of the Penguin Random House group of companies
whose addresses can be found at global.penguinrandomhouse.com.

Penguin Random House UK,
One Embassy Gardens, 8 Viaduct Gardens, London SW11 7BW

penguin.co.uk

Penguin
Random House
UK

First published by Viking 2024
Published in Penguin Books 2025

001

Typeset by Jouve (UK), Milton Keynes
Printed and bound in Great Britain by Clays Ltd, Elcograf S.p.A.

The authorized representative in the EEA is Penguin Random House Ireland, Morrison
Chambers, 32 Nassau Street, Dublin D02 YH68

A CIP catalogue record for this book is available from the British Library

ISBN: 978-1-4059-69833

This book is dedicated to

DAVID JOHN MOORE CORNWELL

Father, husband, brother, son
Ping-pong player, cartoonist, wine-drinker, dog-walker
Germanist
Francophile
Lost boy
Late-life Irishman
Terrible cook

and to

JOHN LE CARRÉ

Novelist

**DISCOVER ONE OF THE MOST ACCLAIMED
THRILLERS OF THE YEAR**

We hope you enjoy this book. Please return or renew it by the due date.

You can renew it at www.norfolk.gov.uk/libraries or by using our free library app.

Otherwise you can phone 0344 800 8020 - please have your library card and PIN ready.

You can sign up for email reminders too.

NORFOLK ITEM

30129 092 952 119

**NORFOLK COUNTY COUNCIL
LIBRARY AND INFORMATION SERVICE**

'Reads like a lost le Carré. Smiley is back at the Circus
in the safest of hands'
Richard Osman

'Harkaway has pulled off the remarkable trick of
providing the reader with something which is satisfyingly
fresh and new, and yet fits seamlessly into the world
of Smiley's Circus in its heyday'
Mick Herron

'A beautifully rendered spy story full of familiar characters
and authentic Cold War tradecraft. It's the missing
chapter of Smiley's battle with Karla that we've
always wanted'
David McCloskey

'Le Carré's legacy is in good hands – Smiley is back
with a vengeance!'
Ian Rankin

'A feat of extraordinary literary alchemy'
Helen Macdonald

'A brilliant and almost uncanny incarnation of le
Carré's voice and world'
William Boyd

'It is all here, everything we revered about le Carré – the
lyrical grace, the exhausted patriotism, the twists and
turns, the characters that burn in your imagination'
Tony Parsons

'An amazing achievement'
Adam Roberts

'Tense and atmospheric, meditative and moving. Fans of
le Carré will have much to rejoice about'
Tan Twan Eng

ABOUT THE AUTHORS

Nick Harkaway is the acclaimed author of *Gnomon*, *The Gone-Away World*, *Angelmaker*, *Tigerman* and *Titanium Noir*, among others. He is the son of John le Carré, and has a unique insight into his father's work. The *Guardian* writes of Harkaway that 'his great gift as a novelist is to merge the pace, wit and clarity of the best "popular" literature with the ambition, complexity and irony of the so-called "literary novel" – a rare combination which le Carré himself also achieved.' He lives in London with his wife and two children.

John le Carré is one of Britain's greatest ever writers. He was born in Dorset in 1931, and over his six-decade career formed a literary world that came to define our age. He published his debut novel, *Call for the Dead*, in 1961 while still working in the secret service. His third novel, *The Spy Who Came in from the Cold*, secured him a worldwide reputation, a fame consolidated by the acclaim for his extraordinary 'Smiley Saga', the series of novels centred on the brilliant spymaster, George Smiley: *Tinker Tailor Soldier Spy*, *The Honourable Schoolboy* and *Smiley's People*. He died on 12 December 2020. His final novel, *Silverview*, was published posthumously in 2021 and completed for publication by Nick Harkaway.

In the spy trade we abandon first what we love the most.

– Smiley's People, John le Carré

I can fake a Picasso as well as anyone.

– attributed to Pablo Picasso

Author's Note: Writing Smiley

'It's a very impressive menu,' my father's first wife, Ann, once told a startled maître d', 'but the question is: can you cook?'

We're about to find out. In some ways I already know: my family is happy with this book. If I'd written something that secured every accolade going and they hated it, that would be a very special kind of Hell. And I also know that there will be forgone conclusions in every direction. There will be people who love the book whatever it is, because their attachment to George Smiley and the Circus is so deep that any slight touch of his hand is enough to bring them joy. There will be others who, for the exact same reason, cannot conceive of reading it, and whose hackles rise at the mention of my absurd hubris. To those people, who will inevitably be given the book by well-meaning family members, and who will have to pretend to be grateful through an instinctive snarl, I can only apologise: I hope that, perhaps in your bath after a particularly dismal day, you pick up the neglected volume on the basis that things can't possibly get any worse, and find that the appetite arrives in the eating.

There were always supposed to be more Smiley books. I know, because I was there. I was born in November 1972 – coincidentally or otherwise, around the time Control died – and I grew up with George. His presence, in various forms, was a friendly ghost at my table. First there was my father's George, voice tight and sometimes raised in outrage, then a moment later coming from the gut to deliver truth, however dark. Next there was Sir Alec Guinness's version, soft, wayward and thoughtful, as if genius could only ever step briefly from fog. Michael Jayston read Smiley in an abridged audiobook, and I listened to the cassettes every night to fall asleep. Then later my father read his own book in the same format, his cadences now mingled with Guinness's – which was, he said, why he couldn't write as many books into the sequence as he'd originally intended. The external Smiley had supplanted the one in his head. Much later again there was Denholm Elliott, then Gary Oldman, and others in different settings and all of them echoed in my ears as I sat down to see whether I could fit some sort of story into that ten-year gap between *The Spy Who Came in from the Cold* and *Tinker Tailor Soldier Spy*.

It was as if Smiley was there, waiting patiently, and I was slightly late. *If you're quite prepared, Nicholas, we may begin.* My Smiley is my father's, but he's also the Smiley we collectively inherit. The character's origins are obscure and much discussed. We know he travels without labels in the guard's van of the social express; that he's academic and not aristocratic; unplaceable, invisible and exceptional. There's a school of thought that has Peter Guillam as my father and Smiley as Sir Maurice Oldfield mixed with Rev. Vivian Green, but any author will tell you that the centre of a novel is always the person into whom they project themselves, however reshaped and reimagined. Smiley was my dad: the too-watchful child, orphaned either in fact or by monstrosity, alone in a crowded room and happy only when, by what seemed like sheer chance, he was delivered into a place of emotional warmth. A brilliant mind on a grey, unrelenting day: let that skeleton be fleshed out by the syncretic body of Smiley seen through the performances of half a dozen superb actors. The voice was clear.

What about Karla? There's a cast-iron rule that he's unknowable. Karla is the opacity of the authoritarian regime, its capricious violence, its ubiquity, its weight. Like the shark in *Jaws*, he only becomes less alarming the more often you see him up close. And yet their enmity must have a starting point. The man must become the monster over time. Canonically, Smiley first tries to get Karla to defect in 1955, and when that happens his feelings towards this Russian officer – a single case among many – are almost collegial. Two decades later, they've become each other's shadows, defining the decline of one empire and the stifling brutality of another. What happens in between? That's part of what we're here to discover.

And, of course, Smiley stories are not in the end about spying. Smiley's Circus was the depiction of intelligence work, which for a lot of people – whether they know it or not – framed the Cold War. His was the grim, unrelenting and unacknowledged theatre of espionage, bounded by the threat of nuclear annihilation, fought through a mosaic of countries shoehorned into a binary international conflict, and ultimately unwinnable because victory of any real meaning lay in another arena entirely. The novels were both a snapshot of the moment and a window on the soul. Success, tacitly, meant something else: finding humanity in the deadlocked shadows, making the world better rather than worse as you go along, looking for a way to be kind in a context which favoured the cruel. My father's later books are overtly and specifically political, but the Circus stories are every bit as angry – they just don't restrict themselves to one target at a time. The Cold War as it was is over, so *Karla's Choice* cannot on the face of things be an image of the now. On the other hand, the pressing need to choose compassion – be it for conscripted enemies, refugees, future generations or ourselves – has never been more stark. Eric Hobsbawn said the twentieth century was short, but you could answer that we're still waiting for it to end.

In that respect, Smiley is again its definitional protagonist. The shape of his life is – to put it mildly, as he no doubt would – rather unclear. He was born in 1907 (*Call for the Dead*) unless it was in 1917 (arguably implied in *Tinker Tailor Soldier Spy*). But he's also of the same generation as Karla, who served as a kitchen boy on a train in 1904 (also in *Tinker Tailor*) – from which one could put his birthday sometime in the late 1890s. And so it goes: things change, and what we remember with absolute clarity turns out to be a shape in the mist.

That's very pretty, but what's the hard line? Why does Smiley's birthday move? On the face of it, because my father wasn't building a franchise. The point for him wasn't the professional's perfect construction of a world but the artist's telling of stories to make you feel. Go a little further, though, and you see something else: the critical dates of Smiley's life change because his age, across books, stays the same. Smiley is in his fifties the way Sherlock Holmes lives in Baker Street or Poirot is Belgian. *Karla's Choice*, therefore, follows a tonal rule of continuity: does it feel right? Is this Smiley as we recognise him? Can you read this book and move on to *Tinker Tailor* or back to *Spy*, and recognise the Circus as you might with another le Carré novel? As a practical matter, that means accepting the sweep of events and letting the specifics shift, so that the whole makes sense even if the details aren't perfectly identical – which, in one direction or another, they can't be. The perfectionist in me is outraged. The writer is delighted. The story comes first, the details must bend. The job is to produce a volume with a beginning, a middle and an end. It must move you, hold on to you and leave you wanting more.

Let's see if it does.

Prologue

The boy was wild and perfect, standing on the central table and clapping his hands. He had the eyes of a saint, Frau Möller recalled afterwards, an earthly saint like Francis, or a great thinker like Galileo. She had noticed him when he came in, past her little alcove by the door. She was not there to oversee the youth club. The young were specifically enjoined by the Party to organise themselves. Spaces were to be set aside for self-education and cultural awareness, and music was a part of that. If these gatherings became rowdy and inappropriate – if they were not strictly what had been envisaged by the committee – that was no concern of hers. She was employed only to keep the coats and close up. She had no other role.

But the boy had caught her attention because he was beautiful. She did not think he was German; he did not look German. If she had to guess, she would say he was from further east, perhaps even Odessa. He had what she called in her mind an Eastern face, with wide cheeks and high, hard edges. The beauty was more than physical, but it was also physical, of the kind that is rare in men but extraordinary when possessed. She had seen it before and was sorry for it. Men with that beauty were often fools because they rarely if ever heard the word 'no'. People made way for them and cosseted them without ever realising what they were doing, because the beauty was itself a form of compulsion. And also, sometimes, hurt them, for the same reason. Frau Möller had seen that too.

It was not a good night for music. The band was not good quality, but had agreed to come at the last minute because a Yugoslav group – probably no better – were supposed to be playing but had not arrived. Drugs, Frau Möller had heard: hash-ish in a guitar case. That was musicians: if it was not one thing it was another.

But the boy had not cared if the music was good or bad. He wanted only to have a high time and he had carried the whole club with him, the way such people do. He had begun to clap along with the indifferent guitar until others did as well, then to urge the band to be bolder in their choices; then to dance, and he had found a pretty girl to dance with and then all the boys were dancing with her and then all the girls were dancing with them. He had bought expensive drinks and then he had climbed up on the refectory table that ran across the middle of the room and begun stamping his feet. The beer in his hand splashed over his half-open shirt, so that he looked as disgraceful and salty as Aph-rodite coming up out of the sea in the main room of the state museum, and the whole dingy little den had pulsed with the rhythm of a heart, and only then was he satisfied. He sprawled in a chair, looking up at the pretty chaos he had made, and Frau Möller watched his wild eyes and wondered if he were crying.

And when, at the height of the feast, three men had entered – serious men, older and quite humourless – they had not cared about the dissolute behaviour in front of them, just about the boy. They had beckoned him over and said something, and he had not been alarmed. He had nodded: of course. He would be delighted to accompany them. He had expected them earlier. Would they like to have a drink first? Which to her amazement they had, everyone drinking together. And then – after that one drink – they had all left in good order, the boy sharing a joke with her on the way out, of which she remembered only the punch-line: 'But, of course, Mutti, because until now everything was satisfactory!'

Still laughing, he had gone out of the door into the Prenz-lauer cold.

I.

Crossing Primrose Hill on her way to the offices of Bánáti &
Clay, where her employer Mr Bánáti presided over the careers of
London's less dazzling literary stars, Susanna Gero had the
instinct that London was only now waking from a deep winter
sleep. In the yellow windows of flats and houses along the lower
edge of the hill, she could see people setting about the day. Low
above St Pancras, the sun was doing its best. Her mother would
have called it adequate, which was her favourite damnation.
Many things were adequate, and none of them was any better
than this Monday morning.

She turned towards Ormonde Terrace, shortening her stride.
This was the price of walking to the top of the hill for the view:
you had to come down again, along the slurried path which was
perilous even in flat shoes. She kept her head over her feet and
spread her arms, hoping no one was looking out of the terrace
windows and comparing her with the penguins half a mile away in
London Zoo. She had walked to school in snow every winter for
the first half of her life; she would not now be defeated by mud.

When she reached the office, she expected to find Mr Bánáti at
his desk, which was the one in the centre, her own to the left and
the third to the right. Instead the door was locked and she had to
open up and turn on the lights, which made her immediately
uncomfortable. Mr Bánáti woke early – the army, he had told
her – and performed a series of ludicrous exercises devised by a
Swiss. Then he drank coffee, ate whatever they sent from the
bakery on the high street and read books, mostly submissions
from new writers hoping for representation. The office was as
prim and tidy as the postbag was immense: there was an old

English woman called Wright who came late three nights a week to dust, with an actual scarf tied on top of her head in the classic style. By the time Susanna arrived each morning there was always a stack of discarded typescripts on the right side of his desk for repatriation, and very occasionally one on the left side for her attention. The two piles would be separated by the eight-by-ten-inch portrait photograph that was his only personal affectation. It showed a boy and a woman, the print older than the modern frame, and its presence indicated a kind of punctuation mark in his discussion with himself: I have done this work, I have arrived at this point, and now I may rest – but only for a short time, because literature never sleeps. And then, when she arrived, they would discuss the submissions.

'What do you think of our Miss Chancellor? Does she have what it takes?' Or 'Our Mr Simmonds: will he do well? Shall we admit him to the sanctum?'

'No,' she had replied with certainty, for Simmonds was on his third offering and each was worse than the last. Miss Chancellor, she allowed, was not awful.

This morning the desk was bare save for the photograph and a single soft pencil, Mr Bánáti's editing tool of choice, awaiting the call to arms. This simplicity was as mendacious as it was complete. The composure of the office was superficial and ended at the scratched green leather desktop. In the drawers, which smelled of wood polish, was chaos: more pencils; cufflinks, biscuits in and out of tins, mints and a spare pair of braces; shoe cream, reading glasses, a stapler, bills and invoices; and a locked cash box, heavy with coins, to which he had lost the key.

She was still wearing her coat, but she was cold. The fog was in here too, invisible but sharp on the tips of her front teeth. She felt an urge to turn around and walk back out into the street, to be anywhere that was not here, and as always there was no hard boundary in her between the idea and the act. It is the thing that separates the displaced from others: the deeper understanding of flight. You don't ask if it's necessary. If it is unnecessary, you can by definition return. You walk out and just keep walking, and know that the world is burned behind you. You go to the edge of town and find a farmer's truck, look up into the driver's expressionless face and his unlit Bulgarian cigarette, like the barrel of a disinterested gun. Tell him your lie: my people are in Tatabánya, in Győr. I need to go home. It does not matter that he believes you, only that he can say he did. In the passenger seat you share space with his rubber overboots and his liquor, travel past cars sunk in the mud and over the rutted tracks of Russian tanks. Go around this village because they are said to be there, head for that one. The day becomes night and you get stopped at a roadblock by patriotic farmers with patriotic rifles, but which patriotism? To which Hungary do they belong? There are so many. Mihály the driver is a known face. When he says you are a cousin, they know he is lying but everything is better. They laugh: lucky Mihály. You get out near Fertőd, his lips brief on your forehead like a holy blessing as he points the way, his breath a puff of smoke. Sad eyes to watch you leave, almost in the shadow of the palace. Walk the last miles and cross the border among the trees, get where you are going without realising it so you're still hiding and jumping at shadows, until you are stopped by a policeman in an Austrian uniform and you cry, cry, cry on his bemused shoulder, into rough wool lapels. Never see Mihály again, never try to find him because that will bring him trouble. Write to your mother and receive a message informing you of her arrest, of your father's. Wait, and wait, and wait to hear of their release, and keep waiting, until you forget that's what you're doing, and just live.

She looked at her own reflection in the window glass. You are twenty-three years old, not sixteen. The window fits snugly in the frame, the glass cut to the right size and of respectable quality. This is London, not Budapest. The year is nineteen sixty-three. Stay, then, this time.

She picked up the cloth and the brass key on the window ledge and bled the air from the top of the radiator, hearing it gurgle, snatching her hand away as the hot water reached the lock and bubbled out. Warmth made the room less alarming, and the sun was high enough for the sixty-watt bulbs to make it brighter rather than darker. She put coffee on the stove and lifted a stack of novels at random from the third desk where they waited. This was Mr Clay's desk, which was never used because Mr Clay was a *ruse de guerre*. People liked an agency better, Mr Bánáti said, if there were two names over the door, and better still if the whimsical artistry of the first, Mitteleuropäisch name was counterbalanced by Saxon practicality in the second. She sampled three offerings at random from the pile – never go from the top down, you'll either dismiss what's at the bottom because it's all the way underground or over-rate it because you've mined so far to get there – and put them aside. She stood in front of the empty desk.

The photograph was lying on its back as if he had been look-ing at it. For a moment she wondered whether he had taken the pencil and drawn a moustache over the glass, whether this morning whatever history was between them had come bub-bling to the surface. Except, not this morning. Last night, it must have been, after she went home: he must have returned to the office and sat here, late. Perhaps he did it a lot, and she had never seen the traces before. But her instinct said that he did not, that this was new, and that it was the kind of new that meant trouble. And, as she reached this conclusion, there came a knock at the door.

Susanna had her excuses ready: Mr Bánáti is indisposed, a family matter. She had no idea if he had family. She assumed yes – the woman and the boy – but he had never spoken of them. She assumed also, from the name, that he was Hungarian, like her; that he had penetrated the meagre disguise of removing the letter z from 'Zsuzsanna' and that he had hired her on that basis – but it was not discussed. In their silence they had achieved, she thought, the kind of affection that arises from having no deeper obligations, so that each was, for the other, a refuge from more difficult things. They didn't talk about the old country or why they weren't there. Everyone has reasons and only a fool expects them to be the same ones.

She opened the door and said good morning, and the man standing there said good morning too. He smiled and she smiled, and they were both doing very well with the polite exchanges, so that she felt they were conspiring nicely to make everything normal, despite the empty office behind her and his impending disappointment when he inquired for Mr Bánáti, or asked whether his typescript had found favour. Not yet, she would tell him, take his name and promise to put the book at the top of the pile. Perhaps she even would, or perhaps Bánáti had already turned it down. It was all of a muchness: an ordinary day.

But then he broke ranks, completely betrayed her and their burgeoning complicity. His gaze travelled to her face and properly took her in for the first time, and – just as she realised she had noticed him through the window a few moments before and recognised him with a young but not inexperienced woman's unfailing instinct for difficult older men – she saw or felt the bomb go off behind his eyes. His hand rose awkwardly, almost unwilled, towards her and she caught it, feeling the hard skin on the fingertips and acknowledging someone who had what Mr Bánáti occasionally referred to as a real job. She was staring at him just as he was at her, with a frank, un-English curiosity on both sides, as if a greater intimacy between them was not only inevitable but had in some sense already taken place. It was not, thank God, about sex. There was no hint of an embarrassing romantic aspiration in either his posture or his gaze. It was something entirely more disturbing and out of place: a fever of need which passed beyond lechery into the alarming territory of belief.

He was short and heavy and smelled of Ropotamo cigarettes, the unmistakable scent carrying to her as he first threw out and then withdrew the hand, with a brief flutter as it came back to his chest suggesting that even this retreat was unclear to him and might be revised. It was the same indecision that had attracted her gaze in the street outside, as he went first across the road from the bus stop to the butcher, then to the news agent, then finally from the news agent to the bus stop again, so that she had idly watched his progress while the coffee gurgled and he doubled back on himself, now reversing, now resuming, always glancing to the sky, to the ground, and into the eyes of any passer-by who might have whatever answer he was seeking, so intimate in his regard that they scuttled around him like good Christmas church-goers around a tramp.

Then there had come a period of exhaustion or paralysis, when he leaned on a wall and stared down at his shoes: dark, modest shoes to match the cigarettes, and trousers which were good, but hardly fine. A long mackintosh, buttoned and undistinguished, hung from his hunched shoulders to his knees. A preposterous loden hat, probably Austrian because it looked expensive, completed the set. A worn, sad man going on sixty, with a craggy Slav face and inherited Slav pain written all over it. She thought of old boys in coffee houses still lamenting the siege of 1541.

And now those fingers, callused at the tips and swollen around the knuckles either from arthritis or boxing, or both, laced around one another in his excitement.

'You are Ana, and your mother was Cintia, and your grand-mother was Eniko, and in another life I was your father, and you are a sign from God.' Having delivered himself of this informa-tion, he gazed at her, awaiting a suitable response. She did not immediately have one.

She supposed she was, or could be, Ana. Her mother and grandmother, though: those were wrong. She couldn't speak with absolute certainty on being a sign from God but had strong reservations, so she began to tell him no – but when she started her denial he threw himself, to her vast embarrassment, down on the floor, making with his body the full pilgrim's prostration, arms spread in the sign of the Cross as if she were a holy relic he had travelled hundreds of miles to see.

'Miki!' he said abruptly, to the worn, deep-green carpet and the moth traps. 'I am Miki. I am here to kill your Mr Bánáti on the personal instruction of a senior officer of the Thirteenth Directorate of the Committee for State Security of the Union of Soviet Socialist Republics. But I have changed my mind. I am Miki, and God has told me I will not be a murderer any more.'

The next thing she did was – Toby Esterhase later told her, as if she hadn't already known – completely mad. Looking at the moment in her own rear-view mirror, she concluded that it had been waiting for her since the night she had fled Budapest, and only now managed to get its teeth into her at last. She could, quite self-evidently, have called the police. Failing that, she could have required of Miki that he make his own arrangements, and report to her again when he had done so. He was, after all, a fully capable foreign spy, and he no doubt knew any number of ways to hand himself in. None of these required of her any personal engagement with the deeper circumstance.

In the event, she told Miki to stay where he was – actually to come inside and sit in one of the chairs – informing him that if he wanted to be useful he could read some of the slush pile. She locked him in, then took herself out and down the street, rushing the fifteen-minute walk to the mansion block where Mr Bánáti had his flat. She was furious with him for being in such danger, and for not telling her that this sort of thing could happen in publishing. She fully intended to give him hell about it, but it would wait until after she had made sure he was safe. She would not – could not – accept that he should be injured. That was, for reasons she could not at this moment properly express, quite unacceptable.

His spare key was on the office ring, and the concierge knew her from occasional social events for particularly exalted clients held on the premises. Taking the lift to the third floor, she found the light out and the day only somewhat seeping in along the east–west corridor. She walked to Number 6 and knocked. There was no reply. She knocked again, louder, wondering if Bánáti was alone or engaged in a personal matter. His social calendar was quite full, and he seemed especially popular with a category of English women over thirty who aspired to the description 'Bohemian'.

'Mr Bánáti,' she called. 'I'm so sorry, it's Susanna. Zsuzsanna Gero, from the office. There's an urgent matter. I'm afraid it won't wait. Can you hear me?' And, when no one answered, she added, 'I'm going to unlock the door.'

She waited a count of five and put the key in the lock, waited another five in the hope that the door would open from within, then turned it. The door was light on its hinges.

Her mind offered images of what she might see. Bánáti sleeping on his own sofa in his underwear, his socks and suspenders visible at the bottom of the blanket. Bánáti naked, halfway to open the door. Bánáti with a hole in his face like the old man at the roadside halfway between Csorna and Kapuvár. Strangled, stabbed, hanged, poisoned, shattered: Bánáti as a museum of punishment, though she realised she still had no idea what sin he might be punished for. The promulgation of decadent quasi-erotic literature. Bad jokes at parties. Crimes against proletarian dignity, mostly his own. Because proletarian was what he was. Of that, she had no doubt. László Bánáti hadn't come from one of the high estates. He wasn't even from the city. He had told her he grew up in farm country, and she believed it. I grew up thin, he'd said, patting his stomach. The harvest was never as good as it should have been.

She hunched her shoulders, ready to turn away from a corpse or an unexpectedly naked employer, and went in.

She wondered if she should take off her shoes. There were slippers by the door, a basket of woollen ones for guests, with leather soles. Oompah slippers. Christmas Eve slippers. She left them where they were.

Grey winter light from modern, south-facing windows. White carpet, no bloodstains. No mud or heavy footprints in the deep pile. White leather sofa, chrome legs. Matching chairs, three black and two white. No spatter of red. And no middle-aged feet, no ladies' undergarments. A long bar in dark wood, for serving breakfast or cocktails, or both. Bánáti was proud of it, of its novelty. He liked to be up to date. Glasses rinsed and put away. No open bottle of champagne. No ice pick.

By the window, an ashtray in thick brown glass, clean. A silver platter made of six small bowls, engraved and very fine, with nuts and olives in it. Magazines, ranging from the glossy to the crudely printed but high-brow. She called out again, this time not expecting an answer.

She felt a breath of movement in the air, and heard a sound, so low and indistinct that it barely qualified, and stopped cold.

Why was she here? Obviously, to warn Bánáti. But if Miki was to be taken at face value, why did Bánáti need to be warned? The source of the danger was presently sitting at her desk, in the grip of whatever pathological religious revelation had taken him. Unless Russian murderers, like the ones she had heard of as a girl, travelled not singly but in groups. In which case there might be one here, or more than one, and she was a fool.

The same soughing again, from the next room. She must leave, obviously. She must get out and call for help. Take refuge, let someone else deal with the rest of Miki's story, let someone else find Bánáti's body, or Bánáti alive.

She went forward instead. Cold air, indisputable now, washed along her arms and across the back of her neck. He has a cat. He has a dog. Someone, unrelatedly, is robbing him. I'm imagining everything.

She opened the door to the bedroom and almost screamed on seeing a tall figure standing just inside, wearing Bánáti's Burberry and hat. She reared back, almost falling, clipped her elbow on the doorframe and yelped, then a moment later recognised her assailant as a coat rack.

She went in again, still shaking.

The window was open six inches, and the blinds were moving in time with the breeze. The bed had been slept in and remade. Halfway along there was a rectangular indentation in the eiderdown: a box, or, more likely, a suitcase.

She looked around for anything else. Bánáti, at the office, was only neat superficially. There would be a place – a cupboard, a room, a drawer – where his uncompleted thoughts and ideas were piled one on top of another. Or perhaps he had left a note.

There was a small study on the other side of the hall. She went in and sat down at the desk, opening everything at once. The same clutter: pens, chocolate, old pairs of spectacles. A silk tie an author had given him for his birthday. A stack of postcards, unmarked, from tourist spots. Bánáti liked to use them instead of plain ones when he was sending a book for someone's consideration. Another copy of the photograph in an identical frame. More pencils.

And, held together by a single rubber band: a small bundle of letters in French, postmarked Vienna, and addressed to Mr László Bánáti, London.

She clutched them to her chest and ran like hell.

Just under an hour later, Susanna climbed the slippery stone steps of a corner building in West Hampstead. Miki trailed behind her, wide-eyed like a tourist, as if the ferns in pots were the equal of Buckingham Palace. She thought he probably wasn't right in the head, and on the way here, first walking and then sitting with him on the lower deck of a juddering Routemaster bus, with László Bánáti's letters clutched to her chest, she had asked herself repeatedly whether she should just tell him no. No to religious epiphanies and Russian spies, no to her unwelcome memories, and no to his ridiculous hat. But Miki had invoked a bond between them which – however fantastical and fevered – she also felt. The British talked about refugees, because refuge was what you wanted, and the Hungarian word was *menekült*, 'one who has fled' – but in German you were a *Flüchtling*, which was the same and yet also, more deeply, a citizen of the nation of escape. We are both sudden escapers, she thought, and accepted that she had obligations on that score.

Bánáti was gone. He had not called. Had stayed late on the Friday, which was against his habits, had packed a suitcase and disappeared. Had been, now that she thought of it, distracted for the last few days, as if he had known somehow of Miki's coming. She had found nothing in her cursory and inappropriate search of his correspondence at the office, nothing in his wastepaper basket, nothing in the drawers; less than nothing, because the heavy cash box – ludicrous by its permanent closure but reassuring by its weight, as if the whole edifice of Bánáti & Clay rested stoutly on a brace of gold ingots held in that secret space – had gone.

Miki had watched her investigations with the politeness that professionals reserve for rank amateurs taking their first steps in the field, so much so that she had suffered a spasm of horrified conjecture, asking herself whether he might after all be on the hunt, might be using her to track down the missing Bánáti, having concocted this ingenious deception. In which case he must by now be realising that he had come to the wrong shop, because it was increasingly obvious that she had no idea where Bánáti might have gone, or who he was, or how to find him; and in which case surely he would now move to silence the witness to his failed plan. But he showed no sign of doing so, just sat meekly opposite her on the patterned felt seats, awaiting her next command. Like Faust, she conjured him: in the name of Ana, who I am not, and her mother, who wisely chose a different husband, and her mother's mother, who no doubt also had views – do my bidding. And he did, which made no sense at all.

She had not the head for this – for hiding and jumping at shadows – not any more and perhaps never, and, if she was going to do the right thing in the end, the right thing now was to get help. She needed someone to trust, and Bánáti was by definition unavailable. She needed something like a friend.

And so to the corner building of the red-brick terrace in Broomsleigh Street which housed the Adams Secretarial Agency, wherein Genevieve Adams, a small and angular Nonconformist, had for two decades provided structure in the lives of the powerful with the stark and simple clarity of a plain carriage clock. She had with equal scrupulousness run the offices of a bishop and a titan of industry; two high court judges had been unable to function without her magical appointment book, and one had eventually graduated to the Law Lords and retained her for five years there, before a fall from a horse during a state function had sadly brought his career to a close. Miss Adams had then, under the will, been responsible for the retirement of the horse, until it too was returned to sender. Now she specialised in the supply of reliable administrative minds trained to a standard she considered sufficient, and took on not only British girls running from families that disapproved of education and careerism in young women but also recent arrivals with the dust of travel still on their shoes.

Somewhere along life's road – from what source, exactly, was unknown, though everything from the Metropolitan Police to the back rooms of West End theatres had been extensively discussed – she had acquired a business partner who was as unlike Miss Adams herself as you were like to find.

Rose Jeremy was wide and strong, with large hands and a thick mop of curly brown hair that was only now going grey, and if she held to a religious doctrine it was uniquely her own. She grieved for someone, regularly and sitting by herself looking out of the front window, into what recollection or absence was not discussed. In her grief, as in the rest of her life, she was forthright and unashamed. You could bring Mrs Jeremy any problem that was too embarrassingly human for Miss Adams. She was a keeper of secrets and a mender of hearts, and, if the situation demanded, a thrower-out of undesirable lovers. Susanna had seen her do it, first politely and then with emphasis. The young man taken by the scruff and shown the door had barely touched the ground from the living room to the street. It was rumoured that Mrs Jeremy regularly won arm-wrestling contests in public houses; that she had served with distinction in the war; and that Jeremy had at one time perhaps been her first name. It did not matter if any of these things were true. Miss Adams would see you employed, and there was no snarl of paper, no ticklish issue of regulation or etiquette, however complex, that she could not in due time untangle. But Mrs Jeremy could answer questions you didn't know how to ask, and, within the compass of her sight, no evil – however trivial or commonly accepted – could hold dominion.

Susanna, as a graduate and former inmate – the agency provided accommodation for unmarried girls on its middle floors – was always welcome and still had a key, but it was the rule that anyone bringing a guest should ring the bell. Male guests were notionally out of bounds in all circumstances, though this diktat was strictly applied only in the context of males who were not desired as guests. To Susanna's mind Miki was not so much a guest as a misdelivered parcel, or a particularly alarming pet someone had asked her to look after, but in any case the bell was required. She leaned on it, and a moment later the door was opened by Mrs Jeremy, whose smile never wavered as her eye settled on the man, on the dark shoes and lined face, on something undefined under his left armpit and something else below the knee, and finally on his gnarled hands.

'Oh, yes?' Mrs Jeremy said.

'He's with me,' Susanna replied. 'Harmless,' which was on the face of it absurd, but Susanna believed that in the immediate context it was true.

'I am Miki,' Miki said, and Susanna put her hand on his shoulder before he could add that he was a professional murderer seeking new employment and that she was a sign from God.

Mrs Jeremy's brown eyes considered her and Miki both, summing up the distance between them, then searching Susanna's face for reservation or concealed dismay. Finally she sighed.

'Waifs and strays, is it?'

'Yes,' Susanna agreed, pleased to have it said aloud. 'Waifs and strays.'

On the west side of the Circus main building was the switchboard, operated between six a.m. and midnight by the Housekeeping Section and thereafter under the purview of the night-duty officer. With the notable exception of the direct line on Control's desk, which went to the Ministry and in wartime to Downing Street, telephone calls to and from the Circus were routed through this room. In times of crisis – of which the recent decade had thrown up more than was desirable, from Suez to Cuba and all points in between – as many as a dozen operators could work the board. In general it was restricted to four.

At five minutes after one, according to the log book, Lily Rippon answered a call to one of the numbers the Post Office kindly reserved for Circus use, while listing them, even internally, to fictional businesses in the North.

'Anderson Ltd?'

'I need to talk to Mrs Kemp,' a woman said. 'It's about a friend.'

'I'll put you straight through,' Lily responded; 'just give me your number in case we're disconnected.' She listened and wrote down the number, which, if the woman was staying on script, would be her identifier, corresponding with a Registry entry listing the real name and address. Then she disconnected her microphone and opened an internal circuit. Kemp: Head of Section. Friend. Possible Russian involvement. 'Mrs McCraig?' she said. 'It's for you. The Chorus Line.'

The Housekeeping Section occupied an anomalous position within the Circus. Responsible in concept for no intelligence gathering at all, it operated notionally on the same level as Banking, where men no longer viable in the field but without the chops for planning or oversight were parked until they could draw a pension. Staffed for the most part by women who had put on a uniform during the war and never spiritually removed it, or by their daughters, it did the kind of work the more hot-blooded in the Circus hierarchy tended to overlook. It was Housekeeping that identified, obtained and modified domestic properties suitable as safe houses. It was Housekeeping that procured plane tickets, general-use vehicles and detailed survey maps, and maintained the absurd warehouse in Eltham which held among other things the public telephone directories of every nation in Europe; and Housekeeping also that in the first instance recruited and vetted clerical staff into the Circus pool and the embassies, and subsequently kept an eye on them in case they went to the bad – or, more hopefully, in case they should ever, in the course of their onward employment, run across anything that had, however diffusely, the smell of someone else's tradecraft.

In practice, therefore, the Head of Housekeeping not only kept the Circus lights on and fended off the day-to-day miserliness of Treasury, but also presided de facto over one of the largest unitary passive security networks in the world. The Chorus Line did not propose to occupy centre stage, but from time to time it provided the absolutely necessary beginning or ending of a show.

'Connect me,' Millie McCraig said. 'But stay on the line and take notes.'

A few moments later she emerged from her office and marched upstairs, carrying a tray of tea from the shiny catering urn in the kitchen. Ten minutes after that, she returned and issued a series of instructions. The first was that Lily was to misfile those notes until further notice, then take the rest of the day off. This, McCraig gave Lily to understand, came directly from Control.

Second, she wanted an available safe house in the London area prepared for one occupant plus a babysitter. Then she went back into her office and placed a call to Oliver Mendel, newly returned to Scotland Yard's Special Branch after some time in an undisclosed wilderness, asking politely that he get over to Broomsleigh Street with dispatch.

'How much dispatch?' Mendel asked.

Ideally an hour ago, Millie McCraig told him, but second best would be now.

'All right,' Control had said, in his meagre office on the fifth floor. The year wasn't yet far enough advanced for the room to be too hot, so it was still bitter, and Control wore a lank wool cardigan which somehow failed to hide the shape of his ribs. When he turned his head, his spectacles caught the light of his desk lamp and his other features all but vanished. 'I want him. But I want him to myself, you understand? Nobody else. As far as the rest of the Circus is concerned, he's just another third-rater. And perhaps that will turn out to be the truth. For general consumption: an allied service burned him and he's too flat-footed to go back in. Or maybe they were a bit public and he's rightly frit. He's low grade, hardly worth the investment of our time; we're going to wring him out and get him a civilian job. Codename . . . something from Gilbert and Sullivan. Frederick. Marmaduke. Stanley. Process the paperwork as if you've got better things to do. Line him up for Sarratt as normal but we won't send him till I'm ready.'

Millie McCraig nodded. 'He'll need a babysitter.'

'Tom Lake from Travel. Get him up from Brixton and tell him I said so. Tell him it's a punishment detail and he's to make that clear. He's offended me with his barbarous atheism. Is he an atheist?'

'I don't know. Probably.'

'Well, if not, then I object to his snivelling piety. You don't want to write that down?'

'No need, thank you.'

'One more thing: I want Smiley.'

'I'll get Sam Collins.'

'I ask for Amadeus and you offer me Clementi. No, Millie, not Collins. Not Collins, not Haydon, not Esterhase, not that bloody fool Alleline. And not Bobby Maston either, or the publican at the Dog and Duck. George Smiley.' He flapped an exasperated, almost translucent hand as if too tired for her disobedience. 'Smiley. Cause it to happen.'

'You realise you can't just order him back?'

'I'm not ordering him back. I'm ordering you to bring him back.' Behind the spectacles, the nasty, knowing eyes looked direct into hers.

'He's not going to pack his life in just because I ask him to.'

Truth, alas. One dark autumn morning last year after all the bad things, from a standing start and in defiance of her own simple religious conviction, she had suggested that they might just pack it all in and run away together forever. They could go to New Zealand, she said, where her sister had a farm. Smiley had been very polite.

'Indeed. But I fancy you can deliver him to me for a week or so. Even forty-eight hours. Can't you?'

She knew she should deny it, and let George go.

'Yes,' she said.

The Circus, after everything that had happened, was enjoying a small heyday. Control's preference for patient intelligence gathering over the interventionist American style only looked wiser in the light of Khrushchev and Kennedy, and if certain persons – he meant Bill Haydon – wanted to see more action, they could find ways to see it without overturning the world.

Haydon himself had handed the Cairo office to Percy Alleline, and where he was now headed no man knew. Venezuela, Roddy Martindale said with authority, running liquor into Cuba and seeding networks from Caracas to Recife. Nonsense, Brookes retorted: it would be Addis for certain; the Soviets were looking hard at Africa. To which Haydon when it was put to him replied he was fine with both, so long as there was canvas, women and wine, and the wiser sort of watcher deduced that it was neither.

But what about Smiley's job, they asked instead, will he get that? Not yet, not unless, who else, and why shouldn't he? And a dozen other questions and speculations that fed the grey gossips of St James's between the fish course and the brandy, but shed light on nothing at all.

In August last year, almost on the anniversary of the Wall, a senior Soviet military man with superb access had offered his clandestine services to Great Britain in the cause of righteousness and Estonian liberty. His first product was an assessment of Baltic shipyard capacity and scope of air cover in the North Atlantic that made the Admiralty weak at the knees. Control recorded General Vladimir as four separate sources in Moscow, Leningrad and Riga, and allocated separate funds and lines of communication to each one, like a mother bear burying her cubs to the eyes in the snow.

Fate sought to balance the scales a month later when the network in Belgrade that Jim Prideaux had set up in fifty-seven was blown, and there were rumours of a new broom in the Soviet cupboard: a cold, sophisticated mind drawing together the disparate lineages of the Kremlin's spies – but there were always rumours. In truth it looked like sheer carelessness on the Serb end; the network hadn't been producing much since sixty-one, and there'd been talk of winding it up anyway.

A fortnight after that, the Circus was on the rise again, when a Czech trade delegation in France decided to attend a celebrated brothel, and compromised themselves with extreme thoroughness right under the nose of the Paris resident. 'I couldn't have arranged it,' the resident reported. 'I'm just bloody lucky, and so are you.' He asked for, and received, a team of Czech-speaking inquisitors for debrief in place, and a line from the reptile fund for continuing exploitation. Economic mysteries behind the Iron Curtain shimmered and were laid bare.

The fly in the ointment was Hans-Dieter Mundt: senior Stasi officer, deeply secret Circus asset and acknowledged full-time bastard, personally responsible for the deaths, as October turned and the year grew dark, of Alec Leamas and Liz Gold.

It had been Control's intention that Smiley should have the running of Mundt within the East German apparat, but by the end of the month it had become clear that other arrangements would be necessary. Control found himself with the choice – taking as a given that he did not wish to bring anyone else in on the secret – of appointing Peter Guillam to handle Mundt or assuming the role personally. But Guillam in Control's eyes was still a young hothead, too enamoured of the mythology of the wartime Circus. At twenty-nine, he was barely even an adult. He had also loved Alec Leamas and now loathed Mundt.

'How, if I asked you, Peter?' Control wondered in his office, a week after Guy Fawkes Night. 'How would that sit?'

'Badly,' Guillam replied. 'But I'd still do it, of course.'

'Of course, you would. But what about slip-ups?'

'What about them?'

'It wouldn't require a lot, you see. A word out of place, and he'd be for the chop. It's not as if they care much about evidence, Fiedler to the contrary. It's all theatre of loyalty over there. The right slip-ups and you'd find justice for Alec lickety-split.'

'We don't do justice, though, do we?' Guillam suggested. 'That's another department.'

For which questionable assurance he was rewarded with the directorship of Causse-Bergen International Furs, a respectable front company with offices on the grimmer bank of the Spree.

In Egypt, in Poland, in Japan, the networks thrived and the intelligence product flowed. Perhaps Control, in his tower on the fifth floor, still fretted at the wretched end of Operation

Jackknife in fifty-nine, but he was alone. Intelligence work was not, the operations men told one another with a hint of pride, a safe drawing-room entertainment. They had not signed up to it for the avoidance of risk.

Of the fate of Alec Leamas a few scant months before, no one spoke. If Peter Guillam sat on Parliament Hill one dismal night and poured half a bottle of Scotch into the City of London's grass, and raised the rest in toast towards the Post Office Tower and St Paul's, his actions went unremarked. If Jim Prideaux, in the Czechoslovak capital of Prague, leaned on the icy Charles Bridge with his eyes on the river, and sang the 'Anne-Marie of the Second Legion' to a wary crow, even the Státní Bezpečnost were unable to draw informative conclusions – though no doubt reports were filed.

Shortly after her meeting with Control, Millie McCraig went out of the Circus to the narrow garage by the stage door of the Prince Edward Theatre where she kept her car. She also had said a private farewell to Alec Leamas during this recent winter, but it had required no particular place or ritual. Sometime between Christmas and New Year, walking to the shops or dusting her late husband's office – not preserved, just unexorcised, and one day soon she would, she really would, sort all that out – she had added Alec to her personal list of the fallen, engraved him on a wall that existed only for her, and called him a bloody fool. When you keep house for secret soldiers, you have to live with secret funerals.

She started the car and took the Oxford road. The sun was washing the shop windows and potholes with fierce winter light. Inexplicably, in spite of death, the world continued.

Susanna, in Broomsleigh Street, was staring at Miki's fingers. They had taken tea with shortbread – a marked concession on Miss Adams's part, for whom shortbread was generally reserved for elevenses – and since Miki was feeling his religion, they had talked about God more than was entirely comfortable. Then they had moved on to home cooking and finally to cricket, with Miki politely uncomprehending but willing to learn. Now even that had fallen away. Miki had closed his eyes and seemed to be prepared to wait forever. In the silence, Susanna found herself fascinated by his nails. In contrast to the hard work in his hands, they were well-kept and pink, but curled around his fingertips to the midline so that they resembled the windscreen of a French bubble car.

She heard the main door open and a woman's voice call out to let them know she was back. 'I think I got it,' the woman said. 'They liked me, I know that. I'm worried about the shorthand, though. Can someone help me brush up?' As she said 'up', she came through the door, sidestepping until she was standing behind Miki. She was tall, with broad shoulders like a swimmer's. 'Because I don't think I've got it right, Miss Adams, I can't keep all the Pitman in my head.'

'Not to worry, Sally,' called a man's voice, 'I don't think that's going to be a problem. There's not so much call for it, nowadays, though they do ask.' And now he was through the door as well, a slight figure in a blue suit, with a thin face and thin, greying hair cut close to the scalp. To Susanna he had the look of a professional mourner. 'I'm Inspector Oliver Mendel,' he said to the room at large. 'And this is my sergeant, Sally Roberts. Welcome to London, Mr Bortnik, and thank you for staying quite exactly as you are.'

Sally Roberts laid her right arm like the diagonal of a three-point seat belt down and across Miki's chest, the left side of her head resting gently against his own. Her other hand was on his left shoulder, or perhaps his neck. 'Nice to meet you, Miki. Are you married? Don't worry, I'm not after your virtue. That's it. Nice and easy.' Her hand slipped inside his coat to remove the gun, keeping contact with his chest as it moved back up so that

23

the barrel lay down along his body. When she reached the collar-bone, it went around his shoulder and into her coat pocket. 'Now, is there anything else I need to take notice of, or are we an honest man?'

'Left ankle,' Rose Jeremy said, and Sally watched as Miki removed a short, wide-bladed knife in a sheath and laid it next to his shortbread. 'Good lad,' she said, as it went into her other coat pocket. 'That the lot?'

Miki nodded.

'Check, anyway,' Mendel ordered, but she already was. He turned to Susanna. 'Well,' he said, 'aren't you having a day?'

And for the first time in a hundred years, she laughed. It came from the stomach, a witch's laugh rather than a wife's: another thing her mother would have sighed at. She saw Sally Roberts watching her. 'What?'

'She's wondering if you'll cry next,' Mendel explained. 'It wouldn't be unreasonable.'

Susanna felt her shoulders lift in a shrug. 'No,' she said, and saw Roberts's lips quirk in something that wasn't quite a smile.

They went outside. It was unobtrusively busy for the hour. Two men were fixing a fence opposite, their van, beneath the grime, promising repairs and decoration work. A few houses down, there was an unfamiliar fellow tinkering under the bonnet of a car, and, in the other direction, two more were replacing the lamps in the black iron Victorian street lights. The decorators waved, and crossed over.

'Nice day for it,' Mendel said to them.

'Don't worry, I hear it's rain later.' As if they were old friends. Sally Roberts escorted Miki gently to the van.

'All right, then,' Mendel said, pointing to his own car. 'Westward ho.'

They got in and set off, as Susanna had half expected, heading east.

*

George Smiley's letter of resignation from the Circus had been just long enough, and professional to the point of affectless. In the light of a recent track record he did not himself regard as exemplary – he did not mention Leamas or Operation Windfall by name – he felt the interests of all parties would be best served by his departure. He was keen to spend more time with Ann, he had always intended to devote a decade to his *Germanistik*, a man reaches a certain age, et cetera. Smiley regretted, and one felt that he really did. Control replied towards the end of January, without personal comment, and the thing was done. It was a sad conclusion to a storied career, but mistakes have their price. If the stones of Cambridge Circus accused, perhaps they were right. Someone had to carry the can.

Smiley had until then moved like a kind of fog among Lady Ann's smart set, but in his unemployment it appeared that there might be, after all, a man inside the mist. Not a wag, not by any measure, and not a dancer or a gay blade, but surely enough an affable, intelligent fellow with a wit so dry you could mistake it – many had – for dullness. But if you did – so went the word that winter – if you did, well, then: the joke was on you.

It began to be whispered among Ann's cousins that Smiley, for all that these recent years had been spent in some abhorrently complex corner of the Treasury calculating milk futures or the export value of the pilchard, had very briefly been something almost daring in forty-four. He denied it, but, of course, George would. And, having denied it, quite coincidentally, he was lured one crisp noontide into a pistol-shooting challenge along the yew lane of her uncle's ancient manse, empty ginger-beer bottles arranged at thirty feet. He missed all but one of them with such good humour and clear bewilderment that the onlookers concluded he could have had the lot, and smartly too, had he not wanted to stay below the line.

And Ann? How was the lovely Ann? Freshly besotted, it appeared. She had her George all to herself, his eyes no longer straying faithlessly to the grey pages of Ministry reports or the pink ones of the *Financial Times*, to the balance of trade or all tomorrow's speeches in Westminster, or whatever it was that a round-faced, round-bodied man in middle age might absurdly think more important than a wife like her. In the mornings, with Smiley buried in a commentary on Opitz reputedly by Zincgref but displaying in his candid opinion strong overtones of Heinsius, she assured him by quiet solicitousness and fond, frequent touches of the hand that he was, of himself, enough. In the afternoons they were so frequently absent from the main rooms that one of her friends was moved to inquire whether, given the terrain, she wouldn't rather wait until nightfall, to which Ann responded tartly that – however things might look – there was never any competence to which George Smiley truly set his mind in which he did not excel. And if that was only mostly true, it hardly mattered. That winter, it was true enough. Having done away with the Circus as his too-demanding mistress, Smiley lived between libraries and love, and came as close to contentment as a man of his peculiar constitution is able. Without a tie and with several pairs of spectacles distributed around his reading-room lair, you might have taken him for anything from a schoolmaster recovering after the term time's excessive use of restorative alcohol to a bibliophile ticket collector newly pensioned from the Cornish Riviera Express.

In the early spring of nineteen sixty-three, there was a rumour – unconfirmed and a little scandalous – that George Smiley might almost be happy.

'George,' Ann said, her forehead close to the lead-light window, 'look who's here.'

Someone she didn't like, or she would just have used the name. Someone who made her nervous, which was no one. Smiley had been awaiting the inevitable Peter Guillam, arriving in motor-cycle leathers full of high drama with the almost filial piety of their long professional friendship. 'Come on, George, old boy. I'm sure you've had your fill by now. Time to get back to it: there's a job of work to be done.' But Guillam went in fear of Ann, not vice versa: the wife of my not-father is definitionally my not-mother. Besides – an unwanted operational skill recalled – the arrival had been a car.

He went to the window and let his shoulder touch hers so that their hands found one another. He could feel the cold of the quarries by his cheek.

On the gravel below was an achingly stylish MGA coupé, and a narrow woman in black driving trousers and a matching turtle-neck jumper. In defiance of decorum, the driver marched straight past the staff and into the hallway. Smiley could hear her giving them hell on the floor below.

'Don't be absurd. I'm here to talk to Smiley. You needn't announce me – he'll know by now, you've made such a fuss. All right, you big baby, if you must, you must. But pick up your feet, man, I've no time for your nonsense! McCraig. Amelia McCraig. Go!'

Ann looked anything but amused. 'What's she doing here?'

'We shall no doubt be told.'

'She's going to ask you to come back.'

'She already has. I said no.'

'That just means this time she's got a better angle.'

'Then let's hope it will be good enough that she hears the reply.'

'Third time's a charm,' Ann muttered, but she opened the door and positively beamed. 'Millie, darling, always a pleasure. Come in and sit down. You're lucky to have caught us, we're off to the most glamorous party in the Alps. I love your car, so racy. I told George we should get something with real legs. He said I had great legs, what on earth would we do with another pair?'

'Spares,' McCraig said blandly, 'so that yours don't get over-used. Please don't trouble with the hospitalities, Lady Ann, I'm afraid I've business with your husband. Old business, I promise, not new. George, five minutes. Then St Moritz can have you back.'

'Five minutes,' Ann said, before Smiley could speak. 'I'll leave you to it, then. Always a pleasure, Millie. And I do love that car. Spotless. So *you*.'

She smiled sincerely and saw herself out into the hall.

Smiley waited until McCraig was sitting. There were two sofas at right angles to one another with a low table in between for cups and decency. She chose the one perpendicular to the door so that he could take the other looking straight at it. The cushions were enormous, printed with rich red peonies, and she had a sudden image of him as a pudgy middle-aged orphan sitting in the master's office on arrival, awaiting dispensation. His hands touched at the fingertips, the thumbs resting against his chest in an attitude of prayer. To her suppressed irritation, the line of his gaze never dropped below the shoulder.

'It's new business,' she said. 'I lied. I'm sorry.'

'Come on, Millie,' Smiley said. 'It's done. Let the old dog sit by the cooker – don't ask him to go and chase rabbits with the younger ones. It's embarrassing all round. Even for the rabbits.'

'You're not old,' she growled at him.

'But I am tired. It's all right for things to change. People to move on. Sometimes it's best.'

'Is that you talking? Or her?'

'It's us, Millie. Ann and I have had our difficulties, but we're not divisible, in the end. I pulled her into my way of living for ten years and it didn't work. Now I'm letting her pull me and I find it rather fine. Mirth isn't fatal, as it turns out. Contrary to what you may have been told.'

'I know that.'

'Good, then. Let be. It's lovely to see you, but I'm not coming back.'

'That's not what he's asking.'

'Control did send you?'

'Yes.'

'I'm surprised. I thought he'd start with Peter, or maybe Toby. My protégés. He's a don, after all: he sees the world in terms of disciples and lineages.'

'Peter says you're well out of it. He's angry about Alec.'

'He's right to be.'

'Why?'

'You know why. You were there. Control made a decision and I went along with it. We chose to win a bloody battle with more blood. When I came to my senses, I realised I'd crossed a line. I tell myself the Circus must triumph because the other side is monstrous; that London and Washington must defeat Moscow because we understand the obligation of the ruler to the ruled, and they do not. But, come to it, we abandoned our obligations and chose to be every bit as monstrous ourselves in quest of victory, and I said nothing. In saying nothing I also, for that matter, barred you and Peter from any objections you might have made. Alec was the price. "I bad thee, when I was distracted of my wits."'

'I wouldn't have said anything.'

'Or perhaps you would. We don't know, because I stood for you and I chose collaboration with what I can now only think of as evil.'

'What if I left too?'

'Then the Circus would be poorer by one extremely able officer.'

'And what about you? What will you do?'

'I am destined for moderate things. I find the prospect enchanting.'

'You know what I meant.'

'And so do you.' He shrugged and settled a little more into the ridiculous cushions. 'Come on, Millie. Say what you came to say.'

'So you can go to St Moritz.'

'It's Geneva, actually. Some sort of art thing for Ann. Then onwards to Austria for me. Goethe, set to music at the Opera House. And, after that, the Wolfgangsee – too cold for swimming, alas, we shall have to do that next time. Very fine.'

For a moment, she hated him. Bad enough when he had loved honour more; worse now that he loved Ann. Although she supposed he always had, and now that he had surrendered it was just less painful for him. She took the moment and held it, used it and applied the knife.

'There's a girl, Susanna Gero. She's Hungarian. She works for a fleshy sort of literary agent named László Bánáti here in London.' She waited.

Smiley shrugged: carry on.

'This morning a man presented himself at her door and told her he'd come to kill her boss on behalf of Moscow Centre, but he wasn't going to do it because it was a dirty job and she was a message from God. She went to someone on my list for advice and they called the Chorus Line and got me. I went to the fifth floor. The man – Mikhail Bortnik – is in Cornhill. Control's keeping him very close. The girl's with Mendel and that Amazon sergeant of his: Roberts.'

'That sounds very good.'

'It does, except that Bánáti's missing, presumed on the lam, and no one has the faintest idea who he is or why Moscow'd want him dead. No Radio Salvation Budapest, no cheeky émigré newspapers. He's not much to look at, and he should be.'

'Perhaps it's a personal matter. Settling an old score.'

'What person? Agapov? Pogodin? And, if so, why now?'

'Excellent operational questions. The Circus is in good hands.'

'Control wants you to take it.'

'I'm sure he does. Who has my job, by the way?'

'It's a temporary appointment.'

'Temporarily, then. Haydon? Prideaux? Sam Collins, if he wants a younger man. Esterhase, if he trusts him. Not Alleline, surely; they loathe one another.'

'Oakmoor,' Millie replied.

'Quite so. A comfortable woollen glove for his iron hand. Un-alarming and unambitious. It's a subtler choice than you might think. Not everybody in an organisation needs to be a bright star – someone has to plod along and fill in all the gaps. Most of spying is ordinary, and the extraordinary is rarely good news. Oakmoor will do well for him, if that's what he wants.'

'Control –'

'Wants me back. You said.'

'I was going to say to hell with Control. Never mind what he wants or why. Never mind any of that. This is me talking. I want you to come back, just for this. For the girl.'

'Gero? Why?'

'Who else is going to walk her in, George? Who? On that list? Bill? Bill's going to walk into the Circus and be presented with a pretty Hungarian girl up to her neck in a Moscow assassination plot and he'll take care of her? Look after her? Make sure at the end of all this she's alive and she can sleep nights and not look over her shoulder the rest of her days? Toby? Sam? There's not one of them'll give a damn about her. But you will, won't you? Because there are responsibilities. You said it, not me. Because not to give a damn would be monstrous. Am I wrong? You know I'm not. That's what I want from you, George Smiley. Walk her in, get everything from her and see her safe out. Forty-eight hours. And I'll never ask again.'

Smiley opened his mouth to say that if he took forty-eight hours he'd miss the party, and then wondered who it was who had been about to speak.

'It won't be forty-eight hours,' he said at last. 'Control will try to get me to handle Bortnik too. There'll be complications.'

'Not necessarily.'

'Yes, necessarily. I want Connie involved from the beginning, otherwise we'll only have to brief her in later. Toby Esterhase for the Hungarian connection in London, for the same reason.'

'Control will say it's too many.'

'Control said I was retired. Now you ask me back.'

McCraig looked away. 'Gero, George. Safely in, safely out.'

She did not say that was her price for absolution.

From the window of the library where Smiley's books were still open, awaiting their last-minute transfer to a travelling case, Ann watched her husband walk Millie McCraig back to the car. His head was down towards his stomach, his shoulders more rounded even than usual. McCraig's driving shoes clipped on the gravel, but nothing in her spoke of having given an inch. He held the door for her and slammed it shut, and she went neatly around the circle and out on to the drive.

Smiley did not watch her go but turned immediately to the house, his eyes questing, finding Ann at the window and answering her gaze with apology as he came inside.

'Damn,' Ann whispered to the books and the pages of notes. 'Damn, damn, damn.'

Her hands clenched, and the burning in her chest and the scream in her throat threatened to overwhelm her, but she held on, and felt them sink down and down into the pit where she kept such things. She practised with her reflection in the glass. Of course. Of course, darling. I'll meet you in Austria. Don't worry, I'm sure Gloria will take care of me. Of course.

She held her own eyes until she could believe every word. She would not crack. If she could not induce Smiley to stay by her side with her laughter, she absolutely declined to keep him with her tears.

2.

For Smiley, the experience of returning to the Circus that evening was like a willed drowning. It was as if, as he climbed St Martin's Lane in the direction of his old office, he were making his way down on to the plain of an abyssal sea. For the last months he had lived in a daylight world, had espoused its meanings and attitudes, and enjoyed the simple pleasures of other men. He had gone to Jermyn Street and bought a coat because it pleased him rather than because it looked like every other coat on every other traveller. He had ordered memorably when eating out, and had asked for small alterations to suit his taste: the kind of things that are not troublesome, but are likely to be recalled by waiters in any subsequent inquiry, and thus also by the maître d', and so attached to names and fellow diners. He had argued with taxi drivers, helped strangers with shopping, given directions, and in general allowed himself to be known and notable in the ordinary passages of life. He had, reciprocally, stopped paying attention to the minor and irrelevant doings of others, so that ten days ago he could not have told you whether the man browsing in a bookshop in Cecil Court was interested in Ovid or Euclid or the history of English cricket, or merely killing time while he waited for an appointment.

Now, as he approached the familiar door, he found that he was once again engaging in the exercise of paranoia, which had governed his former life. Deliberately, he let the nature and movements of his fellow pedestrians function as a random factor in his own movements, making up ridiculous rules as he went along. He turned right on Litchfield Street because the man in front of him wore tan leather shoes, then left after the White

Swan because he was overtaken by a cyclist. Then he crossed the road after seeing an even number of pedestrians, before digressing to Seven Dials to pay homage, because there were, superficially, only six. It was Control's amusement to send the new agents out to find the last, and send them back to Sarratt if they couldn't.

This winding route allowed him to cross over his own track more than once and look back the way he had come, to see whether he could detect – in spite of his own frequent assertion that with any respectable operation you never would – someone following him in the street. The habit was easy to resume, but the understanding which should underpin it – the deep knowledge that nowhere, not London nor Paris nor Washington, was entirely safe – required of him an act of decision. At the corner of Tower Street, he had the sense of standing and looking up at the surface of the water, the sun pale above black waves, but not yet having breathed in and resumed his life below. The shadow in the doorway was still just some fellow cleaning the brass, and the woman running was hoping to catch a bus, not to draw his eye for the approach of some confederate from the blind side. The boy walking hunched and alone was just a boy on his way home to the housing estate, and the beggar on the corner slept under bridges and had no reporting responsibility to anyone. And that tread beside him, light and sure, was the memory of a friend, and nothing more.

With due attention, he considered each until all the threats they might represent were once again real in his mind, and even these were only an earnest of wilier foes unseen. The notion of constant danger was a madness that men in his profession must both inhabit and put aside, and the truth was more complex: that the world could change in an instant from clear and kind to desperate and cold, and the trick to survival lay in knowing that instant before it happened, and not when. This was a skill he had once possessed, but could not guarantee until he tested it again. By the time he reached the Circus he was, as he had been for the three preceding decades of his life, afraid.

He leaned on the door to push it open, and was surprised by how easily it gave. He wondered if they had cleaned the hinges, or if he had grown stronger or just heavier.

Standing blinking on the far side in the sudden illumination of the Circus foyer, he realised abruptly that he had no idea where to go. He had passed through the security check by rote, greeting Scanlon the marine at the desk, and now stood marooned on a desert island of his own habits. He owned no office here, and no office owned him. Up the main stairs, he supposed, to occupy his old room, but, as he turned in that direction and lifted his foot to the first step, he was struck with an almost animal unwillingness. Somewhere up there, six months ago, Control had instructed him to initiate the closing act of Operation Windfall. He could recall the moment and accept that it was past, could know that it was not in any meaningful sense still there waiting. It made no difference to the knotted refusal of his body. After a moment he felt someone in the dead space behind him, then beside him and then climbing ahead with that same light tread, and an alpinist's disregard for the scale of merely man-made structures. Smiley knew the tempo of those feet. He knew the double-time of the man's breathing with each upward exertion, and knew above all that he wasn't there. Alec Leamas had, in Berlin, definitively found a wall he could not climb.

'Mr Smiley, sir?' There was a young man leaning around the partition of the entrance hall, a brutally chopped-in fortification whose false-wood panels were insufficient to hide its shame. 'I'm Glenn, sir. Please come this way.' Glenn was small and had the air of the second tier of Empire.

'I don't believe we've met,' Smiley suggested.

'Uh, no, sir,' Glenn said. 'I'm new.' He had a foolscap document wallet under one arm, pale green, and he hugged it as he talked as if it would tell him everything was going to be all right. 'We've set you up in the Conservatory, sir, if you don't mind. I know it's only temporary.'

The Conservatory was a long extension, part way between a Nissen hut and a lean-to, which smelled of creosote and covered what had at one time been a small, unlovely garden behind the Circus. Used for overflow personnel when some part of the main building was undergoing maintenance or renovation, it was celebratedly grim.

'Thank you,' Smiley said. 'I do know the way. Would you mind asking Housekeeping for two or three additional lamps?'

'Of course, sir.'

'I take it Control is engaged.'

'Yes, sir. I'm told he won't be long.'

'Some cushions, then, if you can,' Smiley said, letting himself through into the service corridor without waiting for a reply.

The corridor led around the back of Banking Section and down a flight of three linoleum steps. The carpet at the bottom was a dark-green artificial felt he distantly recalled was also used in airports. It was hard-wearing and made a faint, unpleasant sound when you walked on it, as if it was hissing at you. Four modern desks, pale wood veneers already peeling away from the board underneath, were lined up along the outside wall, so that anyone using them had their back to the main Circus building and could take advantage of the heat leaking through the single-course brick. Smiley selected the furthest from the door, and hung his coat on the peg next to it like a schoolboy. The surface was bare apart from an internal phone and a sheet of toughened glass. In the drawer was a block of plain paper and a new box of soft pencils. While he waited, he sharpened one of the pencils with his pocket knife, letting the wedges of wood fall on to the desk.

A little while later, Glenn reappeared with two desk lamps held like dead pheasants, and the day's newspapers. Behind him was someone from Housekeeping's lower echelon, bearing two chair cushions in penitent's brown hemp.

'Tea, sir?' said Glenn.

Smiley nodded, and began spreading open the papers along the empty desks.

In his hibernation Smiley had avoided news, which revealed things he no longer wished to understand or think about. The weight of the globe was no longer his to carry, and he had gladly let it drop. Now he read, not intensely but with a wide, searching innocence, allowing headlines and single-inch notes to drop down into the part of himself which gathered and retained them, against the day when such trifles as the mood of Zahir Shah or the price of American chocolate might imply some shadow on the stone that he must read.

A policeman like Oliver Mendel had as his province the past. Even Special Branch was – in its own right, when not doing favours for more covert services – tasked with the business of uncovering old truths and delivering remedies. The Circus by contrast was charged not with justice but anticipation. Its job was to find the green shoots of tomorrow beneath this morning's snow. Setting aside all the clever tricks and tradecraft, that in the end was all: to pass to the Ministry not only the capabilities of today but an under-standing of the other fellow's intent, and some inkling of the news not yet printed. In this, the business of intelligence gathering was partly journalistic, with strict rules on verification; on sources and their reliability; and on the impartiality of reports. 'Two hundred words,' Steed-Asprey used to say, 'and *no* adjectives.' On the other hand, to be useful, intelligence must also be given a frame in which to sit, must be woven into an existing understanding, which could be gained only by knowledge and experience of the world, and so analysis could seem almost oracular. Connie Sachs, the reigning queen of Research, required her recruits to respond first of all immediately, with their instincts, and then subsequently with deep inquiry into the files at Registry, and then to blend the two before offering a formal answer to anyone.

When Millie McCraig made her way to the Conservatory, Smiley was standing with eyes on the middle pages, gazing at London political gossip, Hong Kong horse races and Beirut scandals with the same empty curiosity he devoted to Soviet border patrols.

'George?' she murmured.

His head turned and his eyes settled on the here and now, and she saw his fingers touch lightly at the knot of his tie.

'She's arriving in two minutes. What name are you using?'

'My own,' Smiley replied. 'This is just temporary, after all.' He held up a placating hand. 'With Gero, at least.'

McCraig swallowed her objections. 'Do you want to walk her in yourself?'

He nodded, and followed her back up the linoleum steps.

Susanna's first sight of Smiley was therefore on the pavement at Monmouth Street, and she was not impressed. She was sitting in the back seat of Inspector Mendel's Austin A110 with Sally Roberts. Mendel had pulled them up on to the kerb. She had no idea now where Miki was; he had been removed from Broomsleigh Street in a dusty blue decorator's van bearing the logo ATKINS & SON, with a phone number illegible under the grime.

She saw Millie McCraig first, and only afterwards a figure she took to be a doorman or a janitor: a stout, hurried little man with pouchy cheeks and thick-framed spectacles who opened her door and put out his hand to lift her up out of the car. She judged he was wearing a second-hand suit. It was well-made but not for him.

'This is Mr Smiley,' McCraig said. 'He'll take care of you.'

'Please come this way, Miss Gero,' the janitor said, and led her with old world courtesy along and across the road to a side door.

The building was one of those British Imperial legacies, a red-brick palace built for men who believed themselves rulers of creation, and now in these candle-end days serving out its time until it was demolished or converted into a department store. The side entrance opened into a servants' corridor with glossy white walls that hinted at a green undercoat, and a dark carpet whose only function was to dampen the footsteps of the staff. Narrow windows high up gave on to a neighbouring wall, and baleful fluorescent lights in strips along the ceiling made the whole length a dismal monochrome. The janitor led the way, making small talk. How was your journey in? How long have you been in London and what do you make of it? Apart from the shooting, Mrs Lincoln, how did you feel about the play?

Susanna said she was fine. She said she was concerned about Mr Bánáti. The janitor agreed that Mr Bánáti should be found as soon as possible. He conducted her through a pair of swing doors and abruptly they were above stairs, in a long, serious passageway panelled in dark wood, locked offices along each side, though through the occasional propped-open door she could see more wood, and bookshelves, maps and papers. At the far end there was an open space, rows of secretarial desks in lines, and she wondered if there had ever been a moment when Miss Adams contemplated her for this appointment, or whether she as a Hungarian girl did not meet the relevant criteria.

'George, my dear man! What on earth are you doing here?' It was a voice that belonged on horseback, equally ready to command cavalry or hounds.

The janitor turned, and she turned with him, into the face of a tall, blond-haired Englishman of high estate, with a strong forehead and startlingly arrogant blue eyes. He was younger than the janitor – perhaps only by a little – but he wore his years as if borrowing them. His mouth twitched at her assessing gaze; inclining his body slightly, in something not quite a bow, he put out his hand.

'Hello,' he said, meaning: would she like to go to bed? 'I'm Bill.' His handshake was perfect, like the rest of him; just strong enough to show intent, just long enough to make an impact, and then gone while you were still wondering what would happen next.

It would be great fun. She had no doubt about that at all. There was a clear wickedness in him, fine and full and above all fraught with competence. An energetic affair, robustly satisfying in all the right superficial ways, followed – she knew this to a certainty as well – by an aching, tempestuous separation over some betrayal, and a ghastly hangover. Her twenty-year-old self would have found him intoxicating. Now, a scant few years later, the idea left her pre-emptively exhausted. Send me – she thought – send me a kind young solicitor with good prospects and the heart of a sinner, and deliver me from drama. Amen.

'Hello,' she said, meaning: no.

'Christ,' Bill muttered. 'You saw me coming, didn't you? Who is she, George? Control got you hand-picking flowers for a new Dame Blanche?'

'I believe Miss Hofbauer is interviewing for a position with Connie,' the janitor said. 'Millie asked me to walk her in; it was on my way.'

'I didn't think your way brought you here at all any more.'

'You know how it is. Even when you've retired there's always old business. Well, I suppose you don't know. I'm breaking new ground for both of us.'

'How is it?' Bill seemed, for the first time, genuinely interested. 'Not being inside the door?'

'Oh, recommended.'

'There's a meeting on the fifth floor, I hear. Will you be there?'

'If asked, of course.'

'Righto. See you, if.' The blue eyes again, leaving a last reminder: a lady is always entitled to change her mind. 'Miss Hofbauer.'

The janitor said goodbye to Bill and waited until he had entirely left before turning to look at her. She thought he might congratulate her, but instead he just looked, and she assumed he judged. Perhaps he would say 'adequate' in that familiar voice, and she would wake and find herself back ten years ago in her mother's house. What did he want from her, if not that? She had followed his lead, accepted her new name without saying 'Miss who?' and politely declined his blond sex-maniac friend. Had that been a test? Had all of it been a test? And, if so, had she passed or failed? But the janitor gave no sign.

He led her instead down another service corridor and into a meagre *appentis* with a run of desks and two chairs looking at one another alongside a tray of what passed in Britain for sandwiches. He gestured her to the chair facing into the room, and, to her astonishment, sat down in the other.

'I must have the story from you direct, Miss Gero,' he murmured. 'Please be as complete as you can. I shall make notes but not interrupt. When you have finished, or if it occurs to me as we go, I shall ask questions. Please understand these questions are not accusations. They are merely aids to memory, and in some cases they may be requests that you reconsider any polite obfuscations which might arise if, for example, you and your employer were lovers.' He raised a hand. 'I understand that is not the case. It is, however, a live example of the sort of thing people in our situation needlessly conceal, to the great complication of the work that must be done. Can we proceed on the basis that there is no cause for alarm between us?'

She nodded. 'Yes.'

'Let me begin, then, by saying thank you. You made a series of decisions today which are helpful to your adopted country and brave in the face of remarkable events. You kept a cool head and did it right. It is not everyone who manages even one part of that, let alone all of it, with all the pieces in the correct order.'

That made her smile, and he smiled in response, and extended his hand. She looked at it and wondered if he wanted her to shake it.

'I gather that you retrieved from Mr Bánáti's home a small collection of letters. I wonder if I might trouble you.'

She realised she still had them, because, until now, no one had asked. She reached into her bag and handed them over.

'Why these, rather than anything else?'

'I don't know.'

'The first you saw? The only collection of letters? Or were you looking for something in particular, and these answered?'

She thought back. 'The postmark.'

'Vienna has a particular resonance of some kind?'

'Yes.' But she'd run out and didn't know what it was. Just that Bánáti receiving letters from Vienna and keeping them separate was important, though whether it would actually matter she didn't know.

'It was quite bold,' Smiley added. 'Going to the flat. Though I wonder if you just didn't really think about it that way, at the time.'

She said she thought she had.

'But you went anyway. Do you mind if I ask why?'

Because Bánáti was in trouble and he's my boss. He pays my bills. Because I locked Miki in the office and that made it perfectly safe. She opened her mouth to explain.

'I wanted to get it right this time.'

She slammed her mouth closed, and heard it click. Don't ask me what that means, she thought. I don't think I can say, 'I don't know' again and not start screaming.

Smiley did not ask. 'Very well. In the past I have suggested that those I interview regard me as a priest confessor or a doctor, if those things fitted into their lives. Perhaps – if they are equal to the feat of self-deception – as an old, old friend. Sometimes they prefer to imagine I am not here at all, and therefore that they are speaking to the wind, or to the wallpaper. In all these cases, I make no objection. If at any point you are hesitant to answer, please do not evade or deceive. This service does not engage in criminal investigation and has no interest – for another example – in any minor irregularities around your declarations at ports of entry. In the event that a question entails an answer you prefer not to make, knock once on the table and we shall return to it after suitable assurances have been given. Do you anticipate such a situation arising? No? Very good. Before we begin: can I offer you something to eat, and is there anyone you would like us to call?'

She stared, bewildered, not by the question – although, what a question – but by him. This was the man, she realised, that she had been brought to meet. The one who would put it all right, in whom Mrs McCraig, the friend of Miss Adams, placed her trust; and whom Mrs Jeremy regarded as something close to a god. This, in other words, was one of England's secret chiefs, bathed in power. Here in his office he looked, she thought, less like a janitor and more like a greengrocer.

'No,' she said, at last. 'There's no one. Please go ahead.' And then her hand, of its own accord, snatched up a sandwich and crammed it into her mouth, so that for a few moments she could not answer his questions in any case.

Smiley listened as she told it for what must have been the third, even the fourth time. By now, parts of it at least had set in her mind in shapes that were slightly different from what had actually taken place; from what she had seen, thought and done. Memory was a liar to itself. Once or twice he stopped her to draw her out, magnifying her impatience to reach the crisis as it had impressed itself upon her. He tripped her, trivially, on the time, and liked how she cast about, returned to first principles, and gave a provisional estimate in place of a false certainty. Later on, in the midst of her harrowing visit to Bánáti's flat, he pursued the question of the office cash box.

'Did it rattle?'

She opened her mouth and then stopped. Her hands came up, tracing the shape in physical recollection, then tensed as she considered the weight. Heavier than she had expected but not impossibly so.

'No.'

'Not at all? No loose change?'

Not loose, she said, but solid. She had thought, ludicrously, of bullion wrapped in cloth.

'A thud, perhaps,' Smiley offered. 'A book.'

Not a book. The weight was too concentrated. A little less than a kilo, she said, without hesitation, then waved her hands. Two pounds, in British. She had learned weights from her mother, then for a second time after she came here. Smiley again made her stop the narration while he purloined several bags of sugar from the tea trolley, and found her estimates very accurate. She said Bánáti had joked about it with her: shall we read this manuscript or just weigh it, Susanna?

Without pausing to make a bridge between the questions, Smiley asked whether she thought there had been anyone in Bánáti's flat before she arrived. No, she thought not, but she couldn't be sure; she hadn't spent much time there. Smiley nodded at this corroboration of her innocent relationship with her employer, and let the tale flow on.

Alongside the words, he was listening to the woman who spoke them, to the tilt of her head and the line of her eyes, and the times when she stopped to reconsider, catching herself in elision or fabrication. She was unsparing and fluent, ruthless with the boundaries of what she knew or assumed. All in all, he couldn't have asked for better. When she ran dry, a portraitist who specialised in sketching from descriptions of faces, arranged by Millie McCraig, produced an image of the missing man. Photographs, Smiley had already established, were hard to come by: Bánáti existed for the most part in the blurred background of publishing lunches.

On a Banda master sheet, emerging from the artist's pencil, was a handsome face in early age: rectangular, with sharp eyebrows and a downturned but merry mouth. Smiley reckoned the man ten years his senior. The lines from the nose to the ends of the lips were pronounced, the chin solid and lightly cleft. In the cinema, he might be the hero's wise counsellor. In a storybook, a friendly king or a magical hermit. Susanna had described him, and, without knowing it, also what he meant to her: a good employer in the London sea, a kind man who did not abuse her trust – who reminded her, without forcing her to consider them, of the places she had left behind.

As the artist worked, Smiley received a note of the first preliminary conversation between Miki Bortnik and Andy Royal, the inquisitor he had assigned to the case. Royal noted with approval that it was refreshing to be allowed contact with his subject so soon after arrival, and said that Bortnik was unusually forthcoming.

The standard of care with defectors was to treat them as mendacious from heel to crown. In the normal flow of events, Miki would have been driven via a nauseating and elliptical route to Sarratt, the sprawling country pile north-east of Beaconsfield which served the Circus both as training ground and unlisted prison. Depending on which possible mood the arrivals team wanted to project, he might enter by the main gate and be walked past the neoclassical house, with its implications of majesty and civilisation, or on the farm side between the seed-stock barns and the ominous agricultural hulks where, by arrangement, someone could be feeding bone meal to the pigs. Sarratt was a wartime institution with a wartime sensibility, and, in Royal's view – as in Smiley's – was prone to physical interrogation where none was required.

Recently there'd been a move among the younger inquisitors to a modern perception which emphasised the psychological. Royal, newly promoted, was of this party and wanted a score. Smiley had asked for him by name because he shared the understanding that in the interrogator's arena it was empathy, not ruthlessness, that saw results. In his experience, the first twenty-four hours of any interrogation were definitive. Within that time any person under questioning was cut adrift from their understanding of the world, whether or not they had arrived at their present state by choice, and would reach as a frozen swimmer does for any friendly hand. Human beings are not naturally silent, and in the sudden reversal of total vulnerability even less so, so that hardened spies would often answer with a kind of fool's licence in exchange for nothing more than a kind word and a bowl of soup, as if an outer layer of the world's lessons had been stripped away and the honest soul was all that remained. A defector by definition wants to spend his coin before his former masters can steal back its value, and is the more ready to open up. Sometime on the second or third day, that changed: there was guile again, and often resentment, and the job became not a confession but a negotiation, from which neither side would ever emerge entirely satisfied. You give me this, I give you that; but the very act of trade made the product suspect. With that in mind, Smiley had asked Royal to visit Miki at the safe house – as it were, at home – and begin the debrief immediately so as to catch him in the fullest flood of disorientation and confession.

Miki's story so far was simple: he'd been a peasant and an altar boy, then a soldier, and then almost by accident ended up working as a legman for the Soviet resident in Kabul. He'd been drafted in to help with an abduction there, and had attracted the attention of a senior member of the Thirteenth Directorate named Pogodin. Would Miki like to be reassigned, into a job which could lead to a desk as he got older, maybe significant promotion? Thank you very much, yes, indeed. His life had taken a positive turn. He'd been paid more, shown more respect, and the actual work was comparatively light. For the most part Pogodin used him as a courier for instructions to Directorate officers under official cover. Once or twice a year it was the other thing, and he would be issued with a temporary passport for each job – sometimes French, sometimes Dutch, whatever – to be destroyed as soon as he returned to the Motherland. Miki had realised that there was a narrow window in each assignment between initial reconnaissance of the target and completion when – so long as he was careful – he could relax, take in the sights and even do some shopping.

Recently, it had all got a little more nervy. There'd been tension for years between Pogodin and the other man, Agapov, who had inherited the Thirteenth Directorate from Rudnev in fifty-five, and the word was it had come to a head. Miki stayed out of it, and made himself a known quantity: capable, only moderately ambitious and without emotional attachments to anything except the service which had given his life a shape. He was trusted, and rightly so. In earnest of which he had been given this most recent mission by a senior official personally, and told to keep it entirely secret. This official had been unfamiliar to Miki, and had not followed the usual form. He didn't come across as political, didn't seem to care about the small formalities of submission. He had looked ordinary and spoken quietly, but his tone had been of such stark authority that Miki found himself doubting it could possibly be earned. A front, had been his first reaction; a bluff. Yet, looking around, Miki had realised that, while he might not know the official himself, he recognised the men who travelled with him. They were a hard bunch, but even they were respectful of the one whose company they kept, and from this Miki reckoned the fellow was quite serious, quite natural in his power, and not in any way to be trifled with.

'We are cleaning house,' the official had told Miki. 'At this time there is an appetite from the high offices of the Party to demonstrate the continuing effectiveness of the security apparatus after a period of upheaval, and remove certain annoyances which have been present since Stalin's time. Certain persons who have criminally absconded from Russia and her allies and been tried for their crimes in absentia will now face proportionate retribution under the law. You will carry out one such sentence. Is this understood?'

And to this, in the first instance, Miki had replied with an enthusiastic yes. It was only later that he changed his mind.

His disaffection had come suddenly, and Miki was unable to explain it, which was why he attributed it to a divine intervention. He had left Moscow fully intending to carry out his instructions. He had arrived in London still on task. Somewhere between Heathrow and West Hampstead, between the business travellers' hotel where he was registered as Gustav Florin and the bus stop outside László Bánáti's office, something had changed. He had looked at the people around him, who were honest, boring and largely content, and realised that they were not afraid. There was no caution in their conversations. Their eyes did not automatically seek out mirrors, angles of observation, watchers and listeners. They were like children, and, where before that naivety had always irritated him, now he saw it differently. It was not merely the arrogance of Capital. It was the absence of a state mechanism of coercive control.

He had stayed on the bus and let it take him all the way to the very end of its route, then wandered through the grim streets of an inner-city area whose name he didn't know. It was familiarly run down, the housing blocks familiarly unmaintained, the decay almost comforting. But the boys slouching in the central plaza of a tower complex had a looseness about them, a sense of possibility he was beginning to envy. He took another bus all the way to the edge of the city, and another, and another, looking for oppression. London was grey and drab and unfriendly. It was colourful and imperious and loud. The food was terrible, but there was a lot of it. In Paris he had been angry at the ostentatious clothes, the smell of cooking from the cafés. West Berlin was a showcase pointed at the East, a petty deception. But London was just London, first city of the so-called sick man of Europe, and it wasn't showing off to anyone. It was flawed, perhaps miserable, but its people were unbowed. Suddenly he was furious not with the British but with Moscow, for every hour of his life that he had spent minding his tongue.

Then he had seen Susanna. Maybe she was not, after all, the

girl he had taken her for. It didn't matter. That face, in that place at that time, had told him all he needed to know: God had expectations.

Miki, having delivered this information, needed a cup of tea with something medicinal to wash it down. Royal waited patiently while he stretched his legs and did some deep-knee bends, averring that God also encouraged physical fitness. Finally, they returned to the conversation: what about Moscow? What expectations had Moscow had? And was Bánáti the only person on Miki's docket?

Yes, but he was aware of others with similar briefs. He could go into detail, and did, and Royal noted a short list of names before asking for the specifics of Miki's mission.

Bánáti was to take his own life. Evidence should indicate some sort of financial misconduct, or perhaps a sexual crime. Something explicative and embarrassing to make the British look away. Papers in his office and home in so far as possible were to be destroyed to complete the impression of a man concealing his own disgrace. This had struck Miki as unusual. Centre punishment killings were normally quite overt: the standard was a soft bullet to the face to destroy the features, expressing the justified anger of Mother Russia and forcing her enemies to bury their dead in closed coffins.

Did Miki know why?

He had not asked and no information had been supplied. He had been given a light background on the target. Would Royal like to hear it? Royal would.

So far as Miki knew, Bánáti was from a village outside Debrecen but had spent time in Moscow. Royal asked whether he might have been an infiltrator for an unfriendly power, perhaps for Admiral Miklós Horthy, the de facto ruler of interwar Hungary and something of a minor Fascist in his own right. Miki didn't know. It was implied, maybe, but that could be a mystification. Many things were, Miki said. Only God saw truly. Did God have anything to add about Bánáti? No, God was pretty relaxed about him, but Miki had more to say.

Bánáti spoke Russian, French and English as well as Hungarian. He was supposedly a civilian counter-revolutionary with no connection to the Thirteenth Directorate. But Miki had noticed that the job was rated 'Hard', a distinction more usually reserved for former army men – or, more rarely, professionals from his own service. Centre had given him a photograph of Bánáti, but it had been nearly useless, taken a long time ago. Yes, the picture was in his hotel room. It was procedure to destroy it only after the job was finished, in case he needed to reacquire. That it was useless for acquisition in the first place did not change the procedure.

What conclusions did Miki himself draw from all this?

Here, Royal reported, Miki became shy. He said he was not accustomed to making such assessments. It didn't help, he said, to think too much about such orders. Royal noted in the margin that he thought Miki didn't want to revisit the chain of cause and effect in case it turned out his divine inspiration was nothing so grand. He guided the conversation to happier things. What would Miki like to do in England once he was settled? Would he go back to farming? Never, Miki said. If he never saw another cart of manure again in his life, he would die happy. He was an urbanite. Even a little sophisticated, however much his father's ghost would shake its hoary head. Royal suggested commerce, even publishing, assuming there might be a niche left open by the as-yet-undiscussed closure of Bánáti & Clay. Miki stared at his boots. Come on, Royal suggested, I'm your friend. Your facilitator. If you've got a secret love, now's the time. What is it? You want to go to university? Become an intellectual? Join a bank? You want to work for us direct? Go back in the field? What is it?

I have seen the films of Ealing Studios, Miki said finally. Your Peter Sellers. Your Lionel Jeffries. You have seen these also?

Yes, Royal said. Very funny. I like *The Lavender Hill Mob*, myself.

I also am very funny, Miki explained. People do not know this about me.

Royal made a show of noting it down.

I wish to be in a film with Peter Sellers, Miki said.

Royal chose to end his interim report there, with the po-faced suggestion that this request be referred to Sam Collins and Toby Esterhase, who – as Royal put it – enjoyed connections in areas of British society less directly strategic or governmental in nature.

Smiley felt eyes on him, and looked up.

'George,' Millie McCraig said gently. 'He's ready for you.'

With a brief word of thanks – and a reminder of deepest secrecy – to the portrait artist, Smiley left Susanna in the hands of two Housekeeping stalwarts, the meek Lily and a fearsome middle-aged woman named Alison, who according to legend was the only Conservative Party member to take arms against Mosley at Cable Street. Susanna was worn out and very pale, and Alison was talking about a proper meal, and some sleep on the put-me-up in the Housekeeping rest room.

Having seen Susanna and observed her, Smiley was content in the first premises. In the absence of any reason to believe otherwise, he accepted that she was what she appeared to be, and the story had played out as she said. He followed McCraig up the stairs. The whole building seemed flat, the colours faded and the varnish chipped.

'Who's in the room?' he asked.

'Control and Oakmoor. Esterhase, as you asked. Connie.'

'And Bill's here. I thought he was in Cairo.'

'Reassigned. His tour was up.'

Smiley nodded. 'I suppose it was. It's fine, anyway. Bill's an agile mind, and he knows Moscow.'

McCraig carried on. 'They *are* aware of Bánáti, but they *don't* know about Susanna, nor that we have Miki Bortnik. You are thoroughly enjoined to keep it that way.' And, at Smiley's look: 'It's the order of the day, George. Compartmentalisation. The right hand may not know what the left hand does. Only Control sees everything and he passes on what he wants to whoever he thinks should have it, no one else. Oakmoor runs around apologising to everyone. It's driving them all bonkers, but the fifth floor makes the rules.'

'So they believe I'm here to find Bánáti. Why?'

'What do you mean, why?'

'Why me? He has a dozen capable people. He could pass the whole thing to the sister service. Why me?'

She stopped walking for a moment and looked at him. 'Because it's you, George. He doesn't care what you do. He just wants you here doing it. He'd no more let you go than he would sign his real name or move the Circus to Welwyn Garden City. You do understand that?'

Smiley must have heard, but it was as if he hadn't.

'He could have Bill look into it, even.'

'Bill's on a plane next week. New posting.'

'I'm going to Geneva.'

She nodded yes, as if it didn't matter. Smiley shrugged.

'And you were concerned he'd seduce Susanna before he left. That's fast work, even for Bill.'

'No, it isn't. What did he want, by the way?'

'We walked into him. Or vice versa. I had to improvise a story about a Miss Hofbauer interviewing for something with Connie. Will it pass?'

'On paper, yes. We have an open brief to pad out Connie's section in the Balkans. Bill went for her like a shark, I take it?'

'Something like that.'

'And how was she?'

'Oh, adept,' Smiley said, with regret. 'Really very good indeed.'

'Come on, Smiley,' Control cried, like a ringmaster, as Smiley entered. 'Tell us about László Bánáti. That's what you're here for.' He sat back, as if annoyed to have waited.

Smiley took his time finding a chair down the table from the others. He was closest to Connie, furthest from Control. Oakmoor stood behind Control in the butler's position, and Toby Esterhase was sitting in the middle, turning his head like a dog watching a tennis match. At nearly forty, Toby had forsaken the barely submerged fury of his Vienna days, and now exuded a drawing-room superficiality which matched his clothes, if not his history.

Smiley pursed his lips and allowed himself to fall into the familiar rhythm. 'A Hungarian émigré living here in London. Targeted, we are told, by a Moscow assassin. We don't know why. Or, I don't. Good evening, everyone.' He folded his arms.

'A credible source identifies Bánáti as the target of a Russian operative travelling on a Greek passport,' Control snapped. 'Oliver Mendel informs us that Bánáti is missing from his flat and from his office. Not seen since Friday.'

'Dead,' Haydon said, closing the door. 'Nice to see you, George, mystery solved.'

'He might be,' Smiley agreed, as Haydon selected a place near the head of the table and stood behind it, fussing with his jacket. 'But even in that case, our question does not change. Why now, and why Bánáti at all? Who is he, that someone in Moscow would commission his murder?'

'He's not ours,' Oakmoor said. 'Not even a little bit. Right, Toby?'

'Not the littlest bit that we know of,' Toby said, pressing his thumb and forefinger together in the air to demark the quantum of ownership. 'Not through the groups, anyway. Not the Budapest Salvation Committee, not Új Magyar Hajnal. Not any of those crazy bastards in between either. Sure, he knows them to say hi. You can't eat Hungarian food in London without you meet those people. Sure as hell you can't draw a pay cheque without they ask you for money. You wave, talk about one day this, one day that. But no more. I keep looking, okay? Legacy, that's a different matter. If he has a history with us from the war, maybe – for that you have to apply elsewhere. They don't give *me* the files.'

'But your best guess?' Oakmoor pressed. 'Perhaps an allied service? What sort of fellow is he? Fish or fowl?'

Toby extended his hand palm down and turned it this way, that way.

'Hungary, Mr Oakmoor, that's a tricky question, you know? We got an excess of recent history. More factions than fingers to count them. Maybe this Bánáti has opinions, but he doesn't share them. Maybe he just wants a quiet life. God knows: don't we all, some days? Until this morning if you show me this fellow I say fine, he's just this fellow. But if Moscow knows his name so well that they want to put it on a tombstone –' Toby shrugged. 'Then I'm a little anxious about him, I would say.'

'For Christ's sake, George,' Haydon remonstrated abruptly, 'you were well out of it. Stay that way! This is small potatoes. Take Ann to the Griechenbeisl as planned, eat melted cheese – with small bloody potatoes, if that's your fancy – and drink the wine of the country. Some of the Rotgipfler is really very good.'

Control scowled. 'Haydon.'

But Bill was not to be put off. 'No, fair's fair. George served his time, there's no conscription into our line. Leave him be. What do you say, George? When you come back, my odious cousin Miles Sercombe wants to set you up with his banking pals, and you ought to let him. Money for old rope. I'm told it buys things. First editions with hand-painted illustrations. Museum quality. Just knock on the desk if I'm getting too steamy. Or diamonds for Ann, what about that? She'd enjoy that, a few pointless fripperies to make her feel spoiled. Comfort isn't a dirty word, George. You're allowed a life after spying.'

'I am out, Bill,' Smiley replied. 'This is purely temporary. A stop-gap.'

'I'm trying to get you to cry off, you see. It's a nefarious plan. How am I doing?'

'Oh, quite well.'

'Balls.' He glanced at Control. 'You got your hooks in him again, didn't you? Damned old slave-driver.'

'Quiet down, Bill,' Control said, without apparent emphasis, and Haydon subsided into his chair, lips pressed in a flat line.

'Connie,' Control said.

'Not much to go on,' Connie replied. 'Arrived London in the mid-fifties with a bit of money but not a lot, set up shop and got to work. Pays taxes handsomely and without delay. Copulates in much the same way, generally with artistic wives in their forties. Never with clients and only occasionally with editors. Office in West Hampstead, rented through a local agency, money paid from the company account on the nose each month. Bills likewise. Supposedly left Hungary in a hurry, apparently owing to not wanting to have his balls pulled up around his ears by the bloody ÁVH. We can all sympathise with that. Name not known in our line of work at all. The sister service haven't heard of him; they want to know why we're asking, I said apply through channels. The Americans don't know him either, or that's what they say, and I believe them – he's hardly their speed. Too suburban. No shooty-bangs.'

'Perhaps that is all,' Smiley suggested, inviting anyone to agree. 'Perhaps Moscow is just culling the herd. Reminding everyone to walk softly, and they picked his name out of a hat.'

Control looked around the table. 'A helpless lamb on the run from wolves. An honest man, Con?'

She shrugged: there's a first time for everything. But, by all the measures in the Circus toolkit, Connie said, László Bánáti wasn't anyone at all. He had never been seen with any known Soviet assets, nor was he active in opposition to the Bloc. He was to all outward appearances a completely apolitical refugee.

'It does happen,' Smiley said. 'You can have too much experience to care any more.'

'Can you?' Control murmured, loud enough to be heard. 'I'd no idea.'

Connie hastened to resume. Bánáti, she said, was so clearly just a man getting on with life that his inoffensiveness only compounded her anxiety.

'I wanted him to be in secret love,' Connie said. 'A fine mistress in the Home Counties, a scandal all his own. Or some strapping soldier with a wife and four children in Plymouth. But all he seemed to do was sit about. Maybe he liked making earthenware pots or stitching kilts. Perhaps he kept a pony, bet everything at the races. But he didn't, you see. Not that anyone knew. So, all right. Who was he in Hungary before he left? He brought a bit of cash out with him, so it couldn't have been so bad. Was he boring there too? We had a look, but Hungary isn't an easy place to operate in, is it, Toby?'

Toby shook his head. 'Sheer bloody hell. You get a network up, then the next day someone is arrested. It's not because they know, it's because they don't. It's not that they break our tradecraft, more like everyone takes turns. Say you're the Hungarian secret police, okay? You torture a fellow properly, because if you don't, that's already treason, but you go as easy as you can, because tomorrow you're sharing his cell and hoping the fellow who has your job can see the future as clear as you do. Exhausting, from an operational point of view. Also expensive. And what do we get for our trouble? Shipping manifests and corn reports, written by dock masters who don't dare tell the truth and collective farm managers who don't know it, for an audience of administrators who dare not read them in case the truth that they contain today is a Capitalist sabotage tomorrow. A total backwater, God save me for saying so. You can't get any sense out of that place.' He looked away.

The door opened silently to admit Millie McCraig with a sheaf of Banda machine copies of the portrait artist's sketch. They were warm and smelled of methylated spirits. The ink was dark purple. 'The man himself,' she said, passing them out. 'Mendel says he may have a photograph,' she added to Smiley. 'He's waiting downstairs when you finish here. The second and third pages are self-explanatory. Beard, moustache and so on.' She nodded to Control, and made a precise exit.

'Handsome,' Connie noted, leafing through. 'Good luck to my soldier, or what have you. Quite the grey Adonis.'

'Bloody hell,' Haydon said a moment later. He scowled at Control. 'It's dark as night in here – are you economising on the bloody bulbs?' He pushed his chair back, snatched up a lamp from behind him and set it as close to the paper as he could, then glared down, shielding his eyes from the bounce. He stared at the picture again. Then: 'Toby, take a look at Number 3. There, with a nasty revolutionary beard on his face. You have it?'

Esterhase shook his head.

'Damn. Before your time, I suppose. George, then, surely you see it? He's put on a few pounds of decent living, and he's older – aren't we all? But still.'

Smiley looked, and didn't, but that was classic Bill: he knew things without being able to say how, and thought they must be plain to everyone because they were so obvious to him. He was a little bit witchy, Connie liked to say. Some Irish green in that blue blood.

'Bánáti, my foot,' Haydon said at last, when he realised no one was going to say it for him. 'And not László either. That's Róka. Ferenc Róka. One of the Hotel Tourmaline crowd.'

In the twenties and thirties, Soviet Russia had become a hub for leftist émigrés from Germany and the new Eastern nations created in the Treaty of Trianon, which ended the First World War between the Allies and Hungary. Activists and poets who might otherwise occupy the jails of Miklós Horthy or Adolf Hitler took themselves to Moscow, which pronounced itself their natural home. There, above the Filippov Café in Tverskaya Street, one-time supplier of patisseries to the Tzars, stood the venerable Hotel Lux, whose long-term inmates – or what was left of them, after Stalin's extreme weeding of suspected traitors – were sent home in triumph after the next war, to be rulers of their satellite nations.

On the far side of the Hermitage Garden, the former Hotel Tourmaline was co-opted as the Lux's unacknowledged mirror; a shadowy reflection which served as a safe house of first resort for those who might go back into their home nations, or even the West, without acknowledging their affiliation. While the dignitaries of the Lux issued statements to the world press and prepared for office, the denizens of the Tourmaline slipped away to training camps and less distinguished universities, slowly laundering their own life stories until they became translucent and eventually invisible, making new selves abroad. The Circus had run down a half-dozen of them over the years – Vienna Station under Jim Prideaux considered it something of a blood sport – all under non-official cover and all reporting ultimately to Andrei Alexeyevich Rudnev, then head of the rising Thirteenth Directorate. He, together with Victor Pogodin and Demyan Agapov, had comprised a nexus within Moscow Centre, seeking to loosen the grip of fully military intelligence on the Party structure. Then, in the turbulent mid-fifties, Rudnev had overreached and been shot. The Tourmaline networks were orphaned or broken up, and Smiley had swept up another four or five graduates of the school in places as far flung as Addis and Hong Kong.

'Róka was one of the Hungarian originals,' Connie said. 'If it is him. Spanish Civil War, then fought the Arrow Cross in the streets of Budapest. A proper hero, in his day. Lost both times, of course. We thought he was in Brazil.'

'Brazil's all very well,' Haydon rejoined, 'but as it turns out he came here instead. So was he making a few bob and enjoying the upright moral fabric of the world of not-so-literary publishing – *honi soit qui mal y pense*, by the way – or did he come to do the devil's work? Inquiring minds want to know. Mine, in particular.'

Control turned his eyes on Smiley.

*

The big meeting was over, and the little one had just begun. Haydon had briefly dickered with Control, arguing once more that he could usefully take on the Bánáti – no, the *Róka* inquiry – before his flight out. 'And George can go to bloody Geneva like he's supposed to.'

Haydon's loyalty to this idea was so focused that Smiley wondered if Ann had put him up to it. Even if it would be unlike her to reach into his Circus life through Bill – they were some sort of cousin, but Ann was everyone's cousin – those rules applied to the time before he had retired. Now, he thought, she might – and the idea made him smile.

Or it could just be Bill. Bill loathed idleness, and the quiet sort of Soviet operation even more. Bloody dishonest way of spying, he had once told Smiley. Recruit someone, run them, get them out. That was the proper thing. Long, slow infiltrations were different. They ruined the world, Bill said. Made you doubt your fellow man. Smiley was never sure whether he actually liked Haydon or just enjoyed his bombastic nonsense; whether, under cover of Bill's volume, Smiley's own voice was more easily raised.

Control, in any case, would have none of it. 'You'll go where you're sent,' he'd told Haydon with some asperity; 'it's more important than a ragged-trousered legacy agent from Stalin's time. George can handle Róka for me. He owes us that much.'

Yes, Smiley thought, that's it exactly. I served you for twenty-five years and more, but all that creates is a greater obligation to keep going. The salamander lives in the fire because it has forgotten how to live any other way.

So now was the moment Smiley had both looked forward to and dreaded: a face-to-face conversation, alone, with Control. They sat not in the meeting room but in Control's same drab office, with its row of filing cabinets like the Callanish Stones. The long-case clock beside the fireplace tocked lugubriously over the sound of the wind. They were practically under the eaves, and there was an easterly blowing. Control liked to say it whispered secrets from Moscow. They'd been there for nearly ten minutes, and still no one spoke.

Control's silences were the stuff of legend within the Circus. He made you imagine his questions and answer them, so that you performed your own interrogation. Accustomed and even a little jaded, Smiley had composed himself, not to wait but simply to sit. The key to getting any kind of traction with Control lay in recognising the absence of words not as prelude but as the meeting in itself, and making him say what he wanted.

A year and a half ago, Smiley had not exercised this discipline with sufficient rigour. Control had called him in one afternoon and announced that he was considering a particular operation and Smiley wouldn't like it. It was necessary, but still very bad. Control would handle the detail and all Smiley need do was pick up the pieces afterwards. No need for both of them to carry it.

This had been, in retrospect, chum. Control had bloodied the water, and Smiley had been lured into asking and then demanding that he share the burden. Together they had sent Alec Leamas to Berlin with orders to take down the Stasi's most effective attack dog, Hans-Dieter Mundt, and when Leamas arrived, Mundt had been ready for him.

'I think I decline,' Smiley said, when Control opened his mouth to speak. If it was a rarity for anyone to out-wait Control, no one interrupted him, ever. 'You said I owed you this. In fact, I do not. I already have done what was necessary – not that it was ever important that I do it, except to you. The problem is clear, your sources are gathered in, and I no longer work here. Thank you for the opportunity to say goodbye. And to remind myself of how very much I did not wish to return.'

He went to gather up his things, when Control erupted from his chair, his voice shockingly loud, cracking as he shouted, 'Sit down!' like an affronted prince.

Smiley, if he felt the tug of obedience in his knees, stayed on his feet, and the ghost of Leamas stretched between them.

'I chose his clothes,' Smiley said at last. 'For the burial. His step-mother was supposed to do it. I understand they didn't get along. In the end she sent a telegram saying she wasn't coming. She gave excellent reasons. But that left me in Alec's flat, alone with a dozen pairs of shoes: French, British, German, Italian, Czech. They say you're supposed to begin with the shoes. I don't know why. I picked some black ones from Oslo. They weren't the newest, but I thought I remembered them. Then I muddled through a suit and so on. I think I rather overdressed him, in the end.' He shook his head. 'I found I didn't want him to be cold, you see. I'm not religious. Well, you know my feelings on that: it's one of the unkindnesses of modern life that there's no excuse for it, any more. But I couldn't shake the idea that Alec did a lot of standing around waiting, and he needed comfortable shoes and a good winter coat.' He looked at his own shoes. Church's, made soft by time.

'That's why I left. It's why I'm not coming back. This business has forgotten its root – or, I suppose I should say, you have.'

'Hardly,' Control growled.

Smiley's voice, when he allowed himself anger, was high and tight. It sounded childish in his own ears, and far too much like Control's only a moment before. He hated the sound of it but couldn't hold it in.

'You lied to our own agent! You told him I wasn't part of it any more, then had me scurry around behind his back, and he died! He died of our deceptions! *I* acquiesced in it, but *you* still think it was right.'

'And wasn't it?' Control sounded curious, as if he was honestly trying to puzzle out the contours of Smiley's objection.

'Our side is the one that takes care. That gets people back and knows its own human limit, that some prices are simply too high. Better to lose than become the enemy. That's why we deserve to win at all. Because we acknowledge limits.'

'Do you think Moscow would too?' Control seemed genuinely curious. 'If we offered it to them?'

'I don't know. Perhaps.'

'And, if they did, would we still deserve to win?'

'If they did, would we still need to be at odds?' Smiley waved it away. 'Those are questions for you, now. High matters of policy. I just know I decline to set out any more pairs of shoes.' He glared into the bars of the fire.

'What did you do with the others?'

'What?'

'With the other pairs of shoes. Oh, sit down. Please. What did you do?'

Smiley shrugged, and let himself bend. 'I gave them to House-keeping, of course. Everything like that. Worn shoes are operational resources, aren't they? Although a part of me is superstitious about it. Oh, not actually,' he added, as Control's eyebrows rose. 'I just wonder whether somewhere there's a little Russian fellow with a magnifying glass who has photographs of all our footprints. Cracks in the soles. And one day Alec's shoes will kill another man. It wouldn't be the strangest thing. Doesn't the Stasi keep an archive of scents?'

'Yes,' Control said. 'I understand they do.'

For a while, they both stared at the space between them.

'I'll make you a deal,' Control said at last.

'You already have. And it's done. I told Millie I'd walk Susanna through the door. I have. I'll talk to Mendel, look for Róka until the day after tomorrow. But that's all. I'm not coming back. I'm not going to chase him across half of Europe for you. You have plenty of people to do that. Younger and less compromised.'

'I don't trust other people. I trust you.'

'Why?'

'You know perfectly well why! And, if that wasn't enough, I think retiring from the service to waste yourself among the glit-tering idiots of our aristocracy is a penetration strategy too oblique even for Moscow Centre. So find Róka for me. Use what-ever resources you need, call on whoever you want. If he's nobody, then fine. It's finished. If you go out there and it means something – anything – you can do what you like with the knowledge. No broader objective. No requirement to generate product. You do whatever you think should be done. Show me the Smiley way. Show them.'

'It's not the Smiley way. It's just decency.'

Smiley was expecting scorn, and the busy practitioner's dismissal of lofty club-room lawyering, but Control wrong-footed him. He nodded as if surrendering.

'Then do that, George. Go and be decent, and maybe we'll all learn something.'

Far, far too late, Smiley saw the trap, and he couldn't even complain about it, because he had made it for himself. On his lips were the words 'I have to go to Geneva.' But now, instead of being the honest man's reply, they were the shirker's. His moral objection was turned against him. He could ignore a hollow command to do the wrong thing; it was far harder to set aside a plea that he seek out the right one. And, in the face of Alec's shoes, perhaps impossible.

3.

Smiley went back down the stairs and dictated a short message of apology to Ann: she had been right, and he had been wrong. Control had put him on the spot and he didn't see how he could refuse the task if things worked out that way. He trusted they wouldn't. He still hoped to see her in Geneva in time for the party; he would let her know. This did not indicate a change of heart on the new direction of their life, which he enjoyed and to which he was committed. He was not returning to the Circus.

He left the task of putting that into a telegram format to the owlish night clerk, then called their hotel in Paris and arranged to have flowers waiting in the room.

In the last few years, since he had for the most part sworn off field work of his own, Smiley had often found himself roaming the corridors of the Circus by night, waiting for news of one agent or another. The field men had the hardest part, lurking in a border hut out of sight lest their own presence tip the guards on the other side to the game; walking once and only once every day under a particular window, looking for a cross of masking tape on one of the panes or a postcard propped on the ledge; driving a single drawing pin into soft wood and waiting for a chalked countersign to declare: 'Yes, I am alive. The work goes on.' To say nothing of the raw danger. But it was hard too in operations, sitting in a painted box of an office, isolated by distance and time from the moves on the board, knowing that when you found out what was happening, what inspired improvisations were in play or what dreadful choices were being made, it was already too late. You could not act today, only plan and replan tomorrow, for mitigation, celebration or revenge.

He looked in on Susanna and found her sleeping, Alison sitting quietly in a chair by the window, then took himself to the second floor and the dim offices of Northern Section, which appropriately enough dealt with the Soviet Union and her satellites. Northern was the heart of the Cold War Circus. You could hear the ribs of the building creak and the water pipes moan, and their burning Victorian radiators hiss and whisper; and you could feel that you were in some way part of something, some enormous sleeping mystery that was the greater cause, that gave meaning to failure as well as success. There he stood, with his hands by his sides, for one moment not thinking or reaching, just standing still. It was a state he found difficult, and always had, which was one of the things Control used adeptly against him. The hiatus lasted forever, and forever ended when a car hooted on the street. A chorus of distant indignation brought him back to himself, possessed now of clarity.

The discovery that Bánáti was a Soviet agent of some vintage had on the instant changed Smiley's priorities and – he realised here and now – should change his approach. The missing man was no longer missing by any reasonable measure. He was a trained operator on the run. He had somehow transgressed against Moscow Centre and was in their bad books, which meant an opportunity for the Circus. This in turn implied a dual responsibility for Smiley: on the one hand, to catch up with him, to bring him in; on the other, to know what had gone before, and the reason behind what was happening now.

The shift also affected how things stood with Miki Bortnik. Miki was not on the face of it hugely exciting from a pure intelligence standpoint. Men in his position were secret but did not themselves possess many secrets. Royal could spend weeks on him, unbuttoning every assignment he had worked in the last five years, even the last ten, and then feed the results to Research Section to be cross-referenced with known activity. It was solid intelligence analysis of the workaday kind that yielded slow but inevitable progress over time. It would not tilt the game board on its own.

In the context of a live operation to locate and obtain Ferenc Róka, however, Miki was a trump card to be played as soon as possible, before his usefulness could spoil.

The Cornhill safe house was on the second floor of a grimly functional modern infill, of which the ground floor was a new Italian restaurant, already looking tired. Administratively a curiosity, the City was run not by a local council but by the Corporation of London, which preferred to limit the number of residential dwellings within the Square Mile. This resulted in the absence of the kind of community that existed in Brick Lane, Stockwell or Kentish Town, where new faces were an object of interest. Amid the old-established financial institutions and their livery company neighbours, locals were few, temporary and isolate, and the arrivals and departures of Circus personnel went unregarded. Smiley rang the bell and walked up, passing a genial kitchen porter with a suckling pig on the stairs.

He knocked and announced himself as Mr Nelson, like the admiral, come about the accounts. The door opened to reveal a young man with wide shoulders, an impeccably bland business suit and a sailor's haircut, who ushered him inside.

'Hullo, Andrew,' Smiley said. 'Nice to see you.'

'Always a pleasure,' Tom Lake replied.

Lake had arrived in the Circus by an indirect route, beginning in something that wasn't quite the Special Boat Section but had the same flavour of serious intentions. His family had a tradition of military competence at the sharp end, and the local church had a row of embroidered kneelers to attest to their bravery. He'd done embassy security for a while in Ankara and Beirut, then passed briefly into the sister service – as Haydon had it, trying on every damn glass slipper in the game.

Haydon had actually wanted Lake for the Middle East office,

and there'd been a tussle with Prideaux, who fancied him for Prague. Oblivious in the meanwhile, Lake went to work babysitting ticklish lamplighter operations in neutral countries, picking up a motley of criminal aptitudes from light burglary to the placement of concealed microphones, but chaffing at the necessarily slow process of deep intelligence. Before Haydon and Prideaux could settle their differences, the head of Travel had quietly offered him the chance to do dirty deeds dirt cheap in the old Special Operations style, and Lake had jumped at it.

Travel Section was more commonly known – to Control's seething irritation – by Haydon's nickname, scalphunters, and was set apart from the official Circus at a grim schoolhouse in Brixton. It handled all things too hot for regular spies, including high-risk blackmail, murders, and anything else Control wanted kept completely off book. The agents who worked there had their own name for the place, Scalpel, and they liked to think they were the last line, although wider opinion was not on their side. When Lake took their shilling, just about the only nose not out of joint was Toby Esterhase's, and only because Toby liked having friends in every household.

'How was your night?' Smiley inquired.

'Uneventful,' Lake said. 'I was on first, then Jimmy Little took over for the graveyard shift. I'm on again now.'

'I'm Mr Nelson, and you are Andrew, no second name given, is that right? No slip-ups?'

'No slip-ups,' Lake agreed. 'And Miki's not shopping. Calls me Andrew, doesn't ask for more. Doesn't want to be buddies forever. Got him settled last night after that first chat, gave him a spot of breakfast this morning. Happy as a clam. Apparently God is too.'

'So he's still divinely inspired?'

'Oh, they're on first-name terms,' Lake agreed. 'From here on out, Miki and God, they're basically a partnership. That's what life is in Britain, you know: it's God and Audrey Hepburn on one side of the tea table, me and the Duke of Buckingham on the other. Can I get you anything? Miki fancied himself a croissant. I told him a bacon roll was more the speed, but as it happens there's a French place round the corner, so his luck's in. Yours too.'

'I'm fine, thank you.'

Lake half bowed, and gestured Smiley through into the main room.

Miki Bortnik was a little older than Smiley but barrel-chested and physical, while Smiley himself was soft. The difference was frankly intimidating, even with Lake unobtrusive in the background. Miki's hands were thick and the fingers curled in habitual readiness to make a fist, or a blade. All in all, he was what people in their shared profession called 'capable', and Smiley knew him without knowing him: from a cold childhood belonging to another century, to the march on Berlin and the disappointment of victory without spoils or welcome, to the strange nomadic life of a Moscow murderer, where the only people you met were witnesses and marks. Now he sat, knees apart, and spread New Zealand butter on French bread. The remainder of the loaf rested on the low coffee table in front of him, and Miki seemed almost diffident at the idea he could help himself to jam from the jar. Lake had told him there was another in the kitchen, but Miki had needed to be shown. He was a strong man, both in will and body, and no doubt a force in his own profession, but now he was in a castaway place, lost between worlds.

Smiley did not sit and did not negotiate. It was an occasional stumbling block for intelligence operatives in the debrief of defectors that many if not most Soviet agents, however experienced with the less absolute structures of authority in the West, believed that the power and mandate of the security establishment there must ultimately mirror their own. At the bottom of everything, they assumed, there was still the state, and to maintain otherwise was to attempt a deception. With this in mind,

Smiley chose not to acknowledge the possibility that Miki might be unwilling to lie to his former masters direct. He had come as a secret plenipotentiary to exact the price of defection; it was not high or unreasonable but nor was it insignificant, and above all it was not optional. He spoke without preamble or caveat, in the tone of military orders, and Miki's head came up like a grateful dog's. Here, at last, was the opening of the door.

'You will directly after this conversation enact the necessary steps to call a crash meeting with your handler in London. As a deniable agent in the country only temporarily and without diplomatic status, you will set the time and place. During this meeting you will maintain the appearance of loyalty to the Thirteenth Intelligence Directorate. You will report that you made contact with your target, but were prevented from concluding your mission by the chance arrival of the London police to attend a domestic disturbance in the next-door flat. It is your professional judgement that with full information you can reacquire the target and successfully and unobtrusively complete your assigned task before returning to Moscow. You will not arrange a follow-up meeting but call for this information to be passed to you via a dead letter box in order to minimise contact between yourself and agents operating under official cover. Do you understand?'

'Yes, commissar,' Miki said. If Smiley found the title uncomfortable, he did not show it.

'The purpose of this deception is that you should acquire as much detail about the man Bánáti as possible. You should not deviate from the normal practice or give any indication of greater urgency than is natural. If you feel it is appropriate, you may reveal that you know his real identity as Ferenc Róka, a Moscow Centre agent from the Rudnev era of the Thirteenth Directorate. In this case you will imply that this information was given to you in a verbal statement by the assigning officer to impress upon you the seriousness of the mission, a tactic you now deploy in your turn. Can you follow these instructions?'

'I can.'

'This is in any case a minor operation, but you will at all times be discreetly accompanied by officers of my service, and the risk to you personally so long as you abide by my instructions is negligible. However, before you go, you will provide us with a list of all such emergency-contact protocols with which you are familiar. You may withhold other intelligence until your return so that you can be sure of our continued interest. After you have done this, the Soviet agent Bortnik will go missing and another man of similar age and appearance will begin a new career in another field.'

'I wish to make a film,' Miki said. 'I wish to be actor.'

Smiley appeared to treat this with great seriousness. He withdrew from his pocket a small policeman's notebook and a pen.

'What manner of film, please?'

From Miki's face it was apparent that he had not considered the question. 'With Peter Sellers. A popular film.'

'Not an immoral or licentious film?'

Miki shook his head: no.

'Nor a politically inflammatory project espousing anarchic disregard for proper public order? Not making farce of the institutions of the state?'

Miki, again, stoutly denied the idea. Smiley closed his notebook and put it away.

'This is not impossible,' he said.

Miki stood, and made a serious, clumsy salute in the British mode.

'For the Queen,' Miki said, as if someone ought to, and Smiley felt he had recruited a child.

For his final act of the night, Smiley placed a call to a retired officer of his own service, seeking any history of Ferenc Róka which was not written down. Kingdom Steed-Asprey was himself something of an institution. He was only the second head of the Circus after its foundation, and had run the whole outfit during the war years with a fraught mixture of restraint and absurd daring. Intelligence, in a hot war, was even more critical than in a cold one, but you had to use it improvisationally as often as with deliberation: take advantage of slips and blunders while the target was exposed, or miss an opportunity to turn the course of the world. He was credited with a series of last-minute deceptions and misdirections which had made an actual difference, and Smiley had reported to him directly after his own appalling six months behind the lines. Like Control, and for that matter like Smiley, Steed-Asprey had arrived in post by way of academia, and thence he had returned as some form of emeritus versed in the Greats. Recent circumstances had been unkind, and he was on a leave of absence from which the Master of his college candidly did not expect him to return. He was, after all, an old man. But he was by the same token a repository of yesterday's secrets, and if Bill Haydon might recognise Ferenc Róka – or if Smiley might have, on another day or in another life – old Steed-Asprey could probably tell you his shoe size and his favourite brand of cigarettes.

'Come whenever you like,' Steed-Asprey said. His voice was surprisingly clear. 'Cassie's not well. I imagine you've heard. She doesn't really sleep nights, not the way one ought. The doctors say it's tension; I think they mean pain. Anyway, come on by. Jean – that's our nurse – she's a good scout. She'll let you in.'

Smiley drove himself. As so often in his life, he was reluctant in that moment to share his space or his thoughts with anyone. The car was two years old: a Hillman, in mint green with a cream roof and an American-style wraparound rear window. The gear shift, like a white billiard ball, was too big for his left hand, but he enjoyed the friendly geometry of the double steering wheel, and while driving it he felt a kind of sanctuary. The murmur of the road, the beat of the tyres and the steady passage of motorway signs, turnings and street lamps soothed him and gave him space in which to think. Bánáti – Róka – where are you going, and why?

Heading west and north, the road was empty.

The drive took forty minutes, and when he arrived the cottage was white and miserable under the night sky, lighthouse paint over plucked cement that didn't look like stone. When the door opened the smell of the dogs was awful: two grossly fat bassets, barely able to walk. The nurse, Jean, didn't seem to smell them. Smiley remembered, as a boy, working in a mortuary: you'd hardly notice all day, then come home and suddenly the stink on your clothes would make you gag.

Steed-Asprey was waiting in the living room with a tray of biscuits and tea from Fortnum's. They drank and ate, and Smiley wondered if he'd ever touch shortbread again.

'How have you been?' Steed-Asprey said. 'I heard you stepped away.' He was a little man with an athlete's body turned brittle, and a cap of neat silver hair.

'Oh, I did,' Smiley said. 'I have. Permanently. This is just a favour for Control.'

The tired eyes begged to disagree.

'That man does not understand favours, Smiley. He doesn't do halves or compromises. You give him something and he wants another one straight away. Cry God, Faustus, and right speedily, or he'll have your soul again!'

'It's spoken for, thank you.'

'Yes, so I hear! The daughter of the House of Sercombe is filled with spring, and some career in vapid financial instruments beckons. Children? Oh, don't look so appalled, you've time. Good for you! Live well, Smiley; really do. I'm afraid my Cassie's not in great shape these days. Age, you know.' He gestured towards the nurse. 'Do you want to come and say hello, before we get to it? I think she'd like that.'

Smiley wanted to scream no, but he said yes, and followed the old man into the back part of the house. The corridor was dim, and there was a path worn in the middle of the carpet by too many hasty comings and goings.

In the back room there was a hospital bed with a lever to raise and lower it, and in or on it lay Cassandra Steed-Asprey, propped on a wealth of pillows. Someone had taken pains with her hair, but the back was a mess of tangles again already, and there was far too much of it left on the brush on the bedside table.

'George is here, darling,' Steed-Asprey said. 'Come to say hello.'

Cassie looked at Smiley with bright eyes. 'George,' she said. 'How are you? How's Ann?'

'Both well, thank you.'

'You mustn't ask about me. I don't lie, you see.'

'You look splendid.'

'Thank you, but you mustn't lie either. Kingdom lies all the time. He says I'm going to be all right. I'm very ill, of course.'

Smiley nodded.

'Kingdom, the bad vase is on the mantel again. I've told her it mustn't be.'

There was an inoffensive Doulton vase full of flowers over the fire. The smoke from the banked logs was the only thing in the house that didn't smell of sickness.

Steed-Asprey picked up the vase. 'I'll take it away.'

'No, then I can't know where it is.'

'I'll break it.'

Cassie nodded assent. 'It's a bad vase, you see, George. Very bad. Bad things come with it, into the room. I don't like it, and it comes back whatever anyone does. Break it now, darling, in front of me, so I know. Do it!' There was an avidness in her face, a kind of hunger. Steed-Asprey solemnly took the flowers out of the vase and wrapped them in a hand towel, then opened the door and tapped the vase sharply against the edge of the frame. The pieces fell to the floor, and he picked them up and held them out for inspection. 'There we are. Good?'

Cassie let out a moan and twisted in the bed. 'It always comes back,' she said, her voice rising, and Steed-Asprey herded Smiley back into the corridor and along to the living room again.

'She gets these ideas,' he explained, as if ideas in general were to be avoided. 'Birds bring her messages. Robins especially. And other things – shadows on the wall and so on. Devils, sometimes. She does like the flowers, though, so I get them from the market every day. I'm afraid it's quite expensive in chinaware. My only vice, any more.' His face was perfectly relaxed. Smiley wondered how much effort it took to keep it that way. Probably just about everything he had. From out of the bedroom at the back came a low wail, and the sound of Jean hushing and gentling. A moment later, an argument, loud and bitter, the words indistinct but ugly.

'The children don't come,' Steed-Asprey said abruptly. 'After the last time, I told 'em not to. She was having a bad day, told them – well, all sorts of wretchedly unkind things. It's not good for them, or her; for anyone, really. So it's just me, you see, all the hours of the day. Thanks for coming.'

'I had no idea,' Smiley responded truthfully. 'It was just the work.'

'Oh, quite,' Steed-Asprey said. 'Quite. You want to know about Róka.'

Smiley matched Steed-Asprey's expression, and said yes. He saw relief in the journey into memory: surcease of sorrow.

'And you have the basics? Born Austria-Hungary, red from crown to ankle? Spanish Civil War in Barcelona – proper hot-war spying, that was. All that?'

'I'm sure it's in the file,' Smiley said. 'I wanted your impression. Your feel for the man, if you had one. Not just the agent but the person.'

'I didn't play cards with him, George. We weren't huggermugger in the backstreets of Lisbon or what have you. He was an enemy spy.'

'But an anti-Fascist first. We must have been allies for longer than we were enemies, in your time. Or, for as long as. I'll take

74

anything. When I said "Ferenc Róka" on the phone, you knew immediately who he was. There's a story. Something that makes him worth a piece of your mind, even now.'

'Jean, can you put the kettle on again? It's gone cold. Or perhaps something stronger, Smiley? I might have a tot. It's after midnight, so I think we can say the yard-arm is duly passed.'

There was a whisper of fear in the older man's eyes, and Smiley realised he was afraid that once the story was told he'd be left alone again to his life.

'It occurs to me that we should have debriefed you rather more thoroughly. Perhaps we still should. I could ask Connie to send some of the young ones down to take notes. Generational intelligence, as it were. And it strikes me at the same time the Circus ought to do a little more for you. I don't mean money,' although actually he did mean that too. 'I mean company for Cassie. Some of her old friends. It might help.' And it would help you, he thought, help you carry this appalling house in its appalling hour.

It took a few moments before Steed-Asprey could be persuaded to take on the gift. He poured Scotch for both of them, almost pungent enough to taste.

'Róka,' he said finally, instead of thank you. 'It was just a bit before I stepped down. The French had a spy in Moscow, terrific access, but fond of filthy lucre, so he was putting himself about a bit. After a while we realised he was selling the same product twice, once to the French and once to us. And the problem, you see, was that the details that came out didn't match. Their reports and our reports were different. Bill had confirmed ours through one of the networks he set up out of Vienna with Jim, so it looked pretty strongly as if the French had a traitor in their head office, probably quite high on the ladder. We ran a triangulation – times, dates, access – and worked out who it had to be. Assistant to one of their top operations men. I wanted to turn him and leave him in place; that way we'd see what the French were getting and what the Russians were doing with it. We'd know what they didn't want us to see. One always likes to keep an eye on one's allies, doesn't one? Just to be sure. The Minister wouldn't buy. Politically culpable negligence in the face of a deep security flaw in the NATO apparatus, he said. We were to inform the French authorities immediately. Of course, when we did, it all came tumbling down. The French bungled it and Moscow plugged the leak at their end. They couldn't get their double agent out, but they got word to the rest of the network. When the Sûreté smashed down the door, the top man was gone. You couldn't have done it better, George. He must have had all of ten minutes, but it was as if he'd never existed. That was Ferenc Róka, although we didn't get confirmation until, oh, two months later. You're quite right, I suppose: the same game you were playing in Germany, he did back home in forty-four. One of their best. A gun and a codebook, that's all, and his undying commitment to whatever the hell it is these people love.'

He had more but not much. Before Paris, Róka had been in charge of something in Hungary, something on the daylight side.

'And then?'

'Oh, fell from grace. Had to run. Well, that's how it goes for those fellows, isn't it? Loyalty no issue. The revolution eats its young, and all that.'

Smiley asked if Róka had had a family.

'A mistress, in the forties,' Steed-Asprey recalled. 'When he was playing hide-and-seek with German intelligence. I suppose probably he had a whole string of 'em, women who'd hide him and look out for him for a couple of days – but one acknowledged queen of his heart. Ilyana? Katrina? I'm afraid she hasn't stayed with me. I owe her an apology. A poetess and a war widow, they said, already had a child. A great beauty – square shoulders, tiny waist and all that Magyar fire.'

Róka and the poetess had made a go of it after the war. He was godfather to the child, and she, for sheer talent, was given a teaching position at the university. Smiley prodded gently on the boy's name. Steed-Asprey took his time, and then said 'Leó', proud to have remembered something so far off the track.

'Then it all changed,' he added. 'Fifty-one? Two? Something like that.'

'Changed, how?'

'Oh, you know. In Stalin's time you couldn't trust your weight to anything over there. One day you're a prince, the next you're a villain, and nothing in between. No law, no evidence, just fear. Denounce your neighbour before he does you the same way. Róka's timing was off, or his aim. Pointed the finger in the wrong direction, got it cut off for his trouble. Oh, not literally. Metaphor, you see.'

'Can you remember the pretext? What he got wrong?'

'Not a chance,' Steed-Asprey said. He patted the side of his head as if it were one of the vile dogs. 'I was never much for the rhetoric, you know. All that brotherhood of man, but somehow it means firing squads. Cassie might have. Taught Connie Sachs everything she knows, didn't she? My Cassie. Best of the first generation. No chance of that now, I'm afraid.'

From somewhere in the house, very softly, came the sound of weeping. Smiley wasn't sure if it was the patient or the nurse.

Driving back was an effort of will, and Smiley was grateful for the empty road. He could smell the house on his coat, and knew it had become part of his work, that he'd never take pleasure in it again. He opened the window and let the cold air keep his eyes open all the way back to town.

Toby Esterhase was in one of the meeting rooms on the third floor. There was an ugly set of laminate cabinets along one wall, with an unpersuasive modern veneer, but the rest of the room was still as it had been a hundred years ago, with a simple fireplace and a dark piece of slate for a hearth. Toby had taken off his jacket and put it on a coat hanger by the mantel, and from somewhere he'd conjured a wool blanket and a couple of actual

77

pillows. His office these days was in Acton with the rest of the lamplighters, although Toby's portfolio was rather less defined.

'George,' he said, sitting up and clapping his hands once. 'Get in here, there's a draught. What can I do for you? Coffee? An alcohol? Or a quiet place to hide from Control and get your feet under you?'

'Róka,' Smiley said, obediently closing the door.

Esterhase spread his hands, palm up, like a head waiter regretting a bad meal. 'I speak to my people, George. There's only so many ways to be Hungarian in this country. Sure, they know Bánáti. For the most part not so impressed. The kind of fellow who drinks your booze late and won't leave. Maybe he collects gossip on the side, you know? Maybe he pays a little too much attention to who talks politics with whom. Maybe he sends letters home. But maybe not. Maybe just too many sisters, too many wives. That kind of thing. To hear Bill talk you'd think he was the best of us. I like to believe I'm the sneakiest Hungarian in London. I feel a little threatened, actually.'

Smiley shook his head, hands reaching for something in the air. 'Róka was kicked out of Hungary for backing the wrong horse. Left behind a woman, an academic. She had a son, supposedly not his.'

Toby shrugged. He had the blanket around his shoulders like a shawl. 'Old story, very sad.'

'Steed-Asprey says she was a poet or an artist. A professor. There can't have been so many in Budapest at the right time.'

'Sure. Gossip, George. We can find her. In the morning that's easy. Right now, I call anyone, they want to know where's the fire, you get me? And then when I tell them there's no fire, there's the risk that we light one. Honestly, George, if you don't got Mendel calling you with a corpse or a killer, I say go to sleep. Get some rest. They can make up another room for you here.'

'I can go home,' Smiley pointed out. 'It's not far.'

'But here you are.'

'Where's Peter Guillam, by the way?'

'Berlin,' Esterhase said, giving the name its German pronunciation. 'Non-official cover, some sort of trade thing. He loses money, it's embarrassing. Control calls it an apprenticeship.'

'I'm sure he does.'

'Go home, George. You sound like Bill, and that's never a good sign with you. In the morning we do spy work, okay? Tonight it's enough. Even you've got to sleep sometime.'

Smiley, for a wonder, did not object.

The Smiley home in Bywater Street was starkly empty and a little grim; the heating was always doubtful however often he prevailed on Nuts and Bolts to come and take deep soundings and put it right. He'd have to find a daylight-world plumber, he realised, and perhaps their skills would extend to an actual solution. In the meantime the air was cool and carried that musty smell of Thames mud which blew down Smith Street. The place had an unloved chill about it, and he realised it was as neglected now as it had been when he and Ann were at odds. Perhaps that was a sign: it was time to move, to admit that these few rooms had had their day, in sickness or in health, and a new age was beckoning. He climbed the stairs, almost enjoying the idea. Bricks carried memories, and perhaps in tomorrow's world he would not have a great need for them.

He got into bed and found he couldn't sleep. The kiss of the pillow was chilly on his ear. He wanted to talk to Ann, to reassure her – to reassure himself – but she would still be in their cabin on the overnight ferry. She'd be at the hotel tomorrow, and he'd have to wait until then. At his bedside there was a small pile of books: a collection of German poetry, one of Ann's thrillers and a pretty Baedeker. He picked up the last and inhaled the pages, then read the introduction to the section on Austria. It was the book that had first taken him there, what seemed like a long time ago. A war and Alec Leamas ago, he thought, must be long enough to count.

Smiley woke just after seven with the shame that is felt only by those who work too hard, the sense that he had indulged a weakness by sleeping. He washed and dressed, and found the coat still smelled of Steed-Asprey's house and couldn't put it on. He folded it and sent it to be cleaned, then with a familiar inevitability drew on his old, anonymous commuter's drab from the hall cupboard. He heard Leamas laughing at the neatly mended hem and the old-fashioned style. *For Christ's sake, Smiley, you're a spy, not a mourner! It's nineteen sixty-three. Get something a tiny bit sharp! Live a little. It doesn't all have to be shades of dust and bone.*

A spy and a mourner, apparently, he told the ghost, *and I'm sorry.*

No skin off my nose, old boy. I'm not the one who's been talked back into it, am I? Not this time.

He closed the door and realised that his left hand in his pocket was reaching into a small paper bag of the kind used for penny sweets. This one contained shavings of dry wood. Holding a few in his palm, he looked at them stupidly, and found his right hand moving of its own accord to pluck two narrow splinters and push them into the crack between the door and the frame, above and below the lock. Recognition blossomed in him, and a kind of shame. The splinters were a precaution against the covert invasion of his home. When had he stopped using them? It wasn't safe, even for a retired man. Ann had asked him to, he recalled. She had said it was morbid, and he supposed it was, but for now – for this brief window of his old life in his new one – it was once more a necessity.

The driver's seat of the Hillman was mortally cold.

Entering the daytime Circus was a new kind of penance. Smiley had feared too much recognition, the loud approval of his colleagues. Instead, new faces regarded him from the main desk, and a new guard made him wait. Inside, a group of junior officers in a huddle saw him and quickly looked away, identifying an apostate, at odds with the diktat of Control, and therefore likely at any moment to be struck by lightning. He found himself looking for someone he knew, for Guillam or Jim Prideaux, or, for one appalling, vertiginous moment, for Leamas himself. He wanted to chat, to exchange the irritations of his moment with someone who understood. He wanted Ann. She'd be in Paris by now, in the hotel. He liked to think the flowers had made her smile.

Back at the Conservatory, Smiley took breakfast, and midway through found Oliver Mendel peering in at the doorway. Mendel, overnight, had been working the interior angle, which meant canvassing police departments for any sign of Róka. He'd begun just after dropping Susanna at the Circus by sending Sally Roberts to the local station at West Hampstead, where despite the late hour she immediately struck gold. A man answering to Róka's description had been seen on Saturday standing at the edge of the sports ground on Shirland Road, watching the local boys at play. A sharp-eyed parent reported him as a possible sexual menace, though Mendel observed sourly that it hadn't stopped them sending their children to public school. The desk sergeant had told two constables to make a low-key approach – 'a bit of village green', as Roberts had it – and they noted that he was carrying an orange string bag with a brand-new football in it. This did not allay their suspicions. They had inquired whether he had a child in the group, to which he replied that he hadn't. He was foreign, overdressed and polite.

'We're still to call him Bánáti,' Mendel asked, 'externally, I mean?'

'Yes,' Smiley agreed. 'Bánáti, to the world. Róka, only to us, and to anyone who already knows. Which would be revealing, if it came up.'

When pressed, the gentleman said he had acquired the football as a gift for his godson, Leó. The senior constable, Brand, then had an educational chat about how you said the name: Layoh, Brand later demonstrated to his sergeant. Not like the proper way at all.

How old was Leó? In his twenties. Wasn't that a bit old for a football? Probably, but the gent didn't expect to give it to him anyway. Leó was a long way away. So why buy it? Because they had played football together, back in the day. It would mean something to them both.

At this point Constable Brand and his brother officer were less concerned about the gentleman as a predator and more as a possible breach of the peace. He was obviously very emotional, even granting that he was from overseas, and you didn't want an affray if he became upset.

Would it be impolite to ask, if the gentleman was in such a hurry to find Leó, why was he standing here watching a bunch of children play?

That was a very good question, the gentleman said. Memory, of course, and an old man's folly. But: yes. He should go. He had a great deal to do.

He shook their hands and went – which was fair, as they could hardly arrest him for anything. Brand had been reasonably certain he was crying. Not your intense sort of crying, more like when it's become something you do all the time.

'Off his game,' Roberts recorded. 'By reason of personal emotional distress. In our line we'd say that's trouble.'

End of report.

While Roberts was handling the locals, Mendel had put on a fresh jacket and taken himself somewhere he wasn't welcome.

The Diplomatic Advisory Unit of the Metropolitan Police was known generally as the Shepherds, because their job was to watch the flock, and within the Circus as the Sheepdogs, because they made a lot of noise and often had the wool pulled over their eyes. The Shepherds notionally had the unenviable task of looking after accredited foreign dignitaries who frequently had no desire for their company. In fact, their responsibilities were only partially concerned with the well-being of their charges and rather more with making sure that *soi-disant* diplomats restricted themselves to the sorts of mischief that were appropriate to their stations, and keeping a note of their doings with particular emphasis on any which seemed out of the ordinary.

The Shepherds did not care for Special Branch at any time, and still less in the early evening, when all good coppers – certainly, all good senior ones – should be knocking off. Assistant Chief Inspector Allen had made it no secret that he considered the Branch to be cowboys, and disliked both their heavy hand and their unwillingness to share information in a timely fashion. Mendel had had to make a string of apologies just to get ten minutes with the man before he went home, and they sat on opposite sides of Allen's desk in frozen opposition while Mendel explained what he wanted and handed over Róka's picture.

'What's all this about?' Allen demanded. 'I'm not helping until I'm read in.' He was the other sort of policeman, and he had his uniforms tailored.

'Possible kidnapping,' Mendel said. 'The man's missing. We're tracing his movements.'

'And why would his movements include anyone within my purview?'

'That's rather the question,' Mendel agreed. 'And why would anyone kidnap him? I don't want to cast stones, but he's hardly a Rockefeller, now is he? You might rob him, certainly, but he's got no one to pay his ransom. No one to deliver it to, for that matter. By all accounts he couples like a stoat, so I thought p'raps a jealous husband. But not so far as anyone can tell us. Which leaves me with power, and I ask myself: what sort of power might that be? He's Hungarian, so one's eyes do rather turn eastwards, just by precaution. It's not our best work,' he conceded, like a penitent son with one more venture in mind, 'but it is a line of inquiry. And I thought – since in all honesty it's unlikely it'll go anywhere – it crossed my mind that it might be a venue for my lot and your lot to communicate without friction. And, of course, there's the possibility it throws up something in your bailiwick and we hand the whole thing back to you wrapped up in a bow. Tea and medals all round.'

Allen scowled. 'Your colleagues in the Branch have tradition-ally been unforthcoming with us, Inspector Mendel,' he reported. 'Far too fond of other entities, if you understand me. Entities whose role may be akin to police work but who do not abide by the rules of policing. Looking at some of the operations the Branch has carried out, one might ask whether you were really coppers at all.'

Mendel nodded as if this was the very bane of his life. 'Oh, yes, sir. It's a bloody mess more than half the time. Only ever called in too late, and now it's ours to unpick, if you see what I mean. And plenty of things get done that shouldn't. For my own part, I have to say it's people, not sections, that I put my trust in.'

There was a long pause while Allen gave thought to this fea-therlight compliment. *And I shall wish I'd never said it*, Mendel told himself, *when it all comes down. Which it inevitably will.*

'I shall want a quid pro quo one day, Inspector,' Allen said.

'Understood, sir.'

'And, more than that, I want not to find your boys falling out of the trees on one of my protectees, even if he's involved. Every-thing of that sort through channels.'

Mendel nodded, thinking: *Like hell*, and judged Allen was prob-ably thinking the same.

'Then I'll see what's what and have anything sent over.'

'I appreciate your consideration, sir.'

They parted in cordial loathing.

This morning Mendel's desk phone had rung early, and he heard Allen's voice in a state of what could almost have been excite-ment. According to the Shepherds' log sergeant, there'd been no communication with the official Hungarian presence in London at all, but a week ago the team charged with the well-being of

Second Secretary Commercial Antonov at the Soviet Embassy had followed him to a department store in the West End, where he'd taken a tedious and highly unlikely interest in buying a present for his wife in Moscow. After half an hour looking at scarves and earrings, he'd chosen to sit in the café on the third floor. There he had struck up a casual conversation with another shopper, which had lasted for no more than ten minutes. Despite the fine weather it had been a sombre sort of meeting, especially for two fellows who hardly know one another choosing to have a chat over coffee, and the other man had left without saying goodbye. Yes, they had photographed the contact; that was protocol. Seeing his picture, the two officers immediately identified Bánáti.

'Did they follow him?' Mendel demanded. 'Do they know where he went?'

No, Allen reported curtly. Procedure was to stay on Antonov and let other agencies handle any forward investigation.

'How was he travelling? Did they at least notice that?'

'Yes, because they're police, Inspector Mendel. They spoke to the doorman as Antonov was leaving in the embassy car. Subject was collected by a Renault Dauphine with a radio. Private hire, probably one of the ones that used to be Welbeck Motors.' The notorious Welbeck having been found guilty of unlawfully plying for trade, and dissolved at the behest of the London Hackney Cab industry. 'There you are. We've practically done it all for you.'

Mendel wanted to slam the phone down, but in all honesty Allen was right. The Shepherds had played it exactly by the book.

He sent Sally Roberts back to West Hampstead with the listing of all the private-hire licences for the area, then called Millie McCraig and had her ask Susanna whether 'Mr Bánáti' had a standing relationship with a local car service. Susanna said yes: Artemis Transport, and she had the number in her head. By the time Mendel got hold of Sally Roberts, she was already in the Artemis offices, the company having been high on the list. She put the owner on the phone and Mendel focused every bit of police intent he had down the line. Two minutes later, the man was reading directly from the log book.

Right after his meeting with Antonov, Róka had travelled to an address in Brick Lane that Mendel instantly recognised as a venue for more or less overt criminal behaviour.

'The Cattermoles,' he told Smiley. 'Not your sort at all. Crooks. Protection, dirty casinos, pornography, all that. A nice line in patriotic thuggery, if there's a marching band nearby.'

'And how would they respond to László Bánáti?'

'Depends what he was asking. Strictly commercial, and plenty of money in it, I imagine they'd overlook him being foreign. We do occasionally see old German handguns and such when someone knocks over a Post Office van. They'd buy if he was selling.'

'What about parcels? Papers?'

Mendel made a maybe-maybe not gesture with one hand. 'I'll have to ask.'

'Will they talk to us?'

Mendel snorted lightly. 'They will if I bloody tell them so. But getting a straight answer will take a bit longer. It's not as if all their lads file reports. They'll have to put the word out.'

Smiley nodded, and Mendel saw him depart again, inside his head, seeing things that weren't there.

'I'll pop on over there and let you know,' Mendel suggested, and left without waiting for the answering nod.

4.

Antonov, Dmitri Petrovich, was Head of Station for the regular Moscow Centre apparat in London, and the ultimate conduit for whatever sources Mother Russia might have in mainland Britain.

'Dreadful man,' Connie Sachs lamented to Smiley; 'used to be in Paris and he was dreadful there. Drones on about the inherent strength of proletarian-led industrial facilities as if we didn't all know he's a bloody spy.'

'Where was he before Paris?'

'Oh, everywhere, George, all around the world. The rumour is that when he first went overseas they kept the wife – Lena – in Moscow so he wouldn't think of running away. They do that with everyone, of course, but apparently he adores her and what's more it's reciprocated – there's no accounting for taste – so it must have seemed like having him by the short hairs. But little Lena was the daughter of one of the original cadres, and Stalin used to sit her on his knee when she was a child and tell her stories of his revolutionary struggle. Then later she was in one of the women's brigades, supposed to be an auxiliary but ended up a sniper with the Belarusian partisans. She knew all the old men, you see, and, while Dmitri was away, she went and dug them out of their wretched hero's apartments in the Arbat and got them to talk about their glory, reminded them of who they used to be. Who she was, and how wonderful was this Antonov she'd married, how special, how loyal, a real hero in waiting, and old soldiers love to feel strong, don't they? Strong and capable and on the inside of the door. So heigh-ho and up he rises, from post to post and onward to glory. In a few years he'll be back in Moscow at the top of the pole.'

'And in reality?'

'He's able enough not to trip over her ambition. And nasty, when he needs to be.' But not a mover, Connie said. Not a grand planner. And that suited Moscow Centre quite well, because they liked ambition but not in others.

'And Bánáti. What could Bánáti want with Antonov?'

'He's not Bánáti, George, he's Róka. What does Moscow want with him? We have to assume it's espionage. What sort, I can't tell you.' She waggled her fingers. 'No evidence.'

'All right, what's their cover: how do they know one another?'

'Antonov puts himself about in the London scene. The right sort of gathering isn't complete without some dips, is it? And if the Russians are coming, then maybe the French will show up, or the Americans, to fly the flag, and before you know it everyone's there and some awful little play about nothing is in the diary pages. You know how it goes.'

'Do you think that's what it is? Cocktail parties?'

She looked at him curiously. 'Have you gone soft, darling? In some little retirement cottage?'

'We've mostly been staying with Ann's family, as it happens.'

'Well, then: no, I bloody don't,' Connie said.

Miki Bortnik's meeting was set for four that afternoon at the Hotel Five Star Marylebone Station, a dismal travellers' rest on Melcombe Place with a bright yellow awning which belied its age. In the meantime, Smiley braced Susanna Gero once again. Had she ever carried parcels for Bánáti? All the time. Could she remember the destinations? The regular ones, of course: mostly publishers, sometimes authors. Had she ever been asked to do anything that struck her as unusual? Yes, probably. She had been required to visit Baker Street Police Station twice to bail out clients; to pay a bill at a noted London restaurant featuring a fifty-pound flat fee for 'sundries', which upon closer examination was hush money to an affronted prostitute; and to supply at short notice two live chickens to a house in Belgravia, purpose mercifully obscure. These things were definitely unusual in ordinary life, but she had the sense that in publishing they hardly touched the sides.

Susanna looked back at Smiley and wondered what he was thinking. His voice was still gentle and he was the same shy, kind and yet almost resentful tortoise of a man he had been when he brought her in, but now there was something else in his quiet: a watchfulness that touched everything, as if a fog were paying attention to the house it surrounded. Had she and Bánáti ever discussed politics? No, they had been pleased not to. Had they talked about his life before London? Yes, in general terms. A farm boy, then a soldier and by dint of that a thinker. A reader in fox-holes and thereafter always a student. Her mother had been a great reader. Bánáti would have liked her. In another life, perhaps she could have introduced them.

Smiley pressed: did Bánáti read for pleasure, and, if so, what? She had no idea. Poetry, she thought, but perhaps his flat would reveal that. She had handed over the key. In turn, she asked questions of her own.

'Have you found him?'

Smiley shook his head. 'I think he intends not to be very easy to find. You had no indication that he was proposing to disappear? No financial troubles? No sudden worries at all?'

'He was worried,' she said, seeing it now for herself. Not tired, fool girl, not sleeping poorly or hung over. 'Frightened, I think.'

'For himself?'

'No.' Again, the answer came before she knew she had it. 'For someone else. A friend.'

'A family member?'

'Maybe. I don't know.'

'Did he have a family?' *He had me.* The reaction was almost jealous, and she blinked it away, embarrassed. Five years sharing an office was not ownership.

'No.' Except he must have, whether of the body or the heart.

Everyone did, willingly or not. The only question was whether you knew what they were, or who, or how great was the distance that separated you. 'But I don't think he knew he was going away until very recently. He made appointments.' Though she supposed he could have made them precisely because he knew they would be found. His appointment book would be at the office, she said. She could go and get it and look.

Smiley picked up the phone and murmured into it, and a few minutes later the very book appeared, with Susanna's own handwriting in it. Yes, she realised. They have his whole office, probably the flat as well, right here, to look at and understand. They really want to find him. She considered the letters she had taken from the flat, and wanted to laugh. Such a prize, at such high if imaginary risk, and they had probably just backed up a lorry and collected everything.

And then, at long last, she began to wonder what Mr Bánáti must have done to merit such concern.

'Oh, I'm sure it's nothing,' Smiley replied, when she asked the question aloud. 'But we need to talk to him, anyway. It's how we work.'

She realised he thought of her as belonging to yesterday, as no longer part of what was happening, and then that perhaps she was, and perhaps she should be. Bánáti was gone, and Smiley did not appear to think he would come back, at least to Bánáti & Clay, which meant – what? Had she inherited the clients? Should she just keep the office open, pay herself from the incomings and save the rest? Could she take on new clients?

She imagined herself in ten years, still running the office for a ghost. She wanted to ask Smiley what to do, but found he had already slipped away.

The appointment book listed four lunches in the next week. Susanna had identified three of them as clients, but the fourth, PL, was not known to her. Smiley, therefore, took himself to

Charlotte Street at the appointed time, and sat down at Bánáti's table to wait. PL, it turned out, was Posie Lloyd, an ash-blonde woman in her forties, and Smiley explained that he was Mr Clay, Mr Bánáti's partner, stepping in because Bánáti had been called away on a family emergency.

'I'm sorry that we couldn't reach you,' Smiley said, 'but poor László had to leave in such a hurry that all our affairs are quite up in the air. I've been pretty much at my wit's end since Friday, in fact.'

'How awful,' Posie Lloyd said, still standing. She was handsome, with a strong nose and a warm, deep voice. In a white shirt and a modern grey jacket over what Ann would have called a country skirt, she looked like an echo of women Smiley had known in the war years, determined and sharp. Her right hand, wrapped around her left, was holding her wedding ring.

'I appreciate I haven't László's sparkle,' Smiley went on, 'and I'm afraid I do have to leave at two fifteen sharp, so this will of necessity be a brief lunch, but, if you'd care to join me, I wondered if you might help me make some educated guesses about his thinking on various projects, as I gather you were friends?'

'Acquaintances, really,' Posie Lloyd said, and Smiley held both hands out as if catching a beach ball.

'Quite so. Please, do sit down. I gather the trout is really very good.'

She had ordered turbot and white burgundy and spoken freely. Bánáti was a charming rogue who wore his age well. Some men quite let themselves go at sixty. She was sure Smiley hadn't, but some did. Smiley, for whom sixty was still some years off, agreed that it was so. She had met Bánáti at a book launch – Posie had been at school with the author – and they'd found themselves simpatico. He was terrible in the best possible way. He wore velvet and she loved velvet. He was energetic. They had been making time for lunch in a good hotel every so often when she was in town. They talked politics and French poets. Baudelaire and Rimbaud. They went to bed.

What were Bánáti's politics?

Various. He was broadly of the left but loved an aristocrat. Well, she was almost an aristocrat and he didn't have a problem with her. He made his living from aristocrats dishing the dirt, though what he really wanted to do was to bring the lesser-known authors of middle Europe to the British intellectual awareness. Everyone reads Kafka but no one talks about Baum or Winsloe, or even Sándor Petőfi. He was an idealist. He wanted a better world. And he was Hungarian, so he knew a thing or two about the other sort of world, didn't he? He was an émigré, although he sometimes called himself a refugee. He wasn't keen on the Americans. She thought it was because they'd carved up Hungary in nineteen eighteen. He'd been to America in the fifties and hadn't liked it. The West Coast, she thought. Hollywood. That was no time to be a Hungarian lefty in America, was it? What with McCarthy. So he'd come here.

Did he have a family?

Not much of one, not that she knew of, but he was a very private man. And then:

'Who are you, really?'

Smiley's face suggested it was a question he asked himself from time to time.

'I know you're not Mr Clay. László told me there wasn't one. It was his joke. Is he in trouble?'

'Yes.'

'With you?'

'No.'

'Are you trying to help him?'

'If I can.'

'But, really, are you?' Her eyes were shrewd.

'If I can find him, I can offer him help. Whether he accepts –' Smiley opened his hands again, acknowledging the limits of power.

'And if I don't tell you any more? Will policemen stream in through all the doors and windows and drag me away?'

Smiley said it seemed unlikely.

'Is he bad? László?'

'Perhaps.'

And when Smiley didn't elaborate, she sighed. All the good men were a little bit bad, she supposed. As to Bánáti's family: not much to say. Parents long gone, obviously, and there was an old lover – his great love – from whom he was halfway estranged. A godson, Leó, who gave him trouble. A wild boy, Bánáti said: the great hope of the world.

'Estranged, how?'

'Literally, I think. Some bad blood from when he was in Budapest, or from his not being there enough. Both. You know what passions are, I suppose.' Turning her head, she considered him frankly as a romantic specimen. 'Have you ever loved unwisely, Mr Clay?'

'Alas, no. Tragically conservative. So they weren't in touch?'

'Yes, I thought you had. She wrote to him about the boy all the time. It was always Leó this and Leó that, Leó himself not being the world's greatest correspondent, apparently. Sounds like a real disaster. All the excitement, all the time: girls, boys, booze and ideas. Last one probably the killer.'

Smiley said children were a joyful trouble, and Posie Lloyd asked if he had any. He invented a boy and a girl in their teens and entertained her briefly with a shameful prank they had played on him, which he had not had the heart to condemn as he should, and she averred that she also would have spared the rod.

Was Bánáti religious, then, if he was a godfather? No, not that she'd ever seen, but he took the responsibility seriously. Yes, she had wondered if it might be a fig leaf for an actual son, but it hardly mattered. The boy was grown, and back in the old country, and Bánáti was here. In any case, they were pragmatic with each other. She had no claim on his past any more than he had on her present. She tapped the wedding ring.

'Not just for show. I do love him, but he travels. Work. I don't ask and he doesn't tell, and vice versa. How about you?'

'And before László arrived here, you say he was in America?'

'Your turn.'

'I'm afraid I'm woefully dull.'

'Christ, you're telling the truth, aren't you? I've met people like you: honest as the day is long except when you lie.'

'Bánáti. America.'

'I had the sense that he'd been in a lot of places. He was in the Hungarian government, he said, and got booted out. And I think he was rather brave in the war. Maybe less in it than around it, given what Hungary was like. He had a bullet wound in his left leg. Not a complicated one, but it must have been a bloody great hole at the time.'

'Definitely a bullet?'

'I was in the Nursing Reserve,' Posie Lloyd said, with sudden heat. 'I know what a damn bullet wound looks like. And, for that matter, since you fellows put all your girls through my unit, I know what a spy looks like too.'

Then she looked around hastily in case she'd spoken too loudly. They sat with the word for a while.

'Sorry,' she muttered.

'Is there anything else you can tell me, about László?'

'Of course there is. I'm sleeping with him.'

'If we find him – if I can help him – would you like me to let you know?'

She thought about it.

'No. He can come and find me himself. And if you find him with his face shot off somewhere, definitely don't tell me that. I don't want to think about it.'

Smiley paid the bill and gave her a number to call if Bánáti got in touch. She peered at him.

'Do you think I will?'

'I'm sure you will.'

'Seems a bit cheeky. What makes you so certain?'

'Ask for Mr Barraclough. They'll put you right through.'

'Give my love to your children,' she said, as they parted, and he wasn't sure whether she meant it to sting.

The Five Star Marylebone Station Hotel was a tall, narrow building on six floors, with a grand foyer which overplayed its hand. The rooms were awkward and decorated in the modern style, acid yellow and burnt orange, with weird plastic furniture like gigantic tennis balls. Only the mattresses were traditional: flat, flaccid lozenges lying inert on their imported pine frames. On the walls were black-and-white photographs of pretty men and women in jeans playing music and dancing. The overall effect was that of a Baptist widow dressed by a well-meaning but much younger friend.

Smiley watched while Toby Esterhase prepared the ground, first with a microphone drilled into the lemon wall of the adjoining room until it sat just under the plaster of the one Miki Bortnik had taken for two nights, then another fitted seamlessly into the same cable that provided a meagre overhead light in the bedroom, and finally one more built into the starter switch of the fluorescent strip light over the shaving mirror.

In theory, operating on home soil, the Circus could simply require assistance from just about anyone – but the paper trail would eventually find its way to the sister service, whose myrmidons would want to know all, and under Control's edict of silence that was not to be countenanced. In practice, it hardly mattered. Esterhase was a master of his craft. Ten minutes with the owner, and the hotel staff were treating the whole business – up to and including the minor renovations he had made overnight – as one of those things guests did. When Smiley asked how, precisely, he had achieved this level of cooperation, Toby was evasive.

'George, the hotel trade, it has exigencies. They don't like to be on the wrong side of the right people. They respect their guests quite entirely, of course. But, then, at the same time, well: it depends on the guest. Now, come on over here, you need to meet Diane.'

Diane was a grey-haired woman in her sixties who had replaced the day concierge. She had a ferocious face, very lined and with a downturned mouth, and she smoked constantly, lighting a new cigarette from the dog-end of the last.

'I live on the coast,' she told Smiley, when he inquired politely after her journey in. 'Had to come up special. But that's how it is with Toby. I don't mind.'

Diane would receive Antonov, then place a call to the café where Miki and Tom Lake were waiting, to let them know the meet was on. Smiley watched her settle in, moving the pens and the register, positioning the chair and scowling at the hotel porters until they straightened automatically as her gaze passed across them. Every time he looked back at her, she was more and more a creature of the place, or perhaps had more thoroughly made the place her own.

'Come on, George,' Esterhase murmured. 'Leave the stage to the actors.'

In Miki's room, Esterhase produced a roll of low-tack cellophane and began removing the frames from the pictures. Working to Smiley's instruction, he cleaned each sheet of glass and then stretched a layer of the plastic over it before reattaching the frame.

The cellophane was something from the Cousins, who were known to spend all their many dollars on toys. It was almost a novelty item in the secret world, now being deployed in law enforcement for the capture of fingerprints. Smiley had immediately recognised it as a rat trap for spies of his generation. The habit was burned into him, as into his contemporaries, to make any notes required against a glass surface, using a single sheet of paper at a time, so that a soft pencil would leave no trace of what was written anywhere except on the page, which he could then track, file or destroy. When he travelled, he made do with pictures taken from the walls of his hotel rooms, and took care to clean them twice daily with his handkerchief as well as after each use. With this security in place, he was sometimes more confiding and more speculative to his written record than he was to any human being.

'This is a really dirty trick, George,' Esterhase said admiringly, looking down at the finished pictures. 'I feel almost ashamed, I would say.'

The thin plastic layer was undetectable unless you knew to look for it. If they were lucky, it would carry a full, if jumbled, record of the note-taker's candid opinions. The secret world was not immune to change, and yesterday's certainties became tomorrow's pitfalls. Smiley hoped that Antonov, trained within the rigid structures of Moscow Centre, might be less adaptable to the possibilities of modern espionage.

'Forty-one minutes to go,' Esterhase murmured. 'You okay there, George? You're very quiet. Give me proof of life. How are you feeling? How's our man?'

Miki was on his mark in Euston. According to the protocol, Antonov should arrive first and wait in the lobby, having temporarily eluded his Shepherds. Only if he was confident the coast was clear would he dismiss his own security to a reasonable distance and signal that the meeting could go ahead by placing his hat on his lap and putting his gloves in it.

Lake had reported that Miki was in good spirits.

'It's God again,' Lake explained on the phone. 'God says he's doing the right thing, so he isn't even really lying. He asked if I'd take him to the Orthodox Cathedral in Gunnersbury so he could have a quick word, after. Oh, and he's started writing his film. Says would Mr Sellers want a role for Sophia Loren. I told him he can hash that out when they meet.'

In the hotel room, Esterhase was still waiting for an answer.

'He's fine,' Smiley said.

Forty minutes later, Diane confirmed that Antonov had given Miki the all-clear, and the two of them were now sharing the lift to the second floor. Lake, watching Miki's back, had walked past the entrance on the far side of the road, and spotted Antonov's perimeter man smoking on a station bench.

'Bit pro forma, if I'm honest,' Lake murmured disapprovingly, having come in by the back way. 'He's not giving his all, is what I'm saying. I wondered if he might be a dummy, so to speak, and the real lad's lurking in the shadows.'

Smiley raised his eyebrows. 'And?'

Lake shrugged. 'Never say never,' he acknowledged, 'but nothing jumps out.'

'They're in the room,' Esterhase said. 'They speak Russian, of course. You want me to give you the play-by-play?'

Smiley said yes. Esterhase sat down and put one side of the headphones on, leaving the other ear clear. The magnetic tapes were already rolling.

'Antonov is a scold. He's not comfortable outside protocol. Why is Miki dragging him into a hands-off operation? What's so damned important? He's a respectable spy under proper cover and so and so and so. Honestly that man really doesn't want to say goodbye to Harrods. More of the same: what will people think if they see him going into a hotel room with a dirty foreign traveller? Miki says in this hotel they will assume he is a homosexual. Antonov doesn't like that either. Boo hoo. Miki says maybe Antonov prefers it if Miki just goes to Moscow direct: if you won't help me, that's a matter for the competent authorities within the Thirteenth Directorate as per, and now he's citing regulations. He's very good, George, a total pain in the backside. I like him.' A pause, and then Esterhase held up a finger. 'Miki is giving his credentials: I am a great hero of Soviet ultra-jurisdictional executions, I hunt the wily counter-revolutionary in the long shadows of the Capitalist jungle. I'm paraphrasing, George, okay? Antonov now also has a go: I personally cleaned Stalin's boots and shot a lot of Hungarians in fifty-six. I'm glad he added the date, you know, because really it could be any time. We Hungarians are always in season. You with me, George? You follow?'

Smiley said yes, I follow.

'Miki: Now here I am on this critical operation and Moscow has pissed it up a wall. That's not the Russian expression. He actually says they did this with their sleeves down and left him with the nose. Antonov says sure, that's normal. Damn right, says Miki, but don't let's talk treason in case Moscow can hear us. Big laugh. Now we are all pals together because who hasn't had a boss who leaves you with the nose all the time? Saving your presence, I don't talk about you here. Antonov says he will help if he can, but he's still hedging. Miki please should pass him the big picture of the pretty girl; he has his own paper. Good for you, George, your horrible cellophane is in play. They sit, no one is comfortable: the fellowship of bad furniture. If this is progress, you can have it. To be completely honest, in this one instance I am not entirely unsympathetic. Now . . . now Miki tells Antonov about his mission. From the top: Centre says to Miki to show this old spy where the white crawfish sleeps. That's to teach someone a lesson. Miki says his lessons are very final for the student. Just in case Antonov never met a hitman before. No one in our line likes to be thought naive, do they, George? So Antonov is a little huffy now. We are men of the world, he says, we understand unpleasant necessity. Sure, he understands it but has he ever done it? I don't think so. That man has no mud on his shoes. Miki also does not think so . . . here we go. Miki: Except this time I arrive and Moscow already blew it. Somehow the guy knows to run before I reach him. His place is empty, his office too. He's got a pretty receptionist but he's not with her, by the way that's a crime against the state all on its own. Big laugh, very funny sex joke. Here's the pinch . . . Miki: This man Róka is in the wind but it's a very small wind. There are indications that my target is hiding here in London with sympathisers, so what I need, distinguished Second Secretary Commercial Antonov, what I need is every last morsel that you have locally on Róka so that I find him and get the job done. Then you and I don't got to tell Moscow about the state of their sleeves. Instead of pissy self-justifying bullshit, we get caviar and medals. Can you do this for a brother officer in the name of proletarian solidarity and also promotion? Antonov isn't sure. How is this such an emergency? It's an emergency because the mission comes from the top. This was made clear to Miki in Moscow. All and any means and don't come back until it's done. So how about it?' There was a long pause. 'George, I tell you, I would completely buy this, Miki lies like an Austrian countess. Are you sure he's on our side? Antonov now: Marxism–Leninism is a fundamental attribute of the material universe, the inevitability of victory is assured by scientific knowledge. All intelligent men know this. My God, it's like Sunday school.'

'Antonov's nervous,' Smiley said. 'He needs to cover his own back.'

Toby shook his head in wonder. 'Now they talk race horses. Antonov does not approve of gambling. This will be news to every second bookie in London. Whose microphones exactly is he worried about? Ours or theirs?'

Smiley was polishing his glasses, his familiar habit under stress. Unfolding the soft lining of his tie; huffing lightly on the lens; folding the soft cloth around the glass, and then a fastidious movement with one finger, the nail holding the fabric to the rim. Then the other lens. Toby tutted.

'My God, this fellow. He's making heavy weather, doesn't want to play. Antonov: We make light but in Moscow Centre these days they pay much more attention than they used to. They are acute. There is a new scrutiny. Antonov does not wish to fall foul of this new scrutiny. You think we just bust him right now? Disgraceful conduct from a so-called diplomat, hobnobbing with professional assassins, we are all shocked, tell us everything or it's persona non grata and no more Harrods.'

'What's Miki saying now?'

'He says he has regrettable obligations. Is this you, George? Miki doesn't talk regrettable.'

'It was a fallback,' Smiley said. 'In case Antonov was sticky about handing over the information.'

'Well, thank God for you, George, because sticky is exactly it. Miki says he finds in Róka's apartment a piece of scrap paper with a note for a meeting in Knightsbridge with Second Secretary Antonov. This is a problem for Miki, because if he has to make a report of failure this will inevitably be a necessary component. It is obvious to Miki what happens: Róka meets with Antonov for completely legitimate reasons which unfortunately will now have the flavour of collaboration. Miki doesn't wish to get Antonov in trouble, but certain parties in the apparat will draw certain conclusions or will affect to draw such conclusions in furtherance of their internal political agenda. That's a nice way of saying Antonov is for the chop. Jesus, George, that's a hard ball for you, I think I like it.'

And then quiet, for the first time. Smiley could imagine them not looking at one another in the room below: Miki, still genial and bland, and Antonov, contemplating his own murder. Would he look afraid or stern or something else? And how had they reached this point so quickly, with Smiley already exerting mortal pressure on a man he didn't know?

Esterhase pumped his fist in the air silently. Score. 'Antonov says he will arrange it. He says Miki will owe him one, or Miki's section. Miki says of course, and when the job is done all credit will be shared, but not shared like politics, shared like soldiers. I think now Antonov wants to give him a hug. They are fellow warriors forever. Okay, says Miki, now tell me what Róka wanted from you when you met. Give me the skinny. Antonov: In fact, it was a complete shock actually that Róka was here. I was not briefed. How was I not briefed about a Moscow agent in my backyard? Once again, they leave poor Antonov with the nose; it's the story of his life. Oh, but actually it's tough all over. This happens now, Antonov says. He hears about it from brother officers. New networks outside established structures. New men and new protocols. A new centre within Centre. Exhausting, but if you don't like it maybe you go to sleep forever. So, sure, he says: Róka gives me a signal, I don't know what the hell, but we meet because it's protocol. Miki: What signal? Antonov: He calls one of my juniors and leaves a message. It's a code phrase, not new but old, but who knows? I go to the meeting, I'm not entirely comfortable; it feels like he's gone to seed. Shadows under his eyes, and he talks like a crazy person. I say what the hell are you doing here? Róka says he is doing special work in furtherance of the international revolution. What special work? It is top secret, Róka says. Sure, but give me for instance. Róka doesn't want to say. Finally it turns out he does nothing at all. He is specifically ordered not to recruit, not to solicit sources. Every three months he sends a report: it never says anything. Moscow sends back "Confirm". That's it. They want him here, but they don't tell him why. He's waiting, but he doesn't know what for. How does he send these reports, Antonov wants to know. Róka says he has a contact in Paris. He just sends a postcard, code phrases. That's it. Now Antonov to Miki: This guy also is left with the nose. Miki makes like he doesn't care. He is an assassin, not a psychotherapist. Get on with it. Okay, says Antonov, okay. As for what he wants, that actually is completely crazy. Antonov: Róka wants me to call the Stasi and order them to release a boy. Róka is sure they have arrested this boy, but no one seems to know about it. The reason for this request is so secret I must not discuss it with anyone. How does this square with Róka's bullshit secret work? He cannot explain: it is too secret. Antonov says surely this is a matter for Róka's Paris contact. Róka says his direct contact is unavailable, but this boy is an irreplaceable asset who must be protected. Miki: Did you believe this? Antonov: Not even a little. So now Antonov tells Róka he can't do it; Róka changes his tone. In that case there is something else he needs. Can Antonov please supply the locations of the following individuals vital to the safeguarding of Soviet security? Miki says what individuals?

Antonov says he had a list. Mostly old Tourmaline spies, mostly dead. A couple of soldiers, a political, Antonov doesn't know if they're dead too. He doesn't keep track of provincials. Miki: So what did you tell him? Antonov says he tells Róka to go to hell. Kicks him out in the street, except they are in the Harvey Nichols Café pretending they do sale shopping, so in fact he just makes faces and they part ways. End of story. What does Antonov think it was all about? He has no idea. He says Róka was obviously at the end of his rope. Sometimes that happens with old agents – they get a little bit bonkers. It's very sad. Róka was a great soldier of the Soviet Union, Antonov respects his history and blah blah blah, now we do a eulogy for the guy they conspire to assassinate. Miki has no time for this crap. Thank you, comrade, send me the damn files, we are brothers in arms but also your balls are in the vice, how does this evening suit you? Antonov says call it nine p.m. He puts his notes in his pocket, don't want to leave his big secrets in this nasty hotel where men find love. Oh, except he has to stay a while because that's protocol. Miki says enjoy the minibar because he will leave first. Antonov must stay in the room for ten minutes. That's the door . . . And we wait.'

They waited, Smiley as always beset by absurd scenarios: one of the microphones falling out of the wall; a helpful hotel employee entering the room and asking whether Antonov would like to join the gentlemen upstairs. It was the impossible that tripped you – the unforeseeable or the ridiculous more often than the sublime.

Ten minutes later, Antonov let himself out, and tipped Diane an appropriate amount to make himself forgettable.

'And done,' Toby said. 'Done.'

5.

Sitting alone in the midst of a working office, Susanna Gero understood she was in some manner cast away. Smiley had come, wanting to know about Leó, the ne'er-do-well godson, and Irén, his mother. How deep, he had asked, was the connection? Deep as can be, she said. Where was Leó? She didn't know, realising only now that Mr Bánáti had confined himself to generalities where Leó was concerned. Love, yes, but not life. Did she think Irén an ex-girlfriend? A former love? Yes. She had never asked, but it went almost without saying. Irén was the yardstick by which others were measured. Her opinion, ungiven and unobtainable, had governed the fate of manuscripts and clients. Smiley seemed pleased. Then: would Susanna mind getting in touch with the phone people and asking for an itemised bill? Susanna would not, and did, and when McCraig came on the line as well, the accounts department agreed to rush the job so she could have it picked up this afternoon. By the by, had Bánáti used the phone a lot? She supposed he had. More, recently, than otherwise? Perhaps, yes. She hadn't noticed at the time. She worried that she should have, and Smiley told her: not at all.

Then that was, seemingly, that. He thanked her for her service to the nation. There would be some tidy-up questions from another officer, Mr Glenn. She had done well. She had achieved. She should not expect to know the ending of the story, even if Mr Bánáti should return. In this work, Smiley told her, we do not often have the luxury of neat conclusions. He shook her hand and she read into it without difficulty the form and function of a love affair's ending.

Then he had passed her to a green young fellow with poorly

executed hair who quizzed her artlessly on her work for Mr Bánáti, making it clear that her employer was under considerable suspicion and she, perforce, must clear her name, before pressing her to sign a series of aggressive documents in which she agreed never to speak to anyone in the world about anything, ever again. And now she was, like a patient low on the risk register, awaiting discharge without urgency. She was being released into the wild. Mrs Jeremy, the young man had explained, would come to pick her up, and she should absolutely call the local police if at any point she felt threatened, but there would be no need.

So here she sat, a part of her life made terrifying, and then closed.

'The quiet becomes suddenly difficult,' a voice said, and she saw Millie McCraig in the doorway. 'When you find yourself without work. You can feel a bit adrift.'

Susanna nodded. The older woman shrugged.

'I can help with that, if you like.'

'How?'

'Oh, somehow. I don't know yet, but for example: Bánáti & Clay still exists. Perhaps it can continue to do so even in the absence of Bánáti. You have full authority, you know, over the bank account. Suppose Mr Clay were to die and his daughter take over his share? I mean you,' she added, when Susanna didn't immediately respond. 'You'd be Miss Clay.'

'What would you get out of it?'

'You'd be part of the Chorus Line, so you'd report to me. And you'd occasionally take on a client or a junior agent at my request; put them on the payroll, make announcements about them. Give references. All above board, and government sanctioned, of course. But it would add a dimension to your life, if that's what you want. A sense of doing more than just what everyone does.'

'Why?'

'I like working with people I know, and you're in front of me and you need a way forward. The world isn't easy. I can't change that, but I can change the things that are within my power. Connie does it in Research and I do it here.'

'Your Mr Smiley doesn't trust me.'

'He doesn't distrust you. I think he quite approves of you, in a way, but it's his job to see the invisible. So he looks at you and he sees a young woman who ran away from Hungary and found a life for herself here, and that appeals to him. He believes in the West. But then he looks again and he sees someone who carried packages for a man wanted by Moscow Centre – and who, when a killer presented himself on her doorstep, did not have the vapours and call the police. Instead she sequestered him in her office, secured documents from the home of his target and presented herself at the headquarters of the Secret Intelligence Service. Looked at that way, Miss Gero, you're rather alarming. A little too competent. A little suspicious.'

'Because I didn't faint.'

'Because you did better than anyone had any right to expect, unless you're more than you appear.'

'Is Mr Bánáti more than he appears?'

McCraig shrugged again. 'At this point? No.'

Which was, Susanna realised, an answer with a variety of meanings.

'I don't know what to do,' she said.

'Good. If you did, I'd be rather concerned. I've spoken to Rose Jeremy. She says you can stay at the Adams place for the foreseeable, just to be safe. If László Bánáti contacts you, if you even think he's trying to, I do need to know about it. He may prefer not, but he's in danger and he's being a fool. If you see him, you call me right away. I'll give you a number. You ask for Accounts Payable and say where you are. Any other information afterwards, all right? Even if it's an emergency – particularly if it's an emergency, actually – location comes first. You trust me to know how to handle all the complexities, whatever they are, because I do.'

'And if he doesn't try?'

'Which he won't, by the way. Then you sit tight, consider your soul, and come back to me when you know what you want.'

What she actually wanted in that moment was a copy of Bánáti's portrait, which had struck her forcefully when she saw the completed version because she had no images of either of her parents. She thought they had both died from hard labour; another émigré had told her so, but she had been angry and not inclined to believe him, and had refused the detail. Now, the imperfect yet vital sketch which had sprung from her description of Bánáti seemed like a connection that mattered, and she was ashamed that she didn't know how to ask for one, or whether it would be too secret for sentimental use.

What I want could take a while, Susanna thought, and McCraig's face seemed to tell her: I know that too.

Research Section was the most catholic of the Circus's many faces. Connie, herself as blue-blooded as Haydon, had little interest in the bland opinions of her peers. Perhaps more than anyone else in the Circus, she had as her credo the truth: the best information, with the best explanations, given without partiality, fear or favour. If the Soviet military was moving materiel near Kiev, she could look to Richards or Heumann; if the Chinese border seemed restive, then de Salis, Braques or Lee. But for something which superficially made no sense, when the fog of espionage covered the field and the enemy could be identified only by his footsteps, she had the Bad Aunts. Drawn from every region and class of the fallen Empire which would hear her call, the Aunts were a brain trust dedicated to answering questions which would stump more conventional analysis. Smiley knew both of the women Connie had brought in for this emergency: Katrin, a tiny, bird-boned survivor of Mitteleuropa's hideous mid-century, whose age – unlike Connie's – seemed inversely proportional to her vigour; and Jessica, who had travelled with her parents not on the *Empire Windrush* but a year earlier on the SS *Ormonde*, whose long fingers with their curved, up-turned tips always made Smiley think of piano, who loved crosswords and wooden puzzles and picked up languages the way others do postcards.

Patterned on the eclectic muddle of human curiosity which had twenty years earlier broken the Enigma code, the Bad Aunts were speculative, wayward and uncomfortable, and capable on the right day of delivering forecasts of deeper futures than anyone had any right to ask. That was what mattered, Connie said, and if getting to that point meant bringing in people who couldn't be 'properly cleared' because they were too Jewish or too Jamaican or too intimate with other women, then she would have her section on the far side of the road, and the Lords and Ladies of Control's court could tiptoe through the midden in their cork-heel'd shoes and ask at her door for the truths they needed.

The Aunts endured their exile in a double-width flat on the third floor which had once been some sort of club. The plaster coping was florid, and where the white paint was flaking away you could still see gloss black underneath.

'Tiger-print flock on all the walls,' Connie had told him once, in lascivious horror. 'I almost wish we'd left it there.'

Now, Róka's life was spread out across four rooms. The first was bric-a-brac from his flat. There were manuscripts, published books and magazines, and on a separate table the contents of his drawers, bins and overcoat pockets: chequebook stubs, matches, handkerchiefs, half-finished rolls of strong mints and a quite garish spare tie. Drawing pins, yes, but no chalk. Paperclips. A roll of masking tape, a little piece of gardening twine. It would do, Smiley supposed, for a man in their line. He thought of the cash box, and the weight of it. He might hope for codebooks, though he very much doubted they would be so lucky. He thought it might be a pistol, one of the small Russian sidearms developed for use away from the front line. If fate was kind, Róka would have no call to use it.

The next room was Jessica's, and she sat in silence, reading and discarding Hungarian notes and English memoirs, royalty statements, shopping lists and the endless litany of the day to day. She already had the phone bill and was halfway through, finger pressed against the page as she matched an international number to the office of a small press in Milan. She looked unnaturally still, wrapped in a pale shawl against the damp that somehow always came in.

'Can I bring you anything?' Smiley asked. Jessica smiled, and shook her head.

In the third room, Katrin had the personal correspondence, all of it, the letters Susanna had taken from Róka's flat now pinned to the wall, in deference to their standing as witnesses to the most proximate recent events. She glanced up and snorted gently.

'Smiley!' she said, with reproach. 'You are too soon! We are still making the whole truth from pieces. Don't you know you will see us folding the lady into the box so we can cut her in half? Go away! The magic is not ready. Too soon.'

She shaped her hand as if releasing a butterfly, and shooed him away.

Smiley returned to the bric-a-brac room, which must, he realised, be Connie's domain. She liked to sleep briefly in the middle of the day, and Control encouraged it because, if she didn't, she tended to wander. Later, she'd read everything from Jessica and Katrin, and anything else she could lay her hands on, so that she would become, for the short time it was required of her, an oracle of Róka's past. For now, she wanted not facts but identity, the smell and shape of the man, and the answer to the same question they had asked in Control's meeting room: was he fish or fowl? It was Connie's gift that in between the broken pencils and the used cinema tickets and all the friendly useless clutter of an ongoing life, she would find the truth of him and lay it bare.

Absently, and wary of Katrin's injunction not to spoil the trick,

Smiley wandered to and fro like a customer at a church sale, picking up salt cellars and pairs of reading glasses as if they could whisper to him the secrets he desired. At length, with Antonov's account of the meeting with Róka uppermost in his mind, he fixed on a particular item: the photograph of the woman and the boy in its frame, which Róka had had both on his office desk and in his home. Smiley turned the picture over and over in his hands, smelling the polish on the metal, testing the edges. He opened the frame, hoping for inclusions, but found nothing. The photograph perplexed him because it was wrong along every axis. The paper was English, and recent, the printing bright and sharp, and the cut and make of the clothes were more Bethnal Green than Budapest. Moreover, it was absurd to imagine that a seasoned campaigner like Róka would permit himself, not once but twice, such a wild breach of his own cover. Yet, on the other hand, if they were part of that cover, even notionally, why did he never make a point of calling them? What could be more natural? In fact, the calls from his office were, at least on the surface, scrupulously clean. There weren't even any wrong numbers.

Smiley found the other copy, in its almost identical frame, and turned it over. On the back was a sticker, giving the name of a developing and printing service near Róka's flat. He put the picture in his pocket, and, before he left, sat down at the tiny table in the corner where there was a live telephone. Consulting his notes, he dialled the number for Posie Lloyd. She answered quickly, and he wondered if that was happenstance, or whether she was hovering by the phone.

'Mrs Lloyd?'

'Oh,' she said, 'it's you.'

'I'm afraid so.'

'Don't be, it's fine. Have you found him?'

'No. I just wondered if he'd used your phone recently, perhaps for a business call.'

A long silence. 'He doesn't come to the house. It's a rule.'

Smiley waited.

'All right, we broke the rules. He did. He came here last week. Thursday. I wasn't expecting him, he just rang the bloody bell. I told him he couldn't come in. He said of course not, he just wanted to look at me. Well. I said what exactly did he want to look at, and it all went where you'd imagine. We made love, and afterwards he realised he was late and could he very quickly make a call. He went into the next room.'

'You weren't curious.'

'No.'

Again, he waited.

'I couldn't understand what they were saying. Hungarian, I suppose. It wasn't nearly as quick as he'd said. I was cross because it would show up and Harry would ask about it. I had to work out some excuse about a dress. It was a Paris number.'

'Can you think of anything? Did he mention Leó?'

'Yes. Quite a lot. It got heated, you see, really emotional, and he shouted. Leó blah blah blah, Leó this, Leó that. Whoever it was didn't give an inch, it just got worse and worse. Leó, and Leó and *kérem*. That's Hungarian for "please".'

'Did he mention any other names? Places? Anything at all might help.'

She was silent for a long time, and Smiley worried that she might just have left the phone and walked away.

'I thought he said "Bogdan". That's a name, isn't it? Bogdan? But you know what it's like when you're listening to a language you don't speak. The words make shapes and your brain keeps trying to pretend it understands. If you just listen hard enough, you'll get it. And he was crying. It could just have been that.'

'Did you ask what was wrong?'

'Yes. Of course.'

'What did he say?'

'He said it was nothing I needed to worry about. I said, "Is Leó okay?" And he said he was sure it would be fine. You could tell he didn't. I asked about Bogdan too. He said I'd misheard. I should have told you at lunch.'

'Yes.'

'You don't understand. He cried. It was awful. I didn't want to think about it. I'm sorry, I'm sure that sounds absurd.'

Smiley said not, asked her for the time of day, and let her go. He wrote a note of the entire conversation and passed it immediately to Jessica, marked URGENT. Róka had considered this call special, had distanced himself from it, and in the emerging timeline of events had perhaps known it was the thing for which he would be punished, because it was after this, after saying goodbye to Posie, that he had gone missing – and, at the other end of things, that Miki Bortnik had been given his assignment.

Was it the person he spoke to who occupied some dangerous position in Moscow's secret hierarchy? Or was it this other man, Bogdan? But in that moment Róka had transgressed some higher authority, and been willing to do it.

Marshall Photo of West End Lane was a single frontage of surprising depth, so that Smiley walked between long lines of glass showcases featuring camera bodies and lenses by Nikon and Canon, and a special section for the newer Minoltas alongside a glossy cardboard print of John Glenn. Tripods and monoculars, either for birdwatchers or perverts, filled a final display beside the till.

'Good morning,' Smiley said. 'I wonder if I might have a word with the owner.'

The boy behind the counter shrugged narrow shoulders. 'Allan! Customer wants a chat!' From behind a curtain of faded rainbow ribbons, a man's voice growled something. 'I dunno,' the boy said. 'You want me to ask?'

But Allan had evidently concluded this was no way to run a business, for he swatted the boy to take his place and came around the counter with his hand out. Smiley shook it. Clever fingers, like a pianist's or a tailor's. Mendel had checked him out – it wasn't unusual for a place like this to have a secondary trade in light pornography – but, according to the local station, Marshall wasn't the type. He was a lay preacher and a good egg.

'Help you, sir?' His eyebrows raised in punctuation. And then, with a fond glance towards the curtain, 'My son. Cheeky sod.'

'I do hope so,' Smiley said, and, without further introduction, produced the photograph from his case. 'I'm trying to identify these people,' he explained. 'I'm looking for a missing person, and he had this on his desk. You see it has your sticker on the back. Anything would help. If you could remember what else was on the same film, or even when it was printed.'

Allan Marshall acknowledged the sticker, but, when he turned over the picture, he laughed, and then put his hand to his mouth. 'I'm sorry, it's not funny, I'm sure. Sounds like serious business. But I'm afraid you'll have no luck there. It's not a proper photograph. Or, it is, but you'll not find anything by it. I took this myself: it's my wife and our other son, you see. We put them in the frames we sell, and people take 'em out when they buy the picture.' He gestured towards the far wall, and three rows of ugly modern frames in chrome and brass, each with an image proudly displayed.

'That one was last year. I swap them over at Christmas, use a cartoon of a reindeer because that never changes, then I print up the new image to keep it all fresh. And, of course, I do portraits, so it's all advertising, isn't it?' He shrugged. 'But it won't tell you anything about your missing fellow, I'm afraid.'

Smiley wasn't sure. Róka had reportedly treated the picture with the respect due a holy relic. Granting he hadn't been in love with Mrs Marshall, and that he wasn't so terrible a field man as to draw that much attention to some significant part of his own tradecraft, it must instead be a placeholder, its importance not in what it showed but what it signified. A woman and a boy child, always close to his heart. Leó and his mother, in some moment of joy László Bánáti could not acknowledge, because they were of the history of Ferenc Róka.

While Smiley devilled in West Hampstead, in Paris, Sam Collins opened up at the club in the early afternoon. His bar staff were reliable and the doormen positively subtle, but Sam didn't like letting anyone else begin the day. He told Louis the manager that if somebody had to find a corpse at one of the tables, left over from the night before, he wanted it to be him. It was a joke between them, one which Louis evidently didn't think was funny, and Sam, as his boss, was happy to insist he laughed at. The truth was that Sam wanted to sniff the air and run his finger along the bar counter. The club was his place, and he believed with a certainty that could only be considered superstitious that if someone was watching him or setting him up, he'd know from that first moment in his day. Then too there was always the possibility that someone in or around the Circus would use it as an emergency dead drop. They weren't supposed to, but, if it was going to happen, Sam should be the one to stumble on it, not anyone else. In his darkest imaginings, he saw crucial intelligence from Egypt smuggled out across the Med and up the train line from Naples, while the hounds of Moscow Centre bayed and pursued, and some nameless agent managing to get his package to Club Nid de Chouette Saint-Germain, only to have the cleaners throw it out with the dirty bottles. The fate of Western civilisation sent to landfill because Sam let someone else turn the key.

He made himself coffee from the absurd copper machine behind the bar, and sat, drinking it and smelling stale cigarettes and sour wine. A moment later, he had to leave the cup, because the house phone was ringing.

'Le Nid,' Sam said; and, in French, 'How can we help you?'

He heard Jessica's voice, and felt his eyebrows climb slightly on his face. Unlike many in the Circus, Sam loved the Aunts. They were mad, bad and insufferable in the pursuit of intelligence, and as far as he was concerned that was all that mattered. She asked if he was a bookshop, and he apologised and said he wasn't. Jessica sounded very confused. Surely an owl's nest must be a bookshop? No, Sam said, it was a club, dancing and drinks, perhaps she'd like to come? With his spare hand, he was jotting down notes on a single sheet of paper as she objected: bookshop, then the phone number, and finally the name of her friend who had given her his number: Leó. Was there really no Leó there? He asked her again if perhaps she'd enjoy the club, and said she had a pretty voice. She told him he was a lecher and she'd never been so offended in her life.

'Righto,' Sam said, and she rang off.

He cleaned the bar counter with a cloth, rubbing hard on the copper until he was sure no trace of the note remained. Then he waited twenty minutes until Louis arrived and told him to open all the windows because the place stank, and that he was going for a stroll along the river.

Collins was of a younger Circus generation, only a few years earlier than Guillam, but of a completely different stripe. Guillam was one of their classic adventurers, stalwart and oddly straightforward for someone in their profession. Sam was the opposite. His father had been a local politician and Sam liked to say he was as bent as a thrupenny bit. Sam's mother, daughter of the grand house in their town, had married the man in error, and shortly removed herself, leaving Sam prenticed to the old bastard. Thirty years on, Sam was dapper, credible and, so far as he was able to determine, absolutely devoid of conscience. He liked to win, and he liked to see the other fellow lose, and that was all. In the Circus, he'd found a place to put his talents to work, and it might be the only thing on earth he gave a damn about, at least for now. His favoured beat was the Far East, but spies proposed and Control disposed, and here he was in Paris, though at least with Paris being what it was you could get decent Vietnamese food.

Leaving the club, he did actually turn towards the river, but then broke left into the narrow streets between the club and Saint-Sulpice, until he rounded a corner into a pretty little square and saw the place he was looking for, hard against the back of some preposterous Napoleonic offices. He went in, and heard a bell ring somewhere inside. The place was dim, cosy and smelled mostly the way a bookshop should, though with a hint of modern glue bindings stinking up the main window. There was a woman behind the counter, in her forties and intellectual to look at. She reminded Sam of the matron at the small prep school he had attended, where his father had conducted a successful raid on the sports fund, and then, when the shortfall was discovered, turned around and given half of it back as an emergency donation, not incidentally locking in his nomination for town mayor. The rest of the money bought a fine night at a London casino for both of them. Sam had been fourteen.

'Good morning,' Sam said, though it was by now afternoon. 'I'm looking for a full edition of the serialised *Le Bossu*, by Féval. I wondered if you might know where to start.' She nodded, but didn't, which was why he'd asked. It was hardly a simple request. She made an approving sort of fuss – how exciting, such an excellent story – and Sam could hear light footsteps as the owner padded down the spiral stairs from above. Carpet slippers, was his first thought: old, comfortable, striped velvet. Then unfashionably baggy slacks, and finally a cardigan so awful it wouldn't have looked out of place on Control; no spectacles, which Sam thought was a shame; and surprisingly trim, almost military hair, some last vestige of another life refusing to let go.

'Good afternoon,' the man said in French; 'welcome. What can I do for you?' His accent was solid, but the delivery wasn't. If anything it was too good, without the laziness that ownership gives to native speakers.

'This is Mr Grodescu,' the woman confided; 'he can help you better than I can.'

They shook hands, Grodescu's grip almost completely limp,

as if to let you know his intellect left him too exhausted for physical touch. Sam gave his cover name, Daniel, and repeated that he was hoping to find or collect the full run of Féval's adventure in its original magazine publication. He'd chosen it in part because it was tricky but ultimately deliverable, and also because if he ended up buying a couple of issues he actually wouldn't mind. Grodescu said he would be on the lookout. Buying individual issues over time would be cheaper, of course, but unreliable. Some were naturally more scarce than others, and it was a very long book. On the other hand, should monsieur succeed, his investment would more than pay for itself – not that one would willingly part with such a treasure. He took Sam's number at the club and agreed to call as and when. They chatted amicably, regretting the madness of government and the paucity of good cinema.

At length, Sam thanked him and took his leave, and then – as Grodescu had his foot in the air to go back upstairs, he slapped his forehead. 'What about Leó?' he demanded, and saw in the reflection in the window Grodescu's head come round on his shoulders like a hawk's. Sam was still looking away from him. '*Anna Karenina!*' he proclaimed, pointing at a new edition in the window. 'Can you get me an early translation?'

Grodescu visibly swallowed his irritation, and they embarked on a second round of quality, price and delivery. This time, Grodescu's eyes were sharp on Sam, and Sam took care to be exactly the same ordinary fellow who'd first walked in, even going so far as to buy the modern Tolstoy as a reading copy in expectation of his prize. He went back to the club, wrote the whole thing up and put it in the pocket of a coat left behind a week ago. Later, someone would be in to collect it. Top line: CONFIRM. In Sam's judgement Grodescu was an active Moscow Centre spy and needed careful watching. He'd known who Leó was, without a doubt – which was more than Sam did. Any further detail would require a serious operation and the connivance of the French. He scented deep water, and was unsurprised later in the evening when the order came back: HOLD.

Returning to the Research annexe, Smiley found a slim file set aside for him personally. Opening it, he discovered a photographic copy of Antonov's notes in the original Cyrillic, and a faithful English translation with the text arranged in the same approximate spatial relationships on the page. There had been two sheets, Jessica's accompanying summary explained, and the second set had been written over the top of the first, resulting – along with Antonov's questionable penmanship – in a delay in her transcription. The first page was Antonov's direct aide-memoire of Miki's request, peppered with official irritation. It was the second, dashed off almost as an afterthought, which arrested Smiley's attention. This was the kind of indiscretion which was possible only when brute habit told you there was no risk of interception – precisely what he had been hoping for, and incidentally most feared in himself. It consisted of a list of three names, written diagonally across the top of the page:

Leonov;
Gurin;
and
Grodescu.

The first was no mystery at all. Yuri Leonov was Moscow Centre's Head of Station in Brussels: a muscular ex-soldier who had – per Katrin's note – been the Centre case officer for several of the Tourmaline set until the early fifties. The second was also easy: Aslaan Gurin held the same role in Rome, although rumour had it he was considered superannuated, and overdue to be pensioned off.

Grodescu was new, but Smiley saw that Jessica had already run him down, and had Collins do a sniff test. Very slick, Sam said, to the point of invisible. A real top-drawer item, everything held in so tight you found yourself questioning your instincts – which, from Collins, who prided himself on an almost mystical alertness to human mendacity, was the ultimate compliment.

Smiley's contemplative mood was broken by Tom Lake, who was at a loose end while Miki was being debriefed. 'Royal says I loom,' Lake complained. 'I don't loom, I'm just not short.' Smiley said he was sure that was true.

Wanting to make himself useful, Lake had joined Esterhase's people in canvassing the émigré groups, although by then the picture was already pretty clear. Róka had gone from being an unenthusiastic member of the Hungarian diaspora to asking for help, and the crowd had not opened its arms. Lake's experience was typical. Toby had sent him to talk to Andrea Medve, known as Mama Andi, who ran a social evening in Kilburn for Middle Europeans looking to reconnect with their Lost Hundred. Toby referred to her as London's Habsburg marriage broker.

Tall and ageless but admitting to forty-nine, Mama Andi had taken one look at Lake and made it clear he could ask as many questions as he liked, so long as they could share a bottle of wine. Over the first glass, Lake had shown her Bánáti's picture. Yes, she said immediately. Not a regular but not a stranger either. László, no second name given. Flirt, gentleman, probably a thief. Why a thief? Instinct, darling, Mama Andi said. There's a class of man who makes love to you all night and steals your pearls before dawn. Not for himself. For the cause. And when Lake asked what cause, she said that was quite irrelevant.

Had he been in recently? She didn't know. Maurice might. Maurice being her business partner and lover, who liked Lake a fair bit less than she did. Yes, sure: Maurice knew László. Yes, he came in a fortnight ago. How did he seem? Not good. What sort of not good? Maurice wasn't sure he wanted to say. Mama Andi told him he did, and Maurice looked like a man who knew it was only getting worse from here.

'Always before he's king of the world. Sometimes he brings people from work, they make a party. British people mostly, excited for exotic Hungarian music, get drunk, make passes at the staff. This time he comes alone. He gives me ten pounds. Maurice, he says, I need help. Sure, for ten pounds, a lot of help. That's a fee, he says. For introductions. I say I don't do that kind of work. I think he means hookers. He says no, not that, thank you, he got all he needs in that department. What, then? And he says he needs friends. I say, well, okay, but friends, that's more expensive. He laughs. I'm funny.

' "Someone I love is in trouble," he says, "I need someone who knows someone."

'So I say you got all these British friends, László. I see you with them. You bring them here, they love it, so now go to them. They can help you. Britain has wheels in wheels, I tell him. Things here get done some crazy British way. Ask them, not Maurice. But this is no good for him. He says he needs new friends in Europe. What Europe? He says the East. I don't like this. How come he doesn't have those kinds of friends already? Maybe he does and they don't want anything to do with him. Maybe they're right! How come he needs new friends, I say, but I ask nice, like it's funny. He says this person is in trouble in Berlin, on the wrong side. So now do I know anyone who knows someone who knows? No, I damn well don't. Maurice is no spy! No Stasi friends, not even one of those damn Stasi priests who pretend they don't know who they're talking to. I got no Soviet friends either, no cousins, uncles, old buddies. Maurice is patriot. I'm a little angry now.

' "Everyone knows someone," László says. Then why doesn't he ask his own damn someone?' Maurice sighed. 'So now I feel like an arsehole.'

'Why?'

'Because now he says he already asked and they don't help. He asked and he gets nothing, and this person he loves is still in trouble on the other side. He says he's not a good person to know, that's why he keeps to himself. Trouble follows, he says, that's why he don't make friends before. I feel a little bit bad. A lot.'

Lake nodded. 'So what did you do?'

'He didn't ask me, is what he did,' Mama Andi said, and Maurice flinched.

'Andi is busy. I ask around. Tell a few people. If they can help, go sit at his table. I say it's a favour to me. Not a big one, I don't want to be involved, but I tell them maybe go, hear what he says. Like that.'

'And did they?'

Maurice ducked, and Andi's face went stony. She glowered at Maurice until he got up and walked away, and then she poured two glasses and made Lake drink a toast to László Bánáti, alone at his table until closing.

'Like a bloody funeral,' Lake muttered, and Jessica appeared to tell them it was time.

Connie stood with her back to the door, reaching out to drive a coloured drawing pin into the cork. In her off-hand was a sheaf of notes, and she was muttering as she transferred information from the page to the board. She did this when she was rapt in the study of a new problem: held conversations with her subject, murmured his secrets back to him, or accused him of crossing her in love.

She was taller than Smiley was, quite a bit, and only two years older but not carrying it well. She liked to drape herself in soft clothes to hide the painful shape of her hips. Her joints were drying up, and in the two decades since the war her drinking had become habitual, with the relentless rhythm of the addict. Trauma, her personnel file said. Loyalty unquestionable. Alcohol may become a problem over time; refer to Chief. Smiley had written it himself and hated every word.

'It's a song of sorrows, George,' Connie said. 'It really is. The saga of the East in a single life.' She seemed to forget where she was going: one, two, and then she was back again, eyes sharp. 'Are you going?' She meant, will you hunt him down?

Smiley said no, that was someone else's job. A younger man, not retired. Connie's eyes blinked slowly, and she nodded: of course. Right you are.

'I only ask because whoever does go wants to be careful. Antonov got a warning from little Lena and now he's warning Miki too. She says it's not a good time to test Moscow's patience. The loud voices are going silent. Falling asleep, she says, and not always waking up. The wind's changing, George. Whoever does go, tell them to take care?'

Smiley said he would, and Connie seemed to realise they weren't alone. She raised her voice and stiffened her back like a sergeant.

'Let's do sources,' she declared, to the room in general. 'Reliable-ish. We have Antonov's file, which is good but comes from the Russians, and they do lie to one another. The Party is fate and disagreement is recidivism, so, when the facts don't support the apparat, that's a flaw in the history that needs to be amended. Next we have our Registry records from the time, some good spying going on back then, full marks to J. Prideaux and his partner in crime. The public prints, also under the Soviet thumb. Defectors' gossip, Foreign Office observations, each as real as the other. A collage, not a photograph. Mind you, photographs lie too, don't they? So who do we trust? We trust Connie. Where was I?'

'Róka,' Smiley prompted, and she nodded.

'Róka was a farm boy and then a soldier. Caught his Communism early. You don't remember nineteen seventeen, do you, George? I'm just old enough, you see. The strange hope: a new way of doing things, never before seen. Or a new barbarism, if you believed *The Times*. A wicked king in ruins, a bold economic plan and the promise of freedom; Vladimir Ilyich so dashing in a driving cap, like a movie star. All turned to lies, alas, though I'm sure they meant it at the time. The human factor forever getting in the way of perfection. But, oh, Ferenc Róka. Born in the old Habsburg Empire, grew up with all that wounded pride and lost potential, hope squandered by a bully who liked the clink of his own medals. So Róka joined the Party in the twenties, carried messages hither and yon. Then, in nineteen thirty-six, he took his rifle and his overcoat and went to Spain to fight Franco. Up and down the mountains, and canny he got, so very canny. And who should he meet in Spain but Andrei Alexeyevich Rudnev, senior officer in the foreign intelligence service of the Soviet Union, and, more particularly, the Thirteenth Directorate. Lies, damned lies, and infiltration a speciality. That's not how Antonov's file puts it, but we know, don't we? Would Comrade Róka like to carry on making a real difference in the Struggle? Yes, Comrade Róka very much would. Then come to Moscow, young fella-me-lad, it's a man's life in the Committee for State Security – which he does, and right handily, at a dingy little clubhouse off the main drag called without irony the Hotel Tourmaline. Pop around the corner and you can meet all the bright new faces of the International, although don't get overfond of them because Comrade Stalin tends to have them knocked off by the dozen when he's feeling antsy.'

She put her hand out, and Katrin passed her a teacup. She sipped, grimaced in disappointment and put it down.

'Then off he goes to spy, the young pilot of the ship of the world. Bit of France here, bit of America there, bit of Palestine, even, in the glory days. In thirty-eight – NB not thirty-nine, that's a little British foible, rather insular of us – the war breaks out, and he goes back to Hungary to smite the unrighteous: first Horthy's men beasting the neighbours for supplies and recruits, then the Arrow Cross thugs when they start to take over, and then the actual Nazis in forty-four.'

She drifted for a moment, seeing other lives.

'They keep files on all of them, you know, George: the Russians do. There's a room in Moscow where they have the names of all the Nazis they didn't hang, and whenever one of them rises up, they get a tap on the shoulder. We know who you were. We know the rank, the number, and the names of the dead. Do as you're bid, or we'll tell. Maybe Róka has a copy in his head. Do we want those secrets, if he does? Would we do anything better? Would the Americans? Or would we do exactly the same? Mundt's on that list, of course. Do you think he pulled the trigger himself, or just watched, when poor Alec died? He was security for the Nazis before ever he was a proud advocate of Soviet Communism. Do you think they don't know? Of course they do. That's why they like him, because he's infinitely disposable at any time.'

Smiley, very gently, touched her hand.

'Hungary. Forty-four.'

She nodded. 'Oh, it was the *echter Napoleon*, George. The real thing. Tunnels, secret hidey-holes, and we few, we band of brothers, cutting throats in the dark for peace, country and the greater glory of the revolution. Well, who could resist? Certainly not Irén Pártos, dazzling poetess and fiery beauty of the cause, who hid him in her cellar after he caught one in the leg somewhere. She fell in love with him, fought alongside him. Sex, bullets and ideology. And there was the boy, of course, born sometime before the Soviets arrived. Pártos is listed as a war widow. The story was that she married a soldier just before he went to the front, but all the world knows Leó is Róka's child.'

'Why did they lie?'

'Oh, because she was still playing the Hungarian patriot maid: running messages up and down, smuggling guns to the Resistance. With the boy at her tit, no doubt. She could hardly do that and call herself Róka's mistress in sin, whore to a dirty Communist. Besides, a godson makes you a Christian, doesn't it? Without anyone even asking. They made up some noble sacrifice, a peasant she'd loved who threw himself on a grenade for his brothers.

Then, in forty-five, glory and medals. The Soviets liberated Hungary, which is the first time in recorded history anyone's ever shown up for them and it was a bloody mess.' She glanced at Katrin, who shrugged.

'Not history, in Mitteleuropa. This is the English mistake, to separate then from now. In those places there is only now, and it goes back forever. Here is Hungary seven hundred years ago, alone against Subutai and Batu Khan. Over there in fifteen thirty is Hungary, alone again against Suleiman the Magnificent. Here is Hungary in nineteen fourteen, when Franz Ferdinand is murdered, full of the interests of other powers and so the nexus of a war, and here she is again four years later when that war is over and for their sins her empire must cease to exist. Here is the end of the second great war, which was for Hungary also the continuation of the first, and here is Hungary: alone against Stalin's liberating army, which turned out to be just a second occupation. Here is Hungary, the new democracy, asking for peace and liberty in fifty-six, and instead of help? Here is Suez and another army from the East. The story never changes. Only the clock. Always, there is Budapest on the Donau, knocking at the gate of Europe, wanting to come in, and all the pretty palaces of the Rhine and the Seine and the Thames nod their heads and say yes when they mean no. This is the Hungary of Ferenc Róka: the Hungary that will never receive the help it was promised.

'Well,' Connie murmured, 'Stalin was going to help, all right. When people voted for the bourgeois kulaks to run the place, Comrade Stalin gave them the Communists instead, and that's the inevitable process of historical materialism. Destiny in action. And our boy Róka's destiny was very bright! Moscow told him to run for office and they'd see him elected. One doesn't know, of course, but I doubt they even had to stuff the ballots. Not for him, hero as he was. And why not her, you may well ask? Never mind. He was raised to high estate. Or, at least, he got in, which most of them didn't. Hungary wasn't Communist, you see.

Hardly a red anywhere, from Sárvár to Debrecen. So now the Hungarians wanted to get on with perfectly ordinary bourgeois agrarianism – voted in droves, darling, for the Independent Small-holders' Party. A plot of land, a jug of wine, and thou beside me. Brother Joe had marched his troops up the Donau and down again and now they were telling him: "Thanks a lot, Joseph, but your army's a menace and you're a bloody Osset, so take your Revolution and shove it." Which he wasn't, but I'm sure they had a good laugh. Stalin, though, not known for his sense of humour, says he respects the democratic process and the Smallholders can make all the decisions he tells them to. Here's a coalition, by which I mean a dictatorship, and anyone who doesn't like it can make a cogent and sophisticated argument to the firing squad. Which they did, by the bloody hundreds.' She stuck out her tongue and pantomimed a proud patriotic death. 'But Róka was a genuine war hero in his district. An honest spy.' She spread her hands in wonder. 'So they made him a junior assistant under-minister for something or other. Ferenc and Irén and little Leó all lived happily ever after, until the boy was nine or so, at which point Ferenc Róka ballsed it up.'

'How, exactly?'

Even in the Russian files the detail was unclear. With Stalin dying and more than a little mad, Moscow was in turmoil. Regular denunciation of anti-Soviet infiltrators was a necessity for survival across the Eastern Bloc. Róka chose a target, and immediately found he had sorely miscalculated. The man had more pull than he did, and not just a bit but lots. Róka lost his job and was ruled unreliable, unsuitable for public office. A few days later, one of his remaining friends warned him that his downward path had not by any means hit bottom.

'He packed a suitcase and vanished into the night, leaving his beloved and son behind. Another war death for Irén, a lost child-hood for the boy.' Connie spread her fingers to the winds. 'Whither, we knew not. Moscow evidently saw the whole thing for what it was, because he was running around France for them in fifty-three. The Cousins say he was in Egypt for Suez, but they think that about everybody. We lost track of him after Marseilles. The betting was South America, until he turned up two days ago on our bloody doorstep, and here we all are.'

'And where is that, Connie? Where's Róka?'

'In the badlands, George,' Toby Esterhase called from the doorway. 'I'm sorry to interrupt you, Connie, but I need George quite urgently. The Swiss have a body in Zurich, shot twice in the face from very close. A Moscow classic, I would say. The dead man is Harto Latour, a Belgian Finn with a nasty little trade in illegal arms. But he's travelling on a doctored passport that says he's László Bánáti! You see it?' Esterhase was actually bouncing slightly on his toes. 'You see it, George?'

'Where's Mendel?' Smiley asked.

'I called, he's working. Tell me you see it?'

Smiley drew breath, and allowed that he might.

6.

'I'm Róka,' Smiley said, without looking at Esterhase. 'I've been in London for years and kept my head down. Now I'm breaking protocol. I turn up on Antonov's doorstep and he sends me packing. What then?'

'You've got a problem, George, whichever way you butter it,' Esterhase replied. 'Haven't you? Antonov is going to report you; he's the sort of fellow who does.'

Smiley thought of the call to Grodescu, but chose not to disagree. It remained possible that Antonov had been the trigger: a sudden rush of expedient conscience.

Esterhase had the bit between his teeth. 'Róka is calling all the old familiar spies. He's a gift to us, George. Already Connie has half a dozen names. I mean, names we knew, but still a shopping list. You blow the cover on six or seven of your peers in one week, people in our line will get testy. It's natural. So you take to your heels, obviously. Off you go into the night.'

'But where do I go? And, most importantly, how?'

Katrin spoke before Esterhase could answer.

'If all he wants is to disappear, then anywhere. Maybe he's got another legend waiting and he just steps into it, like a man with two wives. He's Róka, after all. Not his first time.'

Esterhase nodded but looked sceptical. 'Sure, he's Róka.'

Smiley ignored him. 'That would be the wise course, certainly. But it's not what he wants. We know that. He has a mission: the boy in Berlin. He tells Antonov that Leó's an asset, which is doubtful. Now he stands revealed. So what does he do next?'

'He needs an old friend,' Connie murmured. 'Jessie, get in here, we're spying. George has got that look. He can see through walls.' She appropriated a fresh cup and poured something into it from a flask, smacking her lips. Jessica leaned on the doorframe.

'Someone overseas,' she said. 'In London, after Antonov, he'd be stepping down the ladder.'

Connie agreed. 'Oh, no one in London. No one in Britain, actually. Paris, but the bookseller has already turned him down. Maybe . . . Istanbul. Hong Kong. Anywhere.'

Smiley nodded, catching the moment in his hand and holding it. He nodded to Esterhase, granting the logic Toby had seen from the first. 'And for that, he needs to travel. He needs documents and money. Well, let's grant he has the money, but he can hardly use Moscow passports when he's on the run from his own side, now can he? So he's going to want local product. Someone who doesn't deal with Moscow, but isn't directly tied to the Circus either. An independent. Who would he go to?' Jessica pointed to Esterhase, who nodded.

'That's a very interesting question, actually. In the freelance industry, there are circles and circles. Different clients, different artisans. Mendel might know.'

'I'm not following,' Lake said. 'What's this got to do with a dead Finn in Zurich? Proper Moscow, that was,' he added, with professional impartiality; 'not like what Miki was about at all. Bang bang, fall down. Much cleaner.'

'In London they wanted him to vanish,' Smiley responded. 'Before he meant anything to anyone. Now the horse has bolted and they don't care about the stable door. As for the rest –'

He gestured to Esterhase to take over.

'Róka has Russian-made passports, but he doesn't want to use them because Moscow knows the names and the numbers. So he goes to someone here in London who can make him what he needs, and he trades the Russian fakes in part payment for the new ones. Off he runs into the dark, but the fellow he trades them to doesn't sit on his hands. He knows the Russian passports are tricky because Róka tells him, but he doesn't want to leave money on the table, so he alters them quickly and sells them on: a new photograph and new numbers, but he leaves the name, because that's a longer job – if you can do it at all. Sadly the Russians have someone in the immigration office in Zurich who's on the lookout for the name, and when he signals Moscow they don't waste time. Bang bang, as you say. Poor Mr Latour says his last goodnight.' Toby opened his hands, passing the story back to Smiley for the conclusion.

'Latour's death tells us that Róka intends to travel and emphasises that Moscow is very keen that he shouldn't talk to us. Or to anyone, ever again. Which means, of course, that we should really try to arrange a conversation. But, more than that, it tells us what to look for here.'

Lake, at last, looked relieved. 'An artist,' he said. 'A paper man.'

Smiley put in a call to Mendel's office and got Sally Roberts, who reported that her chief had spoken with the Cattermoles and two of their criminal lieutenants, who had asserted proudly that they had no truck with drugs, Sicilians or Russian spies. 'So every bloody horrible thing they do is British-made,' Roberts added, and agreed to send a list of local artistic talent who might have escaped the Circus's notice. Smiley called Donal Evans at the sister service with the same inquiry. Evans, unlike Roberts, was prone to asking questions. He was brick-faced and one of those people who will hold the door closed on you because they want to open it for someone else.

'Why, George? Do you see? My governor will want to know the why.'

'I'm afraid I don't know all of it myself, Don. I've retired – you may have heard. Control has me dotting the i's and crossing the t's, and this is one of my chores, but it seems there's a dead arms dealer in the Bahnhofstrasse using a doctored Russian-made passport. Head of Station there thinks the work was done here, but no one we know is owning up. I wondered if you knew someone we wouldn't think of.'

'I'm sure we do,' Evans snapped, 'but there's a sort of a perception over here, George, that you aren't always forthcoming with security. You play fast and loose, and we only get to hear about it later. There's animosity, almost, lurking in the background. We are on the same side, after all. We should be collegial.'

'Indeed, we should,' Smiley agreed. 'Although, as I say, it's really "You should". I'm on my way out of the door. If you can't name anyone we haven't already got, that's perfectly all right. I think tacitly I'm being punished for leaving just as things are hotting up. I'm supposed to be at a party in Geneva. With Ann, you know. So if you're feeling generous, you could hang up on me. That would be fine.'

'If I was supposed to be at a party with Ann, I'm not sure I'd even have called.'

'No. Well, perhaps I shouldn't have. Thank you, anyway, Don. I'm sorry you couldn't help.'

But, given the opportunity to be vindictive, Evans had changed his mind. A few moments later Smiley had his list of possibles pinned to the wall, and Jessica was running a long, sharp finger along the column of text. She had a pair of gold reading glasses and she stuck her chin forward to bring them in front of her eyes. Esterhase stood beside her, a peacock next to an eagle.

Now Jessica looked from one paper to the other and tapped, nail ticking against the plaster underneath. Esterhase nodded agreement. 'Here,' she said. 'By the Bow Road.'

The sign on the door regretted that entry was by appointment only. Smiley had called and been told Mr Vishwakarma was busy all day, which to Toby was practically a printed invitation. 'You know what they say about Hungarians, George? That's a fellow who goes into a revolving door behind you and comes out in front. We shall go in at five past two o'clock.' Smiley had insisted on bringing a babysitter, so Tom Lake was sitting in a car down the road reading the *A to Z* and keeping an eye out for who else came and went. 'We are a little early. Come on, George, let's go for a little walk. We shall take the London air.' Taking Smiley's arm, he walked them down to the corner, where they stood looking at a shuttered pub as if it were the Post Office Tower or Buckingham Palace. 'Post-war infill,' Toby said. 'Too modern for your taste, maybe, George? Come on, now, it's time. Act natural, look busy, okay?'

Vishwakarma's building was large, with heavy, tinted-glass windows which hinted at luxury in the space beyond. The awning was modern and very sharp, black fabric stretched tight like a Smith & Co. umbrella, boasting proudly in stark silver letters the words VISHWAKARMA FRÈRES: LONDON, MILAN, SPIEZ, HONG KONG. The Spiez location, half an hour from the Swiss capital, was a lawyer's reception desk. As far as anyone could tell, the other addresses were entirely aspirational.

Raghuraman Vishwakarma was actually listed twice in the talent chart, once by Evans and once by Roberts. The Circus had somehow missed him altogether. Born Udangudi Balakrishnan Raghuraman Vishwakarma on the Coromandel Coast in nineteen twenty-one, he'd trained in a Madras workshop making plate dies for the Calcutta Mint, then brought his skills to London in the nineteen fifties to seek his fortune. Rejected by Tower Hill and told to find his own way, he'd made ends meet as a backroom jeweller, then a printer of advertising flyers and local news sheets, before beginning to supplement his income with export-only editions of foreign currencies. The sniffers had him down as a pragmatist, but noted you could never be entirely sure someone wasn't harbouring convictions.

Now, Vishwakarma's business had a public face which doubled as a laundromat for his less legal earnings, ostensibly selling hand-painted or block-printed wallpapers to the discerning bourgeoisie. His more lucrative product was exclusively commercial and criminal: he specialised in Swiss francs, which found their way into large-sum illegal cash transactions, generally in the Far and Middle East, thereby avoiding the immediate scrutiny of Bern's watchdogs. Over time he'd taken an interest in escape passports for the upmarket buyer, usually wealthy businessmen who wanted an option if their business fell into disfavour in Beirut or Vientiane and they had to make a discreet and hasty exit. Among the business community a quarter-hour away in the City, his name was extremely well-regarded. More locally, Mendel's colleagues reported that his prosperity had attracted negative notice, and he had filed several complaints with the local police regarding on-street harassment.

'Oh, dear me,' Toby murmured now, looking towards Spitalfields, and when Smiley turned he saw four large men in labourer's jackets approaching the doorway of Vishwakarma Frères. When they got there, they began to raise hell. A moment later, someone spoke through the intercom, quite politely, which made things worse. The shouting took on an ugly inflection, full of wounded Saxon pride, and someone produced a hammer. The security glass shuddered but held. A second blow produced a white crater, as if either the door or the hammer were made of ice.

Esterhase walked straight out into the road, making a beeline for the toughs. Smiley watched him: a short, narrow figure in a fashionable American-style aviator jacket and business trousers. He could have been the hero of Miki Bortnik's cinematic endeavours.

Midway across the road, Toby barked out an order, and all the men turned to look at him in amazement. They should by rights have set on him immediately, just from the tone, but – by the same token of absolute authority – Toby was for a moment someone worth listening to. Then they got his accent, and someone sneered that foreigns were all the same, whether it was bloody Indians or bloody Germans, and Esterhase bristled and pointed out that he was a bloody Hungarian, thank you so much. Then for good measure he added something starkly offensive and stood with one hand on his hip and the other pointing down the road the way they'd come, telling them in broad language to go back there and reconsider their life choices.

It seemed ridiculous, the little man standing up against four big ones, but in Vienna Smiley had seen Esterhase fight. He possessed the athleticism that is given to smaller men, and the complete lack of compunction that comes with knowing the real consequences of loss. The nearest tough raised his fist, and Esterhase leaned in as if confiding something. With surprising slowness his head simply kept going, and the big man's nose flattened. Esterhase's right hand was still pointing away down the street, but now returned to clap his opponent on the shoulder, while the left did something unspeakable, twisting flesh which was either groin or thigh, and in either case obviously tender. A hundred yards away, Lake was still struggling to get the car door open and race to assist, but Esterhase clearly didn't need the help. He brushed past his first victim to the next man, and now there was something very slender, like a sixth finger, protruding from his grip. It settled under the fellow's chin, and dialogue resumed. There was a short, horrified exchange and the whole group retreated in bad order, calling insults as they went. Esterhase fussed with his handkerchief, dabbing spots of blood from the leather of his jacket and complaining that the Circus should pay to have it cleaned. Lake, having got out of the car, now had to get back into it. He looked chagrined at having missed the fun.

'That was garish,' Smiley murmured.

Esterhase's face was round with innocence. 'I don't know what you could possibly mean, George. Entirely coincidental. But, with the matter unfolding right in front of us, I like to fly the flag for rootless cosmopolitans when I can.' He reached out and pushed the buzzer on the intercom. 'Mr Vishwakarma, I am so sorry to interrupt you. My name is Preuss. My friend is Adam Barraclough. We were hoping to speak to you on a business matter and chanced to come along just as your other guests were making their little scene. Do you think we might have a few minutes of your time?'

The door opened to reveal a man in his early forties, small but not round. He wore a pale-blue roll-neck and corduroy trousers which looked casually expensive, but his hand, when Smiley shook it, was hard on the palm and fingers, the grip powerful.

'Please come inside, Mr Barraclough,' he murmured, and then, turning to Esterhase, 'Mr Preuss.'

They went inside, and Vishwakarma closed the glass door behind them, followed by a second door made of metal. The public space was painted a rich cream and illuminated by a sky-light window. Business was evidently conducted in the sunken lounge, around a coffee table, which made for an extremely informal atmosphere. Esterhase sprawled happily, laying his arms along the backs of the sofa as if waiting for more congenial company. From somewhere backstage came the rich, damp odour of ink, and the nameless but immediately recognisable scent of hot metal. On the walls, in frames, there were bright three-colour posters for West End shows.

'What can I do for you gentlemen?' Vishwakarma asked. 'Something in a hessian, perhaps? The gold weave is excellent for London homes. Very warm. No? Well, then.' He poured drinks for all of them without asking, fruit juice in frosted glasses. Smiley eased himself into a chair, seeming to find comfort of itself somewhat uncomfortable.

'You did a print job recently for a person who is by way of being a colleague of mine. I gather it was rather good. I'm hoping to secure something similar. Paper for a Swiss-style property in Cambodia – quite a sizeable amount, and of course, in context, the appearance of authenticity is a serious concern. For which, naturally, we would expect to a pay a premium. I am assuming from my colleague's enthusiasm that we're talking of a pure flax product.'

Vishwakarma had seemed quite bored until the mention of Swiss paper, then attentive. Now, challenged on quality, he waved his hand as if to say that anything else was not worth considering. 'Of course.'

'And it handles ultraviolet quite well, for example.'

Esterhase's eyebrows rose slightly. Under ultraviolet light, the flax paper of a banknote should shine, and even high-quality counterfeits often didn't, because the flax used to make them was too new. It wasn't that Smiley's question was bad – quite the opposite – just that Esterhase hadn't ever imagined him knowing to ask. Vishwakarma, on the other hand, appeared gratified to be dealing with a competent buyer.

'Really very well. We source the cloth from machine shops in the North: too small to supply the brand names in this area' – by which Toby assumed he meant the central banks – 'but the same history in the fabric. The flax is excellent. You're welcome to take some away and make comparisons.'

'Very kind.'

'There are certain proprieties in such a situation, Mr Barraclough. Just as you require a sample, so I also have need of surety. There are supplies to be acquired. Necessary preparations at fixed cost.'

Smiley nodded, and for a while they talked schedules and means of payment, and a mutual break after payment for the delivery of the sample without prejudice.

'I must ask you, Mr Barraclough, how you came to settle on my firm to provide for this necessity?'

'A recommendation, as I say.'

'From a colleague, I think. What colleague would this be?'

Smiley for the first time appeared wrong-footed, and Vishwakarma hastened to reassure him.

'I'm sorry, Mr Barraclough, I did not mean to ask you an inappropriate question. If you prefer not to name the gentleman – or lady – that is quite entirely acceptable. We will find other roads to trust.'

Smiley shook his head. 'I'm afraid it's a habit with me, Mr Vishwakarma, to be overcautious. In this case I fear I've been quite rude. Although it occurs to me that the name he gave you and the one I know may be different, and I don't wish to be a cause of friction in what is otherwise no doubt a productive relationship. Shall I begin by describing him?'

Vishwakarma nodded.

'Handsome, a little older than me, tall but not enormous. Takes care of himself, well-dressed in an artistic mode. He's Hungarian by origin, though I venture he could credibly pass as Russian or Austrian. In London he is most usually known as László Bánáti, though it's not a name his mother would recognise.'

If there was a hesitation in Vishwakarma's face, it was very brief. Esterhase couldn't be sure, and he'd been looking for it.

'I'm sorry, Mr Barraclough, but I don't recall your friend in this context. Are you sure it was wallpaper he wanted from me?'

'Oh, no, indeed. Mr Bánáti is by way of a commercial traveller. In the course of his voyages he occasionally enters countries whose adherence to the standards of law and order is not absolute. To provide for this eventuality, he likes to carry more than one identity document. Ideally, he prefers three or even four. If he's accompanied, that goes for each individual. On this occasion, his usual supplier was unavailable by reason of a conflict of interest, so he came to you as a cash buyer. I say cash, but he might well have provided you with a specimen document from his usual supplier as a contributing factor in his payment. A chance to unlock the secrets of your competitors overseas.'

Vishwakarma sighed, and stood.

'That was a lovely bit of stage business out there, Mr Preuss. I was quite taken in. I hope it wasn't too expensive.' He raised his eyebrows, and Toby made a face which suggested it was the sort of money a gentleman leaves under the plate. Vishwakarma looked genuinely pleased. 'That's excellent. But I have no business with the British government any more. That was made quite clear to me. I regret I cannot help you, Mr Barraclough. Do finish your drinks. There is no hurry, but I'm afraid our commercial dealings can go no further.'

Smiley nodded. 'As a courtesy, then, let me tell you that Harto Latour was found dead this morning,' he said, as if it was the season for it. 'If I were you, I might take some time off. Perhaps shut up shop for a while, until all this blows over.'

Vishwakarma's face remained politely blank, but one hand absently touched the line of his jaw. 'Who is this Latour to me?'

'The Belgian gentleman to whom I assume you gave one of Bánáti's Russian-made passports. Perhaps by way of an intermediary, if you really don't know the name. He's dead. Quite thoroughly so, I gather. The Zurich police are very agitated about it, not happy with Moscow at all. It was Moscow, by the way. That's who Bánáti – did he tell you who he really is? – that's who he's hiding from, not me. They blundered in Zurich, probably because they were overeager. If they'd taken the passport – again, that's the one you sold him – we wouldn't have made the connection, or, at least, not fast enough. You might be having a quite different conversation this afternoon. I can see why you might have reservations about talking to me, both professionally and personally. But I'm in a position to help.'

'And how would you help me, exactly?'

'Oh, some additional security. Temporary lodgings, if required. Contingencies.'

'I don't see my business surviving your help, Mr Baraclough.'

'We are hardly criminal investigators. We lean on our brothers in the police service, but I'm afraid the relationship is rather one-sided. Your problem goes away once the Bánáti matter is resolved. After that, you're a high-quality artisan in a limited field. Something of a national treasure, I suppose.'

'With my name on a list.'

'It already is. More than one, actually.'

Vishwakarma nodded but did not concede. 'So you're a commercial traveller also? Like this Bánáti?'

'I was. I'm retiring, as it happens.'

'You ever travel commercially in India? Maybe in the great days before independence?'

'I was never stationed there. I'm not really Empire material, not in that way.'

Vishwakarma looked him over again, and then Esterhase, still fussing with the spots on his coat. Smiley wondered what he saw, and how it differed from what Smiley saw when he regarded himself.

'You know anyone in your line who did?'

'Yes,' Smiley said, thinking of Haydon, or Steed-Asprey.

'Tell them from me they're a bloody-handed bastard,' Vishwakarma said, and turned his head away.

Smiley, for a few moments, imagined doing so. Haydon would be incredulous. Steed-Asprey, alone with the wreckage of his life, perhaps not.

After a while, Vishwakarma blew out a long breath.

'The Russians, you said?'

Smiley nodded.

'But, actually, the damn Russians?'

'I'm afraid so.'

'Well, that's no good for anyone, is it?'

Vishwakarma had made four passports for Róka: three for the man himself, one being Swiss, one Maltese and one Swedish; and the last one was for Leó, which was also Swiss. Leó's photograph, Vishwakarma said, must have been two or three years old, and it was absurd: Adonis as a schoolboy, in a quaint old-fashioned suit.

By a laborious process of cross-checking, Mendel and the Aunts had also established that Róka had departed London by train on the Friday, shortly after his call to the French bookshop. Arriving at the coast, he'd arranged travel simultaneously to Calais, Dieppe and Bilbao. The ferry companies were being as precise as they could, but didn't keep particular note of names except for passengers who booked their travel in private cabins.

Róka, no doubt knowing this, had not, and it was not even a certainty that he had boarded any of these vessels. He could equally have crossed back to the west coast and taken ship to neutral Ireland, whose government might or might not be inclined to cooperate with London. From there, Dublin Airport would readily take him wherever he wished to go.

In response, Smiley fretted. He was comfortable with a slow operational pace when he set it, but disliked having it imposed upon him. In the frigid air of the Conservatory he paced and muttered, inveighing against the weakness of scrutiny at the ports, and at the spectre of Róka undetected in London for the better part of a decade.

'What was he doing here?' he demanded of Glenn, who had no cause to know. 'Antonov's file says he had a legitimate, separate line to Centre, without reference to the local Head of Station. Why? Why, if he was thrown out of Hungary as a traitor? He tells Antonov he's Moscow's watchdog in London, he's waiting for something. Waiting for what? And when?'

'I couldn't say, Mr Smiley,' Glenn ventured, and Smiley barked at him to get out and do something useful. Five minutes later he stamped along to Glenn's shared office and apologised, before bolting back across the road to demand more of Connie and the Aunts. Very gently, Katrin touched her fingers to the letters Susanna Gero had taken from Róka's flat: oné, then two more, and finally a fourth, where the nail rested.

'You should read now, Mr Smiley. The thread of his life on the spinning wheel.' And, at his look, she sighed. 'Connie has confirmed it. The boy is gone.'

My Dear Friend,

It pleases me when you write often, and that you ask about Leó. Your godson continues remarkable in all ways. He has finished his school studies and wishes to attend university to study economics.

He considers this a high science, second only to physics, which he also loves, but he does not wish to be a scientist. He says that science is the foundation of the world but economics is the house. He wishes to be an architect, not an engineer.

Thank you for your help last summer. You were quite right: the man I spoke to was very helpful and all was speedily resolved as soon as he understood the situation. I did not tell Leó that you had done this, but he guessed. He is not a child any more and he understands our lives. Perhaps even he has forgiven you a little that you were not here.

Leó says you should see if there is a British Market for the writing of Darvas. Leó has told me he is a particularly able modern thinker and greatly admired here in Budapest.

Write soon and please tell me you are in love.

I remain, as always, your earnest
– Irén

My Dear Friend,

Thank you for your kind letter. I am pleased that your story contains love as well as success and that you are true to your dreams. When you write of the woman you love, I see her on the page with you and I believe in hope. Tell me more in your next; does she dance? I like to believe you will dance all your life. I believe when we stop dancing we become old, not the other way around.

Do you think you will ever visit us here? The music is not less excellent than it ever was. Old men in cafés play to make your heart break and the real concerts are wondrous.

Leó has completed his first term and all is well with him. He is very popular with the other students. He brought with him a small group from PB to see Budapest and they were a very pretty bunch, very clever and foolish and wise. There was a boy, Piotr, and two girls who were sisters, and more I cannot remember, all bright and sparkling and I felt quite old before them. Leó says you really must read Darvas and find him a publisher in Britain, he is quite

transformative. It is urgent, Leó says, that people find out
about him.

   Do you remember when I first met Leó's father? I danced all night
with him and took him to my bed ever so fast because he was so
splendid, so funny. I remember the smell of him on my pillow. I kept it
under a pudding basin when he went away so that I could breathe him
in while he was gone from me. I miss him. I miss him very much.

   I remain, of course, your friend,
   – Irén

My Dear Friend,

Leó asks if you will come for Christmas. I tell him I do not know. He
is angry. He says you never come and that if you cared for him you
would do so. If you cared for us. I say that you wish to know him
through these letters, that he is important to you. He says that we
cannot be understood only in words, that if you wish to know him
you must be present, that this is an equation even a poet can
understand.

   It has been so long, I think he has forgotten all that was good. He
was still young when you had to leave. The man I love is good to him.
He is a kind man. But now when he is angry Leó rejects him. He says
his true father is the dead soldier and he has no need of any other, not
even you.

   I am sorry for this. I feel I have let you down. Always I try to tell
him that you will come back even when I do not believe, but I am afraid
my own anger shows in flashes. Why could we not come with you? I
know why, and yet I do not accept it. You said it would be hard, but it
cannot be harder than this.

   Leó came in just now and saw that I was writing to you. He says I
must tell you to leave us alone now, to let us be who we are. He says
he has stopped wishing you will come home and now he wishes you
to stay away. I do not think he is lying, but I can see his hope in every
hateful word. If you come home, I think he will forgive himself for

the fact that you went away, and then perhaps also he will forgive
both of us.

In hope,
— Irén

And, finally, dated a fortnight ago:

My Dear Friend,

Please write soon. Things are not so good here and I miss your wise
thoughts. Leó's professor writes to me that he has not been in his
lectures, and it is said he was arrested at a party in the youth club.
Men came and spoke to him and he went with them and no one has
seen him since. The police say they know nothing. State security says
the same, but he was taken and has not returned. I am frightened that
he said the wrong thing in the wrong moment. I am frightened they
have read one of my poems, determined it is counter-revolutionary and
now are punishing me with the suffering they inflict on him. I am
frightened. I should have slept with that fool who says he is the nephew
of a high official. Sometimes I am frightened that my fear will make
something happen. I am afraid of being afraid.

I am sure you will know what to do, but I do not and no one can
help me.

Leó needs you, not anyone else. You are all the hope I have.

— Irén

Across a distance of two weeks, in images conjured, reports
from sympathetic students, the conversation with Antonov and
more letters and half-written notes scratched in increasing fer-
vour, Smiley watched Ferenc Róka go from the steady rhythm
of a settled life to a seized desperation. From the moment Leó
was arrested in Berlin to the night of his departure, Róka gave
everything he could command to the simple task of getting his

son back. He began by inquiring politely with the embassy of the DDR in London. Then he made a series of expensive international calls, to Rome and Vienna, to Hungary and even Moscow. Smiley could feel the slow increase in his agitation and in what he was prepared to risk for some kind of answer.

You started small, he told Róka. *You did everything right, but now you wish you'd been a fool earlier, been bolder, because if, in the intervening time, something happened that is irrevocable, you will never forgive yourself for being wise.*

It wasn't the first time Leó had been in trouble. In fact, it seemed that the path was well-trodden, even familiar; his choices were at best unwise. He'd made a rash marriage at twenty and it had blown up, his wife abandoning not only him but Hungary entirely. Irén, in her letters, suspected she'd always intended this, had married Leó knowing she could use the connection to guarantee her return in the eyes of the authorities, and chosen him because she would feel nothing leaving him behind. Leó thought so, and applauded it too loudly, so that someone turned him in as a co-conspirator in anti-state activity and he was duly tortured. Here, Circus intelligence briefly took over from Irén's narration, in the form of a sampling of state security files purchased by one of Toby and Jim Prideaux's short-lived Hungarian networks, and spotted in the Registry index system by Katrin. The attending doctor noted with disapproval the unscientific use of lit cigarettes on Leó's legs. Only the intervention, at Róka's behest, of a Lux graduate named Vaştag saw him released before he was more seriously maimed. 'An internal miscommunication,' Vaştag wrote, 'has led to a serious miscarriage of socialist jurisprudence. No one is to blame.' Although he did, when it became necessary, blame a junior security officer who subsequently died in the same interview room that had formerly held Leó.

A year later there'd been a problem in Sofia which was made to vanish almost before it arose, and the rumour of a great love affair with another boy; Leó called him a prince among knaves .

and proposed to create a model proletarian village which they would jointly oversee – a commune within Communism. He claimed to have the backing of a senior member of Zhivkov's BCP, but in the event the man seemed to have no idea who he was, and Leó was formally ejected from the country. The year after that he had been quite badly beaten outside a coffee house for making the old joke about Russian and Hungarian shipping on the Danube – 'It is quite equitable: they can go along, we can go across!' It spurred his desire to study in Berlin, and once again Papa Róka obliged, but by this time it was clear that the broken-ness in Leó touched his beauty and the combination was like a lamp in fog. It drew people to him, drew notice and danger more than it shed light. In any room he was always the standout, the exemplar, the teaching opportunity. Any one of his encounters with the security apparatus over the last five years might have been the last, if not for the tenuous limitation imposed by his godfather's Muscovite connections, noted in his file. At every turn, Róka's response was swift and apt, pulling strings, calling old friends, and only turning to the direct line of command when absolutely necessary lest his welcome with Moscow Centre wear itself out. So it was, year on year, with Ferenc Róka doing his special work which consisted of nothing at all, sending home almost by way of apology a dry scatter of usable intelligence gleaned from society parties and wrapped in speculation and outright fabrication, and all the while seeking and receiving a long list of favours and escapes for his wayward, beautiful son.

Until now, when the music inexplicably stopped, and, instead of an angel of Marxist–Leninist absolution, Moscow Centre had dispatched Miki Bortnik in answer to Róka's secular prayers. Róka had known that he was crossing a line, and done it anyway.

It was – it always was – Millie McCraig who finally grew tired of having an angry bear half hibernating in the back of her offices, and set him straight.

'Front and centre, George, for God's sake,' she demanded of him. 'Walk me through it.'

Smiley stared churlishly at the wall, thinking of Ann. McCraig sat down heavily in the second chair. Smiley's watery gaze remained fixed.

'How long does it take to get border information from our NATO partners?'

'If we make a point of it, we can have it when they do. About twenty-four hours. Twice that if we put the Vishwakarma passport names in with a couple of dozen others and say we're just keeping an eye.'

'And the unaligned?'

'Case by case. Wanted in connection with tax fraud is usually our best bet. Nobody likes a slow payer. Three days at best. Or we can make a serious point of it, of course. Suggest he's got a sack of uranium in his sponge bag.'

'Good God, no!' Smiley jolted upright. 'That will just push him further underground.' He glared at her. 'If we are to find him again, we must go where he's going or arrange for him to come to us.'

She nodded. 'How?'

Smiley's shoulders half shrugged. 'We know what he wants: he wants the boy. He can hardly turn up in Berlin and demand that they hand him over, so he's looking for someone to help him. The duty of a case officer: to repay the debt owed to an agent by his agency. But it isn't working.'

McCraig seemed to ponder this. 'Who did he go to first?'

Smiley nodded. 'Grodescu, in Paris – but who's he? Róka was Rudnev's agent originally, but who inherited him? Pogodin? Agapov? Or someone else? Who owns Grodescu?'

'Ask Connie, not me.'

Smiley nodded, and resumed his scrutiny of the Conservatory wall.

'What is it you don't want to do, George?'

Reluctantly, his face seemed to clear.

'Yes,' he said, agreeing with whatever she hadn't said. 'Yes. Thank you. You're quite right.'

'For a brief moment,' Smiley told Control, 'we know more than Moscow Centre. They have a report telling them Róka is dead. They may well believe it unless and until they make a closer consideration of the identity of the man in Zurich. The Swiss police will hardly be in a hurry to inform Moscow of the mistaken identity: they don't like assassinations on their streets, and indeed why should they? And there's no guarantee they'll even notice the passport themselves. Unfortunately, the situation is unlikely to last very long. Ferenc Róka will continue to contact old colleagues and friends, and it's only a matter of time before Centre get wind of it. At that point they will want to know why Miki Bortnik hasn't reported in; they'll speak to Antonov and get the story Miki gave him in Marylebone. That might hold them another day or so. Once they recognise that Bortnik is not hot on his heels they will deduce that he's come to us and all his contact protocols will be not only invalid but actively dangerous. Still, for the next forty-eight hours, perhaps, we have room to move.

'In the deficit column, although we know what Róka wants, we have no idea where he is. Thus we either await him somewhere we know he will go, or draw him to us with something we know he wants. If we can secure Leó, or even any concrete information about him that Róka does not possess, we have it all. And, unlike Róka, who must approach the Stasi indirectly through unofficial channels and old contacts, we happen to have a friend in the building.'

'You want to approach Mundt.'

'I do.'

'And how is he to explain his interest? Especially if it's sensitive.'

'How does he explain any of it? You have a cover story in place, surely. It adds to his mystique if he knows something before anyone else. It makes his sources look very good indeed.'

'But altogether too topical.'

'Not if it's being whispered anyway. Which, soon, it must be. Róka will see to that.'

'In any case our relationship with Mundt has a particular purpose to which this is unrelated.'

Smiley seemed to consider. 'I suppose it probably is. But Antonov said Róka was waiting without knowing what he was waiting for. We don't know either, of course, but we do know where he was waiting: here in London. One might choose to disregard the implication, I suppose. If one were quite confident in one's own house.'

Control conceded with an ill grace that something might be managed.

'Berlin first,' Smiley said. 'If we succeed there, the road is very short. If not, then wherever that takes us.'

But here, Control drew a line. 'Not "wherever", by any means. You know that quite well.'

Smiley opened his mouth to object.

'No! Not under any circumstances. Allied nations, of course. Neutral countries likewise, with due precautions. But you are not at any time to go behind the Iron Curtain, not for so much as a single day. If you deal with Mundt, you do it in West Berlin or through Guillam. If the path takes you to Czecho, you call Jim, and so on. You take Lake with you, maybe Esterhase as well, and you go slow, Smiley. I don't care what party you're missing out on or how cross Ann is. You can deal with that when you get home. You go slow and you stay safe. If in doubt, you call me direct. All right? Am I understood?'

Smiley said all right.

'But you're going. That's the thing. You go, and you bring me Róka and his secrets.' Forgetting that Smiley might by the terms of their agreement choose not to.

'Yes,' Smiley agreed. 'I'm going.'

★

The international line was very poor, and Ann's voice was very quiet. Smiley thought she was loving him; he was afraid she might be crying; but he couldn't hear. He had called her to explain, in so far as that was possible, what he was doing and why: that it was incumbent upon him; that he hated it but could not refuse it; that it was a last goodbye. Replying, she spoke for a long time, and when he broke in to tell her she was too quiet it didn't seem to change anything. He listened to the rhythm of her voice, the ebb and flow of emotion, trying to guess the words. Benediction, ultimatum, forgiveness? Or, worse, indifference. He had no way to tell. When she stopped, he answered the only way he could, with his own truth straight from the heart. She was his world, his hope, his light. He remembered Irén's letter, and almost asked her whether it was too late for them to have a child. Instead he repeated that he had this one thing to do and never again, that he could not hear what she was saying and didn't know if she could hear him, but he trusted, he worshipped, and he was coming as soon as he possibly could. He heard a reply. It could have been no more than punctuation. He said, 'I love you,' and waited for a triple beat; and, after the sound of disconnection, went back, over and again in his mind, to look for it in what she had already said. He was sure it was there, if he could but isolate it from the silence.

7.

Take a perfectly reasonable city and make it impossible: think of Venice, with every second calle or sottoportego opening not on to another road but a canal, and only comparatively few bridges to get you from one maze to another. Berlin was different, the Wall a gash down the centre of its face, but the same rules applied. Streets were broken in the middle by a no man's land of barbed wire and searchlights; schools were cut off from their playgrounds and warehouses from markets. Somewhere, Guillam had heard, there was a boatyard with no route to the water. The map of the war was burned forever on to what should have been reconstruction, and the city existed in a frozen parody of peace.

The first thing Guillam had noticed on arrival was how tiny the place was. Berlin was an island in the East German sea, and only half of it was accessible. You bumped up against edges with surprising frequency. The second thing was colour. The Western zone was almost garish: consciously or otherwise, the inhabitants accented their business clothes with shocks of scarlet and azure; they talked loudly and professed forceful opinions, as if to make the point to the others behind the Wall. By comparison, East Berlin was a muted city. Even if you could find bright colours, you might choose something quieter. It was part of the landscape that standing out was unwelcome: you knew you were observed, but that didn't mean it was wise to court attention. The Friedrichstraße Railway Station, which went to the West, was the truth of the whole damn place: the process of purchasing a ticket and passing through security turned you around and around, so that you might be travelling to the Bundesrepublik but you surely couldn't point to it with your finger, and the cameras and mirrors looked down on the back of your neck. You were seen, and knew you were seen, and could not see in your turn. In the West, colours; in the East, visibility; and, in between, the Wall, like a concrete mirror of everything that was wrong with everything.

'Show up to work. Have meetings. Then knock off early and have some fun,' Control had said. 'Don't overdo it, but let everyone get used to you.' Guillam was to become a familiar piece of the scenery, benign, habitual and unremarked, perhaps just a little bit fast. 'Go to clubs and bars, public lectures. Cafés, if that's your sort of thing. Be a face.' But not a face anyone would know.

His passport identified him as Matthieu Gisriel, originally a specialist in commercial bulk transport born in Strasbourg, but now thanks to family connections the boss of the local office of Causse-Bergen International Furs, and charged with adding a line of surprisingly popular East German stuffed bears to the company's stock. He was not to do anything that could be construed as general intelligence gathering, not even keep his eyes open for local talent. Gisriel had very occasional sanctioned, official contact with the trade ministry in the East, for which he crossed the border with great ceremony and was received with calculated disdain. Otherwise, he was, to all intents and purposes, to hibernate in place; not Mundt's courier but his handler, and his church of last resort should everything come down. In that case, Guillam was to enter East Berlin on a day visa with a British passport, hand it over to Mundt for his exit with the entry stamp still wet, and then go to a different checkpoint and use the Gisriel passport with a fake stamp to get out. He and Mundt didn't look much like one another, but a bad photograph and a hangover made it just about plausible, and if four-fifths of a successful exfiltration was planning, the remaining part was sheer momentum, and the brass neck to carry it off. On a busy day at the checkpoint, the odds were decent, and what border guard in his right mind would expect to see Hans-Dieter Mundt, the Stasi's favourite son, making his way through the wire under British cover? Or, having recognised him, would dare to intervene?

So Guillam idled in strange dead-end streets along the Western side of the Wall, and at night the searchlights as they moved across the no man's land lit his attic window. His dreams were full of Leamas and Karl Riemeck, punctuated by the sound of the watch changing at two a.m. and the gossip of the East German guards. Schulz was a bit of a lad; Friedmann was a political climber; Hecht despised his wife's brother, who lived in the West, but she missed the man and they argued about it. The sergeant had no opinions, and Guillam liked him best.

Guillam knew as well as anyone that Smiley had laid down his arms. He felt he had seen it coming, with the glacial inevitability of serious injury at speed. At any moment, any of the drivers could have turned aside, and yet it was obvious that none of them would, that each was set on the particular choices that would produce collision. Leamas had needed not work but rest: an enforced posting to somewhere warm and stupid; Control was a man obsessed with the intricacies of a game even his opponents might not be aware they were playing; Liz Gold had needed a chance to matter, and God help her she'd found one; and Smiley? Smiley believed not in ideology but – against the evidence – in people, which was a sin no one in the secret world could afford. As for Guillam, he'd thought himself below the fight: a man without responsibility because he was without authority – a mistake he had only belatedly recognised and had sworn he would never make again.

So this voice which called to him from an invisible corner table at his favoured coffee house must be either a ridiculous coincidence, or the beginning of a mental collapse. Smiley was in the Home Counties, making love to Ann.

'Why, it's Monsieur Gisriel, isn't it? We met at the trade fair in Lake Constance. I'm Willow, with Deniston's. It's perfectly all right if you don't remember, of course.'

Guillam turned around and beheld him: hair greying, eyes bright, more meat on the shoulder and less on the belly. A healthier edition for the spring market. The spectacles were new, with a fashionable thickness of tortoiseshell; the coat was almost showy. And yet, of course – it was, after all, still George – these very highlights made him somehow more anonymous rather than less: the vanities of a middle-aged married man seeking to stand out among a crowd of others doing precisely the same.

'Mr Willow!' Guillam replied. 'Certainly I remember you, and your company. John, wasn't it?'

'James,' Smiley said.

'I'm so sorry,' Guillam said. 'James, of course.'

'That's all fine,' Guillam said, as they walked back to his office for the tour he had promised Mr Willow, 'but what on earth are you doing here?'

'Putting something to rest,' Smiley said. 'On a single-case basis.'

'Putting what to rest? What case? Why don't I know about it?'

'I'm told compartmentalisation is the order of the day. What do the Americans call it? Silos. We must all stay in our particular silos. Only Control knows all.'

'And doesn't he bloody love that.'

'Oh, I think he likes the idea of holding all the cards and letting no man see the hand. But, when it comes to it, there's a great deal to hang on to and only so many fingers. Thus, here we are. Did you ever hear of a man named Ferenc Róka?'

Guillam paused, then shook his head: no.

'Before your time. Very nearly the first generation of Soviet intelligence, I suppose. Of the Tourmaline intake; you've heard of that?'

'Soviet training academy in the twenties and thirties. The instructors were a mixture – European pros from the Bismarck era, one or two repentant Chekists. A lot were executed by their own side – early Soviet paranoia. Jim Prideaux had a bee in his bonnet about them, made it his mission to go after the rest. Haydon too. Why don't you talk to Jim?'

'I mayn't go to Czecho. Control has strong views. But perhaps Jim will come to me in Vienna, if necessary. Anyway: a graduate of the Tourmaline was in London until a week ago. No one had any idea. It looks as if he was lying low, though I fancy Control is concerned he may have been a conduit for someone better placed.'

'That's still in his head, then, despite everything. Russian spies in Mayfair.'

'He doesn't insist on it. And, in fairness to him, there are an awful lot of Soviet agents about these days. America, Sweden, Japan. It would be surprising if they weren't at least trying to turn some of ours. A little depressing, even: our dwindling significance measured on a Moscow Centre budget sheet. He says he's taking reasonable precautions.'

'Compartmentalisation. For which read total chaos, by the way. You can't get anything done in London. I can hear the shouting from the Kudamm. Mundt knows, of course. He says it's a ghost story. What spies tell their children to scare them to sleep.'

'Be that as it may. I had to get Control's specific permission to read you into this, by the way, and you're not to share with any colleagues without prior reference to his office.'

'Situation normal.'

Smiley shrugged. 'Ferenc Róka was a talented Moscow spy in the thirties, then a resistance fighter at home during the war. He left Hungary under a cloud – real or confected – and disappeared. Prideaux, incidentally, had him down for South America. Three weeks ago, Róka's godson – possibly or probably his natural child, but at this point it hardly matters – was arrested at a student music event near the Humboldt University. I gather those are not always patriotic string quartets.'

'Kids doing what kids do,' Guillam agreed, with the fastidiousness of one a full half-decade removed from such excess. 'Bloody Babylon.'

'It wasn't Leó's first encounter with security, and Róka always managed to get him out. Hence also Control's feeling that he must still be at least somewhat active. This time, however, Róka has been unsuccessful – the boy is lost in the machine. In response to which his godfather is becoming incrementally more bold – or desperate, if you prefer.'

'Why not both? So you want to pick him up and juice him for whatever he remembers from the old days.'

'Both, indeed. But not just the old days. Róka's intervention this time has triggered some sort of crisis in his own affairs, presumably by doing so in someone else's. Moscow sent a man to close his complaint in a permanent fashion. By good fortune, the fellow they picked had some kind of – well. God told him not to go through with it.'

Guillam nodded. 'Russian Orthodox,' he said, as if this explained everything. 'You don't feel the pull at all, do you? Religion?'

'No,' Smiley said. 'I suppose I may have, when I was a child. But, as instructed, I rather put it away.'

Guillam shrugged. 'And that's the C of E,' he said. 'You want to try it with the blood-and-guts version. My mother's people are Catholics, but even that has nothing on the Eastern sort. It's formidable. That's why Lenin cut down all the spires.'

Smiley seemed to feel one could only sympathise. 'Róka was already gone when his would-be assassin arrived. We must assume he had anticipated the response. So he knows he has the tail end of something. He's very good, by the way – misdirection, fog of espionage, hiding in plain sight. It makes me wonder if Control isn't right, and he really was doing something that matters. But he's in the wind now, invisible. Paris, Lisbon, Madrid . . . Washington or Hong Kong. Who knows? Whatever favour he intends to call in next. So I came here because, in the end, so must he. This is where the game is, after all.'

'The boy.'

'Yes.'

155

'Arrested, you said. In East Berlin.'

'Yes.'

'George –'

'I mayn't go, Peter. I won't jog your elbow.'

'It's risky as hell. Not for me, for him.'

'If he can't do it safely, he's not to do it. If he can find a way that increases his value, so much the better. But what's the point of having an agent if you can't use him?'

A gust of wind snatched at them. On the Spree, gulls were picking at something, perhaps the body of a dog.

'And you don't think you're inclined to risk him because you don't care?'

'Oh, I'm sure I am. I'd trade Mundt for Róka quite happily, even if Róka knows nothing at all. Except that I've already traded Alec for him, which gives him an accounting value, in the heart, far beyond his personal worth. Or his intelligence one, come to that.'

Guillam turned and peered directly at him. To his surprise, Smiley looked back, his wide, soft face open and unembarrassed. Ann was very good for him, Guillam thought, in this new constellation of their lives. Christ. Banking, and not the covert kind but the real thing, with drawing rooms and champagne and pinstriped suits. If fate had a sense of humour, Smiley might find his way on to one of the committees that oversaw the Circus. He could end up, indirectly, as Control's boss.

'What exactly do you want?' Guillam asked.

'At best, I want Leó himself delivered to me. I'll take it from there.'

'You don't ask for much, do you?'

'If he can do anything at all, Peter, he can do that. If he can't, he can at least give us more information.'

'Maybe. He's . . . different. Not what you remember.'

'Different how?'

But Guillam shook his head.

*

Guillam had arrived in Berlin with low expectations. Mundt was a coerced asset and at high risk, and they were notorious for foot-dragging. In the autumn he'd felt what it was to sit in front of the lamps, to watch it all tumble down – and to make matters worse he knew or suspected that his role was specific: when it was done, he could easily be thrown away. He was unlikely, in Guillam's view, to be productive if he could possibly avoid it.

In this, as in everything else, Mundt was perverse. His immediate intelligence output was prodigious, so much so that you might think he'd been waiting for the opportunity: a near-endless catalogue of informers and unconscious sources within the DDR, then a collection of East German listening operations at target embassies in Bonn, Vienna and London, and finally even the names and cover identities of a dozen Stasi assets in the continental United States, which Control had pleasure in passing, with appropriate condolences, to his American counterpart. Mundt had even established his own system specifically to service his betrayal: using his role in the security apparatus, he regularly sent and received legitimate Stasi communiqués to operatives in the West, and these operatives, already blown by Mundt to London, now innocently handed off his reports directly to members of Travel Section, so that the entire network appeared more overtly in the Stasi's own organisational structure than it did in Control's. Guillam's role in actual contact work was minimal. Mundt gave him times and places, and Guillam spoke to Travel and made it so. The conjecture, always in the background – that Mundt was not only a Stasi agent but also a Soviet one inside the Stasi apparat – became instantly more plausible to Guillam. If Mundt was already passing secrets to Moscow, it made perfect sense that he'd have a ready supply and a mode of operation for London. That he was unwilling to acknowledge that his soul was already sold elsewhere and thus must be regarded as extremely shop-soiled was likewise hardly shocking.

All that given, Mundt the man remained frustratingly opaque.

It was the Circus's established practice, in cases of agents recruited by compromise or extortion, to leverage betrayal into a kind of dependency, solving problems as they arose, making gifts and fostering addictions, so that eventually the Circus was vastly more needed for what it provided than it was resented for what it sought in exchange. In this instance, however, Guillam found himself in check. Mundt accepted the situation but went no further. On the rare occasions when they met face to face, Guillam tried and failed to open him up. Did Hans-Dieter have family? Hans-Dieter did not. Friends, then, who might require assistance of any kind, either inside the DDR or without? Again, no. Well, then, he was presumably lonely. Company could be provided. Was there perhaps a flavour of consolation which was unacceptable even to trusted officers which he might wish discreetly laid on? But this too Mundt seemed to find almost quaint, as though watching someone perform painstakingly and by hand a task which, in this modern age, should already be automated.

Mundt had always been a cold fish, almost a parody of the wicked German. A Nazi by inclination and a Stasi officer only by opportunism, he served the Circus with the same affectless efficiency he had offered to his other masters. Where most men had desire, for Mundt there was only persistence, and the absence of his own extinction. If he derived satisfaction from anything external, Guillam suspected it was murder. He was both the perfect agent and the worst, because he was entirely featureless.

Until just after Christmas, when he had become appallingly and inconveniently human.

The first sign of trouble had been at the treff in Yugoslavia. Guillam was to make a rare direct contact with Mundt, who was in Belgrade notionally as Captain Adler of diplomatic security. Mundt had scrapped the first two meetings but made the second fallback, in a nightclub catering mostly to tourists and the foreign investors being romanced by Tito's regime.

'Lush place,' Guillam told Smiley with judicious disapproval.

'Not a choice I'd have made. You have to assume it's overheard wall to wall. Brass and red velvet, little green lamps on the tables and a buzzer for the waiter. They dim the lights at seven, so everyone can undo a collar button and start putting their hand on inviting knees. If you can't find one, the staff will make introductions.'

On the day, Guillam had arrived a half-hour early, intending to sit at the far end of the bar, where he'd be able to see the whole room. He'd been told to expect a brush pass, but Mundt was already there and walked right up to him, greeted him as an old friend, then dragged him to a table for drinks, and to look at some girl: Katinka. They'd just met, Mundt informed him loudly, but he thought they would get married. The girl was laughing, occasionally stopping to press her mouth on Mundt's and kiss it, long and drawn out, as if there was something buried in him that she wanted, then fall back and throw her hands in the air, and vow she had no more idea what was going on than Guillam. It wasn't just not covert; they were drawing a bloody crowd. The girl was beautiful, maybe high, and Mundt, his tie in his pocket and his hair grown longer than the strictly military buzz Guillam remembered, looked like something made in marble by a firm trying out for the Parthenon.

'How do you know him?' Guillam asked, while Mundt argued with the barman over whisky. He reckoned he had to make it look good for five minutes, maybe ten, before he ran like hell.

'From the casino in Pula,' the girl said. 'The Brioni.'

'He was gambling?' Guillam asked. It's a play, he was thinking. It has to be. Mundt's trying to throw someone off, maybe the Russians or Tito's boys, maybe me. He's not actually this mad. But he worried all the same. Sometimes agents did just break, and when that happened you could be in serious trouble.

'Oh, sure. He won big! It was a great time.' She shrugged. 'Still is! You know what?'

'What?'

'He makes love with his hat on. A cowboy hat, like in films. He won it from an American, he says. At the gambling table. He think it is very sexy, wants me to wear it too.'

'And do you?'

'Of course! I am his cowgirl now. We will ranch cattle in the country and make wine. Yee-hah!' She mimed a lasso above her head. Mundt returned with the whiskey bottle, Irish rather than Scotch but still a king's ransom, and Guillam took one shot before making his excuses and going straight to the airport. He took a plane to Vienna and cabled the Circus that their agent might be dangerously unhinged. On the plane he found Mundt's report, shoved into his back pocket during their parting embrace. He went through it in case the material was time-sensitive, decided he had no idea what to make of it and put it in the overnight bag for London, marked for Control's personal attention.

'Advise immediate assessment of Adler's situation by those with full knowledge of history and context,' Guillam wrote primly in his covering note, which was how field men informed the mother organisation that they considered something too tricksy or too bloody alarming to leave to their own harum-scarum operational competences.

The second and deeper indication of trouble was the report itself, which veered from the usual cogent and formidable detail of Mundt's intelligence gathering to rambling passages of self-examination and yawning paranoia. Mundt freely admitted he had no evidence to back it up, but believed he was under intense external scrutiny. *Ich habe da so ein Fingerspitzengefühl*: I know it as a carpenter knows wood. Willy Brandt, two years earlier and with appalling prescience, had said the same about the Wall.

Mundt proposed that Control exert all influences to ascertain whether this scrutiny originated in Moscow or Washington – or even, he suggested, whether he might be the target of a compromise operation mounted by the Central Investigation Department of the Chinese Ministry of State Security. It was normal, Mundt acknowledged, for senior members of his service to spy on one another. If it was only a question of the interception of his post or the bugging of his office, that would be insignificant. But Mundt had a catechism by which he lived. This, he explained, was necessary to a man in his impossible position. For every waking instant he had two parallel processes of thought, one which conducted his business both as a Stasi officer and a British agent; the second which attempted at every turn to see himself through the eyes of a fictional counter-intelligence operative he referred to as 'Gegner', meaning 'enemy'.

And Gegner, like the Stasi itself – which was estimated to have penetrated East German society to a unique and almost unimaginable transparency, to have recruited agents in almost every household – saw everything. Gegner was in the room even when the room was empty. Gegner thought further ahead, more deeply, more wisely. Gegner missed nothing and understood everything; he knew you better than you knew yourself. Gegner heard the words you never spoke and used them to build a case against you.

It was impossible to anticipate Gegner, impossible ultimately to evade him, but it was to this task – Mundt reported – that he dedicated half or more of his mind at all times. And now, when most of the world was still breathing out after the confrontation last year in Cuba, Mundt could feel Gegner close by, his eye turned on Berlin, and on the officer who had been so triumphantly vindicated only months before.

'And you read this on the plane,' Smiley said. 'What did you think of it?'

'I thought he was cracked,' Guillam replied. 'I reckoned a Nazi–East German Communist–Soviet Communist–British agent was just too many of him in one skull. Fully expected to get the extraction signal on New Year's Eve and find him at the checkpoint in a Schornsteinfeger outfit stinking drunk. Actually might have worked. Even border guards are human. Even here.' He thought of Schulz and Friedmann singing in the night.

'But you didn't.'

'No. That doesn't make it better. After Belgrade, Mundt went back to normal. The ice man returns. Irregular but fairly frequent product – send Travel to Paris on Wednesday, then nothing, then two weeks later sort out a meeting in Rome. A week after that, detail on unrest among Serbian proles pinched from a Soviet circular, delivered via a bookmaker in Stockholm. Smart, stable and productive, which just leaves you living in the shadow of some bloody unspecific volcano.'

'And you, Peter?'

'Me?'

'What do your fingertips tell you? What did they tell you in Belgrade?'

'In Belgrade, nothing. There was too much noise, what with Mundt playing Hugh Hefner in a bloody Stetson and saying he was getting married.'

'Yes, I can see that must have been quite the picture.'

Guillam rolled his shoulders as if someone was about to take a swing and he wanted to be loose.

'Vienna was the problem. No one knew I was going there until I arrived. The story was a business emergency – I got the Circus to send a message from the day before saying there was a customs problem on the Danube, missing paperwork. After Belgrade, the first twelve hours were like fresh air. Then the weather came in. My back was itching. Bill Haydon told me when I was still wet behind the ears: when you can feel the space behind you, when it feels crowded, that's when you watch out. It was crowded as hell. I got back to my hotel and I was pretty sure someone had tossed the room, but by then there wasn't anything to find. I didn't know who it was – the Yugoslavs? The Russians? The Austrians? Or the bloody Stasi watching their own man.'

Vienna was neutral ground, and Guillam had no espionage business to conduct there. He visited the customs office and had them give him a collection of vastly complex Austrian forms and asked politely for someone to explain them, a task which fell to a studious but very attractive young woman behind the desk. They agreed to meet up that evening. In the meantime he walked around, drank coffee and let his eyes listen. In the banking district, he went to a bar and took a corner table with a good sight line, memorising faces as they came in. That evening, he and Jelske drank Dôle and she talked about Italian Futurism and its hatred of the female, while he admired the female in front of him and tried to spot familiar faces. Like Smiley, he knew well he wouldn't normally uncover a competent team of watchers, but everyone was human: if he made them work they might slip and show their petticoats.

'They didn't,' Guillam said shortly. 'If they were there at all.'

'And were they? I'm not asking you to know, Peter. Just to guess.'

Guillam thought about it for a longish while. 'Yes,' he said at last. 'They were there. But I got my part wrong. Whatever they were expecting me to do, I didn't.'

He went to the airport direct from Jelske's flat, and at Control's instruction tried to put the whole issue of Gegner out of his mind.

'If we assume there is a Gegner,' Smiley suggested, 'that Mundt isn't wrong, even if he may be coming apart: who is it?'

'Moscow,' Guillam said immediately. 'If we grant that Mundt has a self-preservation deal with the Thirteenth as well as with us, maybe they've got him in the crosshairs after last year. Maybe Leamas was enough for the Stasi, but not for Centre.'

'Agapov and Pogodin,' Smiley said, but Guillam looked surprised.

'Agapov's out,' he said, as if it was obvious. 'Pogodin finally got him. He's under house arrest at his place in Leningrad. Control didn't tell you?'

'Compartmentalisation,' Smiley murmured, thinking of Lena Antonova's warning to her husband, and Miki's new broom. 'He's not sharing anything if he can help it.'

'And that's not making him any friends, I can tell you,' Guillam growled.

'What's the pretext?' Smiley asked, and Guillam for a moment honestly wasn't sure whether he meant Moscow or Control.

'Conduct unbecoming a Bolshevik. Pogodin says he had his hand in the operational till. Maybe he did. It doesn't matter, does it? He's finished.'

'Pogodin is hardly the man for witch hunts. He's military by training; he believes in the loyalty of one officer to another. It's what held him back under Stalin.'

Guillam shrugged. 'Before I left London, Oakmoor had it in his head there was someone else. Said he'd got a feeling in his water, which probably means the Americans told him. Pogodin's deputy, a hard sort of fellow, a true believer. There's a question in the air about the two of them: which is the master, and which the man? But Agapov's gone, as of last month.'

'How reliable is that?'

'I'm hardly first in line. But Control said "very". I don't get paid for opinions, George. I just eat what's on my plate.'

Which, today, apparently meant asking Mundt to arrange an exfiltration.

If Guillam in Mitteleuropa was feeling a crowd in the dead space at his back, Susanna Gero in London was aware of a resounding emptiness, and her emotions, as she lingered in the communal living room of the Adams Secretarial Agency, had passed from a kind of relief into boredom and then exhaustion, and finally to a listless energy she could not name, which left her prowling the Axminsters like a panther in the zoo. On the second evening she cooked for the household as a gesture of gratitude, letting her hands do the work and forgetting for the moment the years-long understanding that the Hungarian approach to paprika and spice was not familiar to sheltered Anglo-Saxon palates from the suburban towns past Reading. Rose Jeremy finished her bowl with loud approval and helped herself to another, but the girls with whom Susanna was sharing living quarters looked at her as if she were a Borgia, or possibly just off her head. Later, doing the dishes, she broke two of them and swore, and Miss Adams sighed and went off to find a dustpan.

'Rage,' Rose Jeremy said, from the doorway.

'What?'

'The word you can't find. It's "rage". You're in a rage because your boss turns out to be something you didn't know about, then you got a peep behind the curtain and it was exciting, and then they dropped you down a hole. Didn't they? So now you can't sit still and you can't stop hitting things or jerking them around because you're so angry you can't even see the edges of it from the inside. Like I said: rage.'

'That's absurd.'

'Is it? Because I don't know you've ever spoken to me like that before. Not one woman to another, as if you're about to take my head off with that scrubber.'

Susanna looked down at clenched fingers.

'I quite like the way it looks on you, to be honest,' Rose Jeremy said. 'Not as if you've got nothing to be angry about, is it? Give me that,' she added, 'I'm not a serving dish, I'm not scared of a little soap.' She turned her broad back and went to work. Susanna, once again watching someone else take over the job she'd thought was hers, almost screamed. And, with that, she found, suddenly, that she could feel it: the boiling frustration and the sense that the world was grossly wrong and must be immediately redressed.

'Oh,' she said, and laughed. It hadn't gone, hadn't lifted at all, but in being recognised it had fitted into the place which was meant for it, and now her feet knew which way they should be pointing, and all that was miserable became, instead, a challenge.

'There it is,' Rose Jeremy murmured, from the sink.

*

165

An hour later Susanna reached that same side door and hammered on it, then waited, and then hammered again and then again. After ten minutes, a narrow man with a stupid face peered out at her.

'Who are you?' she demanded, as he opened his mouth. 'I want to see Smiley.'

'Glenn,' he said, and then put his hand over his mouth for a moment as if he'd let the cat out of the bag. 'Mr Smiley's not here.'

'I want to see him. I need to see him. Right now. It concerns –' She almost said Miki Bortnik, but Smiley had warned her that Miki must be very secret, even here. 'It concerns the matter of my employer László Bánáti and his recent disappearance. It concerns also the matter of certain friends.' She gave it the same inflection she'd heard in the corridor inside, invoking the term of art without knowing what art it referred to. She saw Glenn's eyes widen. Friends evidently had friends in high places.

He opened the door and ushered her in, then shut it as if there might be wolves behind the sleigh. 'Mr Smiley's not here,' he said again.

'Then I'll talk to McCraig,' she snapped, remembering the offer of a job she now knew conclusively she didn't want. Glenn struggled as if standing in a high wind, then opened a green wooden box on the wall and lifted the house phone to his ear. 'Glenn,' he said. 'Miss –' He peered at her.

'Hofbauer,' her mouth responded

'Miss Hofbauer is here for Mr Smiley. I've told her – yes. Yes. Right, I will.' He cradled the phone again, and looked at her almost in awe. 'You're to come with me,' he said, as if she wasn't already.

He led her along the same corridor, but in the daytime it seemed less full of portent and more dusty, until they reached the open space and turned left instead of right, and a narrow set of lift doors opened to reveal enough room for two people, but only if they knew each other well. Glenn gestured her in.

'You're not coming?'

'No,' he said. 'Just you.'

She went in, and extended her hand towards the panel.

'Fifth floor,' Glenn said reverently, and the doors began to close.

The air in the lift carriage tasted of polish and carpet cleaner, but when she drew back her hand from the fine brass panel, her fingertip brought with it the pungent tang of old ash. A smoker's lift, but someone worked very hard to keep it clean and bright.

The ascent was slow, and she thought the carriage must be swaying slightly in its shaft, because the hairs on her neck rose and would not subside, and the floor beneath her feet felt skittish, as if it were balanced on a bed of mercury. She saw ceilings and floors drift downwards past the narrow glass pane, and then at last she had arrived. The carriage jolted once and was still. She pushed her way out to discover a corridor panelled in brown wood, skylight windows shedding just enough illumination on the green clubland carpet to obscure everything else. The tobacco smell was stronger and fresher. What was up here, in the quiet beneath the eaves? Where was she supposed to go?

She heard a voice say her name from somewhere directly in front of her. She craned her neck and realised that on the other side of the corridor, made invisible by a shaft of grey London light, there was a room, and in the doorway a man, slight and uncomfortable and wearing a lank wool cardigan over a Jermyn Street shirt. She thought he was old, at least in his heart. He stood like an old man, as if he had carried too many things in a long, unsatisfactory life. His hands shook by the seams of his trousers.

'Miss Gero,' he said again, and through the haze she saw the lenses of his glasses instead of his eyes. 'Do come in. I'm very pleased to meet you.'

He turned, and she followed him into a large room with a solid desk and gabled windows almost as draughty as the ones she'd grown up with, and around the disused hearth there were two chairs and a low coffee table, and an electric fire which seemed to generate only false expectation.

'Please sit down, and tell me how I can help you.'

'Do you work for Mr Smiley?'

He laughed, a single soft chuff of noise. 'Sometimes I think so.'

He wrapped a dish cloth around the handle of the teapot and poured. He did not ask if she wanted milk or sugar but just added them as a matter of course. He put the cup next to her, then went crabwise around the back of her chair to his table and retrieved a packet of cigarette papers and a rolling tin. He made a cigarette and offered it to her; then, when she declined, immediately put it in his own mouth and lit it. He settled in his chair. She had assumed that he, like Smiley, would ask her questions. He didn't, and she realised that she had in some way relied on it, that until someone asked the questions she wouldn't know the answers. He seemed content to listen to the wind rattling his windows and the scuttling of pigeons overhead. He exhaled smoke in a long, empty sigh, and she felt she was seeing the last breath leave him, and a while later again, and again. Still, he asked her nothing.

Well, what did she want? Unclear. Had she known when she set out an hour ago? She had thought so; now she doubted. It was like explaining your dreams. The experience of clarity was undeniable, and yet the detail faded away as she chased it, vanishing into the smoke. She looked at the rolling tin. There was something engraved on it in ornate italics, something about decades of British coal. The silver plate was tarnished, with bright patches where he held it to make his smokes.

At some point he would finish his cigarette and his cup of tea and then sooner or later he would kick her out. She had to say something. She wanted it to be something important, something that would make him listen.

'I met Bill,' she said, and stared at the words in the air. Of course, he must know that: she'd said she was Hofbauer, and they'd still let

168

her in. There'd been a Hofbauer family in her building in Budapest, in a corner apartment. The light in winter was so stark you
couldn't read in their living room in the middle of the day.

'And what did you think of Bill?'

What did she think of Bill? He was a rogue but not a fool. She
had declined him, but not without cost.

'He's adequate.' Her mother, taking control of her lips.

'Poor Bill.' He laughed again, and she realised she still didn't
have anything to call him. He was just the man. 'Do you enjoy
your work? For Mr Bánáti. Is it satisfying?'

'That's adequate too.'

'And yet when a man came to your door and said he was a murderer, your first thought was to run to Bánáti's home and warn
him. Even knowing it was either unnecessary or quite risky. Why
did you do that, do you think, for an adequate job?'

'I didn't say he was adequate. I said the job was.'

'You like him that much? As a person?'

'Yes.'

'But you're not lovers.'

'No.'

'A paternal relationship, perhaps.'

'I don't know.' What were fathers supposed to be like? Or
daughters, for that matter. Was that something a daughter would
do in a crisis? She supposed it might be, although in American
films it was the other way around. Fathers kept their daughters
safe. It was not appropriate, cinematically, for the relationship to
go the other way, but in real life she thought it would be. People
did things, sometimes stupid things, and care went in whichever
direction it must.

'I wondered if you'd like to do something dangerous again. To
go towards, rather than away. Smiley wanted to keep you out of
this, but he has romantic notions about people. About some sort
of sanctity in civilian life. It did occur to me that you were here
because you wanted to be in it, instead.'

The head turned towards her, and now she saw his eyes. She thought they were brown but wasn't sure. The lids were thickly folded and the eyebrows heavy. The fall of light went across his cheeks and the bridge of his nose but seemed to stop there. It made him look deceitful or bored, or perhaps he was both. And yet his voice was abruptly forceful, as though he'd just arrived in his own body for the first time since they sat down.

'I can offer you that, you see. If you find it attractive. I can offer you a job that's something more than adequate, to replace the one you've lost. Because you have lost it. Your Mr Bánáti – that's not his name – I think it very unlikely he will return to the literary world. I think you had already realised that.'

Yes. Not aloud, not even in so many words. But, yes, she had.

'These days it isn't so dramatic as it was during the war. No parachutes, I'm afraid, no French Resistance. But I can't conceal from you that there would be unpleasantness, and perhaps quite some risk, if you chose to go into the field. In general, even if you just worked here in the Circus, you would be separated from your friends, from everyone you know, to some extent forever more. I don't mean you'd never see them, but you'd have to lie to them about simple things. But you'd be making a difference, if that means anything. You'd have an actual thumb on the scales. And you wouldn't be running away any more, you'd be running towards. Does that sound attractive?'

She hadn't come here for a job. At least, she didn't think so. Why had she come?

'I want to find Mr Bánáti.'

'Even if he isn't your boss any more. And not your lover.'

'Yes.'

'Unfinished business.'

'Yes.'

'Sometimes it's better to leave that behind. Let it stay unfinished.'

'That's what I want. I don't know why.'

'Smiley is looking for your Bánáti. But he doesn't speak Hungarian. Very elevated German, or the gutter dialect, when he wants to, but no Hungarian, no Czech, no Russian. If I order him to take you along, he'll have to do it, but it will compress him. Weigh on him. It will make him feel responsible for you.'

'That's what you want, isn't it?'

The eyes were gone, and the lenses glinted. 'I want everyone to be in the role that best suits them. And to win. It is a war, after all, and if one must fight a war, better to win with all the unpleasantness that implies, than lose, and be subjected to the cost of losing. Don't you think? I believe you know a little of that cost.'

She didn't answer. They drank tea, and listened to the traffic until Millie McCraig came, and sighed, and led her away.

8.

Arriving in Britain after fifty-six had been – as Susanna imagined – like something from the age of sail. She had moved in a haze through one bureaucratic process after another, unsure of why she was heading west and yet sure that she was, as if a wind blew and only her sails could feel it. Nothing made particular sense and nothing was intended, and still things happened. Vienna would have taken her, as it had thousands of others, but she was not Austrian and did not wish to become so. If she was no longer to be in her own house, she would not move in next door. Paris was too stern, Stockholm too northern, Madrid too southern. She would not have said these things aloud, could not have named them, and yet she obeyed their diktat and let the wash carry her from everything she knew to something whose shape she had no idea of, but which was the only destination that would fit. The train line went west, and so would she, until Calais and its absurd, box-shaped ferry with – to her astonishment – a saloon bar on the top deck, where she sat cradling a vile glass of red wine she was not really allowed to drink, though she had lied to the Austrian police about her name and her age and so had temporary papers which made it possible. She stared at the Channel, realising she was not dead and not captive and not anything she had expected, and she had no idea what to do about any of it. A bawdy tourist tried to chat her up; the stern barmaid – the first black woman she had ever seen – sent him packing. She got seasick and didn't care, then fell into the formal business of immigration, no one properly understanding how she'd arrived solo when there was a process – of course, with hundreds of refugees pouring out of her home nation in these weeks – and yet here she was and that was an end of it and something must be done. Two months later she was in Genevieve Adams's office and Rose Jeremy was unpacking every one of the polite lies Susanna had told without seeming to mind about any of them. From there, language classes and a few short contracts and false starts, and time flew, and the seasons turned, and at last there was Bánáti & Clay.

The journey in the opposite direction was jarring in its abruptness. For the Berlin trip McCraig had given her fresh papers, actually drawn up in the name of Hofbauer. She was a probationary interpreter attached to the embassy in Bonn on a trial basis. She would present herself to Smiley as a fait accompli because she was, and he would be instructed to make use of her for insight into Mr Bánáti – whose real name, apparently, was Róka – and for any initial contact which could be facilitated by the presence of a familiar face. McCraig looked irritated, and Susanna gathered she was strongly opposed. She demanded to know why.

'Because it's bloody dangerous,' McCraig said, without particular heat. 'For all of you. It's a mile outside the operational norm. If there's one rule for using civilians, it's that if they want to be involved then they're not allowed.'

'What about training?'

'What, indeed?'

Was there not, she asked, some short, radical introduction to spying that she should undergo? One of Bánáti's clients – Bánáti who was himself apparently a master spy and she had never noticed – had explained in an effort to impress her that he'd been recruited out of university and made to spend a week in a strange installation on the east coast where they were taught unarmed combat during the day, and at night slept in dormitories opposite a row of huts housing over a hundred different kinds of lavatory. There was nothing, he had maintained, which was more likely to blow your cover than an inability to contend with bathroom facilities you supposedly had been using from birth. She relayed this to McCraig, who stared at her in a kind of horrified fascination.

'I'm not familiar with the facility,' McCraig ventured after a while. 'Possibly the Department. Not us, anyway. And, as for training, just do what Smiley says. First, last and always, even if it sounds mad.'

'Even though he doesn't speak Hungarian.'

'He's the best. If you decide to go on with this – make a life of it – they'll put you through the Sarratt course. It takes months and they run you ragged, make you do all sorts of team exercises, kidnap cyclists, talk your way through doors, fight like a tiger. At the end of it, they'll have Smiley come and tell you all the things that can't be taught, which is all the things that matter. And, anyway, you've already got more experience of the real thing than almost anyone who takes the course. You walked out of Hungary in fifty-six. You know what it means to live there and you've been on the run. If that wasn't good enough, you can ask yourself what your Mr Bánáti would do.'

'He never did anything exciting at all. He was just ordinary.' Susanna listened to these words in the air, and looked back at McCraig's faint smile. 'Oh.'

'They're quite alike in some ways, I suspect: Smiley and Róka. You'll see.'

'But what if I have to fight someone?'

'Then you'll be in big trouble, so don't. Not just if you lose – if you win too. So make sure it doesn't happen, all right?' She glowered, then relented. 'Oh, don't be such a damp rag. I'll tell you three things to think about if that ever happens. One: no half-measures. Be final. You don't have the time or the strength to be gentle, so forget it. If it's that bad, do the nastiest thing you can, as hard as you can, and then the next and the next without stopping until you can get away or he's dead. Not down, not staggered – dead in a ditch. Two: don't use your fists to punch or you'll crack your knuckles. Pick up a lump of wood. Use your elbows, the heels of your hands, your knees, I don't care. A hard bit of you on a soft bit of him. Nose is good, mouth is good. If you can cut the forehead with something it'll bleed into his eyes. Small bones in the foot if you've good shoes on. Stamp like a playground bully. Don't go for the groin unless you absolutely have to. He knows how to move it out of the way and it'll give him ideas. If you do, get hold of it, try to twist it off and throw it away, then do something worse, before he recovers. Ears, eyes, nose, fingers. Three: the collarbone is brittle and critical. If in doubt, come down on it hard and try to put it down somewhere near his feet. Use your body weight and give it everything. If you break it, he's gone. Knock him down and kick him in the head until it's over.'

Susanna stared. 'Is that what's on the Sarratt course?'

McCraig shrugged. 'In my day we just made it up as we went along.'

'What day was that?'

The older woman's jaw clenched and her head tugged up in something almost like a twitch. There was a scar on her jaw, fine and white and very faint under well-applied make-up.

'Do what Smiley tells you,' McCraig said. 'He'll bring you home.'

After a while, Susanna asked: 'Why's he doing it?' 'He' being Control. It seemed infantile to her that he had no other name.

'Search me,' McCraig said shortly, and handed her a plane ticket. By early afternoon on the same day she was standing in a good German city, smelling chestnuts in burners and charred meat from a Schnellimbiss and the tang of German petrol, and she was back in Mitteleuropa, astonished at how much she'd missed it and how coming to this place she'd never been before – that hadn't even existed until two years ago – felt like coming home. McCraig had given her a picture of the man she was meeting. She was to call him Mr Prescott. Prescott, who worked for Willow as a driver.

She saw him, carrying a sign which read DENISTON COMPANY, and waved. He funnelled her into a car. 'It's the Hotel Elegant,'

he said, in a deferential chauffeur's singsong. 'Hope that suits.'
She said yes, having no idea, and accepted his hand into the car.

'Well,' Lake said, taking his place in the front. 'This is a startler.
The boss man doesn't like it at all.'

'I'm told he doesn't have to.'

'So's he,' Lake agreed. 'Imagine how that goes down.'

In the event, Smiley was perfectly welcoming, like a relative receiving a guest in a Christmas Eve emergency. If he regarded her presence as an imposition, that was for him alone. He'd changed his coat, she thought, irrelevantly. The expensive one he'd worn in London was gone, replaced with something older, in a coarser wool. The grey collars pushed at the flesh under his chin, and the unbelted shape made him look like an upturned pail. Only the buttons were good. It was a poor man's trick, something her mother had done: to put good buttons on a bad coat. If you didn't look too hard, they made the whole thing seem fine.

He was travelling as James Willow, importing German furs to Britain's shooting classes. 'Tweed has had its day, apparently,' McCraig had said. 'Or that's what you're to tell everyone, every chance you get.'

He greeted her in the lobby of their hotel, and murmured not to worry that her plane had been delayed, he'd been managing. She saw the concierge tut, and felt instantly guilty for being late. The concierge showed her to a small room on the second floor, just down the hall from Smiley's, and gave her a knowing smile. 'Will Fräulein Hofbauer require a second key to her room?' Of course: if everyone assumed she was Bánáti's mistress in London, so too Willow's here. She said no and ushered him out, hoping to convey Miss Adams's professional disdain for all matters of lust. She saw him smirk, and tried to remember that it was good cover. She wondered if Smiley realised, and, if he did, what he felt about it.

*

There were four of them in the little meeting room, each sitting in front of a notepad which already had notes on it from a meeting about quarterly earnings, and all the blunted pencils were embossed with a colophon – CB, for Causse-Bergen. Smiley she already knew, and he was in charge. The Frenchman was Guillam and he wasn't French, and Prescott's real name was Lake. She recognised a pecking order, though it was exquisitely unspoken: Smiley, the wise old owl; Guillam, the sorcerer's apprentice; and Lake, the working man. Lake and Guillam had nodded to each other on arrival, and she thought they might also be lovers. Each had a constant awareness of the other's physical space, of the reach of his arms, and they moved around one another as if they were used to doing it and no longer worried about accidental proximity. No, not lovers, something else. Surgeons. Bath attendants. Barbers. And then she recognised it at last: fighters. These two were like the old wrestlers her father had known. He had been one, she supposed, though it was never discussed, and she assumed he hadn't been very good. But they too had had that ease of broad back and thigh, and no hang-ups about touching their brothers of the ring. She wondered if they knew how obvious it was, how much it gave away. She must ask Smiley; he surely did. His own rejection of physical contact was natural and intense, with her as much as with them, and that too might be a problem if they were supposed to be lovers. Except perhaps it wasn't, because if he was hiding it, that just spoke to guilt, and everyone knew English men were guilty about sex. How many layers of deception did you stop at? How deep did the lie have to go to be deep enough, and could you make it so deep that it no longer worked, because you were hiding the thing you wanted everyone to find out?

'This is Susanna Gero,' Smiley said, though they already knew. 'She was Ferenc Róka's assistant in London, and Control feels she may be helpful in getting him to talk to us. That is, of course, if we can find him at all. In which case we may also seek Susanna's assistance; she has the closest acquaintance with Róka of anyone to whom we have ready access, even if it was under a cover identity. As a Hungarian-born naturalised British citizen, she also speaks respectable Viennese German and native Budapest Hungarian. She is not experienced in Circus protocol or tradecraft. I think we will all do best to think of her as a friendly émigré group of one.' She thought the smile was rueful but not unkind. 'While we are in Berlin, I will ask either Tom or Peter to accompany you at all times if I am not present. Our commercial cover should suffice to explain that. If and when we find ourselves dealing directly with your former employer, that may change, but you must be aware of and accept an element of risk. I promised Millie McCraig I'd get you out of this and you've quite conclusively got yourself in, so I assume that meets with your approval.'

She nodded.

'Very well, then. I will ask you in the first instance to sit with us and offer your opinions. You should not hesitate to intervene if it appears to you that we are missing something obvious in an area where you have direct knowledge. For background: Róka – your Mr Bánáti – is travelling on false passports he got in London and is probably seeking the help of old friends. We have the names he's using, but at best we'll get notifications one or two days late when he crosses a friendly border.'

'False passports,' she echoed. 'Right. Is that what was in the cash box?'

She heard the question and wished she hadn't asked. An amateur question.

But no one laughed. Smiley shook his head. 'He obtained his new documents from a man named Vishwakarma, in Brick Lane. Mr Vishwakarma is inclined to be cooperative. I believe he senses opportunity.'

Guillam snorted something that might have been 'Esterhase'.

Smiley waved this away. 'You were concerned it was the wrong question. Please ask as many of those as you can. In the first instance, Peter has things to do which will take' – he glanced at Guillam – 'twelve hours?'

'At a minimum.'

'And I shall need to make some house calls. Tom will watch my back and you will learn by observation. You will be his cover and he will be yours. A flirtation, perhaps. Or a chore. Try not to overthink. Let the story tell itself.'

Lake, she thought, looked embarrassed, and she wondered which of these possibilities he found more distressing.

'What the hell is Control playing at?' Guillam demanded, twenty minutes later in his private office. 'It's bad enough dealing with one lunatic, I don't need another standing behind me.'

'Control is operating according to the information he holds and his best analysis of what it means,' Smiley said. 'We don't know those things, so we cannot readily assess his rationality. The same applies to Mundt, as it happens. You were quite right, in Belgrade, to ask yourself whether he was playing against you. I don't think he was, but it was the right question.'

'And you think Mundt's right to be worried,' Guillam said.

'Always,' Smiley agreed, 'but, yes, particularly now. Moscow knows as well as we do that the best time to catch someone out is when they think they're in the clear. Which means, by the way, that you need to be careful too. If your judgement is that it's too risky to meet him face to face, we'll find another way. You're the man on the ground. The expert.'

'It's fine. I go in the same way each trip, no more than I absolutely have to, and I do the same things. Mostly argue with junior trade officials about shipping delays. Every so often they give me a hard time at the checkpoint. Sometimes they confiscate my cigarettes and we have a good laugh while we wait for the officer to declare me acceptable. But I don't carry anything real. Not ever. So there's never anything for them to find except the usual. Booze and knickers.'

Smiley's exhalation suggested distaste, and Guillam bristled.

'That's the job, though, isn't it? Be what I look like. So I blandish the flowers of East Berlin with Parisian intimates and talk about my business in the West and how rich it's going to make me. They turn around and tell whoever they report to that I'm a typical Franco-Capitalist erotomane. We're all doing what we're told. Predictable is boring and boring is safe. Except now there's your Hungarian secretary. What's Control thinking?'

'Connie says we have too many bulls in the field and not enough cows.'

'Connie drinks.'

'So would you,' Smiley snapped, abruptly very angry, and Guillam held up his hands in apology.

'Sorry. I'm on edge, George. I don't like surprises.'

After a moment, Smiley's temper went grudgingly back into its burrow. He waved a hand. 'Susanna is not a surprise, Peter. In some ways she's an inevitability. From her point of view, because she wants resolution. From Control's – well, that's more difficult, but to begin with the very obvious, he's not wrong in saying that Róka may talk to her where he would run from us. It's foolish, of course. She can only be here with our connivance, or with Moscow's. In Róka's position, one ought to consider her high risk.'

'But you think he won't.'

'I think there are obligations in life which we cannot help but feel, even when we know better. He left her holding the bag in London, and put her somewhat in harm's way. I'm not sure if she's considered that last. But by any measure he owes her something we greatly desire.'

'What?'

'An explanation, Peter. An account of himself.'

'He'll see her and bolt like a rabbit.'

'That is the wise course.'

'Yes, it bloody is, and you said he was good. Very good.'

Smiley shrugged. 'Would you be able to resist that opportunity to be judged by someone you've wronged? To explain yourself: the rightness of what you did, its overwhelming necessity?'

'Yes,' Guillam said shortly, 'if I were on the run, absolutely.'

Smiley nodded. 'Perhaps you could, at that. But Róka took her on: not just any office help, but a woman running from his own country and in need. Since then, he has not made romantic overtures towards her despite being what Toby would call "very *activ*". Instead he's spent a long time being Bánáti for her – teaching her, making her laugh, making her feel safe. A man with a wayward son and a family he cannot own to, sharing a single room with a young woman day in and day out. If he's not attracted to her, what does she mean to him, I wonder? Is he really so buttoned up that she's just staff after all that time? I'll ask you again another day, Peter, whether you could walk away.'

In the end, Guillam had to acknowledge that the lie was at least persuasive: middle-aged James Willow and his attractive young mistress, in Berlin sourcing fabrics and pelts from the East and taking in the discreet and disgraceful nightlife. Berlin might not be Hamburg, but it wasn't Grantchester either. There was certainly enough sin to be getting on with.

An hour later, through the Circus's regular presence in Berlin, came news that Róka had used one of his passports at the Italian border, and been seen in Rome. He'd evidently doctored the passport himself with reasonable competence, which meant that the names Vishwakarma had given Smiley would no longer reliably obtain. The resident, Clancy, had been unable to persuade the Italian authorities to pick him up without a criminal charge issued by London for an act that would also be illegal under Italian law. Clancy had tried to approach Róka himself, but had found an empty loft in Parione and no sign of the man. Clancy additionally reported that Róka had met with Aslaan Gurin, Moscow's outgoing Head of Station who somehow never actually went. Gurin, Connie's addendum noted piously, was a shameless drunk, but in his day had been a respectable enough Moscow agent all along the Mediterranean coast. He had spied valiantly in the fleshpots of Lisbon and Barcelona during and after thirty-nine–forty-five, when secrets were the only real currency anyone had. Gurin and Róka had gone to a bar and Gurin was drunk when he arrived. Róka had to bribe the doormen to let him in. They'd listened to the music, drunk more and Gurin had propositioned the staff, though what he thought he'd do with them in his condition if they agreed, no one had any idea. Then the meeting had soured. There'd been a row over Leó, and inevitably they'd been ejected. One of the waitresses thought she'd heard another name, but it was Russian and she couldn't remember it. Boris, perhaps, or like *marilenghe*: Furlan.

Also appended was a response to Connie's query from Jim Prideaux. Prideaux knew of Róka, of course, and regarded him as top grade. If he'd been in London, Prideaux said, the Circus needed to count the spoons. The only Bogdan he could think of in Róka's circle was called Molchalin: a minor anti-Communist who stood for the first Hungarian parliament and retired almost immediately when it became apparent that his hopes meant less than nothing in the new Soviet-allied country. Why Róka would be looking for him, Prideaux couldn't guess. Molchalin must be in his eighties now if he was alive, and washed up by definition. Prideaux even thought there was bad blood between them. By his reckoning, it must be someone else.

Lake, on hearing about Rome, was despondent. His Travel instincts told him they should have chased after Róka in the first place, and he even wanted to get on a plane now and follow the trail. His section was the province of agile, enthusiastic bloodhounds, and Lake's tail was up. He thought Clancy had moved too slowly and been wet with the Italian police.

'I wish it had been Paris,' Lake muttered. 'Collins would have got it done.'

Smiley was unruffled.

'He was gone before we knew he was there,' he told Lake gently. 'Which was always the problem. By now he could be any-where. It's the same game it was in London: we must be ahead, or we are too far behind.'

'We would have found something,' Lake asserted; 'there's always something.'

'Oh, indeed,' Smiley agreed. 'There's this.' And he returned, visibly, to his reading.

In London, the Bad Aunts had bent themselves to the recent history of the Hungarian government, and to the story of Róka's misadventure in daylight politics. Jim Prideaux was a top field man with excellent instincts, but the Aunts begged to differ with his encroachment on the field of analysis. What followed, accord-ing to Connie, was cobbled together from Party newspaper reports and the known career trajectories of junior ministers in the fifties, alongside the records and recollections of legitimate Foreign Office dips in Budapest. At the last, Toby Esterhase had run down an elderly woman who had served as a clerk in Hun-gary's Ministry of Works and now lived in Peckham Rye above a florist's. She claimed to know the story well, though Connie wasn't comfortable with her adherence to memory, and thought she might be overstating her knowledge of the fine detail. Over-all, Connie said, this was a best guess: as close as she could get but strictly not verified.

In the elections after the war, Róka found himself encouraged to become a minor office holder in the new Hungarian apparat. By all accounts, he seemed to enjoy the fleshier side of nation-making, and even to have some talent for it, but by fifty-two the failings of the new administration required traditional sacrifices, and Stalin's eye was heavy on Budapest. Visible amends were needed, and the apparat began a frenzy of internal denunciations without merit or sincerity but with terrible vigour. Róka didn't want to participate, but in falling behind, he was himself becom-ing a target. He knew he was in a bind, and he wasn't so proud or so virtuous that he refused to consider the obvious. If he could find someone even halfway a traitor he'd push them in front of the bus, but he had no plausible candidates. His blind spot was the continuing conviction that a denouncement of this kind had to make sense.

Connie guessed he'd had less than a week before the next round of interrogations would have sent him to the cells, and, in fear of his life, he did what a lot of people did. He compromised, and sold out a friend: a Russian-Hungarian named Bogdan Molchalin.

As best anyone could say, they'd met when Róka was fighting his insurgency against the Arrow Cross, and Bogdan had been doing the same on the other side of a Danube tributary. They had from time to time been in contact, and used each other's resources. Bogdan was twenty years older, and as a boy had joined the Tsar's army and fought as a private soldier, most notably on an armoured train in the Russo-Japanese War a dozen years before the Revolution. Even in forty-four, his life had the sense of belonging to an age of adventurers from which the modern world was now profoundly removed. Bogdan was not a Bolshevik but a fiery democrat – a trait inherited from his Hungarian mother – and he'd eventually been booted from the Tsar's army for spreading liberal sedition, which by coincidence had saved him from fighting in Lenin's civil war.

After Horthy's fall and the Soviet invasion in forty-five, Bogdan had gone the same way as Róka, standing as a candidate not for the Hungarian Communist Party but for the somewhat democratic Smallholders. Unlike Róka's, his votes had not been punctiliously counted, and he lost out to a self-appointed shop steward from his district's only factory. Accepting the lie of the land, Bogdan had gone back to his river crossing in a sulk and been seen no more, but Róka in his hour of need realised that the man was a perfect patsy. Bogdan was nothing if not forthright about his political opinions, and if he was White Russian as well as Hungarian that was hardly a point in his favour. Bogdan was a

friend, but, as a committed and conscious advocate for the interests of the bourgeois class, his likely impact on society could be
readily estimated as a negative. In the moral calculus, one could
argue that refusing to denounce him was itself a complicit act.
Róka, on the other hand, had the backing of the Tourmaline set.
He was a proper Muscovite, demonstrably loyal to the Soviet
Bloc above any national allegiance. His word against Bogdan's
was a pushover, and it would buy him breathing space.

As it turned out, the decision was very much the wrong one.
If he hadn't been so frantic, Róka might have asked himself how
Bogdan had survived this far, given his antecedents. Instead, he
ran headlong into a wall. Less than a day after making his report,
he was summoned to a meeting with the senior minister and two
members of the security police. He was informed that the loyalty
of Bogdan Molchalin was not in question, and asked to account
for several aspects of his own conduct. As the interview became
more antagonistic, he realised that he was in serious trouble. He
leaned hard into his Moscow patronage, and found that it had
already been quite effectively countered. The interview panel
informed him that it was only by virtue of his extensive international service to the cause that he was not already in prison
awaiting trial, and that if further information linked him to any
infractions, however minor, he should expect that forbearance to
end. He must discuss this interview and its contents with no one.
They sent him home, and he recognised two things: first, that
somewhere, somehow, Bogdan was significantly protected; and,
second, that he was being invited to run.

And run he had, that time and this. As for Bogdan, no one
knew whether he was still alive, and, if he were, why Róka would
imagine the friend he had betrayed could help him with the son
he was terrified to lose.

That evening, around six, Guillam went to the miserable Café
Beatrice, near but not on the Johannisthaler Chaussee: a grim

corner eatery torn between faux-Viennese and American styles, and overlooked by apartments on the Soviet side of the Wall. The owner, Ludo, was one of Mundt's stringers in the Allied sector. There was no political conviction in his service; Ludo had family in the East, and this was his way of looking out for them.

Guillam had spent the intervening hours typing up a report from a non-existent source in the French Embassy in Bonn, referred to in the Stasi's files as GOTTFRIED. The Gottfried identity was not directly within the French security service, but his job, or hers, allowed access to signals traffic between Bonn and Paris on an irregular basis. If Guillam had been scrutinising the Gottfried product from the outside – the way Mundt's imaginary Gegner might – he would most likely conclude that Gottfried was either a low-level diplomat assigned casually to cover whichever department had a heavy workload, or a senior member of the janitorial complement with trusted access. Gottfried's output was in general frustratingly incomplete, but occasionally offered paper confirmation of carefully selected significant diplomatic information which the East German apparat already knew. Today, Gottfried had very little to say for himself but was asking for money to tide him over, and as an earnest of his commitment was including some secret tittle-tattle. The Americans, Gottfried claimed, were quietly looking for detail on a Humboldt University student from Budapest named Leó, who had been arrested at a youth club cultural evening in the last month. The speculation in the cafés of Bad Godesberg was that Leó might be the illegitimate wartime child of an American officer now favoured for a senior political role in Washington. Surely, Gottfried asserted, that sort of hot tip was worth a few marks in advance.

Mundt would know perfectly well what this meant: that London wanted him to chase down Leó and report. Using the direct connection through Café Beatrice meant it was urgent, and Mundt should if possible facilitate a meeting within twenty-four hours. The shared fiction was that all communication was by sign, countersign and runners, but Guillam suspected Ludo had a burst radio set. In Berlin it wasn't impossible; there was so much traffic the hard part would be finding a clear frequency. Mundt on the other end could send to his heart's content, the secret conductor guiding his violins.

Guillam ate and left a handful of change for the waiter. As he went through the door, he forced himself to look north and east, because Berliners in general did not: the scar of their city's severing was so painful that most of the time they lived inside it and allowed themselves to pretend it wasn't there – but Gisriel wasn't from Berlin, and to him the Wall and the frozen land beyond should still be notable, even fascinating. Gazing at the meagre light from the apartment windows on the Heideweg, Guillam wondered which of them watched over Ludo, awaiting his signal; whether you could see the place where Alec Leamas had died from the window; whether Mundt had Katinka stashed there, and made love to her looking over the Anti-Fascist Defences and the degenerate West.

9.

Smiley and Gero had gone back to their hotel, and Lake to his rather less salubrious one a few streets away, leaving Guillam with the night to himself. He let himself into the lower floor of the office and walked between the crates of furs, the smell rising around him: salt, reindeer leather and the cured pelts of tiger and lynx, white fox and mink. The more ordinary ones were local, the others from Russia herself, from the Caucasus and South Asia, along the Don and the Danube to Hungary, and by road through Czecho to Berlin. All legitimate freight, at least so far as he and the Circus knew, and all of it with the simple purpose of making not money but paper: customs stamps and a trail of receipts and bills of lading to demonstrate the reality of the company. Banking Section took it over in Paris and sold it who knew where, and money flowed back. In the meantime, it filled the warehouse space with that salt and burnt-match taste, and the lingering reflex gasp of ammonia.

He had never been to the spot on the Wall where Leamas died. The place could be significant only to a British agent, so anyone who knew what it was scrupulously avoided it. Guillam had thought about going there one day anyway, just passing by on his way to somewhere, but didn't trust himself not to turn his head. He had instead a kind of ritual where he walked along the canal and imagined the water was concrete and barbed wire.

His mouth was dry, and he wasn't sure how long he'd been standing in the dark, but the scent of furs was in his nose and on his tongue. He looked around, but the mug was gone from his desk, and he realised old Sandra must have taken it when she closed up: the cleaner, probably the only person on earth certified civilian by the Circus and the Stasi both. She was a churchgoer and a very formal old busybody who thought it high time Matthieu Gisriel met a nice girl and settled down. She had a candidate in mind, blocked when he politely told her 'no Lutherans'.

He read a book for an hour, then worked on Gisriel's papers for another. He was thinking of turning in or going to a bar to look for someone Sandra would consider unsuitable when the phone rang. He picked it up.

'Causse-Bergen, Gisriel speaking.'

The voice on the other end was tentative, a woman in middle age. She asked if he was not Udo. He said no, he was Matthieu, she must have the wrong number. She told him she knew quite well what the number was, she had dialled it herself, and announced it quite correctly. Then she had been given the wrong number, and with respect that was no fault of his.

'I want to speak to Udo,' she demanded. 'I know he is there, drinking. Udo Lange. This is his wife, Frau Lange.'

'I assure madame that there is no Udo here.'

Udo, she said, had an appointment tomorrow. She gave him the time, and an address in the far west of the Allied sector. She told Gisriel he was a libertine and God would judge him, and Gisriel responded by putting down the phone.

Drinking – meeting confirmed. Immediate, come now.

Udo – extreme caution.

Libertine – the lobby of the Hotel Störche, three-quarters of a mile into East Berlin.

In a shoebox shoved carelessly into the top of the stationery cupboard, sandwiched between the inner and outer layers of cardboard and further concealed by the galoshes which had accompanied the shoes, Guillam had a genuine East German passport given to him by Mundt. It was at the same time the safest and most perilous false identity he had ever owned. Safe, because it carried Mundt's blessing and would usher him straight through the checkpoints. Perilous, for the same reason, because while it possessed the quality of making him invisible to mundane border guards, if ever the moment should come when such a thing mattered, it was very far from invisible to the Stasi.

He reached into another box and retrieved something almost more illicit, which Mundt had made him promise would under no circumstances make its way back across the Wall: a stamp with rolling numbered dials. Painstakingly, he recalled his conversation with the notional Frau Lange: the digits of the address in West Berlin, and the time, over which she had hesitated. Remembering them in sequence, he entered the setting on the stamp, pressed it against the ink pad and brought it down hard on the next page of the passport. The dials produced a day code, validating the stamp. He waited, then marked an illegible scrawl on the signature line. As with the document itself, all this would pass muster at a high level, so long as Mundt was not directly compromised.

He let the ink dry, then put on a long grey coat and a winter hat. Like the passport, both were authentically of the East, and carried the lingering scents of East German soap and Sonja cooking fat. Smiley, he thought, would approve, although it was Prideaux who had drilled it into him over months that when you went in under local cover, it was the detail that mattered. If you called Moscow the German capital or named Walter Ulbricht the Chancellor in Bonn, they might just think you were drunk, but if your clothes had the wrong cut or your hair was more Paris than Potsdam, you were done.

He looked in the mirror and saw a youngish man with a narrow face, pinched and washed out by the fluorescent light, something military in the jut of the chin. A rising bureaucrat, ambitious but not overbold, and just the sort of person to be taking a late meeting in a respectable socialist hotel.

He changed his shoes last, to a pair which were heavy but surprisingly comfortable. They were authentic too, made four years ago, before the Wall.

Guillam called the Elegant and asked to be connected to Mr Willow's room. Smiley answered in German with Willow's inflection, and Guillam responded in his best Strasbourg-accented English. Would Mr Willow like to come to lunch tomorrow to discuss the advantageous possibilities of shipping via Odessa rather than the overland route? Perhaps he would bring his glamorous assistant? Gisriel would be sure to be suitably accompanied also. Mr Willow agreed, and Gisriel added as an afterthought that he'd heard from their mutual friend Harold and would share the gossip. Harold was not Mundt's official codename but one they had agreed for the duration of Smiley's visit.

'Oh, splendid,' Smiley's voice said. 'Dear old Harold. He's always good for a laugh, isn't he?'

Guillam nearly gagged, and reflected that as far as misdirection went it was cold but excellent.

'I'll give you a call in the morning when I've sorted out a table,' he told Willow, and received a jaunty farewell.

Crossing from West to East was not quite so nervous as the return trip, although Guillam's instincts, as ever, objected to the perversity of the choice. The distances involved were tiny; in the thirties you could have walked from the University to the Großer Stern in under an hour. It was not that you were lost far behind enemy lines. It was that the distinction between the two parts of Berlin was absolute. One was an island of the cosmopolitan lost in the consequences of Germany's worst and most unforgivable decisions. The other was like a model forest made in lead and left unpainted, a cold facsimile which might never let you go. The sensation was not made better by the clear opinion of the guards on the Western side that he must be out of his mind.

Casual traffic between the two halves of the city, in the first months after the Wall went up, was almost nil. The severance was deliberate and total. Little by little, in the time since, compromise had crept in around the edges like damp, so that now – even if families could not share Christmas or visit for funerals – some measure of necessary contact was possible. At an official, international level, it was oddly easier than in the day to day, and the grand international hotels of the East were if anything more offensively luxurious than their counterparts in the West. A small, awkward club existed, of men and a few women, mostly Party members from elsewhere in the DDR but also some Westerners, who were permitted or even required to make regular crossings from one side of the city to the other. Into this foggy category Guillam now inserted himself, crisply laying the East German passport in the hands of a young, fat-faced boy in uniform. It had been dark for hours, and the checkpoint was lit only from above, by the white glare of a bank of floodlights over the official hut. Standing in the light, you couldn't see anything outside it, as if the whole world came down to this alone.

'Purpose of your trip?' the boy asked.

'Hydrological infrastructure,' Guillam said, as if it were bloody obvious. The boy flinched and looked down at the passport, then went back to the hut, leaving Guillam standing in the light, carefully not looking at his watch. *It takes as long as it takes*, he told himself. *You live with it. You endorse it. You respect the necessity or you like being part of a machine that bosses people around. Maybe one day you'll be in charge, you'll have Ulbricht's job.* But the thought occurred to him that he'd forgotten to exchange his French watch for a sober Soviet one. He couldn't remember. Perhaps he wasn't wearing one at all. He couldn't feel it. If he checked, it would look as if he was nervous. It was cold as hell. He stamped his feet, turning in a circle, which was absolutely not allowed. He realised he was humming. What was he humming? Was it the bloody 'Marseillaise'? No, thank God, it wasn't. His Adam's apple bobbled in his neck. Da da DEE da. The 'Volga Boatmen', a bargee's song for hauling river-boats from the bank. 'Let's all go OOOF now . . .' It was a joke in London, the leitmotiv of pompous Soviet pageantry. How did it sound here? He had no idea. He also didn't know the rest of it.

In front of him, beyond the circle of light, someone else took up the tune. Guillam nearly jumped out of his skin. He stopped, and heard someone greet him in Russian. He held up his hands in apology. *Tut mir leid.*

He heard footsteps. Not the boy from the hut but the Russian speaker. A German who spoke Russian? A Lithuanian? Or an actual Soviet officer checking up on the locals?

It takes as long as it takes. Spying is waiting.

He stayed in the circle of light, occasionally shaking his hands down by his hips to keep them warm.

'You don't have a car, Herr Doktor,' the boy's voice said, very formal now that he'd checked the fake passport. Guillam shook his head in vanguardist disapproval.

'I am not a paper-pusher. When I was young I was a miner. I don't need a car to take me two miles – it's not even a proper winter.'

The boy nodded wisely as if Guillam had confirmed something he had always suspected, and waved him through. The walk to the Störche was another thirty-five minutes, and Guillam felt the weight of the East grow on him with every step, until the doorman invited him in, and he looked across the lobby to a cluster of leather chairs by a grand fire where Hans-Dieter Mundt was waiting for him.

In his physical appearance, Mundt looked no different from how he had in Belgrade. A decade older than Guillam, he had wide shoulders and a chiselled, disagreeable face. His hair was a stark blond, as if he'd forgotten which Party now owned him. His fingers were long and narrow, perfect for playing the piano or pulling the trigger on machine guns, if you happened to be murdering Alec Leamas.

'My dear fellow, welcome,' Mundt said in breezy northern *Hochdeutsch*. 'We have a private dining room, so much easier to talk. How have you been?'

'Very good,' Guillam said. 'And I heard you were engaged.'

Mundt's eyes flickered. 'Alas,' he murmured, 'not any more. Shall we go in?'

He gestured, and Guillam realised he was going to have to let Mundt go behind him. His gut told him not to, and his training wanted someone to watch his back. He quashed both, and wandered through the door as if he was shopping in the West End. The private dining room had laminated wood panels, very modern and already chipped in tiny tell-tale impacts along the edges which showed the wood pulp board under the veneer. The tablecloth was the same improbable white as Mundt's teeth when he smiled. Guillam went left, choosing the seat which would put his back to the wall rather than the staff doorway, and Mundt let him. The German shut the door and turned.

'You people are out of your bloody minds,' Mundt said. Guillam flinched, not at the words or even the tone, but because he'd spoken in English. His accent was strong and he struggled with cadence, so that when he came down hard on 'bloody' there was more Rostock in it than London.

'Forgive me, Herr Mundt,' Guillam said, still in German. 'I didn't quite catch that.'

Mundt snorted. 'It's a bit late to be so dainty, okay? If we can't talk English here, then we're screwed anyway. Or maybe I am and you have a deal, I don't know. Maybe you defect. You give me up and get a nice house in Prague or someplace. Maybe you can marry Katinka. That at least would make sense to me.'

Someone knocked at the door, and Mundt barked at Guillam to shut up. He told the waiter to come in and they sat while two bowls of soup arrived with dry bread, but, as soon as the man left, Mundt stood up and started pacing. Guillam instinctively matched him – and Mundt's temper detonated. He ran at Guillam, three quick steps with hands outstretched, and Guillam felt his feet actually leave the ground as the full weight of the other man slammed into his chest. His back hit the laminate panelling and there was a sharp clunk as something broke, mercifully East German joinery rather than bone, and he felt more than saw the cold metal of a Makarov semi-automatic pistol pressed into his neck above the collar, then a nauseating twitch as the barrel twisted upward under his jaw. Mundt screamed directly into his face, not in English or German but a single noise that went on for far too long. They must be able to hear it at the reception desk, in the kitchen. Someone would notice, would remark it, would report it. But of course they wouldn't, because it was Mundt. Screaming was to be expected, and there was no need to report the state to itself.

'You stupid, stupid bastards,' Mundt breathed. 'You damned incompetents! You'll kill me and you'll say "Hans-Dieter was a damn fool, and anyway a Nazi, and to hell with him." But it will be you! You killed me. Not me.'

Guillam inhaled carefully, seeking consent and keeping his hands well away from Mundt's. He could smell the other man's breath, and beneath it the scent of gun oil.

'Why don't you tell me what we've done wrong?' he suggested.

After a long moment, and still holding Guillam against the wall with the pistol, Mundt listed his grievances, like a primary schoolteacher sharing his disappointment. How dare the Circus expose him to this level of risk? Were they professionals at all, or a bunch of stupid old men longing for Empire and expecting everyone to know their place? Leó wasn't any American's by-blow and they ought to know it; he was damn sure they did know it and had set him up. Yes, set him up, made him a target, because Moscow was asking the same damn question: where was Leó Pártos and who had arrested him? And Mundt, who was ultimately the man who arrested everyone, the chief of the security organ of the state, had no idea and looked like a fool, but, worse, he'd nearly tripped over the Russian investigator coming along the track in the opposite direction, and it was all very well saying he could claim Gottfried had put him on to it, but he didn't want them paying close attention to Gottfried either. The Circus was being casual, and this Russian wasn't a casual man. He was small and modest, with pouchy eyes that made him look like an old hunting dog, but he was clever with it and entirely cold. Mundt had recognised him immediately: this was Gegner made flesh. Gegner was here in Berlin, and the Circus had put Mundt directly in his path.

Mundt's body had relaxed now, and his alarming fever had given way to melancholy. The gun was still there, but his finger was off the trigger and his weight was pushing through the grip into Guillam's chest. From that position it would be hard if not impossible to get a shot off before Guillam took it away from him. And Guillam wanted very much to hit him. It would be quite justifiable, to London and probably even to Mundt. He had a brief, glorious vision of pasting him with a sharp elbow, breaking a proud Aryan cheekbone and sending Mundt crashing to the ground. Following him down and finishing the damn job, telling Control he was very sorry, but Mundt had struck first, and here were the bruises on his neck to prove it. He could kill Mundt now, with a clear conscience. He could do it and walk away, tell the staff not to disturb his host, then get back across the border before the body was discovered. Or the East Germans would catch up with him and he would die in a hail of bullets like Alec. He didn't care. It would be worth it.

Except he did care, because now there was intelligence in the room. Not clean intelligence, not clear-cut, but something. He could feel it in the air: a secret of which even Mundt had only the barest hint, the secret Smiley had been chasing in London and now here. Why did Moscow care so much about Leó Pártos and Ferenc Róka? Why was a Soviet heavyweight bothering with a drunken university student and his absentee spy father? If it mattered enough for all this fuss, then it was worth letting Mundt live another day, and, for that matter, himself.

For the first time in this dismal round of crossing and recrossing the Wall while thousands in its Eastern shadow risked their lives to cross it only once, Guillam had the scent of a prize.

'Then you better get yourself under control,' he snapped, to the sledge-dog eyes. 'Do you want to get caught?' It wasn't until he said it that he realised the answer might actually be yes, that some part of Mundt was just exhausted by being so utterly soul-less in the name of survival. Sometimes, if you were in an impossible situation, you gave yourself permission to panto-mime insanity and only later recognised that there'd never been anything false in it at all.

But not tonight, evidently, as Mundt's hand slipped away from Guillam's collar, patting at his lapels on the way down, smooth-ing at him as if it had all been a moment of boyish hijinks. The face returned to a glassy equilibrium.

'The soup is not good,' Mundt said, sounding like an offended dowager. 'I will have them bring the meat course. We will talk. This is normal. There is always work.'

'The poussin,' Smiley said, looking over at Susanna for approval, and the waiter made a noise which suggested he, at least, would consider sleeping with anyone who ordered him a poussin.

They were sitting in Martello's, a storied West Berlin dinner place on the far side of the Tiergarten, and she was practising her cover as a kept woman. When he asked her anything, she made sure to brighten, and when his attention strayed she drooped. If he looked at anyone female between the ages of seventeen and sixty, even to ask for their table or hand over his coat, she assumed a thunderous glower. It was a pattern she'd witnessed around Bánáti's mistresses, and she was doing it well. She still wasn't sure if Smiley knew. He seemed if anything more opaque and unre-markable than ever.

It wasn't that he didn't understand mood and body language. His own use of it was striking. The person he was outside a room vanished as soon as he got inside and understood the flow and priority around him, so that he instantly fitted himself to what-ever shape was most acceptable, be that high-status client or shoeshine man. With that in mind, he ought to be responding to her charade, occasionally meeting her eyes and smirking with the pleasure of ownership – but he was blank, as if flirtation was just beyond him. She had worried briefly that he might think the play was real, that she was actually seeking a liaison, which she was sure would be extremely unprofessional. Then, though, he had offered her his arm as they went into Martello's, and for a moment they had moved together like dancers, with him showing her off as they made their way to the table, and her strutting proudly and defiantly in step. The superficially intimate contact had been bloodless, clinical on both sides, and she'd caught the flicker of his approval as they sat. So why wasn't he responding?

'Are you worried about him?' she asked, when the waiter had gone.

'Oh, no. Matthieu will come through for us, clear as day,' Smiley replied, in Willow's genial tones. 'He knows the supply routes, the border crossings and so on, he's a real operator in Mitteleuropa. If he says Odessa, then Odessa it is.'

She thought about how to compose her next question. 'I'm sure he does, but in any venture like this, there's always risk. We've never used that route before.'

'No, but he has. I'm sure his usual process will serve quite well. And the product is superior. Very fine, indeed. He has a soft white fur – from a fox, I think, or a wolf – that I'm quite eager to see made into something special. New product is everything, after all. You can't just wait for the market to come to you.'

She nodded. 'I'm not sure I've got the nerves for this part of it.'

'You have considerably more to offer in that regard than most, but there's no reason to court it if it makes you uncomfortable. *Unbequem* is the German word. I rather like it, don't you?'

She shrugged, actually considering. 'Yes,' she said, surprised. 'It's a good word.'

The poussin arrived steaming and exceptional, which made conversation and preening both much harder.

'He'll let us know as soon as possible what his thinking is,' Smiley said, when the feast had temporarily abated. 'So that we can prepare any questions. Then, when we've done all we can, you and I – and Mr Prescott, of course – will head onward to our next meeting, and Mr Gisriel will arrange matters here.'

For a moment she couldn't remember who Prescott was, then thought of Lake, sitting alone in one of Berlin's more workmanlike eateries. She wanted to ask whether Lake should have accompanied Guillam, but she couldn't find a way to put it that wasn't absurd, because the answer was obvious. Should Mr Willow's driver work with his business contact on a new bid? Smiley seemed to read the question anyway.

'Mr Gisriel is very adept in his profession,' he said. 'We need have no qualms at all.' Which was how she realised that he was deathly nervous himself.

'Dessertkarte,' the waiter said, from behind her. Smiley glanced at his menu and nodded. 'The crème brûlée, if you please,' he said, and the waiter turned back to Susanna and asked, 'And for your daughter?'

Susanna suddenly found herself blushing, and it only got worse when she saw Smiley was, for the first time ever in her experience, likewise wrong-footed. Of all the constellations they might have played, both of them had avoided that one, and she realised that doing so required an unconscious complicity which made this casual question all the more startling. Yes, she supposed, that also was a way to see them. Smiley was the right age, after all, and his benign indifference to her body, coupled with his solicitude, did answer the role. It was like being on a date, and having someone ask when the wedding was. Too much, too steep, too soon. She felt a powerful sense of infidelity.

They stared at one another in mutual horror, and the waiter

took fright. He began to stammer an apology, and Smiley raised a hand to stem the flood.

'Miss Hofbauer is a work colleague only, I'm afraid,' he murmured. And later, he notably overtipped, which was the best absolution he could manage.

Lake acquired Guillam on the Western side of the Bösebrücke checkpoint just after midnight. In the role of a well-refreshed Prescott, he idled in the street and observed no one, either on foot or in a car, paying any attention. When Guillam rounded the corner and was out of the direct line of sight from East Berlin, Lake fell in beside him and asked for directions, and Guillam suggested they walk together, saying it wasn't out of his way. For the benefit of watchers they knew fine well were not present, or some magical form of surveillance which did not exist, they kept up their performance all the way to Lake's hotel.

'Not a dickiebird,' Lake murmured, as they shook hands at the door.

'All clear,' Guillam agreed, then went back to the office to write up everything he had learned, encipher it and despatch it to London. Smiley would have it direct from him, but Control also demanded his tribute.

Mundt – Guillam related to Smiley the following morning after too little sleep and a shower which, if it wasn't actually cold, sure as hell wasn't as hot as he'd been looking for – had received Guillam's message and gone to work, discovering almost immediately that he was fishing in very deep water indeed.

First, Mundt had taken himself out of the political offices, where he naturally had one of the most luxurious, and gone down two floors to the stark white corridors and institutional hessian of the watch commander's office, to find Bendt Lehmann, whose job included overseeing the overt activities of the Ministry for State Security. More particularly, Lehmann, while he was on shift, was the official keeper of the day book: actually, a lever-arch binder containing the top copies of numbered report forms. It was essentially an index of other books held in records, in which were kept scrupulous accounts of all actions great or small conducted by Stasi officers – including the details of any captures and arrests.

Lehmann was a little fellow, only just tall enough to meet the height requirement, but he was from the mountains near Pirna and his body seemed to possess a climber's indefatigable elasticity. Senior grades were not required to train to the same physical standard as the boys who broke down doors, but, like Mundt, Lehmann did anyway. They were already on easy terms, partly because of this, and partly because Lehmann had good access to the Stasi's archive system, and Mundt had been quietly setting him up to take the fall if his own betrayals should ever lead to another internal investigation.

Mundt had dropped in on Lehmann as if on his way home, and made small talk. Lehmann was a football fanatic, and a follower of the blindingly unsuccessful local Aufbau team. Mundt commiserated, then went to leave, and finally remembered why he was there. He'd had a sniff of something interesting – could Lehmann help him out? Lehmann could. Well, then: going back a fortnight or so, had there been any difficulties involving members of the university staff? Lehmann thought not, but he'd have to check. No, nothing obvious. Could Mundt be more specific? No, this was both highly speculative and highly secret, and indeed Lehmann must consider the conversation entirely off the record, from anyone. This was *unter vier Augen*, no more. Lehmann did a poor job of concealing his excitement. He was, Mundt noted to Guillam later, appallingly loyal. That was part of why Mundt liked him as a patsy: the deeper you went into his life, the more honesty you found, and there was nothing more perfectly calculated to alarm an inquisitor than the consistent appearance of blamelessness. Hence, Mundt had cut loose in Belgrade and made such a messy scene with Katinka: you had to be able to give them something, be punished occasionally, or you were growing too tall and likely to be reaped.

'And what was your punishment,' Guillam had demanded, 'for Belgrade?'

Katinka had been refused residency in the DDR, Mundt said. The marriage was off. He was officially heartbroken. And he had been pointedly informed that psychological counselling was available for officers seeking guidance on proper emotional conduct in public life. This was, he emphasised, an optimal outcome.

Lehmann was frustrated that he couldn't find what Mundt was looking for and began to widen the search, first to academics and intellectuals more loosely associated with the university but living outside Berlin, or even on exchange programmes with other institutions. There was a senior petrochemical engineer presently attached to the faculty in Leningrad. He had a gambling problem and was flagged high risk for recruitment by Fascist intelligence agencies, most likely by America. Was this the connection Mundt was seeking? And when it wasn't, at last, Lehmann asked the question Mundt had been fishing for all along: was it possible that the issue was not with the teaching staff or the researchers but among the undergraduates?

At this, Mundt gave every evidence of being thunderstruck. No, he said, it was impossible, and yet – there was actually nothing to say so, he had just assumed, had read an implication into the report which, now that he considered it – well, Lehmann was right. It could be a student, after all. And Lehmann, sensing that he might just have broken an important case, puffed up with pride and went back to his book.

It took in total twenty-one minutes for Mundt to get what he had come for: confirmation that Leó Pártos was arrested at ten forty-seven p.m. three weeks ago and brought here to Rusche-straße for formal and in-depth interrogation about possible anti-Soviet or anti-Party activity. There was corroboration of the arrest from the old woman who was caretaker at the youth club. She had told her priest all about it, and the priest had a weekly meeting with one of Mundt's quiet listeners. She hadn't been confessing, after all, so it hardly mattered if he shared the detail with a respectable official. Questioning had begun at midnight, gone on for an hour, then a break, then another hour, and then – after some internal discussion – Leó had been released without further action, back into the Prenzlauer wilds. The officer in charge had noted that he was intellectually able and a committed socialist but also a young idiot with a belly full of beer.

'Does that answer your question, Comrade Mundt?' Lehmann had asked breathlessly.

Mundt affected the manner of an impressed sorcerer with his talented apprentice. Indeed, that was very fine, and it set him upon a path that might be very important. Lehmann was a solid officer, and a brother in arms.

But Lehmann didn't look happy, which raised in Mundt an immediate sense of trouble. The little man should have been ecstatic. Mundt had dangled in front of him the strongest indicator yet of promotion and patronage, but his face was very grave, as if he was bringing news of a death. He pulled a couple of annexe files from the cubbies behind the watch commander's station, spreading them out on the desk. His blunt fingers traced lines of handwriting, then skipped, flipping back through the calendar, and traced again.

'What's wrong?' Mundt demanded. 'What's the hold-up?' And Lehmann came within an ace of shushing him. Finally, he turned.

'There is a problem with the book,' Lehmann said.

Lehmann had come on shift at four in the afternoon, and completed the formal handover with Klein, who had the midday shift. The day book had been absent, and Klein explained that it was with the secretaries for transcription and copying to the archive. This was not the established schedule, but Klein had orders. Lehmann assumed out loud that these must have come from Mundt's office, but when he said this Klein became squirrelly, and finally admitted that there was a senior Russian officer here in Ruschestraße making an inspection. What sort of inspection? Klein had not felt strongly enough to ask. All right, where was the written order authorising cooperation at an intergovernmental level? Again, Klein shrugged. It was the Russians, he said. You didn't argue, you just did it. Lehmann got angry, and told him outright that he was a poor officer and a bad German. There were rules, and one of them was that there must always be a paper trail. While they argued, Lehmann heard someone come in, and, when he turned, there was a fellow about his own height in a well-made proletarian jacket, watching in silence.

'Comrade Lehmann has the right of it,' the man said, in accented German. 'But this is not to be discussed further. I wish to be as informal as possible.' And he gave them to understand that it would be easier that way for everyone. Then, without comment, he left, and Lehmann realised he still didn't even have the man's name.

The book had been returned a short while later by a departmental runner, and Lehmann had thought nothing more about it until just now, when he had touched the pages of the entry for Leó Pártos and found them cold. The ink on the entry page was dry, but on the back of the preceding form was a small blot where the binder had been closed over the freshly written words, and the blot was wet. Lehmann pointed to the annexe files spread out on the desk. They did not match the report in what he now suspected was the altered day book. In the annexe files, Leó's arrest was still listed, but his release was more muddy and tagged REFER, which meant that Moscow had a stated interest in the case. Leó's personal file was missing entirely.

Mundt recognised – he told Guillam, without a hint of modesty – that this moment constituted a hinge which could dictate his fortunes going forward. He chose the offensive path, and told Lehmann that the entire encounter and most especially the Russian were now to be considered not merely informal but absolutely secret. Mundt had never come here and Lehmann had never made his discovery. The deception was to apply at the highest level, and included not only officers junior to Lehmann but any superior not directly in his chain of command and above Mundt in authority. Furthermore, it applied specifically to any members of the intelligence services of allied nations not already directly involved. Any inquiries from such officers should be redirected to Mundt in person. He didn't think that would stick for more than a heartbeat if the Soviets put the screws into Lehmann, but he could if necessary point to any infraction as a violation of a direct order, and a minor but offensive sleight by the Russians of East German democratic socialist sovereignty. He took the day book and the relevant annexe entries, and told Lehmann to begin a temporary file.

Returning to his office, Mundt reckoned he had anything from minutes to hours before he got a visit from whoever was operating inside his own agency. He sat down and set to work, establishing what Smiley by this time already knew: that Leó's condition had been queried on three separate occasions since the night of his arrest, and each time the question had been bounced back unanswered, without ever being kicked upstairs to the political floor, which was where it belonged. He looked, and found that the two arresting officers had this morning requested and received permission for temporary secondments to quite prestigious postings with Soviet intelligence overseas, beginning with a covert training programme lasting six months, during which time they were expected to be entirely incommunicado. The paperwork was marked only THIRTEENTH DIRECTORATE, followed by a signature in Cyrillic which he thought was quite poor penmanship and seemed to be a woman's name: Karla. He was just looking for connections to files which might still be available, to piece together

205

what was missing, when a heavy knock told him that his time had run out.

'Come,' he called, without looking up, and then: 'I am quite busy. Please leave whatever it is, and go.' When this was greeted with silence, he glanced over at the door, and reacted with appropriate surprise to what he had been expecting.

Only one of the men in the doorway was familiar. His name was Bezrukov, and he was the Thirteenth Directorate's permanent envoy to the Berlin branch of the Stasi. He was tall and narrow, with stooped shoulders that always reminded Mundt of corn. Mundt regarded Bezrukov as necessary baggage. He was a go-between and of course a spy but hardly a threat. Beside him was a shorter man with no uniform, who gave the impression of a bland and general interest. It was this second man – presumably the same one Lehmann had met earlier – who spoke with a gentle curiosity which to Mundt was immediately suspect.

'Whatever are you working on so late, Comrade Mundt?'

'If you are the ranking Soviet officer blundering around in my files,' Mundt snapped, 'then I think I am tidying up your mess.'

It looked for a moment as if Bezrukov might break and run. Ranking officer, indeed, and evidently someone you just didn't talk to like that, but Mundt, in the legend of his own life on which his fate now rested, was a scarred veteran of overseas missions, internal coups and failed purges, and you didn't talk to him like that either. He waited, and, when nothing happened, he put his head down and went back to the files as if the Russians weren't even in the room. A moment later, Bezrukov felt the need to explain himself.

'Comrade Mundt,' Bezrukov said, 'we wish to discuss with you the matter of the boy Leó Pártos.'

'Well,' Mundt growled, 'if only someone hadn't interfered with my files – badly – I could probably help with that. I take it you wanted the whole trail to disappear? Not just half of it?'

'To disappear,' Bezrukov agreed, 'but also to follow it.' He glanced to the side, as if sharing what was already obvious was a sin for which he must make contrition to his companion. Or, no: his boss.

'We don't have the boy,' Mundt said. 'When I have finished, we will never have had him. But even before your – I'm sorry, your quite amateurish tampering – even before that, he was not held. He was picked up, he answered questions, no further action was taken. That's it.'

Except that you people came calling, once, twice, three times, and now today, when you felt the need to extract two of my officers, and probably bury them.

The second man was still not particularly looking at him, but Mundt didn't think for a second he wasn't paying attention. He had that look of someone who feels his way to things, who gets into the cracks like water and then breaks them open like ice. Finally, he spoke.

'Comrade Mundt,' he said. 'We do thank you for your time and hard work. May I ask: what was it, in our amateurish blundering, that first drew your attention?'

And, again, Mundt felt possible worlds opening and closing in front of him like teeth. Pick a mistake: operationally, there had been plenty; call it coincidence and brazen it out; or fall back on the fabricated Gottfried intelligence. He chose none of the above.

'It didn't,' he admitted, with the shyness of a professional investigator caught playing a long shot. 'I monitor Lehmann.'

The soft eyes blinked very slowly. 'You have concerns.'

Mundt shrugged. 'Slight. A feeling in the small hairs I should dismiss. But I have history.'

'Yet you do not report these concerns.'

Mundt allowed himself a little flare of resentment. 'I dislike the idea of making false accusations against a patriot and a fellow officer.'

And he saw, just for a moment, the slightest twitch in the little man's heels, as if he wore cavalry boots.

Got you, you bastard.

As Guillam talked, Smiley looked into some middle distance of his own. His expression was almost that of one dreaming, but his hands lifted occasionally from his lap as if starting to write something on a blackboard and then retreating. His eyes were half closed, and Susanna wondered whether – it being after midnight and he being over fifty – he was drifting off. The office was spare and not obviously cosy, but, in the orange light of an electric fire and with darkness in the windows, it was their place, and she could imagine sleeping here as a child's adventure. A secret hidey-hole in a fortified city, with all enemies kept safe beyond the walls.

Lake, she thought, was suffering a kind of crisis, because Guillam had done all that was to be done and left him nothing but a shadow. He was clearly unused to it, and itching to make ground. His nervous energy made her look again at herself, at the sudden lurch that had brought her here, one of several in her life which came upon her as it seemed from nowhere and governed everything. What was she doing, here in this room? Watching herself watch the others, and understanding less than nothing. What good was that?

Smiley's eyes came open as if in response, looking directly into her face. 'So, then. What do you make of it?'

'Me?'

'Yes. I know what I think. And Peter and Tom come from the same institution – I taught them, even – so they can hardly be considered entirely independent. You, on the other hand, are only yourself. Your experience is with Róka, and with your own life. You're a Hungarian émigrée woman in Berlin, in this year of our Lord nineteen sixty-three. You must see things differently – or see different things.'

What had she been thinking, as she followed the story? Nothing warm.

'He's dead,' she said flatly, trying not to see Bánáti, or the agony that verdict would ignite within him. 'Leó. They made a mistake. Hit him too hard, killed him. After, they found out Moscow cared about him, maybe they read the file. Realised someone was getting him out of trouble. They panicked and made it go away, put the body in a ditch or a river or . . . wherever. Lied to Mundt, to everyone. Then your little professor came and finished the job. Made them go away too.'

Smiley turned to Guillam. 'Peter?'

Guillam shook his head but not to disagree. 'Mundt thought the same. What he didn't know was why the hell they cared. Why this man from Moscow would show up and hide it all. Who's he hiding it from? Not the Stasi. Not us, even if he suspects Mundt may be a double.'

'I assume Mundt had a theory.'

'Well, it's Gegner, isn't it? So he assumes maximum risk.'

'Did Mundt mean this man was Gegner in particular? Or just that he was Gegner today? Was he focused on him because he was there, or because he guessed who he was?'

'He didn't say. Why, who is he?'

'Oh, he's Karla. A nickname out of the past.'

'You've heard it before?'

'From time to time, yes. Operating in Germany in the first half of forty-five against the Nazi stay-behind men. Then he ran quite a pretty network in North America in fifty-four – Vancouver and Seattle. Although I did rather think he was shot when he got home. He was close with Rudnev.' Smiley shrugged. 'We see through a glass darkly. And now he has the Stasi chasing their own tail. Why?'

Smiley glanced at Guillam, then back to Susanna. She shrugged: don't know. His eyes went to Lake.

'Same reason as us,' Lake said, too promptly. Younger brother,

Susanna thought; younger son. Worried that Smiley favours his firstborn – which he obviously does. She wanted to tell him to be calm, to hold back. Smiley, she was quite certain, admired restraint. 'If he's got the boy, he's got Róka.'

'And what does he want from Róka? Was it Karla who sent Miki Bortnik to London, or someone else?'

'Doesn't matter. Either he wants to shut him up or help him out. It's the same play. To a point,' Lake added placatingly, as Guillam frowned.

'It doesn't matter from Róka's point of view, but it does from ours,' Smiley said. 'On the face of it, Karla is in Berlin to hide whatever happened with Leó. From whom? The two men who arrested him – and they may not be dead, they may actually have been promoted – were already stonewalling Róka's efforts. Karla had no need to intervene for that. And he's not hiding it from us either, because as far as he knows we aren't looking. That leaves his own side. His exposed flank. Which, if he's now in a senior position, is rather interesting to us, isn't it?'

'It's thin,' Guillam objected.

'Oh, it's not even that – but supposition is the nature of the work. If we want to be ahead of the game, we must guess where it will go. A chain of connection ties Ferenc Róka to Karla, and Karla wishes that chain to go unnoticed. We, definitionally, want to know what it is.'

Lake looked very impressed, then caught Susanna's expression and brought himself to heel.

'Was she right, Mr Smiley? About the boy?'

Smiley looked over at Susanna. 'The Stasi aren't shy of physical violence – and intellectually disaster is appealing. Literature tells us sorrow is more profound than joy – a very Russian perception, as it happens. As I live longer, I'm the more convinced that our valorisation of pain is what makes our world so bleak. We anticipate it, we approve of it, and in doing so we make it. We need a better way. So, as a matter of personal policy: Leó is alive.

Although that of itself does not guarantee a happier world.' He waved a hand as if banishing bad dreams. 'But we also must not fall into the trap of thinking that Mundt tells us the whole truth. He is not our man, not our friend. He's not even our agent, really – he spies for himself and gives us the product to secure a commodity he desires: our forbearance. His account of Karla and of his investigation must be suspect. Perhaps there is no Karla; or, there is, but he remains oblivious in Moscow. Perhaps there's no Lehmann, no record of an arrest. Perhaps Mundt personally killed the boy for no better reason than that he could. We accept the existence of Mundt's report, not its veracity. We hypothesise, and we consider the facts, and, in the end, we do the best we can with what we have. But Karla being here now is not good for us. He's paying attention, which means he's seen Latour's picture and knows that Róka is still alive. Whatever time we thought we had in hand has slipped away while we were sleeping. As you say, Tom: whoever has Leó controls the game – and we, alas, do not. Which presents me with an operational challenge. My best hope was to bring Róka to me. Now here I am in front of the haystack again, hoping to find the needle with my fingertips.' He stood, contemplating the view of the Spree Canal through Guillam's window.

'If you can find him, Susanna can talk to him, at least.' Guillam raised his eyebrows, making it a request. She nodded but immediately pictured the scene, her scolding Róka like one of the old women in the market. *Stop this absurd pursuit of your stolen child and come back to the office where you belong. What am I, for God's sake, if not the appropriate surrogate for your paternal affection? You should be ashamed! A man your age. What will everyone think?* And then, more soberly, wished she could upbraid him that way, because he was being a fool and the Russians would kill him. She had seen them do it in fifty-six, and those men hadn't even given cause.

'Yes,' Smiley agreed. 'Susanna, as it turns out, is our best hope to make Róka stop and think. I'm sorry,' he added, in her direction, and she wasn't sure what for.

Smiley, having made his apology, moved his attention to Lake. 'Under the circumstances, it appears we don't have time to play cat and mouse. Tom, I shall need to ask you to do something a little dangerous, if that's all right.'

Lake looked abruptly happier than he had done for days. 'Scalpel, Mr Smiley,' he said immediately. 'The quick and the dead.' Susanna thought it must be an unofficial motto, and saw Guillam wince.

'You be bloody careful,' Guillam snapped. 'You do it smart, and you come back and tell everyone how reckless you were after. I'll even throw in a frosty note for your file. Institutional culture of irresponsibility in Travel Section, blunt-force actions which are superficially effective but detrimental to long-term intelligence gathering. Those lunatics in Brixton will love it. But I want you back, first.'

'It's all right, Peter,' Smiley said. 'Tom is wiser than he gives out. Control assures me.'

'Fine,' Guillam subsided, then: 'Vienna?'

'Yes,' Smiley said. 'As it must be, Vienna.'

Guillam nodded. 'All right. I'd come to the airport, but we don't know each other that well.' It took Susanna a moment to realise he meant Gisriel and Willow. 'Good luck.'

'And you, Peter. Take care of yourself.' Smiley's voice seemed, for a moment, uncharacteristically constricted. Guillam got to his feet.

'It's been good to see you, George. But don't let Control talk you into staying.'

And, after another moment, to Susanna's surprise and Lake's frank amazement, they embraced.

IO.

British European Airways was London as it wanted the jet set to see it: picture-perfect stewardesses with World Service voices shepherding civilisation in the skies. The wing of the Comet as it rose above Tempelhof was speckled gold by the rising sun, and all the grim blot of Berlin fell back behind them, the scar of the Wall drawn in grey and brown across the centre. Susanna tried to find the Causse-Bergen office, and Guillam, and thought she might have: a meagre white box hard by the undesirable bank of the Spree. She looked away.

'But see,' Lake said, from the next seat, 'you need to stay sharp, understand? Vienna isn't like Berlin. It's different.'

She glanced at Smiley, but he had let his chin drop the moment they sat down, and now his chest rose very softly as the plane banked and headed south and east. He seemed in this one moment to be carefree, and even young. She looked back at Lake.

'How, different?'

He was not the poetic sort at all; he had reports in him, she thought, but not songs. His face showed effort and concentration.

'When you were a child, did you ever spread your arms and try to fly on the wind?'

She laughed. 'Of course.'

'Did you ever worry that it might work?'

'No. The wind's not that strong.'

'Some places it is.'

Mountains, she supposed. Or maybe Kansas. 'Some places,' she said.

Lake shrugged. 'Same thing.'

Vienna did not seem like a place where the wind might blow

you off your feet. After the leisurely descent between the mountains to a runway that seemed rather short for rather a long plane, the city itself was surpassingly pretty. The line of the Danube – her river, the Hungarian in her still asserted – flowed past the old town with businesslike certainty, and the city smelled of melted snow, pine and woodsmoke. In the Budapest of her childhood, the Danube was a fundamental truth, running from the countries to the west, which saw themselves as modern, into the Black Sea, in which the rest of the world was reflected, just as Budapest was reflected in Odessa – and, she now realised, just as Vienna was reflected in both, unless it was the other way around. The river was holy and commercial at the same time, and perhaps after all there was no difference. In London, by contrast, the Thames was just mud, and joyless barges chugged along it bringing coal and oil. Londoners didn't look at the river, didn't notice it except when they crossed a bridge and the traffic was slow. Only a madman would swim in the Thames any more. She'd thought it might be different in other towns, but, having asked, found it was not, and stopped talking about it lest the topic become one of those meaningful errors that marked her as a foreigner. Now, she could smell the river again, full and sharp, and the chill along her neck was a homecoming, even at some remove.

With Lake thirty feet behind and superficially hunting for postcards, she and Smiley established themselves as visitors, Mr Willow and Miss Hofbauer roaming the shopping streets near St Stephen's, whose luxury marks, lounging in fine Viennese premises, promised the absolute height of Capitalist sophistication. Willow, as her lover, would halfway ruin himself to buy her things from Hermès or Cartier. As her father, perhaps he might bring her one of their lesser consolations when he returned home after a trip. As Smiley, she thought he barely saw them at all, and was astounded when his face lit from within in some kind of fevered realisation, and he plunged randomly into a boutique selling Italian silk and demanded that she help him pick something for his wife.

It had not consciously occurred to Smiley until that moment, seeing the printed poster of a woman in the window, her face delighted by the fripperies and flounces, that Ann was – if proceeding according to the schedule – here in Vienna, and staying at a hotel not fifteen minutes away. Willow could not go and see her, but, if he used the embassy wisely, Willow could enter, and Smiley – briefly – emerge. It was undoubtedly unprofessional, but as a practical matter the risk was negligible, and it was precisely the sort of concession to humanity that was his due as a consulting ex-spy rather than a full-time member of the Circus.

The sales assistant inside was taller than Ann but had her colour, and with Susanna's doubtful aid he chose and purchased a scarf of blue silk which might do well for convertible motoring, walking in the high passes or aviation. Above all, it was a frivolous, expensive and useless thing, suitable only for the expression of love. He urged more ribbon to the parcel, and excessive curls and loops. When the job was done, it was almost grotesque, and he put it proudly and carefully under his arm. Susanna felt a curious wash of pride, almost affection, as she realised he had done something that was, for him, very difficult.

'Willow,' Smiley said, to the impertinent guard at the gate, 'James. I have an appointment with Sandy Layton.'

The British Embassy in Vienna occupied a cream box which resembled every nearby building without being one of them. The ornamentation which dignified the windows of its neighbours had either been stripped away for security or never added to what might be a poor copy of the Viennese style. Stark, blockish and inelegant, it looked like a barracks pony at a show for retired race horses.

The guard seemed to think he was on to something, perhaps

that Smiley was a clear felon, but a short while later confirmation was forthcoming via the black corded telephone in the security box, and, with a bad grace, the boy let him through.

Inside, the place was no kinder than out. The reception desk was small and screened off, and Smiley stood while the reception-ist licked her index finger before turning each page of the ledger, looking for some detail that did not satisfy her. Eventually, a narrow, reddish face appeared like a dormouse from behind one of the veneered room dividers.

'Mr Willow?'

'Yes,' Smiley said.

'Layton,' the woman said. 'Sandy. With trade,' she added. 'Do come this way. Alice, I'll take this one.'

Alice, perpetually unsatisfied, made a moue of distaste, as if Sandy being involved explained everything. Which no doubt it did, if the embassy diplomats had identified Sandy as belonging as much to the Circus as to the pleasant and upstanding world of international cooperation.

'First right,' Layton said. 'It's a pleasure to see you, sir. We did meet, back in England. Three years ago, I think.'

Smiley distantly recalled her from the graduating class at Sar-ratt: industrious and bland, a combination he greatly admired.

Layton ushered him to a long, narrow room without win-dows, with a desk at the far end and a telex machine which plugged into an alarmingly large green metal cabinet.

'You're to have top-shelf access,' Layton said. 'The cipher clerks are at your disposal if you want them, and so am I. There's a package waiting for you. Arrived in the overnight bag.' She looked doubtfully at the loops and ribbons of Ann's gift.

'Is that something you'd like me to put in the safe?'

'Oh, yes,' Smiley said, after a moment. 'Highly classified.'

He watched her bear it off as if it might at any moment explode.

*

Guillam must have been very quick, to the point that Smiley suspected he had sent a flash message to Control even before briefing Smiley the day before. The care package from London included the best summary of Karla's life Connie and Katrin could provide.

Karla, Soviet agent, real name: unknown. Born turn of the century, possibly just before, which made him a child of the Tsarist times and a first-generation Soviet, with all the undiminished fire that entailed. Exact age: likewise unknown. Rumoured to be one of the original Moscow spies, the founding intake of the Thirteenth Directorate trained by the legendary Arno Berg, himself the star apprentice of Metternich. Fought in Spain in nineteen thirty-six, details: unknown. Infiltrated into Germany through Rostock in nineteen forty-three, tasked with reconnaissance and recruitment for intelligence operations against the Third Reich. In forty-four, thought to have assassinated the local SS commander using a shrapnel bomb placed in the headboard of his bed. During the Russian advance through the Baltics, commanding officer of a small group charged with locating and neutralising Nazi guerrilla units operating around and behind the fluid lines of control. Fleeting appearances after the war in Japan, Hong Kong and finally North America, establishing Soviet radio networks under the tutelage of Andrei Rudnev, Chief, Thirteenth Directorate. Arrested, New Delhi, nineteen fifty-five under the name Heinrich Gerstmann, where he was interviewed, with an eye to recruitment, by one G. Smiley. Result: no further action. Voluntarily returned to Moscow, where until recently he was believed to have been shot.

Smiley looked down at the page. He remembered Gerstmann, of course, and that night in the Delhi jail, though at the time he'd had no idea who he was talking to. If he'd known, they might have had more to say to each other; Smiley was pretty sure they'd just missed meeting in Magdeburg in forty-four, and again in the New Year at Rathenow. Meaningless now, but what about then? Political leaders were advised by their intelligencers, and those intelligencers told their stories from what they knew and had seen. Understanding of the world flowed up the chain of command. If a dozen men and women on what would soon be opposing sides of the East–West divide had had the chance to speak, would the divide have materialised at all? Would the Soviet leadership still have understood 'encirclement' as 'strangulation'?

But no such chance encounter had occurred, and Gerstmann had been just another Soviet officer in distress, struggling to stay above water in the time after Stalin, and – like most of them – all set to fail. Smiley hadn't known it on the day, but he was himself quite ill, and he had not handled the meeting well. Gerstmann sat in absolute silence while Smiley babbled in a fevered semi-dream, and then mutely indicated that the interview was at an end. Smiley, on a human level, had regretted that the man was choosing the firing squad. It seemed such a waste of anybody. Personally, however, he'd felt a little relieved. He thought he'd appeared both indiscreet and foolish, and now those memories would go out of the world with the little man whose quiet had up-ended his own.

But Karla had survived, and here he was, at or near the top. His identity now had meaning that went far beyond Róka and Leó. His history suggested an idealist, one who had lashed himself to the mast of the Communist ship and genuinely believed he was doing right. Like Róka, or Smiley, or Prideaux, or Haydon, or really anyone of their approximate age and profession, he found himself contending with a world that was accelerated, volatile and, in the long history of human horror, uniquely capable of destruction. The combination argued for the possibility of a conflict less ugly, less obviously destined to spiral into dangerously open violence.

By contrast, the word from Moscow was that Karla and Pogodin were at daggers drawn. Pogodin resented the other man's presence and thought him jumped-up: a field agent pretending to operations. Karla's opinion of Pogodin went unvoiced, but over seven years he had by stealth and compromise annihilated Pogodin's political support and broken his cadre within the Thirteenth Directorate, so that now their positions from fifty-five were reversed: it was Pogodin who was alone, isolated, and Pogodin who was casting about desperately for anything that would turn back the tide. Karla must have vulnerabilities. He was a man of a certain age; he had a past and a story. Somewhere, hidden amid his successes and the flaws of other men, there were appetites and consequences waiting to bring him down.

But Pogodin could not find them, and the harder he looked, the more emptiness awaited. Karla had read Richelieu's maxim and understood its reciprocal meaning. If six lines in a man's handwriting were enough to hang him, the man who would be safe from his enemies must leave no such traces, written or otherwise. He must erase even the memories of those around him or – if that cannot be achieved – erase them instead; and this, Karla had done, with appalling completeness. Pogodin had found no one left in Moscow who knew Karla's other lives. He had cut himself out of his own history, and his present was so unreachable it might as well be a city glimpsed in the clouds.

Smiley's hope – it was too much by far to call it a theory – was that this was what Ferenc Róka had quite accidentally threatened to reveal; that Róka could somehow connect the man in Moscow with the life he had lived. If Pogodin could obtain Róka, he would once again have access to the pressures by which Karla might be moved or destroyed. And Pogodin, for the moment, seemed to have no idea that the door was open, that on the right day at the right hour he might walk through it to the very place he wished to see. Instead of Pogodin, it was Smiley who might glimpse through the crack the private world of this Karla, who had so terrified Mundt, and whose dark incurious eyes had once regarded a floundering Smiley across that table in the Delhi jail – and who was the coming man within Moscow Centre's most aggressive secret department.

Whether or not Smiley's conceit regarding Róka proved accurate, the most obvious operational move was perhaps to offer Pogodin a lifeline; to court him, win him and extract him for all that he could reveal – which would be a bountiful harvest of secrets, sure enough. That was Control's end of things, by his own order as much as Smiley's preference. A Prideaux or a Haydon might make that approach, even Sam Collins, if Control wanted a younger man. Not George Smiley, who must stay on the lee side of the Iron Curtain, and was in any case retired to spend time with his family.

Although, if one could seize Pogodin, there was a second game beyond that, where one might leverage Róka and Pogodin together to have Karla into the bargain, and take the whole top off the Thirteenth, to the confusion – convulsion – of the Kremlin.

And then what? Having used the man's loves to bring him down, then what? Would Moscow abruptly suffer a shortage of brutal and brutalised men, thinking to make good whatever sink-holes were in them by destroying the West? By finally achieving Peter the Great's ambitions and standing Russia at the pinnacle of the world? Would the Cold War, with all its terrible arsenals and its power to compress and unshape ordinary lives, come to an end? Would the nuclear demon go back to hell, and the fear of a Russian land invasion sweeping everything before it, not stopping until it reached Normandy and Lagos and Palermo, fade into history because Karla fell to Smiley's most unknightly lance? Or was all this to and fro between them just a way to stay busy while God disposed? There had to be something more, something better, or what was the point?

Leamas was laughing. They were drunk in a bar in Porto, in Hong Kong, in Damascus. They were walking together by the Danube where it wells up in the German hills, while Smiley contemplated proposing to Ann and Leamas urged him not to wait, to find out one way or the other. He was sorting through Alec's shoes in the empty flat, and contemplating the impossibility of death: the death of friends and brothers and fathers, of anyone whose departure from the world makes it dimmer and more awful. He was sitting in a grain cellar in Germany, listening to a man he had met seconds before risking his life to send a patrol the other way: *No, no, down the road, I saw him, on a bicycle. A tall man, perhaps American! It is every citizen's duty to serve the Fatherland. I hope he is shot when you catch him.* He was in Control's ghastly office, eyes unfocused as he gave his account of gunfire at the Wall.

Leamas was still laughing, and there was no malice in it, not even pity. The world was funny, and only Alec got the joke.

'Christ's sake, Smiley! He as much as told you: do it your way. If you've got a better idea, now's the bloody time. I'll back you. To the hilt, to the end of the road. The sticking point. Every last drop of blood.'

But then, abruptly, he was gone. He had not indicated that he was leaving or said his goodbyes; he just wasn't there any more. Smiley wept without moving his hands to his face or writhing, though he imagined doing both and thought he should. It was as if he had no volition at all, and the only life left in him was the water running down his cheeks.

What other way was there? How do you offer peace to an enemy you never wanted, but whom you are already fighting? Who has already wounded you terribly, and proposes to do more of the same? An enemy whose fatal mistake may have been made before you ever knew one another, or discovered your opposition?

'What have you brought me?' Sandy Layton inquired, when Smiley wandered into her office looking for something he couldn't name.

'Nothing,' Smiley said. 'Just thinking.'

She shook her head. 'Vienna's gone funny,' she said. 'Today and yesterday. What's going on?'

'What sort of funny?'

'All the snails have gone back in their shells. Whatever you're here for, it's bringing weather.'

She raised her eyebrows in hope and expectation, but Smiley shook his head. 'I'm afraid I've no idea,' he said, and left her to growl into her breakfast.

That afternoon, in what Susanna took to be an excess of caution, Smiley moved them from the Grand Habsburg Hotel where they had been staying to rooms at the König von Ungarn, which boasted two hundred years in the trade – though, as Lake had pointed out with some relief on arrival, it had seen a bit of work since Mozart stayed there.

'A superstition,' Smiley assured her, 'nothing more.' But she noticed that, while Lake distracted the porter with some preposterous question about room service, Smiley ran his thumb lightly over the glass of the pictures on the walls. His nail slid effortlessly down the surface, and he nodded faintly, as if satisfied.

The porter dismissed, Lake raised his eyebrows.

'I'm sure the Grand Habsburg are merely careful to protect their guests from the risk of splintering,' Smiley replied. 'Happily, the König is a more traditional hotel.'

'I need you to do something for me,' Smiley told Lake a little later, in a private meeting room downstairs. 'And, as I said in Berlin, it will be dangerous.' Smiley held up a hand to forestall Lake's inevitable reply. 'Please hear the whole thing, and give me your professional opinion. Cold-headed. It does nothing for us if you are caught. The outcome is what matters, not the will.'

Lake settled himself, and nodded.

'I should infinitely prefer,' Smiley said, 'to take our time. The best intelligence work is slow. In this case, however, we move to Róka's schedule, and Moscow's. He initiates, they counter, and we come along last, hoping to finesse the product of their recent enmity and take advantage of their mutual efforts at obfuscation. Securing Leó was our best option. We now proceed to the next. We have so far accepted the idea that the participants in this drama are Karla, Róka, Leó and ourselves. We have ignored the other actor on this stage, who is not only influential by her relationships but also formidable in her own right: Irén Pártos, Leó's mother. Irén's significant virtue from our perspective is that we know where she is. Adjunct Professor of Poetry and Literature at Budapest University. At a minimum we can hope to reach Róka through her. Even better, if she can be persuaded to remove herself entirely from Budapest and come to the West. Róka's calculus must then shift in our favour. If he cannot help Leó, he can at least be with Leó's mother and hope that the Circus will be willing to extract his son in exchange for whatever secrets he can supply to us.'

To Susanna's ear, it sounded grimly instrumental, as if Smiley himself felt it was a step in the wrong direction. Last week if she had said something was a necessary evil, she would have meant an irritation. Now she contemplated the last word in all its meanings.

Lake meanwhile had evolved into something new and clinical which was if anything even more alarming. She had expected him to be excited, but the boyishness had evaporated from his face, and for the first time he seemed to belong in Smiley's world, and to understand its offices.

'Talking is fine,' Lake said. 'Train from here to there, go to the baths and a couple of churches, then off to the university. Maybe I'm writing a book about the Ottomans in Europe. Tomb of Gül Baba and, oops, bump into her in the hallway, I've read your poetry, madame, I've never been so honoured in my life. Hungary is misunderstood in London, you must come and lecture,

I know a fellow at SOAS. But that's talking. Getting her out, that's another matter. Moscow must be all over her. The only reason she's still running around loose is because they're expecting their boy to come in and try the same thing – and he knows her, she'll make it easy for him. Me, she'll see coming, one way or another. Maybe she thinks I'm one of theirs, playing at the English bloody fool, maybe she gets it right and wants no part of that either. But in the best case I can hardly pinch a long-distance lorry and hide her under the seat, can I?'

'Suppose it were a kidnapping,' Smiley suggested. 'For the purposes of planning, only. What if we had no cooperation from her at all. Does that make it harder, or easier?'

'If there were three or four of me, and we had a week to plan,' Lake said. 'I might say that was a better option. As it is, no. It's talk; and, if she fancies a midnight flit, it's going to need everything thrown at it, including the embassy in Budapest. They'll scream bloody murder, but we'll have to get her in somehow, pretend she's not there while we change her look and the fuss dies down, then it's the dip two-step: bring someone over on an FO passport, transfer that to Irén and off she goes to London, give it a week and our courier walks out on an ordinary tourist pass we've fitted up in the meantime. That part is someone else's problem. Embassies are strictly off-limits to my lot; I'm told we get mud on the carpets. So from the gate it's lamplighters, and hope they have their little ways. If things really go to hell, it's a straight coin toss: get Irén some ordinary documents and run for the nearest border post. Hope like hell to catch them napping and we're faster than the telephone.' He shrugged. 'Bad odds, Mr Smiley.'

Smiley nodded. 'In the first instance, we need her to use whatever communication channel she has with Róka to tell him that we have information about Leó. Which we do, albeit thus far only of the negative variety. We send him a way to get in touch with us, and then, if we can, we extract the lady. But we can't necessarily trust her. They may well be using Leó as a rod for her back. Bring us your lover and we'll give you your son. How much easier to give them an actual British spy?'

Susanna looked curiously at Lake. *'Beszélsz magyarul?'*

'Yes,' Lake replied in English, 'but not well enough to pass, and we don't let the nice police know we patter local. It gives them the unkind notion we might be a spy.'

Pushing the table back along one wall, they practised Lake's approach to Irén Pártos, with Susanna playing her part and Smiley looking on. Lake's first approach was very distant and properly British, as if he'd suddenly been consumed by the manners of an officer and a gentleman. He was both too elliptical and too formal, so that he seemed to Susanna to be bringing news of a death, without the mercy of bluntness. They did it again, and then again, until she lost patience.

'Irén is Hungarian,' she told Lake, 'and a partisan. She has an acquaintance with sorrow. If you stall, she will assume the worst and she will hate you for being slow. When you tell her it's not that bad, she'll hate you again for making her afraid.'

'And you won't have long,' Smiley added. 'You must think of her as a fellow professional. Which, of course, she is, by the way.'

The next round was better. This time they started at the beginning, and walked through his contrived chance encounter. Lake blundered convincingly and was covered in confusion, then realised who it was exactly that he'd had the honour of knocking over, and his contrition knew no bounds. Smiley warned him not to rehearse that part too much, lest it become obviously false and land them both in trouble, but Lake responded that he needed the springboard, and, anyway, he could always claim to be in love or obsessed. They went again.

'I must talk to you regarding your son,' Lake told Susanna, taking her hand and speaking urgently as he shook it, eyes locked on her own. 'I believe I can assist you, and his father, in securing his release and your safety, but you must trust me. I know this will not be natural for you, but we have very little time. If you are willing to contemplate what I am offering, laugh as if I have embarrassed you.'

She laughed on reflex, because he had. She was for the first time aware of him physically: the scale of him, and the restrained power in his body. It was amazing to her that she had walked alongside this creature and been so distracted that she hadn't noticed him before. She knew it was performance, but it wasn't any less affecting for all that, which offended her and also made it more impressive.

'A little less, Tom, perhaps,' Smiley said, but Susanna disagreed.

'No. It should be big. Too much.' She saw Smiley frown, and tried to put her instinct into words. 'If it's unwise, it feels innocent. If it's within bounds, it's suspect.'

Irén, she thought, would find it no less compelling than she did, and would be instinctively against turning him in. Rash. Young. Beautiful. She had a son like that. Likely Róka had been the same when Irén fell in love with him. This was not a gap in her defences; it was the very thing she defended.

Smiley had already acknowledged that his guess in this might not be the equal of hers. His hand sketched permission in the air: go again. Lake returned to first position, and Susanna once more came into the room as if she had no idea he was waiting. She had to seal her hand against her side to stop it twitching in his direction when he moved, and when he touched her she clamped down hard on a sharp exhalation.

'I must speak with you regarding your son,' Lake said, and she thought: yes. By all means.

Was there a real danger that poor Irén Pártos would want to run off with him, and to hell with Róka? If so, was that intentional? Was Lake doing it on purpose? Was Smiley ordering him to? Or was she the only one who noticed the sudden weight of his presence when he went from babysitter to operational man? He had the same easy movement as the disgraceful Bill, the same comfort in his skin. In Lake, however, it was not a game. It was simply the man himself, laid out like produce on a grocer's board.

'I must tell you something regarding –'

The idea was appealing but unhelpful in the moment. She sighed and let it fade.

'I must speak to you, madame –'

In the event that Irén took the bait, then Lake should organise a second meeting with a very simple protocol: the nearest church at a given time, with a fallback three hours later at another. He would pass by a short while before, and, if he was sure it was safe, go ahead and meet her. If he wasn't, he was to skip the first treff and the fallback entirely and reacquire her near her home, but only if in his judgement the coast was clear. The terms of engagement were deliberately loose, because Smiley wanted Lake to have the maximum latitude.

'If the best you can do is a brief conversation,' Smiley said, 'that's already excellent. I know you're willing to take risks, but, unless the upside is very clear, I'm not interested in courage. We live by results, alas.'

'What about at the meet?' Lake asked. 'What do I tell her? I can hardly say we asked the Stasi Chief of Operations in Berlin, and he says it's all gravy.'

'You tell her the truth,' Smiley said, after some consideration. 'The truth but not all of it. That we have sources which tell us Leó was arrested and released, that the Russians are involved directly and that a man was sent to London on bad business. We know Róka is not ideologically disposed towards the West, but we are willing to help, and he has an acute shortage of other friends. Don't offer money; it will offend her.' He glanced at Susanna for confirmation, and she nodded. 'As far as his connection with Moscow is concerned, that relationship is irretrievable, whatever Róka may wish. Harto Latour is proof enough of that. You can even mention Karla – he's made enough noise in Berlin that knowledge of his presence there hardly implicates Mundt.

Tell her you believe this is their best and only chance at a life, for themselves and for Leó. Which it is, after all, and you must make her feel your conviction.'

Lake nodded. 'She'll push on Leó. She'll want certainty.'

'I'm sure she will. It's better for us if you don't give it to her. Too much clarity is itself suspect. You may allow her to believe that Róka's cooperation can be partial, that he need not disgorge everything he knows, only sufficient to pay for what help we can give. And you should encourage her in what I imagine is her most desperate hope: that Leó is alive.'

Susanna found that her head had snapped around to look at him, but Smiley's whole attention was on Lake. Lake, in turn, looked at his shoes. Don't lie to her. Let her lie to herself. Don't deceive her. Foster her need.

Lake wasn't comfortable. 'And if that's not enough?'

Susanna waited. She knew what he would say. In the event, Lake would have to confess that Leó was missing. To do otherwise would be to cross the line, and, when Irén and Róka arrived in London and discovered they had been deceived, their cooperation would be withdrawn. But once Lake admitted the limits of his knowledge, Irén would throw him out. What they had was just not enough, even in desperation, and, worse: it hinted at the darkest outcome.

Smiley looked back at Lake. 'Then you lie, Tom. It's a bad lie because it is ultimately unsustainable, but we can manufacture support for a few days. A story in the *Daily Mail* somewhere on the second page. Daring escape: a small group of right-thinking students evade the devilish clutches of the oppressive Socialist machine. A tunnel, or, better: a balloon. The press adore balloons; they find the metaphor irresistible. A picture of three young men and an attractive young woman with smudged faces, smiling at an anonymous location in the company of diverse officials. Johann Schmidt times two, Inge Fuchs times one, and Leó Pártos, the Hungarian Houdini who masterminded the whole escape, all now safe and secure in the West. If it were sufficiently blurry, Róka might accept the image as Leó and come. And indeed, even if he had doubts, it's unlikely he could stay away. We'd have our man, for whatever good it would do us once he discovered the truth.' He looked at Susanna. 'But he would be alive.'

Susanna imagined the scene: Bánáti arriving, surrendering all his advantages to hope and then having that hope dashed. It seemed a poor way to discharge her obligations, and likely would get the response it deserved: a quiet damnation, a severance without farewell. Another father left behind, as her own track wound ever on towards some place where she could stop running, start building and actually be someone. Be who? Build what? It seemed unlikely that the answer to either would come from stepping on Bánáti's heart.

She wanted to ask if they'd really do such a thing, but the question was suddenly absurd. They were spies. Deception and betrayal were their legitimate tactics. She wondered what else. Did they assassinate? She looked at Lake, at the easy physical confidence. At the very least they knew how – of course they did. They must. Nations did murder, either in whispers or out loud. She was a fool not to have thought of it before, and, in that light, simply lying to a desperate father was small potatoes.

'The Stasi wouldn't know whether we'd made it up or not,' Lake submitted.

Smiley's gaze went from Lake to Susanna. 'I'm sorry.' And now she knew what he was apologising for, and what she was supposed to do. She was to be a lifeline in that narrow window of time when the mark believed, but could not know, that his son was coming to him. Then, when they manufactured some accident, or some Moscow outrage of revenge, and crushed the hope, she was to be the remedy. She would step into Leó's place and soothe his pain with a daughter's care, and keep the secrets flowing. And she could tell herself it was for the best. If they didn't do it this way, Bánáti would die, and likely Irén, and they would lose mother, father and son to the grave, and all their mysteries with them. Moscow would be the only winner. She could even believe they might bring Leó home, after all. She had every opportunity and every reason to accept.

Save his life, break his heart, then steal the pieces from the dead.

Smiley shook himself.

'Back to it,' he said. 'I'm afraid we can't spare the time.'

A moment later, Lake clasped her arm and drew her in, and again the eyes held her.

'Madame, I must speak with you regarding Leó, your son. It is quite urgent. I believe I can help you. Perhaps we can find a quiet place.'

She felt her anger spark in response, felt the pull of him and the push of revulsion at the lie. She listened to the practised lines and heard the sincerity, the commitment in him, the full belief that what he was saying was the right thing to say, and how he would use that in himself to perpetrate what was by any reasonable standard a deep deception. A deception she was helping him practise on a woman she had no cause to hate and a man who had only ever treated her honestly, and she yanked her hand back, seeing bewilderment in his honest, beautiful, lying face.

Smiley, she could not bear to look at.

'I'm going to take a walk,' she said. 'I'll be back in time for –' Was she really going to say 'dinner'? In time to lie to a woman about her dead son and to call in her living lover to share the pain?

She left it unspoken, and fled.

Susanna found, a few moments later, that she had left the hotel and was walking through the pretty, pointless shopping streets. She had had the presence of mind to bring her coat, and she wondered if she would just keep walking until she was somewhere else, somewhere that was out of this moment in her life. She had, after all, done it before, though a child arriving cap in hand is subject to different scrutinies and demands from those imposed upon a woman in her twenties. She had done it again to get herself into this mess, bolting to Control's office and demanding to continue the story and help Bánáti, and that had brought her here, to this bad solution and its limited outcomes. She should not complain that the world declined to arrange itself to her specification. She could turn once more and run, but, considering it, she found that flight was not what she wanted. She had no desire to retreat before this enemy. She wanted to smash it, drag it down and break it on the ground. She found herself asking what bargain might be made with the universe: if I commit, if I do something more, what will you give me? She knew the mood for a lie. It was the desperation of the victim before the torture, the illusion of hope in the face of a machine that took no notice of circumstance.

She walked, and reason seeped in around the edges of her fury. Very well, let it come. Was Smiley right, after all? Was he doing the only thing that made sense? How better to make it right?

Bánáti as she knew him would do anything for Leó. If his present course was disaster, then it was the nature of that 'anything' that must change. First, he had to be found, and then persuaded. Was Leó's fate itself still amenable to change? That was unknown, and parenthetically she must acknowledge that, without that information, it was possible Bánáti's track also was fixed, that it led into death one way or another. If we're being brutally honest with ourselves, then let us by all means be truly honest.

Grant that salvation is achievable, or else why are we all here? Assume, in spite of evidence, that God, or the universe, looks kindly on strivers. Ask yourself: by what means can he be persuaded, if not the granting of his wish? He will see any defection from his course as damnation. What would Leó say? It depended on the nature of the child. Bánáti's son would answer loudly: don't be such a fool. *Get out, drink wine, live as you can. This storm is greater than you. I don't want to wash ashore and find you drowned looking for me.* Róka's child was another question, abandoned into the care of his mother and the Hungarian state. Though Róka had loved Irén, and still did, which made her by definition a woman of consequence.

She rounded a corner and found St Stephen's outlined against the sky. Inside, someone was rehearsing, a choir with an impossible treble lamenting the Christ, but the master was not satisfied, and the boy kept going back and back, repeating the same few bars.

Without intervention, Róka would do the same. Ask the same question again and again, receive the same answer, until eventually his tradecraft – she heard the word in her head, the argot of her newly acquired profession – until his tradecraft eventually failed him, and he walked into a bullet.

Against which, Smiley would send Lake to lie by omission, by implication, would drag Irén and Róka both to London and keep them safe, squeeze them out and leave them dry and dusty. If he could bring Leó home, it would be forgivable, she supposed, making the lie into a truth. If he could not, then it would be monstrous. And she believed Leó was dead. Every instinct in her, narrative and Hungarian both, cried out that his vanishing was an end point. There was a time before and a time after Leó, and they lived in the second.

Which Róka likely also knew, and could not accept, and so he would reject Lake anyway, reject any lie short of the absolute one: we have your son. He is safe and sound in Charing Cross.

Lake would be pushed to that point, she realised. He would speak to Irén and she, knowing Róka's heartbeat and his soul, would demand more and more clarity, more commitment, and Lake – the good operational man – would ultimately provide it. Smiley was giving him that permission, that latitude. He would come home and apologise: I had to cross the line. *Ego te absolvo.* The historical process requires – no, that excuse belonged to the other side. The political necessity entails.

She saw Róka's face as he received the news. He's not here. We lied.

No, she realised, she could not permit it. Anything at all was better than that. In saying this aloud to her unrevealing reflection in the mirror, she realised that there was another choice if she had the courage – the madness – to take it. It required her to betray Smiley's trust, but he had demonstrably betrayed hers, and there was an older loyalty at stake which she found compelling.

If Róka, in his secret heart, believed as she did but could not speak the words, then perhaps he could hear them from someone who stood outside his family but within his life. Someone who cared enough to do something foolish. Who had no right to his paternal affection, yet upon whom it had already been conferred. Someone who represented a life in place of the one he had already lost and could not relinquish.

She could cross the border into Hungary, and go and meet with Irén Pártos. She, in her own person, was a Hungarian woman. Her voice would confirm it; she knew the streets of the city and its moods, its unspoken and undocumented shibboleths. What if she went, and spoke to Irén, and then perhaps even to Bánáti himself? He must, surely, listen to her. The very insanity of her presence, of her journey across Europe in the company of British spies and her defection again to her own side – which was made up, she supposed, entirely of herself and the family she sought to reunite – was patently absurd, as his own journey was, and this must be persuasive. He could not think any plan so hare-brained was the choice of a master manipulator.

She would not reproach him or demand that he stop. She would not tell him outright that Leó was dead. He would reject it, and rightly. There was a slim chance. People did get lost in the machine, did emerge weeks, months, years later after being misfiled. He would cling to that in the face of every other instinct. No. She would say instead what she knew from Smiley: that his efforts were taking him deeper by far than he had intended; that he was mired in something that would drown him and everyone around him; that his pursuit, now, by these means, only increased the likelihood that Leó would die. He must come back with her, and give up his pride, his ideological faith, for a last throw of the dice. He had already written off his own life for his son. How hard could it be to sacrifice his politics?

She would have Irén for an ally, she thought. Irén must recognise that she stood to lose both the men she loved if everything continued on its present track. Susanna would be offering tacitly the rescue of the man if the boy could not be salvaged, and the hope of preserving both. The cost would be nothing more than or less than leaving Hungary – a cost she could confirm was not beyond paying, although if Irén were to point out that here she was, in Budapest, even now, Susanna would have to concede the city's unexpected gravity.

How? Lake had said the train: good enough. She would need money and a ticket. She had spending money from the Circus, but it was for cups of tea, not travel. She realised she had the accounts of Bánáti & Clay to draw on. She could call the bank. It was not a fortune, not to run for the hills, but it was substantial if one were doing something foolish and needed funds.

She'd have to be able to explain her presence outside Hungary – a cultural exchange, say, a trade conference – but not her need to leave again, because by that point it would be the Circus extracting her with Irén, or Róka extracting them both. For this she did not need to be able to escape the pull of Hungary, only let it drag her in again and hold her close.

She needed a passport. The Hofbauer one would not serve. It belonged to the Circus, and if she was going to do this, then – like Róka – she could not trust a tool she did not control. She needed one that called her what she was, a local, a woman coming home. Róka himself had shown her the solution – but that first step would be hard. It was the point after which she would be travelling downhill until she arrived at Irén's door, and some-where along that slope lay the moment at which she would be entirely on her own.

She turned around and went back to the hotel. There was a bank of phones in the lobby. From there, she called a friend in London and prevailed on her to look in the Brick Lane Yellow Pages for a particular number, which she jotted down on the courtesy pad provided for that purpose. Without breaking her flow – because if she did she was aware that her second thoughts would crash in upon her – she dialled. It was very late, even with the time difference, and she expected to get an answering machine. Instead she heard a soft, cultured voice in English asking to know what he could do to help, and she told him.

'Late tomorrow now,' Vishwakarma said. 'My man will bring it to Vienna. You tell me how you want it delivered.' He paused. 'This isn't the same account number we discussed.'

'We rotate them,' Susanna said. 'For additional security.' Bánáti had a client who swore by this. The man lived partly in Monaco, and his relationship with British taxation was at best tenuous. She had no idea if it worked, and hoped that Vishwakarma knew no more about the financing of espionage operations than she did.

'Of course,' he said. 'Security, I quite understand.' It occurred to her that he didn't care. It didn't matter whether he believed her explanation, only that she supplied one, and filled in the gap.

She rang off and composed herself to a shamed contrition, putting on her best wan little smile as she returned to the practice room. No one – and most certainly not Smiley – must have cause to ask how she had spent that intervening time. It was a young woman's brief attack of conscience in the face of necessity. Understandable, even laudable in another circumstance, and her surrender now to the tides of realpolitik was no less so. A coming of age, she told herself. I have embraced the lie, and now we are the same. Which was true, albeit not along the axis she desperately needed them to assume.

She put her hand against the grain of the door and pushed it open, ducked her head like a penitent sinner and made her entrance quietly, meeting Lake's eyes, and then Smiley's.

'Sorry. I'm not used to this,' she told them. 'I'll do better.' And, indeed, she did. In the space of forty intense minutes, she coached Lake in the niceties of Hungarian womanhood as she understood it through memories of her mother, and insisted on a direct frankness which was quite at odds with Smiley's inclination and Lake's rough-hewn chivalry. After all, it hardly mattered now what she said. It wasn't happening any more. Circumstance would bend to her. This was just performance.

'Irén does not admire nonsense,' she snapped, when Lake was elliptical. 'She will trust the commodity she does not often see. She wants truth, even if it is unpleasant. She is a partisan. She bares her teeth in the face of horror. Again! And this time, make me believe in your respect.'

Lake went again, and then again, until she was satisfied that he had abandoned any notion of gentleness, and Smiley, seeing the work finished, stopped them to rest.

'Very good,' he told her. 'Really, very good indeed. Thank you.'

She was embarrassed by his pride, and almost told him everything, but she had chosen now, and sooner or later you had to do, rather than just imagine.

Did Smiley know? If one were speaking of Control, the question would be easy. Control was heedless of the injuries he did in the course of the work. He moved people by heavy nudges; he was not above the spur or the whip. Control absolutely would have pushed Susanna to her choice, and thought it well done. Smiley, though: would George Smiley, in that strange moment of his long career, when he believed himself no more a master of spies, and aspired instead to something fleshy and trivial in the daylight world; when Alec Leamas's ghost was at his shoulder and he wanted above all to show that the brutal passages of his recent life were an aberration and not his underlying truth – would Smiley, then, have set her on this path?

Among those who knew him best, opinion was unevenly divided. Esterhase said definitely not, and Guillam concurred. Ann kept her silence, as always. Bill Haydon, alone, advanced the notion, with his usual fiery certainty: that Smiley chose to let Susanna know the lie was in play, and reject it, and from that put herself on the board instead. Haydon pointed out that it was only by Smiley's direct intervention that she knew of Raghuraman Vishwakarma at all, let alone how to get in touch with him – an unforgivable lapse in operational security which would be quite alien to clever George – but which, if you accept it as deliberate, implies that Smiley had always allowed for the possibility that he might need her to go rogue, albeit positioned exactly where he could put his hand on her, should the moment arise. And again: would Smiley really have left her angry and untended for so long, even in the planning of Lake's infiltration into Hungary? Would he have made the mistake of taking his eye off his charge, on pain of Millie McCraig's displeasure?

Haydon said not.

However you read the runes, it was that evening in Vienna that the whole business of Róka and Leó Pártos began to come entirely off the rails.

Smiley's plan for his surprise meeting with Ann had been quite uncharacteristically flash. He would arrive at the hotel and give Ann the present from the boutique by St Stephen's. She would admire both the elegance of it and its absolute impracticality, and recognise also that he was committing a deep professional sin in coming to see her. This would impress her as a reconfirmation of his departure from the Circus. They would eat a light supper, and afterwards – still with a sense of stolen time – they would return to her hotel room and make love. Only then would he have to leave her again, and return to the business of Ferenc Róka, and that briefly, for long enough to bring it home. With Róka in hand, he was done, and the mountains – and the rest of his life – would still be waiting.

Standing in the lobby, he had been struck suddenly by a sense of presumption. He should have called ahead, and afforded her the time to prepare. In doing otherwise, he had taken upon himself the big entrance which was her particular joy. Happily, there was still a window. He took himself to the concierge's desk and asked him to telephone the room and inform Lady Ann that she had a visitor, and would she meet him in the jazz bar as soon as possible. The concierge, suitably lubricated with a large note, agreed that this was indeed entirely possible, and showed Smiley to a booth. Smiley sat and waited, and then waited some more, until he was concerned about the timing. He returned to the concierge's desk and found the man looking very grave.

'Lady Ann regrets,' he said, shaking his head. 'She and her husband are engaged.'

This information was so incomprehensible that Smiley for a long moment felt honestly embarrassed. He should have known better, he thought, and what could be more reasonable? It took a full minute for him to realise that he was Ann's husband, and to gather the implication. Then he stood, fingers pressing hard into his palms, his face flaming. The concierge affected a polite ignorance.

He wondered what would happen if he went upstairs anyway and banged on the door, called out to her. He thought perhaps he should, that she would recognise the bravery in it, and the offer. Not forgiveness – that would be mutually owed – but continuation of the track they had been on before Control sent Millie McCraig calling. The life we were going to have. It still exists. It can be chosen now, tonight. If we both are very brave.

But what if she chose otherwise? What if he went, and she did not answer the door? Or, worse, she did, and closed it? Tomorrow might bring better chances. Tonight might bring only pain.

Knowing it was the wrong thing, that tomorrow would be too late, he asked the concierge to put the scarf in the cubbyhole for her room, and turned around. As he left, he thought everybody in the lobby was watching, and seeing his cowardice. He returned to the hotel and slept, telling no one.

With Smiley and Susanna both early to bed, Lake had the jitters. He often did in the run-up to an operation, and the more so when he was in hiatus, everything ready but still awaiting the go code. He paced in his room, then felt sorry for whoever had the one underneath and took himself downstairs to the bar. He set himself a strict maximum of two drinks, played a few rounds of cards for pin money with a bored American woman and her German husband, then took a late walk without a coat, breathing the cold air and making his body work to keep itself warm. It was a trick he'd picked up in his navy days; the training officers, themselves veterans of a dozen bad places, had sworn by it.

He considered heading over to one of the city's rangier areas – Vienna hardly had a bad part of town, but you could always find trouble. He might, he supposed, get into a fist fight, just for practice, but the possibility of police attention or cracked knuckles steered him away. Instead, he walked along the Danube, looking at the ripples and listening to the sound of the shipping. Somewhere east of here the same river ran through the city where Irén Pártos was waiting. The river, it seemed to him, stretched not only geographically but in time, and united him with his future in Budapest.

I must talk to you about your son, Leó. It is quite urgent. We have very little time.

When he was thoroughly freezing, he walked back, warmed up in front of the lobby fire and found himself blissfully exhausted.

The following day, with Layton's help, Smiley located a Hungarian barber in Vienna's outer sprawl, and Lake returned from his chair with a working man's trim that wouldn't stand out in a Budapest street. There was something old world about him in this mode which made Smiley uneasy, having too much of the flavour of bad operations past, where earnest Circus assets had walked, all unknowing, directly into enemy hands.

The thought made him first pettish and then, by compensation, chatty. He and Lake debated over clothes. From a flea market which took place in a churchyard after the morning service, Lake had found a Hungarian suit in his rough size, made seven years before. Smiley worried that it was too familiar, and that people would begin to assume Lake was actually Hungarian. They wanted him to be able to walk unregarded in a crowd, but his cover, of necessity, identified him as a foreigner, and if he blended too well and was then revealed, there might be trouble. A regular Circus agent might have a long-standing persona in a country, but Scalpel agents did not foster connection or favour, leaving a trail behind. They were deniable, and used for precisely the kind of thing Lake was about to attempt: an improvised operation under time constraint which, if it went wrong, would have to be loudly disavowed. On the one hand, that meant Lake could behave like a barbarian if he had to. On the other, it implied an absolute division between himself and the idealised business of formal diplomacy. It was already touch and go whether he should be close to Smiley, who was himself visiting the embassy in Vienna – not precisely the arm's length that protocol normally required.

As if balancing the scales, Lake prevailed on Susanna to sit with him and pass the time of day, to amend the traces of English in his businesslike Hungarian. They walked around Vienna and she made him describe everything as he saw it, then taxed him on his favourite things, his dislikes, the shape of the clouds and the flavours in his coffee. By evening she allowed that he actually could pass as a native, so long as he positioned himself as a big, slow thinker, or perhaps better someone recovering from a minor head injury. Lake received this information with mixed gratitude, although he conceded it was, from an operational standpoint, good to know.

Susanna excused herself from Lake's Hungarian lessons on the pretext of needing to change for dinner. She hadn't done so on any other day, but she thought Smiley and Lake would both accept it as something women did, especially in a crisis. Then, retaining her key in flagrant violation of the hotel rules, she asked the concierge to inform Mr Willow if he asked that she was ill and had retired to her room to sleep. No, she would not need a doctor. Indeed, she was going to take the night air and clear her head. She watched the man decode this and decide she was meeting a younger lover in defiance of the older one she was travelling with, and marvelled at how easily people sold themselves stories that had not been told.

She walked a few hundred metres to the Bar Byron, and sat at a table for two with a three-deci carafe of white wine. Ten minutes later an inoffensive Austrian boy a little younger than she was sat down and asked if she might be Maria. She said no, and he apologised. She suggested he could sit with her while they both waited, and he said he didn't want Maria to misunderstand, because Susanna was very beautiful. She laughed, and he fled, accidentally forgetting a short white envelope, which proved to contain – along with greetings from Raghuraman Vishwakarma – a small bundle of forints and what seemed to her a perfect facsimile of a Hungarian passport. She looked curiously at her own name on the page, then paid her bill and left the wine where it was.

As she climbed the three metal steps to the Budapest train, Susanna still felt the disconnection which had attended her since Lake had touched her arm in the Hotel König von Ungarn meeting room.

I must speak with you regarding your son.

She was aware that she was reacting, that the decisions she had made in the strange, lucid fury which had engulfed her last night were not well-considered – were not really considered at all – and she was content with this. Smiley, she thought, lived with entirely reasonable choices and was unhappy. It was quite proper, and quite English, to prize moderation, but it was not for her.

It is quite urgent. Things are not well with him.

She rode the unreality of her actions, watching herself sit and assume a position of regal unconcern as the train left the station, her ticket and documents ordered in her bag and ready to be checked, until she heard the announcement of their destination over the loudspeaker, first in German, and then finally in a language she could not immediately place, although she understood it and knew it to belong to her.

If you wish to hear what I have to say, please laugh now, as if I have embarrassed you.

She listened to the announcement through the fog of calm, and wondered if it was a heavily accented English, perhaps from Newcastle or Belfast. No. French, then, although it surprised her that she was so at ease with the words. No, not French. Something more specific, more uniquely itself.

And then, as three young men in Austrian police uniforms entered the carriage and asked everyone to have their documents ready, she remembered the man whose shoulder she had wept on seven years before, and from that followed where she was going and why, and she knew the language she was hearing for Hungarian. She very nearly stood up and ran.

I am going to Budapest to see Irén. To talk to Bánáti. To find this man Róka who has changed my life.

She wanted to say she was going home, but home should not be somewhere that made you afraid.

II.

Smiley, with paternal concern, had been to check on Susanna before turning in, and when there was no answer to his knock had prevailed on the household staff to open her door. Discovering her missing, he knew immediately where she had gone, and summoned Lake to a crisis meeting.

Lake was characteristic. His Travel instinct was simple: he wanted to go straight after her and bring her back. Smiley asked how exactly that might be achieved. The last Budapest train was gone, and trying the road border at night would likely see them held until dawn, and, at best, invite a scrutiny they could not afford. More seriously, a brief discussion with the Vienna Südbahnhof stationmaster, in which Smiley presented himself as the loyal retainer of a senior aristocratic family and Susanna their errant child, had confirmed that she was travelling under her own name, as a Hungarian citizen. Lake could hardly just drag her home by her hair.

He bloody could, Lake retorted. He had the Hofbauer passport, which she'd left on the nightstand: he could knock her out and say she was a tourist interrupting her trip for medical reasons, walk her back the way she'd come and get on with it. If he went now, and was lucky by road, he could have her in Frauenkirchen before lunchtime. She'd be in a state tourist hotel, and there was a better than decent chance she wouldn't have had time to contact Irén. The situation was stupid and dangerous, but in Lake's eyes it was still retrievable.

'The Hofbauer passport won't have an entry stamp,' Smiley pointed out. 'We could probably find a way to create the body but not the day code. The operation becomes a lobster pot: entry is easy, but departure is not. Susanna has good instincts but she is not magical and she isn't thinking. If you go in behind her, you will simply be hoovered up in whatever comes. What traps there are have perhaps already been sprung, though the watchers may be as confused as we are.'

'So what do we do? Just wait?'

It seemed to Lake that crisis merely deepened Smiley's calm. It was infuriating, and he wished he could follow the trick of it. Instead, Smiley's apparent indolence was driving him mad, and his fingers kept clenching and unclenching as he paced back and forth in the hotel room.

After an eternal pause, Smiley finally had an answer for him.

'We report events and follow the wise path. I go to the embassy; you watch my back. We inform London of what's happening in case they have a remedy we do not. We look for advantage and information, as always, and, since we no longer control the flow of events, we prepare instead to react. In other words, yes. Susanna has stolen your mission. She intends to conduct it according to her lights. Perhaps she's right. Morally, she has the high ground, which matters less than one would wish. We do whatever we can here, in the hope that we still have an operation to salvage.' For a moment there was something in his set face that might have been fury, like a big fish rolling in the dark of a shadowed pond. 'I trust Control will be satisfied with the burden of his choices.'

Summoned from her bed, Layton put her head in her hands and made a noise of suffering. It was long and low, and almost agricultural in its solemnity. Yes, she had resources, but nothing that was tailored to this. There was a small lamplighter operation which could provide documents and run the usual games into the fleshy side of embassy life: two junior case officers who checked dead letter boxes and serviced existing agents among the diplomats of other nations; and most of all a large contingent of bookish listeners who talked about pitch, frequency and room tone, and tended to the many microphones of Vienna. She could bug, bribe and even suborn to her heart's content, but spontaneous cross-border incursions were something else, a job for the deniable madmen at Travel.

'We're really doing this?' she asked, and then said it again, answering her own question.

With Layton aboard, Smiley went next to the telex room. He sent a flash message to London: YOUR ASSET OFF SCRIPT. CONSEQUENCES AS YET UNKNOWN. For good measure, he wrote another to Jim Prideaux in Prague, asking him directly whether he had anyone in Budapest who could help, if push came to shove. Prideaux was specifically not cleared for Smiley's operation, and in Control's new world of silos he shouldn't be read in, but Smiley chose to exercise his carte blanche. Jim had been a Circus field man since before the war, and gone quietly in and out of Czecho, East Germany and even Russia more times than anyone could count. He knew Hungary as well as anybody, and, in the white-knuckle insanity of an improvised extraction, his help might be the difference between a slim chance and none.

At the same time, at Layton's urging, Smiley sent an alert to Morris, the notional resident at the Budapest embassy. In an ideal world, Morris should have been first, but the truth was he was a stay-behind man in everything but name. After the war, Hungary had been a theatre of operations just like anywhere else, but successive spasms of self-loathing in the apparat had winnowed the Circus presence, not just because local agents were being swept up along with the innocent, but because, as Toby Esterhase had complained in London, you could hardly rely on whatever intelligence you got out. The Hungarian product was so inconsistent that interest among ministerial customers was limited. It would be the perfect counter-intelligence strategy if only it didn't equally degrade the state's ability to get anything done.

Morris had been in post for two years, and in the first, by diligence and graft and close attention to the black market, had managed to get a few tenuous networks up and running. Then they'd all been blown away, and he'd had to start again, and according to Layton he now didn't even try to establish permanent relationships, choosing instead to buy any information he could that looked legitimate through the same quasi-official brokers who supplied the elite with illicit luxuries. One top minister, she said, had had a weakness for prestige automobiles. He didn't drive, he just liked having them, and the Americans had tried bugging a very pretty Bristol in case he disclosed state secrets to his mistress while they made love in the back seat. It might have worked, but by the time the car was in place, the man was in prison, and his successor preferred hunting.

Smiley told Morris there was an operation under way, and to stand by in case he was needed. PREPARE ANY AND ALL AVENUES OF ASSISTANCE. DO NOT INFORM EMBASSY STAFF. DO NOT TAKE EXTERNAL ACTIONS. AWAIT MY INSTRUCTION. CONFIRM.

Morris was rated average by Personnel, and hardly existed for the likes of Haydon and Control. The son of a provincial engineer, he was a striver who prized process over instinct and reportedly had no operational flair. Layton said he was rock solid, and Smiley was prepared to accept her assessment. Morris cabled back CONFIRM, and that was all.

Prideaux's response, thirty minutes later, was in two parts. The first read, in characteristic defiance of communications protocol, GEORGE WHAT THE BLOODY HELL. The second, more informative, was no less in Prideaux's distinctive style. THIEVES AND SCOUNDRELS ONLY. TELL ME WHAT YOU NEED. STANDING BY.

It was now after midnight, and they were stuck on this side of the border until after dawn. With Prideaux, Layton and Morris ready at hand, Smiley began to consider his necessary preparations. He sent a list to each of them, testing the water. Can you get me a car if I need one? A place to hide? Which is the softest border crossing? Tell me about the weather – by which he meant not wind and water but the mood of the Hungarian state and its level of focus, and, even more: can you feel the Russians in the air?

With these matters in hand, he summoned Lake. He needed a walk to clear his head, and had realised that he ought to go back to the König von Ungarn to search Susanna's room in case she had been in contact with Róka. Lake had evidently not considered the idea, and Smiley nodded. Until a few seconds before, he hadn't either.

'In crisis,' he told Lake, 'we tend to become quite linear. It requires a conscious effort to look more widely. Come on. I'm foggy behind the eyes. I need to see the sky.'

They went into the street, letting the cold blow the cobwebs out, and still waiting for any kind of news. Vienna smelled of damp and old stone. The sky was dark above the proud Imperial buildings and the dim yellow of the street lights. A mist or a fine snow made the air glitter as you turned your head. It was, undeniably, very beautiful, and Smiley remembered arriving here years ago, almost a child, and experiencing something like homecoming. He let out a breath, then another, accepting the calm as he found it.

The moment of change was silent, and Smiley could not have said how he knew. He just did, the way he sometimes had before, in a half-dozen cities throughout a long and nervous career. His eye fell on three men idling on the far side of the road, then moved away. A car went past, and another in the opposite direction. Nothing was wrong, and yet something was. Slowly, he turned to Lake and shook his hand as if they were concluding a deal, and Lake, bewildered, returned the gesture. Smiley looked over his shoulder along the street.

'We're blown,' he told Lake. 'They're here. Walk with me.'

Lake turned, and they strolled north together, chatting and gesticulating amiably like two friends in the sunshine.

'I can't see them,' Lake said.

'Nor can I,' Smiley agreed, and Lake immediately nodded. If

Smiley said they were blown then as far as he was concerned that was all. The flight of birds, the Sarratt team had said. Tea leaves. Whatever he does, get your head around it, because it works. When he knows, he knows. And he knows Vienna, Lake appended. This is where he recruited Esterhase.

They turned left, away from the main road and towards the cathedral square. The cafés were closing up, but Vienna was still very much awake, making its nightly transition from stately dowager to hive of licence, and they walked through clouds of spiced tobacco and the smell of nuts roasting in steel cans on the street corners. Then Smiley went right, and Lake found himself struggling to keep up. He quickened his stride, and couldn't believe a small man could cover ground so quickly without running. They ducked into a palatial wine bar, with ceilings like the Sistine Chapel, and Smiley greeted one of the waiters by name. The man's face lit in a smile of greeting, but Smiley bustled past him, murmuring something Lake didn't catch and wasn't sure was even framed in words, just a promissory tone and an invocation of complicity. They passed through the kitchen to the emergency stairs, where a stockroom door gave not on to the street but into another stockroom, this one belonging to a beer cellar. Three workmen on the late shift were eating sausage and bread and drinking from huge glasses. Smiley, voice now gruff, wished them health, but did not slow down. Urging Lake to haste, he slipped out into a gaggle of merry Bavarians celebrating the end of a successful Kur, then immediately reversed into another crowd heading off along a different tack, and Lake found himself instinctively extending his hand like a boy playing at caravans: don't leave me behind. Back along their twisted route, he heard a commotion and raised voices, and the sound of a heavy bottle smashing. He wondered if it was anything to do with them, but Smiley's fingers plucked at his sleeve and he saw in the little face a brisk, energetic impatience: *I thought you Scalpel boys were supposed to be fleet of foot?* He turned his back on the chaos and followed.

After ninety minutes, they had covered what felt to Lake like half of Vienna, from the river to the south-western suburbs, and passed through every night market and off-book watering hole Smiley's art could find. Privately, Lake thought that if he was running a chase team, he'd have given it up in the forty-seventh minute, when – with a brazenness which Lake would have thought quite beyond him – Smiley talked his way past the doormen and walked right through the make-up room at a cabaret, where two dozen women in identical and scandalous blue gauze were being transformed into what, in the dazzle of the main show, would pass for doves. At the far end of the line, when a formidable woman with a brush put her hand in the middle of his chest and demanded to know what the hell he thought he was doing, Smiley doffed his hat and said it was for love, madame, and when she inflated further to denounce him as a lecher, he took the wind out of her sails by stipulating with unheralded classicism that he was speaking not of *eros* but of *agape* and perhaps even *caritas*, and could she please direct him immediately to an exit no one would know about – and she, turning on a sixpence, invoked the blessing of the saints and did exactly that.

Whatever he does, get your head around it, because it works.

Through the back ways of a city he barely knew, with no idea how close behind the dogs might be, Lake followed, and counted himself lucky.

Warm aboard the last nightly tram through Ottakring, wrapped in the temporary invisibility he had created for himself and Lake, Smiley considered his options. He could – almost certainly, he should – head directly for the embassy and look to hear from Susanna in Budapest if her self-assigned mission bore fruit – though he had now to assume she was already under the direct eye of Moscow. She would be arrested, he supposed, and charged with espionage. She was a British citizen but a Hungarian by birth, and travelling on a passport which, though false, identified her by her real name. The Hungarians might take a proprietorial interest and dismiss any British intervention on her behalf, even supposing Control requested one and the ministry was prepared to follow through. And why shouldn't they? Susanna might be a small fish, but undeniably she belonged now to the Circus. She could be brought home whenever they next traded a Soviet illegal. It would almost be no more than a courtesy. But, then again, why bother? She was extremely deniable. And whatever happened, in the meantime her detention would be unpleasant. He thought of the attending doctor at Leó's interrogation, the man's distaste for the methods he was called upon to certify. Smiley would have to confess failure to Millie McCraig, but he could also claim absolution. Control had intervened and Susanna had made her own choices. In the face of both adulthood and authority, Smiley's power was limited.

What would Ann say? Well, he wouldn't tell her. They would not discuss this moment at all. It would be consigned to a time before, part of the Circus era from which they both desired to emerge. His failures and hers could both be written off as past.

Which left only Alec, watching him from the seat at the very back of the tram, arms spread out across the cracked leather and coincidentally across the shoulders of a handsome Italian woman in a fine coat.

What would he say to Alec?

That he had not, in the end, been prepared to risk much to do the right thing. That he preferred his comfortable retirement, and the Sercombe banking connections.

That he had allowed Susanna to act according to her conscience, and in the worst case considered her an acceptable loss in the name of the same greater struggle which had expended Leamas and preserved Mundt. The struggle to which he personally no longer subscribed.

That instead of following the road to its end, he found at the last that he was the sort to wave others on their way.

Alec would shrug. 'Good choice. Mind you, it wasn't always so, was it, now? George Smiley was a field man once. Good as any of them. Better, because he was smart. Still, I suppose everyone slows down, don't they, in the end? Pass the bottle. How's Ann?'

'Ann's fine,' he told the man next to him, and received a bewildered glance in return.

A while later, Smiley dismounted on the Prinz-Eugen-Straße and considered the contents of his pockets. In one, he had a small bundle of banknotes, some Austrian, some German and some Swiss, and his Willow passport, which now must be considered suspect. In the other was an unimpeachable escape passport intended for Ferenc Róka, which identified him as Ernst Grawert, native of a Hungarian town just over the border from Jennersdorf. By necessity it had no photograph, and could be adapted for almost anyone the right age. He had nothing at all for either Irén or Susanna; there were blanks in his case at the hotel, but he'd had no reason to bring them. He could go back, but he had to assume that both the König von Ungarn and the embassy were under heavy surveillance. On the other hand, if he got in touch with Prideaux, or even Morris, he might access their capability without resurfacing. A nice trick, if he could manage it.

He consulted Lake, who was carrying his existing passport in the name of Prescott, and the second one intended for the attempt to recruit Irén, but – like Smiley – no escape document of his own. In other words, they could enter Hungary with identities which were completely clean, but only so long as they were prepared to do so without the easy option to cut and run.

George Smiley was a field man once.

He thought about giving Lake the choice, but realised there was no point. Lake was Scalpel all the way down. This was his feast, his moment to shine. Instead, Smiley turned his back on the Schloss Belvedere and went left, heading for the Südtiroler Platz and the train station hotel. The concierge, well-used to sudden changes of itinerary, was happy to show them to a private lounge where they could wait a few hours for the first of the morning trains east.

Susanna, in the cold morning of a city she both knew and did not, realised that part of her had expected the whole thing to go wrong immediately. She would cross the invisible line, and darkness would fall and sirens wail. Men would appear from nowhere and accuse her, and she would have no answer because she would actually have done the thing for which they berated her, and meant to do more. She intended to undo their works, to take Róka from them and have her desire supersede their will, and that above all was unforgivable.

Instead, she had simply crossed, and here she was in Budapest on an ordinary day with nothing happening at all. It was not unlike Vienna, and seen from a great height she supposed one would find nothing so very different. No one had arrested her or crushed her hands in a press, which was the fate her school-teacher had once told her fell on traitors.

What if the state police just weren't watching for someone like her? What if the appearance of indifference was exactly the truth, and she had succeeded in a silent entry into her old home country? Then she was not doomed, and from that it followed that she could actually change her mind. She could go to the embassy and give them her name and address, and tell them she'd just lost her passport, and please would they bring her back to London? If all that was so, then the Rubicon was still ahead of her, would retreat before her until abruptly it had passed, and she would not know.

It struck her that this was the moment-by-moment reality of Lake's profession: not one leap into danger but thousands, every hour of every day lived in the understanding that the next choice could be the one that failed you, that the next step might find footing, or tumble you over the edge of an unseen cliff.

She had no doubt what she would do. Her certainty had not

ebbed – but where, last night, action had flowed from decision quite naturally, this morning it was hard. Her momentum was gone, and she faced, alone, a wall of the mind. She knew what she meant to do, but she was not yet actually doing it, and she realised she would have to choose again, and again and again, until she was looking into the eyes of Irén Pártos, until she had said everything, and then the choices would finally belong to someone else. Although that too sat ill with her. Irén, after all, was not guaranteed to fall into line.

At one of Bánáti's launches she had met a Frenchman who eventually became her lover. He had recently served five years in their forces, in the parachute regiments, which had left him lean and avid in all aspects of life. He told her that the hardest thing he had been called upon to do was a parachute jump from a hot-air balloon. He'd made dozens of jumps from different kinds of plane, sometimes into the teeth of enemy fire, but the balloon – which had been nothing but a training exercise – had nearly defeated him. The journey up had been calm and very beautiful, the sky clear and the earth below a tapestry, just as it would be in a dream. And then the instructor had told him to jump, and he realised there would be no turbulence; no hard, screaming air, and no engines. Just this placid emptiness into which he would not fly but fall.

Now she stood on the threshold of her rooming house and looked through the door into the street, with Mrs Sipos the landlady behind her smiling and wishing her well. The accommodation agency had placed her here the night before because Mrs Sipos had registered her willingness to accept late last-minute guests. She was lonely, Susanna had immediately realised. Her husband's family had owned land in the country-side, and he had been sent there with their two sons to work. They were permitted to return three times a year, and in the meanwhile she took in lodgers and tourists to make ends meet, and to have someone to talk to.

The door lintel, Susanna thought, is my hot-air balloon. Last night, I flew, and now I have to decide to fall.

'Tomorrow, we will have fresh eggs, maybe,' Mrs Sipos said, her dark eyes looking hopefully for approval. Susanna was her only guest this week and money was tight. Mrs Sipos was not a Party member. She did not really understand politics, and felt that doing so was the responsibility of those who chose it. She had asked Susanna cautiously on arrival whether she might be in government. Susanna's clothes were very fine. Susanna said not directly. She was in trade, she said, and gestured to the river. The river was always a reason for things, and Mrs Sipos nodded, and showed her to her room, then picked up the conversation the next morning as if it had never stopped. By the end of break-fast she had extracted the information that Susanna was in Budapest for a meeting and that she was concerned for a friend, and both of these things seemed to make just as much sense to her as the river.

In Vienna, Susanna thought, Smiley and Lake would know by now. That decision, at least, was already made, and in that thought she found the thread of Susanna of yesterday.

Irén, and Bánáti – and Róka.

Susanna said that eggs sounded lovely, and, yes, please mark her in for another night. She paid in advance, counting the notes on to the hall table, and then stepped out into the street.

The air smelled different from how she thought it should – differently dirty, differently fresh – but the light was the Budapest light she remembered from growing up, and the faces, the wind and the whole world were remarkably unchanged. In a sense, that was the problem, the heart of the modern Hungarian dilemma. Emerging from Horthy, the occupation and the war, Hungarians of her parents' generation had compared the twi-light in which they lived to the total darkness of the before times, and called it good enough. In the fifties they and their children

254

had begun to discover the limits of their dawn, and wanted better, and then the Russians had returned in force. Now they had something like real life, but it was thin – a skin of food, work and progress stretched over dry bones – and it smelled equally of Hungarian rain and Russian petrol.

She looked around. There were workmen digging at the kerb, lifting a heavy stone into place. Pedestrians went to and fro, some faster than others. A car was stopped on the other side of the street. Which of these might be watchers? The woman in soft shoes or the older fellow with an umbrella? The late student dashing to his classes? Was Mrs Sipos even now denouncing her as a foreign agent? Which would be ironic, given that today she was actually neither.

Or else the world was as it seemed, and she was still completely invisible. Just a woman in a long coat, wool-gathering on her way to work. Perhaps, so far, she was in no danger at all.

She tossed her hair and waved at the young, bored security guard at the university main entrance, and, when he waved back hesitatingly, she caught his eye and unloaded a full-wattage smile to distract him from asking who she was. To her delight, he actually blushed, and she passed on, undetected, into the campus.

She had consulted the printed timetable and got someone to help her with the arcane structures which indicated what lecturer was in what room, and she half thought she should get a camera and photograph it for Smiley as an example of high-level Hungarian cryptography. Now she was walking down the third-floor corridor and wondering how on earth to contrive a meeting. Lake had intended a collision, but Susanna couldn't think of a single reason why you'd just carelessly walk into someone else. She had nothing in her hands to look at, no newspaper, no clutch or compact, and no one to talk to who might cause her to turn her head. She imagined herself lurching towards Irén for no good reason, like the monster in an American film, and then trying to persuade a dozen people it was all an accident. Insanity might be their first thought, rather than espionage. Suppose she pretended to talk to someone heading the other way, and walked almost backwards into her target? Or perhaps the wall charts were sufficiently fascinating that a person might suddenly be distracted by whatever they displayed. Each idea seemed idiotic as it presented itself. Then the doors opened all along the corridor, and people started coming out. There was no more time, because here she was.

Irén Pártos at fifty-one had broad shoulders and hips and what once must have been an absurdly tiny waist. She wore a waistcoat like a corset over a long dress, and a poet's headscarf from which emerged a curl of dark hair shot with gothic white. One hand held a cup of black tea strictly upright like a drill sergeant's baton. They were passing within a few feet of one another, and Susanna still had no idea what she was going to do. Perhaps it would be better just to talk to her, to call her by name. I'm an admirer of your poetry. Except – unlike Lake – she had never read any of it. She turned her head, and almost put her foot down wrong, then realised that it would serve and twisted her toes around and under so that she was falling. It was natural, entirely human, that she reach out with both hands for support, and just as natural that she found herself held in an unflinching embrace, her cheek pressed against rough wool lapels and a surprising amount of muscle. She looked up.

'Good morning,' Irén said, as if this was only to be expected.

Her teacup lay shattered on the floor of the main corridor, and now Susanna was apologising for all she was worth and patting at the woman's chest and shoulder with a too-tiny handkerchief she'd taken from her pocket.

'I'm so sorry,' Susanna said. 'Come – no, I insist, come with me, I must help immediately.'

Irén looked helplessly at the two suffused academics she had been walking with, and inclined her head.

'There really is no need,' she said, but Susanna had her by the hand and drew her just far enough away to lean in as if confiding some shameful secret, and murmur Lake's line directly to her right ear.

'I must speak to you regarding your son, Leó, and his father, Ferenc Róka. I am Hungarian, but I have come from London to help you. It is very confusing and difficult and not all the news is good, but it is urgent. I am sorry to surprise you but I didn't know what else to do. If you will speak to me, laugh as though I have said something funny and all is forgiven, and let's go somewhere we can talk.'

She felt Irén go stock-still, and was almost pulled off her feet as the woman's legs locked, and they stopped dead in the middle of the corridor, the stiffness in Irén's arm yanking her around so that they were close like lovers. Irén stared into her face, and Susanna knew to a certainty how impossibly frustrating that moment was, when you found again, in spite of instinct, that very little of the heart or the head can be read in the eyes, and try as you may, you see only white, iris and pupil where there should be truth.

'My son,' Irén whispered. 'My Leó?'

Susanna nodded, and felt herself enfolded in the most indiscreet way imaginable, lifted from her feet and then set down again.

'Come!' Irén said, her voice very loud. 'Come! Your father was a great hero to me in those days! I must hear everything. Everything! No, never mind your classes, they will wait. Hungary first! Come!'

Her hand darted out and wrapped again around Susanna's from above, like a hawk grasping a hare, and she led Susanna down the back stairs and out into the gardens, past the smokers and the engineers.

'What are you?' Irén demanded. 'You are not a spy. You are ridiculous. How do you know my Leó? Are you his lover? His wife? Where is he?' And, when Susanna found herself caught, mouth open, in the face of this barrage, she gave a little growl of exasperation and returned to the beginning. 'What are you?'

Susanna had faced this same question, years ago, from an Austrian policeman whose braid was still wet on his uniform collar from her tears. Not who, because names came later, but what, because that was where the story was.

She gave the same answer.

'I'm a refugee,' she said, using the German word. 'I am escaping from the kind of deception that never leaves you. A lie that runs counter not to truth but life.'

Irén, hearing only the first part, shrugged, and turned away, as if that was that. Susanna had a wild moment when she thought the other woman would tell her to leave, that her indulgence was withdrawn and the time she had allotted to that mysterious acceptance was already at an end.

'We must go to my home,' Irén said. 'I have no more lectures today. Faculty meetings I shall not attend, and they will complain but honestly they will be relieved. I tell them you can have a good poet or a good bureaucrat but you cannot have both. I am not sure that is true but it impresses them a great deal. Come.'

She set off, back straight, along a muddy path across the grass.

Irén's apartment was ten minutes away, and the window glass was old, which was to say it fitted. One pane had been broken, so that in the bottom right of the window was a rectangle of painted wood.

'Is it safe?' Susanna asked, pointing at everything.

Irén didn't answer, but she went to the little stove and fussed with it, turning the handle on the gas cylinder minutely, looking for the place where the screw would bite and allow her to open the flow. When it did, there was a gentle pop, and a smell Susanna hadn't known she was missing. It sat in the back of her mouth, lamp-black and copper, and she felt a familiar, welcome nausea. Irén filled an old kettle and put it above the flame.

In her private space, Irén was no less formidable. Susanna felt she had travelled this immense distance, not in space so much as in heart, to ask about Róka, to carry out the mission – but, now that she was here, Róka seemed almost banal, as if his remarkable presence was a reflection of Irén's, and his weathered physical beauty contrived, whereas hers was a fundamental aspect of light and bone. Susanna wondered, if she had stayed here and survived, and endured whatever fate found her, would she have been on a path to becoming this, whatever it was?

They sat together, watching the flame.

'I'm very tired,' Irén said. 'Do you know why?'

'I know Leó is missing and I know Róka is looking for him.' She hadn't wanted to speak those names yet, but Irén was choosing the pace.

'Róka,' Irén nodded. 'You know a lot.' She didn't ask how, or from whom. The kettle boiled, and she poured black tea from a saucer in through the top. Old tea, dried out to be used at least once more. Susanna's mother had done the same. The flavour would take a long time to arrive, but sometimes it was the best, as if the leaves didn't give up their secrets until they knew you better.

'You are his lover?' Irén asked. 'You are a little young. I do not judge. Blood flow also is important.'

Susanna stared at her. 'No! Oh, no, we're not, I'm not. That isn't it. Not at all.'

She saw the other woman laughing.

'You are a stray,' she said. 'Yes? You were a refugee there.'

Susanna nodded, and put out her hand. 'I'm –' In a moment of indecision, she stumbled over her own name. 'Zsuzsanna.' She saw Irén cock her head, then take her hand.

'Irén. Of course.'

'I work for him, at his office. He's a literary agent. He called himself Bánáti. Then there was a man –' And, again, words poured out of her. She came as far as Berlin and abruptly stopped,

259

truth sticking in the throat. Mundt was a secret, a very great one. If she gave it up and things went wrong, she would put Guillam in mortal danger, which wouldn't do. She had not come here to ruin anyone. The reverse. And, if she carried on past that point, she must explain that she thought Leó was dead, and she would not say that to this woman as part of her own story, as an incidental in her decisions.

Instead, she let her heart ask a question. 'How did you meet him?'

The fine eyebrows rose. 'He was a fool.' As if that explained everything. Susanna looked at her own last twenty-four hours, and thought perhaps it did. 'Róka is like me, he is a socialist. Today in all of Hungary everyone is a socialist and no one is. Back then to be a socialist was a secret. To be a socialist or to be a Jew. What am I? I am a clerk in a government office. I am efficient and unimportant, so no one asks what else. But I have friends and some of these friends have friends who are young Halutzim. Sometimes they ask me to do things. Maybe to be slow one day with a letter. Maybe to forget a name from a list. I do these things. They say will I do more? I say of course. But it is not enough for me. Their work is to escape. They have a factory making Schutzpasses, the Swiss have put a flag on it and say it is official Swiss business. Switzerland is permitted to make a certain number of Schutzpasses. They make this number, and then they keep going and make more. The Swiss endorse this action, give cover. They make an underground railroad to Palestine, to America, to Moscow. It is good work, but running does not interest me. I want to fight. My friends fight but only to make space to leave. I say to them: who is fighting to stay? They say there is a fool called Róka.'

She laughs.

'They were right. He was a fool, and he was fighting. Of course, we fell in love. Who else could we fall in love with? And he was pretty, so it was not hard.'

It hadn't occurred to her to ask. 'Was Róka Jewish?'

Irén looked back as if from a great distance. 'He is Hungarian.' Stress gently but firmly on the second word. At length, whatever she saw in Susanna was good enough, and she sighed. 'He didn't know. His father said not. His mother was dead. Before the war he had not thought so much about it. After . . . he could hardly go to the synagogue and ask, hmm? Maybe the Halutzim could have told him and he was afraid of what they would say. Maybe they were afraid if they said no he would stop helping. He was Jewish enough for the Arrow Cross, for sure. And also for me. My friends offered to get him out. Both of us, when I was pregnant. We said no.' She smoothed her hair with both hands. 'We were together. We fought and we hid and we had a son. That's how we met.'

The tea was ready, pale as corn but almost otherworldly: smoke, salt, tannin and iron.

'You want to talk to Róka?' Irén asked.

'Yes.'

'Why?'

'I want him to stop. To run. To . . . I don't know. He's going to kill himself.'

'This will hurt you.'

She nodded.

'Me also.'

'Then –'

'Because if I tell him to stop, that will hurt him. If I tell him, he will do it, but he will come to hate me. If Leó lives, he will live in spite of Róka's weakness. If he dies, he will die because Róka did not do enough. If I say to stop, I lose them both forever, even if it does not seem so at the time. And then . . . perhaps he can do it. He has done impossible things before. Perhaps he can again, and his stupid plan will save our son. So it seems I am selfish. I cannot kill his love to save his life. Can you?'

Yes. She could. She could live with his despite, if it saved him. She nodded, and Irén let out a breath.

'Is that what you want from me? To urge on him the treason that you cannot?'

'I don't know how. What to say.'

'What do they want you to say?'

She wondered if she should deny that there was a 'they'. But everything she could offer was contingent on Smiley. All the hope and all the bad news she had came from him.

'That we have news of Leó.'

'And do you?'

'He was arrested. And released. No one knows what happened after that.'

Irén's eyes were closed as she drank from her cup.

'And what do you think?'

Her head came up, and her eyes looked directly into Susanna's.

12.

She had come here for this precisely: to tell the truth rather than the lie. Her outrage at Smiley's readiness to deception had carried her, and yet, now, with Irén's teacup in her hand and the taste of coal gas on her tongue, she found it entirely absent. What did she know? That the world was unkind. That Leó was missing. That he had been arrested and was marked as released, and that someone was lying. And, for this, she should sit in Irén's kitchen and tell her that her son was dead. If Smiley's lie was self-serving, what was that?

The longer she waited, the more worthless her answer would be.

'I think he's dead,' she said plainly. 'But I don't know it.'

Irén seemed not to understand, as if Susanna had started speaking another language they did not share. Then all at once she heard it, and Susanna saw her rock back, and then settle herself like a fighter getting ready for the next punch.

'Nor do I,' Irén said. 'Thank you.'

She poured two more cups of tea, then filled the kettle with more water. Irén had more to say now that the shadow on the world was acknowledged, and Susanna felt something in her chest, bright and excited even as she chided herself for it. The sensation was entirely new in her experience, and yet she knew it immediately for the same desire Guillam had described in Berlin: an appetite for knowledge that perhaps existed nowhere else in the world.

She could feel it in the way Irén hesitated, like a child asking for a balloon or a boy inviting you to hold hands. She wanted to say something, to nudge Irén to speak, but she held back. The silence would ask for her, so long as she did not interrupt. It was the longest five heartbeats of her life.

'A man came to me,' Irén said. 'On Friday. A little man with old eyes, like a farmer or a priest. He was strong but grey. Older than me, older than Róka. He had men with him, but they stayed in the street. He came alone. I thought he would interrogate me about Róka. He did not. Instead he asked mé if I knew Bogdan. I say of course I know Bogdan. This man says what do I know? I tell him I am a poet. If I were writing a poem of Bogdan, I would call him the Old Captain because he loved only boats. I would make a story of how the Old Captain made love to the Donau. I would say he was the friend of my husband, his brother in arms, and they were men together in the war. Fools together after. And that is all I know. Would the commissar wish me to write this poem? I am joking. This is what I do when I am afraid. He does not seem to notice. He says, yes, please, I should write it now and give it to him. So I do. This is possible for me. Sometimes poetry is slow and I work it like sheets in the mangle. Sometimes it is very quick and it is done forever and I must not touch it, even if it is imperfect, because I will only make it worse. This time it was quick. I wrote it for him on a piece of notepaper and gave it to him, and then immediately I forgot it. This also is normal. You have experienced it? Sometimes if we are artists we surge into the work and we inhabit it or the other way around and then it is gone and we remember nothing, as if it has wiped us clean. Tomorrow you could show me that poem and I would not be sure it was mine. I hand it over. He reads. He laughs. He says it is very good. And then he asks me again, very serious: this is all I know? I say yes. I say I have in my head just one picture of Bogdan from during the war. I remember his face and his laugh. But I did not know him more than that. I say Bogdan and Róka, they are friends in the alleyways, they share stories, they make insurgency, but at this time I am quite pregnant. I do not wish to be in alleyways with two young men. I am coarse because I think he will

264

laugh, but he does not. He is disappointed in me. I apologise. I do not ever apologise to men for coarseness, but this time I do. He says he is not shocked, just the joke does not suit me. And then he leaves.' She shrugged. 'I have lied to him deeply. It is always better not to know things. I do not know whether he believes me. I wonder if he will come back or if he will send someone, but nothing happens. He takes my poem and he goes away. I did not even think to ask him to help me. To help Leó. I wanted only that he should leave.'

She looked out of the three-quarter window, and Susanna realised she would not answer the question unless it was asked, and that here was another of her points of no return, perhaps the first that was absolute.

It is better not to know things.

She felt it again, in her fingers: that certainty of consequence.

'What would you have said if you were telling the truth?'

Irén nodded, as if this, like the presentiment of Leó's death, now belonged in the open.

'I would have told him the story of Bogdan and his boy on the Russian train.'

It stank, Bogdan had told her, of diesel and frightened men. Looking back, he'd come to think of it not as a train, or even a tank, but as a submarine on rails: a long, narrow tunnel you walked along every day, in the hope that eventually you might come back to the sun. The whole body of the thing was armoured, and the armour made quarters tight. It made the air inside hot and heavy or cold and suffocating. Light came in through narrow horizontal slits and gun ports, and sound was both muffled, so that you couldn't hear the birdsong, and amplified, so that all the impacts were like being inside a giant church bell when it rang. The train had steel plates on the outside and a layer of knotted ropes hanging down to soak up some of the momentum of larger projectiles before they tested the armour. It had an official number, but the men who rode inside called it 'The Dog', because it looked like one, crawling along on its belly to beg for fat from the table; the men, and one boy in the kitchen who peeled vegetables and stewed the slops, and who sang the patriotic songs when they were under attack to stop himself from crying. *Reign to make our foes fear, Orthodox Tsar! May God protect him.*

Bogdan had told him the Tsar was fine, but, if someone was in the business of protecting, they could protect the Dog and all who sailed in her. The Captain told Bogdan to shut up, and then the next day a bullet punched clean through the armour and took the side of his head off, and Bogdan sang whatever the hell he liked. Drinking songs, mostly, but the 'Marseillaise' as well, because you could really drink to the 'Marseillaise'. Trust the French, Bogdan said, to create a marching song that worked with wine.

They were in the train for eleven months, and by the time they were done it was bathed in their blood and piss and tears. The Tsar wanted a port south and west of Vladivostok. The Japanese wanted it too, and so they fought. People in Paris would tell you fourteen eighteen was the first truly mechanised, truly appalling war, but Bogdan was pretty confident his was just as bad.

The boy nearly died twice: once from a fever, and once when the kitchen was set on fire by a bullet passing through a pan of oil and the cook was killed outright. Bogdan had pulled the boy through the door into the next carriage against orders, and been both burned and reprimanded. He counted the cost negligible, and the other men agreed. The boy was their mascot, their shared son. He was an idiot. He'd stowed away for the glory of the Tsar, and they loved his idiocy because they'd all to some extent done the same, and not a man of them was concerned with glory now. The Captain had been, but that was his blood on the wall of the map room, on the far side from the patched hole. They were supposed to get a new officer, but he never came, so they put Bogdan in charge because he could write, and, in the eternal spaces between fire and fear, he taught the boy and any of the men who wanted to learn. Told them, as well, what he thought of tsars, of kings and princes generally. Of his dream of a democratic Russia to equal France or America: prosperous, cultured and free. They laughed at him, Bogdan said. They were farm boys for the most part. They'd settle for land they owned, beer each night and a wife with broad shoulders. Why did he have to make everything complicated?

But the boy listened, and now quoted Locke as often as he hailed the Tsar. Bogdan was proud.

The war wasn't very long, and after it was over Bogdan went home and was told the Tsar could fight any further wars without his kind of backchat. He was flogged for good measure, and left Russia to see what lay beyond. That was the first time he sailed in a ship, as a deckhand. When he was in port, he wrote letters to his parents, and to the boy, and trusted them to the post. The Revolution actually came, and Bogdan missed it, and when the dust settled he found his way to Hungary, because it was his mother's place and he'd heard that Horthy would call elections. By the time it was apparent that Horthy had no such intention, he'd made a home for himself, and he prepared to set his shoulder to the mill of history, whose long, slow turning would grind a strongman honest and give him, at last, the free country of his heart. In between times, he still wrote to the boy, who had long ago become a man. They met only once or twice each decade, but one way and another the relationship survived, and it seemed the boy had made a name for himself in Soviet Russia. He was married, even. Bogdan had been to the wedding, which was very strange, he said, because by then his boy had become so important that even his name was a state secret.

His boy. Somewhere in the intervening years it had become known between them: each was the other's longest-standing friend, and filled a need which was touched by no one else. Survival, gentleness, the shared memory of the stinking heat inside an armoured train. It was almost their distance that made it so; their separation, and the time elapsed. Neither of them could have accepted more. Neither could tolerate less. At the turnings in life's road, they nodded to one another, and carried on. Bogdan the democrat, and the boy who sang songs for the Tsar of all the Russias, and grew up to be a commissar.

A small, clever man with a quiet voice, Susanna thought, whose heels wanted to click together when you talked about the comradeship of soldiers.

'The man who came to see you,' she began, and Irén cut her off.

'Perhaps,' she said, meaning: not aloud. Not even here.

When Bogdan gave them his tale in the war years, the boy's rise had not yet taken place. The story was a gift of Bogdan's most cherished secret, to match their own vulnerability when Leó was born: I too have a son whom I love. The later part they found out in fifty-two. Róka, under pressure to identify traitors who did not exist, chose Bogdan to be his patsy. He hadn't wanted to. Irén said he had cried, and vomited, and then written the report and sat alone in the dark. Half, he thought Bogdan would understand; and, half, he thought the man really might be an agent of the West, perhaps always had been. It didn't matter; he ran full tilt into a wall. Bogdan's boy got wind of it and stopped the whole thing cold, then drove Róka into the wilderness for his sins.

'Then why go to Bogdan now?'

Irén looked at her as if she was an idiot. 'Because it is for his son,' she said. 'It is for family. Even if the boy does not care, if Bogdan asks him, he must at least consider it. He has this power. It is nothing to him to save Leó – not even the time to sign a paper. Just his breath to speak it. But for this Róka must find Bogdan. First, he must ask Bogdan for forgiveness, and then for help. He cannot approach the boy directly. Only Bogdan knows his name.' Irén paused, and then lifted her head. 'I'm sorry,' she told Susanna. 'I am too slow.'

'No,' Susanna said. 'It's fine. Keep going.'

Irén sighed deeply in negation and pointed, and Susanna heard the sound of footsteps outside, then a brisk, official knock on the front door.

'Too slow,' Irén said again. There was another knock, this one heavier and more urgent.

'They are here,' Irén said. 'I suppose there is no use in waiting.'

This, Susanna realised, was her true point of no return. The door was opening under Irén's hand, and behind it must be a reckoning. The men who stood there might even be the same ones who had pursued her seven years ago. Or perhaps they had trained alongside Miki Bortnik, and she had come all this way to meet the end he should have delivered in London. She assumed they would be Russian. If they were Hungarian, then the arithmetic of her damnation changed, though not the sum. They would arrest her. She would go to one of the places they had and experience the reality of state power in the East. Perhaps she would share this experience with Leó. Perhaps not. The cost of her choices would be measured in all the things she had learned, and would now give away, and the danger to everyone along the way: Guillam, Smiley, even Mundt, who of himself was perhaps worth nothing, but upon whom hinged an unknown consequence in lives and hope.

Perhaps they would also arrest Irén, or perhaps they still intended to leave her here, dangling bait for Róka. Perhaps Irén was with them and had told her all that purely to keep her here for this moment. She looked back along the line of the last thirty-six hours and saw that, from the far side of the hinge, everything was inevitable. Her watchers had preserved the illusion of choice, but their grip had held her, all along. Once the door was fully open and they came in, the time of her decisions was past and she would be fully owned by the whims of another.

She thought of Millie McCraig, and looked around for a blunt object. A lump of wood, McCraig had said, but the stove was gas. She picked up a heavy pan instead. *The collarbone is brittle and critical*. She raised the pan and ran past Irén, swinging down hard, and felt the impact not in the steel but in the bones of her forearms as the big man in front of her blocked high and rolled on into the room, cursing as she kicked and struggled. She struck again and he ducked his head into her shoulder and lifted her off her feet, then reversed, dragging her out into the corridor, the whiplash agonising on the bones in her spine. In London, she thought, the doors all along the passageway would open so people could look and argue and get involved, but here the inhabitants recognised the tenor of the state police, and shut themselves in. We don't see it, her mother had told her, because we want it not to be true. She didn't call out, but she flailed and made it hard for him. If they were going to take her, she wanted them to work, to make time for something impossible to save her, so she yawed and scratched and hoped she'd have the opportunity to bite. All the while, she kept expecting a heavy hand around her neck or a blow to her face to silence her, and couldn't understand why it didn't come. Then she was jolted sharply against the wall, and all the wind went out of her as she slid down and stared into her captor's face.

'You,' Lake said distinctly, 'are a pain in my arse.'

She looked at him and then, still not understanding, beyond him, and saw Smiley extend his hand to Irén across the threshold and say something in courtly Austrian German, to which Irén responded with what was almost a blush. *He can't be here*, Susanna thought. *It is specifically forbidden*.

If her own capture was dangerous, Smiley's must be a nightmare. What could possibly induce him to do something so obviously stupid? And, in answering the question, she wished she hadn't asked.

Smiley drew Irén out into the corridor as if offering her a glass slipper. The whole thing was so otherworldly she half expected music, but then instead a service door opened at the near end of the corridor, and four men rushed towards them. The front one flung out his hand, and Susanna saw a flash of bright red hair cut very short, and a face contorted in furious command.

Lake swore and hauled her off the wall. He propelled her almost from her feet with a shove in Smiley's direction, then barrelled along behind her. She heard a shouted order to stop: they were all under arrest. Resistance would be heavily penalised. As opposed to what, she didn't know, and anyway Lake had her by the hand and they were running, running away, which was the only sensible thing. There were more men now, joining the hunt, and the fugitives dived into the stairwell and down towards the street. One of their pursuers had flat feet, and she could hear the syncopated *snap snap snapping* as he slammed the soles of his boots down on to the concrete. Lake stumbled, his chest landing full on her back. It nearly crushed her to the floor, but she rammed her hand on to the wooden rail and shouldered him upright, then carried on, knowing he was close behind. She could hear him breathing, heavy, like a dog after a run. Smiley, in the front, seemed hardly to touch the ground, and he was half carrying Irén.

The door ahead of them was propped open by a man in a workman's donkey jacket and a horrible hat. He reached out to Smiley and pulled him through, then Irén, and then they were all in the street. 'Get a bloody move on,' he yelled, in English, as if giving Smiley orders was the most natural thing in the world.

Outside, the day was so aggressively ordinary she felt the mad urge to slow down lest she disturb everyone with her clatter. She could see the police cars parked next to one another a few yards ahead, and right in front of her two more cars – a Trabant and a Moskvitch 407 – both empty, with the engines running. Smiley took the driver's seat in the first, gesturing for Susanna to get in next to him and for Irén to get in the other with the man in the donkey jacket. The cars had local plates and mud on the wheel arches. They looked modern but not fast. Lake glanced into the Moskvitch and something seemed to pass between him and the driver, because the man half opened his door and then swore and slammed it shut as Lake ran past them to one of the police cars, reached into his pocket and plunged his hand down, first at the back right, and then again at the front right tyre, something flashing briefly as he did so. Then again on the second car, and as he doubled back Smiley had pulled out and was accelerating towards him when the man with flat feet started running again, and Lake jolted hard, his face taking on a grimace Susanna had never seen before and instinctively hated. There was a black mark on his coat just above the hip, and another in the back as he twisted, and she saw it was surrounded by blood. With a shock she realised he'd been shot, twice: once on the stairs, and once now, and he was falling, falling down in the street, and Smiley wasn't slowing.

She lunged for the door, but Smiley caught her and jammed his foot down on the pedal, swearing in a quiet, intense monotone which was more vicious than if he'd shouted, because it hadn't occurred to her that he'd ever use those words, that the loss of control they implied was even possible for him. She heard a whirring sound like a fishing line, then another and another, and a series of little snaps. The wing mirror on her side exploded. Smiley spun the wheel one way and then the other, then round again to turn right at the corner and out of the line of fire. The other car was behind them, and Susanna could see a bright star of broken glass in the middle of the windscreen. The man in the donkey jacket was bent over the wheel, head low and eyes very intense. Irén seemed to be shouting or screaming, her mouth a perfect, consistent O. Lake was back there, on the pavement. They had him.

In the warmth of the Vienna station hotel, Smiley had used a house phone box, much as Susanna had done, to call Morris and declare a full emergency. The code phrases were prearranged, and changed every few months, so that Smiley was sure he was at least one cycle out of date. He had to trust that Morris would untangle his message, and that its very obsolescence would delay Moscow for long enough if they were listening and had somehow had sight of the codebook. He'd told Morris to bring fresh passports, and to pass on to Prideaux that he was running the extraction now, today, and needed local transport and whatever assistance was possible. Prague was six hours away by car, but Prideaux's network in Brno was robust and capable, and with Jim you didn't hold back. You asked for what you wanted, and he got you what was possible.

Jim did not disappoint. The car they'd taken to Irén's apartment had been waiting at the station, handed over by a local boy who gave them the keys and asked in German if they wanted to buy cigarettes or needed any introductions. The car, he said, had been stolen just this side of the Hungarian border. The news would still be in the local police reports, if it had even been missed. There was a map in the glove box, and he had memorised an address. He reeled it off twice, once slowly and once for confirmation. They should not write it down. Someone would meet them there within the next thirty minutes. After that, it was a bust. Smiley shook his hand with an Austrian hundred-schilling note folded tightly into the palm, and felt it vanish like a ferret into a rabbit hole.

'Your friend says it's better not to hang around,' the boy said, and took his own advice.

Of that much, there was no doubt. In Smiley's experience, the narrow window of action lived in the delay between your first movement and your enemy's comprehension of the choice. Once they knew what you were doing, you needed to have done it and be doing something else. And now, with gunfire still ringing in his ears and his foot pressed down hard on the accelerator to little avail, one thing was sure: they knew. The police cars Lake had immobilised would have radios, and the bulletin would already be on air. The fugitives had minutes at best before the streets were blocked.

Behind him, Smiley saw the Moskvitch swerve wildly, and heard the sound of the engine, the revs far higher than they should ever go. The car surged past and cut in dangerously close, then pulled away, and then he was struggling to keep up. The Trabant's engine was as underpowered as the body was flimsy, and the steering column shift slipped in his hands as he changed down and pressed his foot to the floor, praying the whole gearbox wouldn't just be ripped apart. Instead, the engine screamed and the car jolted to follow its stable mate. They zigzagged, dipping on the one side into the narrow streets of the older city, and on the other into the wide, frighteningly exposed avenues of the Communist expansion, but always moving forwards, towards the river. How long had it been? Two minutes? Three? He had to shift again, up for the straight and then down as they turned a corner, and again he was terrified that the car would just give up before they got to where they were going, but he had no choice. There was no time, none at all, and maybe less than that.

Smiley's hope now, as he racked his brains for every instruction he'd ever been given on evasive high-speed driving, and found it amounted to going fast and not hitting anything, was that the answer to the single question he had not found a way to ask in Vienna was no.

If Karla had not yet arrived to take personal charge; if he was just still tying off loose ends in Berlin; if they were dealing not with a full Directorate team but merely local watchers set on by Moscow in the hope of rolling up Róka should he appear; if his own instinct last night had been false, and there'd been no one on them, just shadows on the wall; then he had a chance, however narrow, to get everyone out.

Susanna pressed her hands against the wooden uprights of the car interior as they hurtled around the corners of narrow streets she should have recognised, if only they were moving more slowly. When they turned, she was thrown against the frame. She pressed her feet hard into the seat well, and worried they might actually break through. She thought she had her bearings for a moment when she saw the river appear behind them, then lost her way immediately as they turned right around and she glimpsed the cathedral on the skyline. The man in the donkey jacket pulled out ahead of Smiley and they danced through the city; then, just as she started to hear sirens everywhere and to realise they were done, he swung down an alley into a shipyard and the car vanished through an open warehouse door. Smiley followed, and before the door closed behind them, Susanna saw two young men in fishermen's coats start sweeping water across the ground so that the tracks of the cars on the concrete would disappear. They ran inside and threw the bolts, and a few seconds later she heard the tones of the police cars roaring past. For the longest time, everyone was completely still as they listened to the sirens fade away, and then again as another set came closer and passed them by, until after a minute the only sound was the washing of the river on the far side of the warehouse wall.

She looked around. They were surrounded by crates in orderly rows, and a church-like silence that seemed mad. The man in the donkey jacket wrenched open Smiley's door, and then Susanna's, and said, 'Move faster,' before running back to the other car and dragging Irén to her feet. He pointed to an open drainage hatch in the floor, and Smiley hustled Susanna down a metal ladder and into a low stone corridor that struck her irrelevantly as being just like the Paris catacombs, which she'd visited on holiday. This looked about that old, the stones cut by hand: a sewer; a crypt; a refuge. There was a stain a few inches below the ceiling, and she had a moment of screaming claustrophobia when she saw droplets running down the right-hand wall, and it crashed in on her that it must be the high-water mark. The river was directly on the other side, and this was some sort of flood drain. When the corridor narrowed and she had to turn sideways, she felt her breathing stop as she choked in imagined drowning, and forced herself to look straight ahead over her right shoulder. Feet together and then apart; one step, and then the next, it doesn't matter how the musty brick plucks at the buttons on your coat, how like a coffin or a grave the passage feels. It is escape. One step, and then the next, there is only forward.

The walls diverged again, and, ducking their heads to avoid thick oak sleepers, they half ran, half fell forwards. Susanna kept expecting to hear the *snap snap* of the pistols and feel whatever it felt like to be shot, because it had dawned on her at some point between there and here that Lake had stepped between her and the gun, and the first bullet that had hit him had had her name on it. Ahead of her there was a wall and a series of iron rungs driven directly into the brick. Together, they climbed up and out. She realised they were in a second warehouse, two or three blocks away and from the surface quite separate. A black saloon with East German plates, expensive and imposingly official, was standing by the door. Beyond it was another car with a Czech registration, far less exalted. The man in the donkey jacket slapped Smiley on the shoulder.

'Welcome to the wrong side of the world, George. You must be out of your mind.'

'Jim,' Smiley said. 'You're supposed to be in Prague. And respectable.'

Jim snorted. 'I got on the road as soon as I got your message, just in case. Woke up my man outside Brno. His cows too. His wife gave him hell. Apparently I've turned the milk or something. Don't look at me like that. Same for both of us: it's no harm so long as we don't get caught.' He gestured. 'The boys'll take care of the other cars,' he said. 'A lot of things go missing around here. Sell them, burn them, I don't know. They're good-enough lads and I paid them plenty, but they're local and halfway brigands, so their pledge of eternal loyalty is good for about half an hour. You

276

three take the big car. They'll be looking out at the Austrian border so you don't go that way. There's a map on the passenger seat. Head north and cross into Czecho. From Bratislava I can run you out, no problem. Passports . . . You're a high official, East German. They're your family. But Morris can't get the day codes and nor can I. It's a rotating code and they make a note in a bloody ledger, takes hours. You'll have to swing it. Can you manage?'

He handed over a slim leather slipcase. Smiley looked inside and found a trio of blank passports, the glue still warm in the spines, and a forger's kit: knife, adhesive, tape, white spirit and a stolen border stamp, the drum for the day code conspicuously missing.

'George,' Jim said. 'I'm asking, can you manage? If you don't fancy it, I can try something else. Hide you in a sack under the chickens.'

'This is fine,' Smiley said. 'You've done more than enough. Thank you.'

'We left Tom Lake back there,' Jim said. 'They were picking him up. Alive.'

Smiley nodded. Jim carried on.

'That was proper Scalpel, you know, killing the tyres. They'd have had us otherwise.'

And he knew he wouldn't get away, Susanna thought. I saw him, and he knew.

'Yes,' Smiley said. 'I'll get him back, of course.'

'Do that,' Jim said. 'I'd like to see us win one again. It's been long enough. All right, let's go. Clock's ticking.'

Smiley drove and Susanna sat in the passenger seat. Irén half lay in the back. She almost seemed to be sleeping, and Susanna realised she was exhausted, not from running but from everything, for weeks, maybe years. Her eyes were closed and she was breathing so silently and softly that you might mistake her for dead. The window glass was slightly tinted, and as in Berlin so here: she felt like a princess in a tower, surrounded on all sides but safe within. She knew it for a dangerous illusion but couldn't shake it, even as two more police cars passed them in the opposite direction, lights and sirens on, and she saw the driver of the second one notice her and Smiley and consider the East German plates and the sheer substance of the car. She thought they made eye contact, but wasn't sure if it was possible through the glass; and then she saw him make the decision to ignore the big car and its occupants, to play the odds that if he swung the car around through the centre partition and made them stop, he'd just be irritating some irrelevant high official and losing time on his pursuit. If he hadn't, she realised, that would have been it. They could run but not escape, and there were no more boltholes. She wanted Smiley to accelerate and knew he mustn't, and her eyes fixed on his foot where it rested on the pedal, willing it to stay exactly as it was in spite of her desire. He must feel the same. He was human, and they were running.

A thousand years later, the sirens faded, and Smiley changed lanes, then turned on to the road north. A quarter-hour later they had crossed the river and were picking up speed, with Budapest and its frantic search behind them.

The road was new and starkly industrial, built for heavy Soviet lorries, perhaps even for tanks. She pictured them coming, although that wasn't how it had happened. They'd come from the east, reaching Budapest in what seemed like no time at all, and effectively just made their own road, scattering everything from the border to the capital. Or, at least, she thought so. She'd seen only the tiniest part of it as she ran.

They stopped for half an hour near Tatabánya, on the Nitra road, and Smiley sent her across to a little shop to buy bread. When she got back, he was leaning over the tray of the glove box, cutting her photograph from the Hofbauer passport, placing it into the new one and sticking it down. Irén's was already done, and something in Susanna was still terrified at the barbarous vandalism of her official documents, the hole where Smiley had cut out her picture.

There was a ballpoint pen resting on the dash, as if he had considered and discarded it. He glanced at Susanna and held it up.

'In Hungarian?' he asked.

'Toll,' she said, and he nodded, repeating it until she was satisfied. He hesitated, and then threw the pen out on to the road.

The car smelled outrageously of glue, and he turned the fan up high and opened the windows, then told her to drop the passport in the seat well and move it around against the floor with her feet. 'Not old, not new,' he said, and gave her two more: his own and Irén's.

Twenty minutes later, they reached the tail of the border queue.

The line was forever, and every time they moved forward, Susanna could feel the weight of the mirrors on poles all around, which showed every angle of the checkpoint to the controller sitting in his wooden box, and showed most particularly your back and what was in the space you couldn't see behind you, so that not only could you not hide anything, but the controller knew more about your position than you did yourself. To stand at the checkpoint was to be seen from every angle, to be naked and scrutinized, and, above all, to know that this was happening and that there was no chance you could evade the eye.

They sat in the line, and crawled forwards. Prideaux had said the clock was ticking. Surely it had run out, and that long ago. Yet, if it had, why were they sitting here? If they were already caught, why wait for them to present themselves? And so she had to assume that they had a chance, and that once again she must jump into the still air. She didn't know if it was better to believe in hope or to be pessimistic, and realised that it was this uncertainty that had framed her mother's infuriating fatalism. Not a conviction at all, but the awareness that in the face of something so unpredictable, fatalism was the only truth you could be sure would never let you down.

Now the guard was coming. He had waved away the car in front and was beckoning them even as he walked, rolling his hand – onward, onward – and shuffled back with them until the bonnet of the car was barely a foot from the barrier. Now he came around to the driver's window and tapped on the glass with the barrel of his rifle. The mouth pointed briefly right at her, and it was huge.

Smiley wound down the window and she realised it was happening, this very instant, as he reached over and took her papers and Irén's and passed them to the young, grim-faced boy with his gun now hanging loosely at his right side. One of many young men, as she looked around. A half-dozen, working their way through the queue, and the controller hardly any older, sitting amid the mirrors, knowing everything. So many guns, all aimed slightly away, slightly off and to the ground. And the passports had no day code, because they were fake, and no one had ever used them before, least of all to come into Hungary this morning. Irén was still barely awake, and now turned her face to the cold pillar of the car and rested it there, waiting.

The boy nodded thanks for the passports, saw there were three and peered into the back. His face wrinkled with concern.

'Is madame well?' he asked. 'Do you need a doctor?'

'It's fine,' Susanna said, when Irén did not respond. 'My mother does not like automobiles.'

The guard's forehead wrinkled. She felt her stomach drop into her feet, remembering Lake. *We don't let the nice police know we patter local. It gives them the unkind notion we might be a spy.* Which she hadn't had to think about as Gero, but now she was a German woman.

'Your Hungarian is excellent,' the guard said, and his hand strayed towards the gun.

'It is adequate,' Irén growled from the back. 'No daughter of mine will fail to learn my language.'

The boy flinched slightly, and nodded in understanding, his gaze flicking briefly to Susanna in sympathy. Her face must be a perfect picture of filial horror. Adequate, indeed.

The boy opened their passports with a disinterested formality. The exchange with Irén had embarrassed him, and now he wanted only to wave them through. He nodded, nodded, turned the pages back and forth, and frowned with unwilling reluctance at the entry stamps and the missing day codes. Finally, apologetically, he turned back to Smiley.

'Commissar, these papers are incomplete. There is no day code. You cannot pass through.'

Smiley did not move. He gave no sign of having heard at all. He just waited, as if utterly bored, and the guard made haste to explain.

'The entry visa must have a stamp. No doubt the commissar is aware of the protocol. It is necessary for the maintenance of security in the face of colonialist aggression. Even the dependants and friends of high officials. Even at a friendly border. Please bring the car around to the side. You will be delayed. I am sorry.'

And that was it, Susanna thought. It ended here. They would sit and wait, and sooner or later the passports would fail them. They would be exposed, and arrested, and what happened then would only be bad. She felt a scream inside her and struggled to keep it in.

Smiley finally seemed to notice what was going on, as if the notion of impedance was almost new to him. His hand extended, rigid.

'Pen,' he said. *Toll*, his one word of Hungarian, spoken with a distaste that was almost physical. He still had not turned his head.

'I beg your pardon, commissar?'

Smiley could not know what the question meant. It seemed to make no difference to him either way. Susanna waited until the moment was almost gone, and then she said, 'My father asked you for your pen.' She was lost. She had no idea what was happening. Her voice came out calm, even sympathetic, as if she was really just trying to help.

The boy took his pen from his pocket and handed it over. Smiley received it and then put his hand out again, flat like a table. He closed the fingers once, twice, and opened them again in clear instruction: he wanted the passports as well.

The boy hesitated, and then laid them on the waiting hand. Susanna thought his fingers were shaking. Smiley very deliberately flicked through the pages one by one until he reached the stamp. Resting on the dash, he drew a line through it where the day code should be, then signed underneath: an appallingly elegant signature in the classic nineteenth-century cursive style of peace treaties and royal decrees. Then again. One, two, three. He held each page open so the ink wouldn't smudge. When he was satisfied, he closed the passports, and finally turned his head to look at the boy for the first time. It was the purest expression of power and arrogance Susanna had ever seen.

Smiley waited a beat, and handed back the pen. Then he looked towards the road ahead, raised his hand and flicked two fingers forward as if to say: 'Carry on.'

The boy stepped back and shouted at his partner to raise the gate. Quickly, quickly. That's it: the commissar is in a hurry.

A moment later, the barrier rose, and they drove through.

13.

By evening, Susanna was once again standing on dry land. Prideaux had given her yet another fresh passport, this one issued directly by the British government, and appended her to a departing British Council tour group which had been visiting church altars. Amid the gaggle and clatter of two dozen jocular Nonconformists, she and Irén were to all intents and purposes invisible. Smiley, bickering amiably with the driver over the relative merits of the Phillips and the Wuest Expanded, looked so ordinary she wondered if this wasn't after all his natural home. When the moment came, crossing back into Austria was barely even tedious.

In the aftermath of the escape, the chaos that followed was like calm. She was interviewed, accused, dismissed and finally allowed to sleep, but when she tried she found herself watching Lake – not falling to the ground but practising his lines for the meeting with Irén which she had stolen from him. He was earnest and sincere, which at the time had made her angry. Now she looked at the results of her own intervention, and wondered if they were truly so much better than what he would have done. She had considered the consequences to Róka, to Irén, and determined that what she was doing was a price worth paying, but she had never considered the coin in which it might be paid. Eventually, she slept, without dreaming.

'I don't know what you *thought* you were doing,' the Ambassador snapped, 'but I know what you *are* doing! You're packing a bag and you're leaving, and I shall be speaking to the Minister personally. Do you have any idea what a mess you've made?'

Smiley said yes. On arrival, he had telexed London, and demanded of Control whether they had anyone to trade for Tom Lake. To sweeten the pill, he had at the same time given a short précis of Irén's information, and asked for the Aunts to begin an immediate search. The first part of the message was still unanswered, but that was not necessarily bad news. Lake's colleagues could be window-shopping.

For the rest, Control was furious with him for crossing behind the line, and, as he put it, for dragging Jim Prideaux into a similarly dangerous dereliction. Smiley said yes, he was entirely responsible, and he quite agreed it was the sort of thing you could lose your job over.

The Ambassador was still shouting, and after a while Smiley excused himself.

'What do you mean?' the Ambassador demanded.

'I'm leaving,' Smiley said. 'That is what you wanted, I believe.'

'Where do you think you're going?'

But, while Smiley was prepared to accept reproach, it seemed he felt no need to answer ridiculous questions. He had a note in his pocket from Ann, and he wanted to answer it before he left for the airport.

Ann had moved on from Vienna to an unscheduled stop in St Moritz, where she was, she said, catching the last of the winter's snow. She had met a charming group of people including a defrocked contessa whose pleasure was to move from one European beauty spot to another, living the life. The Contessa had taken a chalet, and invited a selection of persons of interest as guests. Ann was quite honoured to be among them. She'd love it if her George would come along and join her. It was past time he learned to ski. She made no mention of Smiley's attempted visit, and he in any case felt he had failed her more perfectly than she would ever know, even if he had the courage to confess.

He had realised far too late that Ann might have been in very real danger in Vienna. He had accepted the concierge's statement that she was with her husband as evidence of infidelity – and, of course, he'd been right – but it could in the context have been something far more sinister, and that possibility had simply not occurred to him. Smiley had brought his wife to the very battle-front, then lost track of her, and ignored the absence. She might, as he retreated in shame, have been calling out for his help. She might already have been dead, and he had taken flight with his hurt feelings, to the relief of his grey mistress.

He wrote back that he would be free the day after tomorrow, and proposed to join her then, although he could not promise he would risk himself to the joys of the piste. Perhaps, if she would be his instructor. In the meantime, he was going to Lisbon, and would make certain to bring back some Douro wine and, if he could get it, the rare Frasqueira Madeira which was her particular favourite. Then, for what he was sure would be the last time, he put away his future life, and returned to the task.

With Irén's account in hand, Smiley felt he now understood both the distant and the recent past. Leó's disappearance in Berlin had set Róka in motion, just as Leó's problems always did. His requests for help had not been declined, but had bounced off the smooth surface of the East German apparat. Probably the interrogation had been too rough and Leó had died on the spot, or else come to harm after his release, with the Stasi actually having no idea what had happened. Karla had found out only when Róka began raising hell, and even then had hoped he wouldn't have to act. Self-delusion, perhaps, was a universal vice. Likely he had assumed Leó would turn up, probably in someone's bed, but one way or another. In that case, why not let Róka exhaust himself going down his list of old Tourmaline acquaintances, and then use his embarrassment to secure better behaviour in future? It was the daily bread of anyone who ran agents in the field. At worst, Moscow would see some old spies exposed, incidentally clearing the way for men loyal to the new boss. But when Róka called Grodescu and asked after Bogdan, he had inadvertently put his boot on Karla's neck. In his desperation to find his son, Róka risked compromising Karla's identity, and in the moment of his rise to dominance within Moscow Centre any weakness was to be despised. Karla had chosen to conceal his name, and that by itself was reason enough that it must not come to light. *What I hide stays hidden; what I bury is never exposed. You are complicit in my invisibility, because you know if you see me I must close your eyes.* And if that name came with attached vulnerabilities – the wife Irén had mentioned, or other family, or Bogdan's record as a democratic anti-Communist – then Karla's ascendancy could end before it began.

All Smiley needed now was Bogdan. If Karla had squirrelled him away, had brought him to Russia's interior expanse and made him a home, then unearthing him would be the work of a lifetime, if it were even possible. But by the same token in that case there would never have been any danger that Róka might find him, or persuade Bogdan to give up the name. The implication of Karla's actions was twofold: first, that Bogdan remained the contrary fellow Irén remembered, and that he would judge any such submission on its merits; and, second, that he was outside the ordinary bounds of Soviet power, in some location a fugitive like Róka might reasonably expect to reach: a Western nation, or one of the non-aligned. Karla need act as he had only if the danger was real, and that could be the case only if Bogdan might actually be found.

In this, Smiley had resources which Róka simply did not. The Bad Aunts, tackling the problem, had chosen blunt-force research. Working with McCraig, they'd called in every spare member of the Chorus Line, and searched listings from across the continent for Bogdan, and for his boat. For a single person, it was a years-long task, but for several hundred, it wanted only hours. To cut it down still further, they had focused on the south, because Connie insisted that a man in age would prefer mild winters. Katrin objected that this was barely even superstition, and Jessica that, even granting it were so, why would he stay in Europe? But Connie was, as so often, quite right. In the registry of the moorings in Almada where he kept the *Water Nymph*, Bogdan was right there under his own name.

Smiley, therefore, was already in a position to negotiate, and had things he wanted. In the first instance, Lake, then Róka, and – assuming there was a chance he was still alive – Leó, and only thereafter any other matters. Control had conceded the point at the very beginning of all this, to force him to the task. Do it the Smiley way, he'd said, almost goading. Show everyone decency. And Smiley fully intended to do exactly that. Control would want him to leverage Bogdan's knowledge to secure Karla's defection, if there was even the slightest chance it could be done, and in quest of that would sacrifice Lake in a heartbeat. Smiley would not, and knowing that conferred on him a deeper insight into the value of Bogdan's secret. Karla could be damaged, yes, even made vulnerable, but hardly toppled, and in making the attempt Control would overplay his hand and risk a declaration that the families of intelligence officers in general were now legitimate targets. From there, the escalation was obvious, and had no natural ceiling.

For Leamas and for his sins, Smiley wanted to do better, to offer an alternative: a world in which the conflict between two absolutely opposed ideas of well-being was fought within limits. Without them, the result must eventually be destruction. Within them, perhaps there might be peace. If it was hopeless, then it was, but Lake alone made the trick worth trying. Conflict was not always avoidable, but the possibility to withdraw must always exist, or else what was there?

At the airport, Smiley picked up the phone and dialled. He heard the ringing tone and waited, counting steps. Collins had said the phone was by the counter, and Grodescu took his time coming down the stairs in slippers. Seven. Eight. Nine. Smiley let it go on, and then heard the click and pop of connection. The line was crisp. A man's voice, warm and mostly French, gave the name of the shop.

'Hello, Mr Grodescu,' Smiley said. 'My name is James Willow. I believe we have a mutual friend, a Dr Gerstmann. I was visiting him last week, and we had something of a row. In the course of it, I left in a hurry and I managed to leave something of considerable sentimental value behind. I wondered if you might pass him a message for me, to say that I should very much like it back in one piece. As it happens, I believe I've located something that may belong to him, and I wanted to assure him I'd maintain a hands-off policy. It strikes me that our professional competitiveness should have agreed boundaries. I thought, if he agreed, he could let me know. I'm travelling again this week, to Lisbon, and I'll be quite close to the place where he keeps his particular treasure. I thought he might care to join me for a cup of coffee by the river, and bring my item.'

Silence from the other end of the phone. Then the man spoke again, almost irritable.

'There is no Gerstmann here,' he said. 'I regret I cannot assist you.'

'That's all right,' Smiley said. 'I must be mistaken. I'm sorry to have troubled you. You'll keep it in mind, though, in case he comes by.'

'No Gerstmann.'

'Thank you.'

'Adieu.'

Smiley glanced at the departures board, and, seeing his flight listed as ready, wandered to the gate.

Smiley had known Lisbon for more than two decades, much as one knows the owner of the village shop. It was a polite, formal acquaintance, never unfriendly but likewise never personal. Portugal was anti-Communist but strategically non-aligned. The rules here were different, and had been since the thirties: foreign intelligence services were free to act in moderation so long as they were scrupulous in working entirely clear of the Portuguese state. Play how you like, but the ball stays on the field. On the rare occasions when that constraint was ignored, Salazar's PIDE could be very direct in delivering their displeasure. Lisbon was as dazzling and energetic as Paris, and if you put a foot over the line it could be every bit as perilous as Berlin.

As Smiley stepped from the little water taxi on to the stones of the Almada quay, the afternoon sun warmed his face, and he realised that soon, even with his coat folded over his arm, he would be too hot. The wind blew fresh from the sea, but there was precious little shade. Bogdan's flat was nearby, on the fifth floor of a stocky apartment block with a view over the Tagus, where he could see the shipping come and go and look west into the raw Atlantic. A dying place, if one was honest, for a man constructing his own end. Smiley thought he'd seen much worse.

There was a café three hundred yards away along the waterfront, with sunshades in heavy concrete plinths and paper tablecloths held down with ashtrays. The canvas chairs were bleached by years of exposure. Smiley ordered coffee and the local bread, and sat down to wait. The sound of the sea lay under everything, and the wind whistled in gusts around the edges of the buildings. Out on the Tagus River he could see small ships and bigger ones, and beyond them to the west there was nothing between him and New York but the curve of the world. He almost put out his hand, wishing for Ann and knowing she wasn't there.

After half an hour he ordered a second coffee as a kind of sacrifice, as if having it there on the table would conjure the man he awaited. He watched it cool, and declined to rehearse what he would say. He would listen. They would listen to one another.

From that, everything else would follow. Even if Karla did not come, that would be an answer of sorts, and Smiley's presence would speak. It was most important that they understood one another.

He cocked his head, listening. The wind had picked up, he thought. Perhaps there was a storm coming. He had heard that in Lisbon you could watch them arrive: first a sweep of darkness rolling in across the sky, then the plucking of a fiercer gale, and finally rain, like a curtain drawn across the world.

No. It was not wind but something else. A flute, or a distant funfair. Perhaps a spring festival, with a choir. And then, very faintly around the noise of the city, he heard sirens. He wondered where they were going, before a suspicion surfaced in him that he declined to name. He heard shouting and turned to look. Three cars, then four, in the livery of the Portuguese police, pulled up outside Bogdan's building, and an old woman in a care-taker's coat emerged shakily from the porch to weep in the arms of the first bewildered young man. He still did not understand, or would not, until the sun began to drop below the blue horizon, and the shadow and the chill set in.

Later, at the embassy's request, they showed him the scene. A policeman named Caçador brought him up the stairs to the front door, which had not been forced. These locks are not good anyway, Caçador lamented. Anyone could break them. If he was my grandfather, I would have told him to get better.

The apartment was quite small, with a warm, tiled floor. The hallway was painted lemon yellow and filled with boat clutter: ropes, old instruments and tools. Smiley wasn't sure if they were things Molchalin used or things he had collected. Perhaps both. He noticed himself looking at them and knew he was delaying. He was breathing through his mouth, but he could taste the iron already. He swallowed, and Caçador put a hand on his upper arm.

'If you are going to be ill, it's better you go outside.' He hesitated, then added, 'I was. Twice already. It's normal.'

'I'm fine,' Smiley said. 'Thank you.'

There was no room in the hall for Caçador to go past him, so Smiley led the way himself. He turned the handle and stepped through into the main room. There was a round iron table with a white cloth. More boat clutter: an aneroid barometer, a spoked wheel and a pair of flags, one Hungarian and one Russian, crossed as if at the stern of a ship. Wine and two glasses, good Portuguese chicken with the paper bag torn down so they could cut it, and rice in a bowl. The smell of the food wasn't enough to cover the rest. Smiley had to make himself look.

Bogdan sat in the chair facing the window where he could see the sea. His eyes were open and he was almost at attention. His jaw had fallen open so that he might be mid-mouthful. The bullet wound was at the back of the head, where the skull joined the neck, which was not regulation at all. Caçador's Chief said he probably never knew. Lights on, the Chief said, and then: lights off. A family killing, the Chief said, between this and the food. Not like the other fellow.

Smiley asked about the other fellow.

Not the same at all, Caçador said. This one here was fast, almost apologetic. No marks on the face or body, just quick and clean. The man in the harbour was different. Torture, and quite a lot of it. Caçador's Chief was something of an expert, and he said it had been very bad. The only connection was the gun. The same one had been used on both of them.

'What sort of gun?'

A Russian gun, Caçador said, a pistol. They were pretty sure it had belonged to the second man, because they'd found an oilcloth and spare ammunition in his room, but he'd never fired it.

Smiley nodded. Róka's own weapon, then, from the cash box. It made a certain kind of sense.

'But you confirm?' Caçador asked. 'They were friends?'

'Yes,' Smiley said. 'Yes, I'm afraid they were.'

'And the third man? Who killed them? Do you know his name?'

'No,' Smiley said. 'No, no name.'

Caçador thought about it, then shrugged. 'Communists,' he said, as if this explained everything.

For a short while Smiley stood where Karla must have, looking where Bogdan was looking, out at the sea. He held his hand like a pistol and pulled the trigger, and looked again. The waves, of course, had not changed. Smiley thought perhaps he had. He found Karla's choice impossible, for all that he understood the logic. Smiley had made clear that he would extend forbearance, and that his only price would be the same in turn. And this was Karla's response, not merely a solution but an answer, laid out for Smiley to read.

'Thank you,' he told Caçador.

He walked back along the waterfront to the Praça do Comércio, and spent the evening writing up his report for Control. In the morning, he had the news that Lake was dead.

Morris had taken delivery. The Hungarian officer presiding had called first, and asked the embassy whether they cared to acknowledge Lake belonged to them. They said no, which was standard for Scalpel, and the officer explained that in that case Lake would be buried in the paupers' cemetery with the other homeless men. Morris agreed that that would be best, then called his locals and had them steal the coffin overnight. He had had it crated up and added to the diplomatic bag, and had the preposterous experience of walking it through the airport with everyone pretending they had no idea what was inside.

The Circus doctors reported that Lake had probably died shortly after being hit. The second bullet had shattered and perforated his heart. There was very little that could have been done anywhere. In addition, they said, he had injuries on the hands consistent with scratching against a leather boot, which led them to the conclusion he had been attempting to obstruct someone when his strength left him.

In Brixton, they called that sort of thing a good effort, and were glad for him.

McCraig told Susanna that the funeral was family only.

'Will you be going?'

McCraig shrugged, and then her shoulders slumped. 'You bury them here,' she said, touching her heart. 'You remember the names here, if you can.' Touching her temple. 'There's nothing on the headstone that makes any difference. You think it might, but it doesn't. You just have what you have of them, and that's all.'

'I'd like to see Irén. She must be frantic.'

'I'll see what's possible.'

Susanna thought she recognised a closing door, and acknowledged that by any measure she deserved it. She very nearly missed the offer of absolution through good works: a temporary job at a company specialising in the manufacture and sale of high-tolerance machine parts. She had already discarded it, and was looking through her other options with the weary eye of someone choosing between financial records and bulk lamb when Rose Jeremy tapped lightly on the letter in the out tray.

'Decent prospects,' Mrs Jeremy suggested. 'If they take you on long term, the pay's respectable. Promotion. The chance to make a difference.' She tapped again, at the address near Coldharbour Lane. 'Travel,' she said, and shrugged. 'As I say: if you like that sort of thing.'

'It was a waste of bloody time,' Haydon said irritably. 'I wish I had been in bloody Venezuela. At least there I'd have had a shot at something worth while. Control had me make a pass at Pogodin, of all people. What a mess.'

By the time Haydon arrived, he said, it was already too late.

Pogodin had been arrested and summarily executed, along with four of his lieutenants, although the news didn't leak for days. Karla was in Berlin, and this confident absence was only further proof that his ascendancy in the Thirteenth was now complete.

'How about you?' Haydon demanded. 'Good times? Never mind, I don't want to know. I'll see you at the Hall, anyway, won't I?'

'Oh, I'm sure,' Smiley said. 'Yes, of course: the Hall.'

Haydon suggested they go for a drink. 'Wash the failures off our boots, George, and sing of better days.'

Smiley excused himself, and said he needed some air. He went to Bywater Street and sat in the semi-dark of his living room without bothering to turn on the light or start a fire. An hour before sunset he got up again and took a cab to Primrose Hill. Ann's mother had once told him it was where rich men kept their mistresses.

Control was sitting on one of the benches at the very top, with a view south to his own office and St Paul's. Smiley looked for the clocktower of the Brixton Railway Hotel, but knew it was too small and too far away.

'It's confirmed,' Control said. 'The Pártos boy. They were working him over for too long and he just died. Mundt got word to Guillam while you were in Lisbon. Said it was bloody careless and he'd take steps, if Karla hadn't already disappeared the men in question.'

'I'm sure he would.'

'I'm not. I don't believe he's ever had a decent thought in all his life.' Control turned his head. Without his glasses he looked older. The circles under the eyes were an alarming colour, like yellowed bruises. 'Not like you.'

Smiley nodded. 'I'm sorry about that.'

'Mundt did have one other thing to say, if you were wondering. He said Moscow put out an order to leak Bogdan's location if Róka came asking. Karla must have decided to cut right to the chase. Mundt said he didn't connect it with Leó until it was too late. I imagine that's a lie, and he was quite enjoying the show.'

'I suppose so.'

Control nodded. 'I asked you to show me the Smiley way and you showed me. Offered Karla the chance to call it all off. No tricks, just the thing itself. Do you reckon he understood that? Knew you meant it?'

'Yes, I think so.'

'And no quarter given in reply. Well, then: at least I know what he is. A true believer. That's how it ends.'

Smiley looked around for Leamas, but didn't find him.

'No,' he said. 'No, not ends. Not just yet.'

Ann stayed in St Moritz for a fortnight, and reported the slopes unmissable. When she returned, she insisted she was not angry, and Smiley believed her. They went to dinner at a new place, one she said was going to be the next thing. They talked about nothing very much until coffee, when she laid her hand on his cheek.

'Why do you run, George?'

'I don't.'

'Yes, you do. I thought for the longest time it wasn't deliberate. I still think that, but it also is. There's some part of you that doesn't want to be happy, that feels guilty about it. Why should you be happy when someone else is miserable? When Alec is dead. So you leave me and you go to your grey mistress.'

Smiley said the Circus wasn't grey but red brick, and felt more than ever in his life like a fool. Ann laughed with genuine fondness.

'But it is, George. That's how I think of it when you go: he's leaving me for her. For shadows and sorrows. I like bright colours. I like to play and be warm and I like it when you're there with me. But you . . . some part of you belongs in the cold, doesn't it? Not mountain cold, not sunsets and snow and the smell of woodsmoke, but city cold, all wet black mud and damp that gets into your gloves and under your door. Faceless men in rooms deciding the future of the world, except that they're not. The world turns and confounds them every time, and you're left to tidy up. And you don't even know who's opposite you across the board. What's his name, George? Does he even have one?'

'I don't know. He does exist. But he doesn't let anyone know his name.'

'Why not?'

'Bill would say because he's afraid. I don't think he's afraid of anything. I think he likes control, to know more than anyone else.'

She laughed again. 'Do you love him?'

Smiley stared at her.

'Oh, don't be so provincial, George. I don't mean are you lovers. I mean are you tied to one another the way you're tied to me? Does he have a wife at home who never sees him? Who wonders all this about you? Does he tell her "I must defeat the dog Smiley and then I can come to bed"?'

'I don't know that either.'

'Now I've made you sad. Look, I don't mean to. Maybe this is how it is for us. You and your grey mistress, me and my pretty boys. Two perfectly respectable other loves within a marriage. If that's what you want.'

'It isn't. Desperately.'

'Then you have to let her down, George. You have to put her away and decide, today and every day, that you don't belong to her. It isn't once, you see. Not for you or for me. It's every time, or we'll spin apart.'

'I will.'

She kissed him then, her lips heavy and hungry against his. 'Now?'

'I have –'

She sighed, then patted his hand. 'Oh, I know, George. You have one more thing you need to do.'

Acknowledgements

In so very many ways, this book is owed to a multitude – to my father, obviously; and to the actors who have played Smiley and Guillam and Esterhase, Connie Sachs and Ann and Maria Ostrakova and all the rest; to my brothers – Simon, who suggested I write it, and Steve, who is wrestling the same bear up a different hill; to Penguin Random House and others for having faith that I could; to everyone who reads it.

My amazing wife, Clare, took on the directorship of John le Carré Limited last year, making her my boss – and me hers – in one stroke. Untangle that and make it simple if you will – which she does, to my enduring benefit and delight. Our children bring chaos, heart and education at every turn, for which I should thank them too.

My agent, Patrick Walsh, and Jonny Geller – who represents the company – danced a tango of support, comment and negotiation which reminds me how superb they both are.

I shamelessly leaned on my friend Leena Karnik to help me with the naming of Raghuraman Vishwakarma – who I hope will make a further appearance, both because I like him, and because the deeper I went into it the more fascinating his backstory became – and Biraj Patnaik was kind enough to advise as well. Needless to say, any blunders or infelicities are mine, not theirs.

My editors Harriet Bourton and Edd Kirke in the UK, and Brian Tart in the US, produced the kind of feedback you read about in the lives of storied writers – short, cogent and above all actionable advice, by which the narrative and the prose greatly profited. The excellent Donna Poppy, who copyedited, kept me grammatically honest and creatively tidy – at least in so far as either is possible.

Joe Hill – one of the few people on earth who can claim to understand the scale of my fear around this book – read it early, and responded swiftly and with vigorous enjoyment. The man's a treasure.

Finally, there's one more person who lives in the text, though she would object to the limelight. My mother was not only my father's collaborator, woven into the story of Smiley's struggle with Karla; she was also the person who sat patiently with the six-year-old me as *Smiley's People* was being written in the study next door, and untangled the first long story I ever wrote for school. My effort had been roundly rejected by the teacher as making no sense – unsurprising, given that I had attempted to condense the creation of a 300-page novel into a single lesson, and had handwriting like the tracks of a drunken earthworm. Over what seemed to me then like days, she questioned, noted and transcribed, finally printing the whole thing on a dedicated word-processing machine about the size of Stonehenge. Whenever I work, the pattern of review and surgical correction is owed to her.

To all these, and to others who lifted heavy weights for me along the way:

Thank you.

NH
London
2024

THE GEORGE SMILEY SAGA

THE SPY WHO CAME IN FROM THE COLD

JOHN LE CARRÉ

'A portrait of a man who has lived by lies and subterfuge for so long, he's forgotten how to tell the truth' *Time*

Alec Leamas is tired. It's the 1960s, he's been out in the cold for years, spying in the shadow of the Berlin Wall for his British masters. He has seen too many good agents murdered for their troubles. Now Control wants to bring him in at last – but only after one final assignment. He must travel deep into the heart of Communist Germany and betray his country, a job that he will do with his usual cynical professionalism. But when George Smiley tries to help a young woman Leamas has befriended, Leamas's mission may prove to be the worst thing he could ever have done. In le Carré's breakthrough work of 1963, the spy story is reborn as a gritty and terrible tale of men who are caught up in politics beyond their imagining.

'The best spy story I have ever read' Graham Greene

THE GEORGE SMILEY SAGA

TINKER TAILOR SOLDIER SPY

JOHN LE CARRÉ

'A masterpiece' *Guardian*

A mole, implanted by Moscow Centre, has infiltrated the highest ranks of the British Intelligence Service, almost destroying it in the process. And so, former spymaster George Smiley has been brought out of retirement in order to hunt down the traitor at the very heart of the Circus – even though it may be one of those closest to him.

A stunning salvo in le Carré's acclaimed Smiley Saga, *Tinker Tailor Soldier Spy* sees the ratcheting up of the stealthy Cold War cat-and-mouse game between the taciturn Smiley and his wily Soviet counterpart.

'A great thriller, the best le Carré has written' *Spectator*